# YOU KNOW IT'S GOING TO BE A LONG NIGHT WHEN...

"I need you," Lorraine said, her voice strained. "I'll text the address. Hurry. They want to kill him. We can't let it happen. I won't."

"Kill him?" I repeated, but she was gone.

My lust forgotten, I tossed my phone onto the seat along with my water bottle and slid behind the wheel. Damon grabbed the door to keep me from closing it.

"Kill him? Who? What's going on?" He looked like a panther about to spring on prey, all coiled up to leap, muscles bulging, face intense. He was a testosterone explosion held in place by a very fine body.

"That is none of your business." I slid the key home in the ignition and turned the engine over. It rumbled to life. I glanced up at him. "You should move."

He gripped the top of the door tighter. "I want to know what that meant. Who is killing who?" His deep voice was so hard, it could have cut diamonds.

"Whom," I corrected. I put the Thunderbird in reverse and started backing up.

"Rebecca, wait! You don't know the danger—"

I didn't hear any more. The big block V8 engine roared like a lion as I hit the gas and drowned out his words. Damon swore and the hand not holding the door started glowing blue.

Oh, no he didn't. I gunned the engine and he yelped, leaping aside as I twisted the wheel, my tires squealing protest. As soon as I had room, I jammed the car into drive and floored it. The door swung wide, and I grabbed the handle and yanked it shut. I think Damon might have screamed my name, but I didn't stop.

I made it to the driveway before a meteor of blue struck the trees on the left side of the entrance. They crashed into the road. I wasn't sure I even had time to brake.

Good thing I didn't consider it.

# PUTTING THE FUN IN FUNERAL

## EVERYDAY DISASTERS
### BOOK ONE

## DIANA PHARAOH FRANCIS

BOOK VIEW CAFE

# PRAISE FOR
# DIANA PHARAOH FRANCIS

OMG! I had such a fun time reading this book ... I laughed so hard! Oh god, to be like the heroine, being so open about hating someone - no being nice, just honest ... freaking hilarious!!

*— ~AMAZON REVIEWER*

This entire story is amazing. Loved the world building. Please tell me there will be more?? I need lots more of this world. Beck is one hell of a heroine and I want to know more about her new life and adventures.

*— ~AMAZON REVIEWER*

I'm a little obsessed with this new series. I love pretty much everything Diana writes but this one was so much fun. I loved the light-heated title but the story was so great and much deeper and more intriguing then I expected. I'm really looking forward to the next book and learning more about the world.

*— ~AMAZON REVIEWER*

# MORE BOOKS BY DIANA PHARAOH FRANCIS

From Book View Café and Lucky Foot Press

EVERYDAY DISASTERS

*Putting the Fun in Funeral*

*Putting the Chic in Psychic*

*Putting the Ice in Nice* (Forthcoming)

MISSION: MAGIC

*The Incubus Trap* (Forthcoming)

*The Elf Deception* (Forthcoming)

*The Giant Riot* (Forthcoming)

THE PATH SERIES

*Path of Fate* (Forthcoming)

*Path of Honor* (Forthcoming)

*Path of Blood* (Forthcoming)

*The Quick and Dirty Guide to Character Creation* (Forthcoming)

Books from Other Publishers

DIAMOND CITY MAGIC SERIES

*Trace of Magic*

*Edge of Dreams*

*Whisper of Shadows*

*Shades of Memory*

*Shatter of Light*

CROSSPOINTE CHRONICLES

*The Cipher*

*The Black Ship*

*The Turning Tide*

*The Hollow Crown*

HORNGATE WITCHES SERIES

*Bitter Night*

*Crimson Wind*

*Shadow City*

*Blood Winter*

MAGICFALL SERIES

*The Witchkin Murders*

*PUTTING THE FUN IN FUNERAL*
*Everyday Disasters: Book 1*
Diana Pharaoh Francis
Copyright 2018 by Diana Pharaoh Francis
9781944756079
Published by Book View Café in conjunction with Lucky Foot Press 2023

PRODUCTION TEAM:
Cover illustration and design by Lyn Forester
Copyediting and proofreading by Patricia Rice
Ebook design and formatting by Jennifer Stevenson
Print design and formatting by Diana Pharaoh Francis



This book is a work of fiction. All characters, locations, and events portrayed in this book are fictional or used in an imaginary manner to entertain, and any resemblance to any real people, situations, or incidents is purely coincidental.

Lucky Foot Press
*in conjunction with*
Book View Café
304 S. Jones Blvd. Suite #2906
Las Vegas NV 89107
www.bookviewcafe.com

🌼 Created with Vellum

*For Christy Keyes*

# CHAPTER ONE

"Tell me about your mother."

"She's dead."

Detective Ballard gave me a studiously bland look. "I'm aware. Do you think this is funny?"

I pretended to consider. "Funny—no. Ironic? Yes."

"Do you care to explain yourself?"

"Because I get to plan her funeral." I already was. It would have to be the tackiest, white-trashiest, low-rent trailer park sort of affair for kicking off the dearly departed. I'd definitely serve beer. Oh, and champagne. With Funions and pork rinds and pigs in blankets and deep-fried Twinkies. And confetti. Maybe fireworks. Or pumpkin chunkin'. I could go with a viewing and dress her in Daisy Duke shorts and a tube top. Add some blue eye shadow and crimson lipstick for that extra-special touch.

Regret slid through me. No. She'd need to be cremated. *I* needed her cremated, just to be sure she couldn't come back as a zombie or vampire. Maybe I'd be allowed to light the match on the fire.

"Miss Wyatt?" The detective said, tapping my knee and interrupting my happy daydream.

I focused on her. She could have used some under-eye concealer. Maybe a little lipstick. And some rouge. The woman looked like death. "What?"

"I asked how you would categorize your relationship with your mother?"

"She pretty much hated everything about me, and I tried my damnedest to earn her malice."

Her brows rose at my candor. "So you didn't get along with her?"

Was she deaf or just stupid? "Didn't I just say that?"

"Did you?"

The detective needed her ass kicked. "Yes."

". . . relationship contentious . . . ." she muttered as she wrote in her notebook.

Such a mild word. Like my mother hadn't been the wicked witch of the west. Like she hadn't spent every minute of every day criticizing and castigating [me] and moaning over my flaws and failures, which were all I was to her. I don't even know why she'd had me. Or kept me.

"Did she have any other family? Do you have siblings?"

"Don't know and no." Because if there was one thing that was true about my mother, it is that she kept her life a secret from me.

"What about friends? Or enemies? Anyone you can think of who might want to hurt her?"

"Grab a phonebook and start with the A's," I suggested.

The detective looked up from beneath her brows. "Your cooperation could go a long way in solving your mother's murder. Don't you want to find her killer?" Her tone implied heavily that I might just be the killer. Not that I could blame her. I was a perfect suspect. Luckily I had a perfect alibi.

"If the killer walked in right now, I'd probably offer to suck his dick," I said. "That's how much better my life will be without my mother."

Which was pathetic. And also a challenge the universe had no intention of losing. Not only could my life get much worse, it Murphy's Law said it probably would.

"Where were you yesterday?"

"I already told you. Twice."

"I'd like to hear it again."

"Yeah? I'd like a mansion in Monaco and naked hot-tub time with Ryan Reynolds, but neither of those are going to happen either."

Detective Ballard visibly gritted her teeth then changed tack. "Was your mother seeing anyone romantically?"

"Check her nightstand. Bet she's got a rainbow of vibrators in there."

The detective's mouth dropped open then snapped shut. "I'd think that you'd be a little bit serious about finding your mother's murderer."

"What you think isn't my problem, is it?"

"It is if I arrest you for obstructing a murder investigation."

I stood up. "And we're done."

The detective stood up, tapping her pen against her notebook. "Sit down. I still have questions for you, Miss Wyatt."

I cocked an eyebrow at her in disbelief. She did not know when she'd lost. Up to me to teach her, then. "Here's the answer to all of your idiot questions. Ready? Going to write it down in your little book so you don't forget? Here we go, then. Fuck. Off. There. You now have all the answers you're going to get from me. Now get out."

"Can you tell me who the beneficiaries of her will are?"

The detective was tenacious. I had to give her that. I glared, flipped her off, then spun around and walked into the back room, slamming the door behind me.

I leaned against the door and took a deep breath, my heart pounding. My mother was dead. It was my own personal miracle. I was shaking. I held up my hand to watch it tremble and laughed quietly at myself. God, how long had I been hoping and praying for karma to come and dump my mother in its cosmic woodchipper?

Leaving the door, I wound through the maze of antiques, expensive knickknacks, unusual finds, and everything else I'd packed in the back warehouse of my store until I made it to my office. A Louis XV desk and chair in honey-colored birdseye maple sat in the middle, surrounded by crowded shelves of my favorite finds. I'm an estate broker, selling people's things when they downsize or die. I've found some amazing and strange things over the years and keep them in my eclectic collection.

I grabbed the phone and punched in a number.

"Lorraine? Get over here. Now. Bring champagne. Mother is dead." I depressed the talk button to cut off questions and made two more calls to Jennifer and Stacey, repeating myself both times.

After that, I went to the back door of the warehouse and unlocked it, dropping a spell on it to warn me if anybody besides my three best friends should try to enter. I ran up the steel grate stairs to my home. Inside the utility room I toed off my shoes, then went down the short hallway to slide open the rustic barn doors to my living room.

The place was perfect. The walls were unpainted brick with giant, industrial windows along every exterior wall. Each was five feet wide and twenty feet tall, crisscrossed by mullions. I'd put up a few walls for three bathrooms and three bedrooms, but the rest of my loft was open. More of my weird and strange collection clung to every stray surface, horizontal and vertical. I had a giant nearly square cushy white suede couch in the middle of the loft space with a giant ottoman inside that pretty much made the whole thing a walled bed. The girls and I had spent many a Saturday night drinking, watching movies, and dishing dirt there.

I waltzed through my house to the kitchen, on the other side of my living room. It was a large, gourmet space since I liked to cook. I dug out glasses, shoved more champagne into the wine fridge—I kept one chilling all the time, just in case a reason to celebrate popped up—and grabbed some of my triple chocolate cookie dough out of the freezer and set the balls onto a cookie sheet before tossing it into the oven.

Next I turned on the stereo, flipping until I found the mix I wanted, all of which were songs about winning. Halestorm kicked it off, followed by Beyonce. I ran down the front stairs into the store to make sure Detective Stick Up Her Ass had left, which she had. A cruiser was still parked outside, its lights flashing. No doubt to make sure I wasn't off on a killing spree. I locked the doors and flipped the closed sign then snapped off the lights. It was only three hours until closing anyhow.

I glanced once more out the door, just in time to see a news van pull into the parking lot. Hadn't taken those vampires long. I stuck my tongue out at them and closed the shades.

# CHAPTER TWO

"Here's to no more tirades about your crappy whore friends while we're standing there," Stacey said, clinking her glass against ours. Champagne sloshed over the edge, and I nudged it back with a subtle swipe of magic. I avoided public magic at all costs, but the couch was suede and custom made.

"And here's to no more bribes or threats to us and everybody we know to stay out of your life," said Jen.

"Oh, and no more siccing the cops on you, suing you, getting your power and lights turned off, your cars towed, your houses quarantined—"

"Don't forget the bedbug infestations. That had her handwriting all over it," Lorraine said, interrupting me.

"She was awful to you guys. Why in the hell didn't you guys run for the hills?" I asked, not for the first time in our long friendship.

"Because these bitches don't run, and we're like the marines—no friend left behind," Jen said, throwing a cheese puff at me. "And anyway, all the things she did to us pale in comparison to what she was doing to you."

"What do you mean?" I'd kept all the bad stuff hidden.

"Oh, please. It's not like we didn't know she was fucking with you. Afterward, you'd be sick in bed for entire weekends and vacations. Half the time at school you'd have bruises and lacerations and you *should* have been in bed," Lorraine said, scowling at me.

"You *should* have been in a hospital," Stacey corrected.

I'd never been sick. That's just what I told them. If I hadn't, they'd have demanded to know more and I was never going to tell the real truth about what happened when I said I was sick.

"Man, I'd have been out of that house like my ass was on fire," Lorraine said. "I still don't get why you stayed."

Because as much as my mother had hated my three friends, she'd used them to blackmail me into staying put. All the things she'd done to them were half because she wanted to get rid of them and half so I'd know she was serious when she threatened them with real harm. Like burning their houses down around them. Or getting them fired from jobs. Framing them for murder. She even had some guy roofie Jen and take nasty sex photos of her. My mother really was mean. I'd paid big to get the pictures and all the evidence of their existence without Jen ever knowing about it. My mother gloated the whole time. At least the scum fuck she hired never got his dick hard from that day onward. I can be vicious too.

"I'm a sadomasochist," I declared in response to Lorraine's comment. "Obviously. With twisted-mother issues. Somebody get me in to see Dr. Phil. Or is it Dr. Oz? Better yet, find me a really hot sex therapist and we'll both head straight to the couch and work my issues out, all naked and sweaty."

"One of these days, we want to know the real reason you stayed," Jennifer said, giving me a shrewd look that said she could see right through my bullshit. "And then we'll all go piss on her grave."

I snorted at the mental picture of the four of us squatting on a grave together. Champagne came out my nose.

"I hate peeing outside," Stacey said. "It always ends up running down my leg."

"Clearly you need more practice," Lorraine said, passing me a napkin to sop the champagne dripping from my nose. I gave up trying to keep the couch clean at that point. It's a little OCD to worry about it, anyhow, when I have the magic to clean it into pristine condition without hardly a thought.

"No thanks. But I'm willing to suffer for the sake of peeing on your mom's grave," Stacey said to me.

"Maybe we should do it weekly," Jen said, filling my glass again. She froze as she drew away, her eyes widening. "You don't think she could possibly haunt us, do you? I mean, she's mean enough to hang out and torture us for eternity if she can."

"If she does, I swear I'll build one of those backpack things from *Ghostbusters* and suck her up," I said.

"Do you think there's any possibility she was wearing a g-string and nothing else when they found her?" Lorraine asked longingly and then sat up. "No, wait! Maybe she was wearing a dog collar with spikes, thigh-high stiletto boots, and a ball gag? Oh, God—we have *got* to get ahold of the crime scene pictures and see for ourselves. Stace, don't you have a friend in the copshop? Doesn't he owe you a favor?"

"Mike isn't talking to me," Stacey said, toying with her blonde ringlets. "He's mad about Luke."

"Luke? Your stepbrother?" I asked, not seeing how the pieces fit.

"Mike thinks Luke has a thing for me. He also thinks I have the secret hots for Luke."

"Is he right?" Jennifer asked, wagging her brows.

Stacey shrugged. "Luke is hot as sin. Can't argue that. But he's my stepbrother. And he has sex with just about anything that moves—male or female, often in groups. I know because he tells me," she said before any of us could ask. "Sometimes he shows me videos. He's a slut. I am so *not* going there."

"Tell Mike that," I suggested. The cop was a beautiful specimen with broad shoulders, a lean waist, legs like tree trunks, a square, chiseled face, and an ass made to be grabbed. Unfortunately, he was also a straight arrow and didn't approve of Stacey's friends—especially me, Lorraine, and Jen. Somehow he had this idea that Stacey was some sort of innocent angel and we were the devils out to corrupt her. It's the blonde ringlets and the fact that she's only five foot two. She looks like a little angel. If only he knew.

She rolled her eyes at me. "He wouldn't believe it if I swore on a stack of bibles. And anyhow, what's the point? He's not going to let me play ride 'em cowboy unless we get married, and *that* is never going to happen. Not without brain damage, anyhow."

"He'd probably only want to do it missionary in the dark anyway," Lorraine said, nodding sagely. "And only to make you pregnant. Can you imagine him going down on you?" She shook her head. "At least Luke would keep your engine lubed."

"Luckily I don't have to pick either one of them," Stacey said loftily.

"Still, would be nice to get ahold of the crime scene photos," Jen said. "They didn't tell you anything about how she died or where or anything?"

I shook my head. "Just that she was murdered." I frowned. "You don't suppose they were lying about that, do you?"

"Possible, but I doubt it," Jen said. "Otherwise they harassed a victim's kid for no good reason. That would be stupid. It would end up smeared all over the papers. Probably will anyway." She grabbed her phone and started texting. Her sister was a reporter for the local news station.

A minute later, she got a text back. "Val wants to interview you." Jen looked at me. "Tomorrow morning? Here?"

"I have to open the store tomorrow, and I've got two sales this weekend. I don't have time."

"Nine a.m. it is," she said, her fingers flying. "She'll bring doughnuts. And your quadruple espresso mocha latte."

I scowled at her. "What am I going to say? Mom was a bitch, and I'm glad she's dead? I'd lose all my business. Her friends and clients all shop here."

"Don't worry. Val knows how evil your mom was. She needs a scoop, and interviewing you gets her that. Plus you get a plug for the store. You know, grieving daughter carrying bravely on. Val will softball you. If she doesn't, she knows I'll kick her ass."

I still didn't like it, but I also wasn't getting out of it, so there wasn't any point arguing. I sighed and grabbed another handful of potato chips. "Fine, but you have to do my hair and makeup for it."

"And dress you," Lorraine said. "Otherwise you'll wear jeans and a torn T-shirt."

"Aren't those in right now?" I asked.

"Only if you're flashing back to the eighties. Don't worry; we've got your back. You'll look totally killer."

"Don't put me in black. I don't want to look like I'm mourning."

"Would we do that?" Lorraine asked. "Trust us."

# CHAPTER THREE

The interview went off well. I managed not to giggle every time Val gave me the sad-sympathetic face, and not once did I break into dance, though my toes were tapping. The girls had put me in an indigo sheath that hugged my curves like a horny man's hands. I wore black heels and pearls, along with a black lace bolero, and I looked amazing, if I do say so myself.

I'm not pixie cute like Stacey, nor Amazon beautiful like Jen. Lorraine is mother earth gorgeous, and I'm your basic California-style surfer girl, except that I've never even seen a surfboard. I'm medium tall, with thick blonde hair that hangs in a long bob to my shoulders. It's my best asset, if you ask me. I'm on the too-thin side, but my mother's death will change that. I'm also extremely athletic—mother's fault again. The woman was a sadist. I still don't know if it was personal or if she generally liked to torture people. Maybe it was both.

The girls had spent the night, waking early to shove me into the shower and make me presentable. The back buzzer of the warehouse started going off so much with flower deliveries that I finally turned it off. They could pile the offerings outside if they wanted. I'd be having them carted over to the hospital anyhow. No sense wasting flowers.

Luckily, Jen, Lorraine, and Stacey kept a supply of clothing at my place, and while Val interviewed me, they ran interference with the other press and everybody else who had descended to offer their condolences. Some of them even seemed genuinely to have liked the bitch, which only goes to show how fake people can be.

Kevin showed up just before ten. He was my store manager. He wore a green sweater vest and a bow tie. He squeezed in and slammed the front door. "What in the name of Jesus is going on out there?" he asked. "Are we giving away free condoms today or something?"

"My mother died," I said baldly. "Murdered."

He stutter-stepped and looked at me. When it was obvious I wasn't kidding, he looked up. "There is a God." Then back at me. "Congratulations." With that, he jigged to his office, singing "Ding Dong the Witch Is Dead" off key.

Val watched him go. "He took the news well."

I grinned. "Almost as well as I did."

"Jen's been turning cartwheels. Literally. She also keeps giggling. My sister does not giggle."

"Some things just have to be celebrated."

"Amen to that. Thanks for giving me the scoop. And congratulations."

I ushered her out and then started going over my day. Unfortunately, thanks to my mother, my schedule was shot to hell. The day got worse when less than a half hour later, Detective Ballard showed up again, this time with her partner.

I rolled my eyes as she entered the store first, the door chiming softly. The place was swarming with customers.

Kevin had chased out the reporters who tried to horn their way in. They could buy or they could leave, was his motto.

My employees had really stepped up. Angie was manning the register, and Kevin was helping customers. Monica and Dean were on their way in, along with Randy and George. The store needed all the extra coverage it could get today, what with the flood of rubberneckers.

I had retreated to Kevin's office to call my mother's house. Specifically, I'd called Deirdre, the housekeeper, to make sure everything was OK and that the animals were getting cared for. She didn't offer me condolences, and I didn't pretend I needed any. Her voice was crisp.

"The mistress was found on the back patio," she said without waiting for me to ask. "The police have been here since early yesterday, and I don't know when they'll wrap up."

"You're feeding them?" I asked, already knowing she was.

"Certainly," she said, sounding insulted.

"Then they'll take as long as humanly possible. Your food is legendary. If you need me for anything, let me know," I said. "I wish I could tell you what's going to happen with her estate, but I have no idea."

The employees were likely going to get sacked, including Deirdre. That was the only thing that sucked about my mother's death. I knew I wasn't going to inherit a damned thing, which was more than fine by me, but I hated that everybody on the estate would likely lose their jobs.

"We will be fine, Miss Rebecca," Deirdre said.

"All the same, you know how to reach me. Any references you need, you can count on me."

I hung up and went to the doorway of Kevin's office, watching as Detective Ballard and her partner wound their way through the maze of people and displays to me. I was aware of Ballard's partner's slow up-and-down scrutiny. His gaze lingered on my legs, which my dress and heels showed off to perfection. They are almost my best feature, according to the girl squad, second only to my ass.

I didn't greet either one of them as they stopped in front of me. I just waited with that distantly bored look that used to piss my mother off to no end. It clearly grated on Detective Ballard, whose lips thinned. She looked like she'd eaten a raw onion.

"Miss Wyatt," her partner said, offering his hand. "I'm Detective Jeffers."

I gave him a limp-fish handshake.

"I believe you know my partner," he said, letting go and motioning toward his dark-skinned companion. She still looked awful, like sleep was a wish and never a reality. She nodded at me.

"I wonder if you might have somewhere private we could talk."

"I do," I said and didn't move.

He frowned. The man wasn't bad looking. Sort of in the bad boy handsome-pretty club, with a crooked nose and a cleft chin. I hated cleft chins. His eyes were a mossy brown, and his hair looked due for a cut. He was broad shouldered and lean waisted, like he took physical fitness seriously, unlike the doughnut-glutton cops of legend.

"We'd like to ask you a few more questions," Detective Jeffers prompted me.

"You mean questions about my relationship with my mother and whether I might want to kill her?"

Jeffers cut a sharp look at Ballard, who didn't look the slightest bit cowed. OK, I had to admit I was impressed by that. The woman owned her shit.

"I'm sure Detective Ballard didn't intend to make any accusations."

"Sure she did. Didn't you?"

Ballard shrugged unrepentantly. "We haven't ruled you out. You could take a polygraph test."

"I could also tell you to fuck off again."

Ballard's mouth tightened and I couldn't tell if she was trying to stop a smile or a grimace.

"We'd appreciate your cooperation," Jeffers said smoothly. "The faster we find your mother's killer, the sooner this zoo is over." He waved at the reporters clustered outside.

He'd found my weak spot. I sighed. "This way."

Kevin's office was a fishbowl. I led the detectives back into the warehouse to my office. I made a pot of coffee and poured a round for each of us before parking behind my desk.

"Miss Wyatt—" Jeffers began. I cut him off.

"Fair warning. I am not particularly patient, so better ask questions I haven't already answered." I looked at Ballard. "Go ahead."

Her brows rose. Jeffers glared at my dismissal, and I ignored him. He'd probably expected to charm me. He had that aura around him, like he thought he was God's gift. I bet his invitations to bed didn't get a lot of refusals. I liked Ballard better.

She flipped open her notebook and jumped back in where she'd left off yesterday. "Was your mother seeing anyone romantically?"

"I don't know."

A sharp look. "Any previous boyfriends or lovers who might be holding a grudge?"

"I don't know."

"What about friends?"

"I don't know."

Ballard dropped her notebook into her lap and gave me a disgusted look. "I thought you were ready to cooperate."

"I am cooperating. I'm answering your questions, aren't I?"

"*I don't know* is not an answer."

"Of course it is. It's just not the answer you want."

"Miss Wyatt—may I call you Rebecca? Surely you know more about your mother's life than you've told us," Jeffers inserted smoothly.

I leveled an impatient look at him. "Surely I don't. And no, you may not call me Rebecca. It's Beck. I hate Rebecca."

"Let me guess: your mother called you Rebecca," Ballard said dryly.

Nail on the head. "Do you have more questions?"

The other woman sighed. "How about you tell us what you do know."

"My mother was a very successful real estate agent, and she was stupid wealthy. She never talked about family, and I never met any. She saw a lot of people socially and threw a lot of parties, but I couldn't say if she had any actual friends. I doubt it, but then she was a different person with me than with other people. As far as I could tell, she was frigid, cruel, impatient, and she enjoyed watching people suffer, especially me. You should talk to her housekeeper, Deirdre. She'd know more."

Ballard was writing notes, nodding. "We already have." She looked at me. "The housekeeper tells us you were a regular visitor. Seems odd since you disliked her so much."

"I didn't dislike her. I despised her. And yes, I went to see her once a week, sometimes more often."

"Why?"

"She didn't give me a lot of choice."

"How so?" Jeffers asked, leaning forward like I was going to offer some great revelation.

"She threatened to have me blackballed and put me out of business."

Ballard's brows rose. "Could she do that?"

"Yep."

Both of them looked disbelieving, and I didn't bother to explain. I could tell them that my mother had made of point of referring clients to me so that I grew dependent on the same clientele. I couldn't tell them that she had dirt on just about everybody in town and that they'd do what she wanted to keep their secrets from getting out. If that meant blackballing me, that was a small enough price to pay. The ones she didn't have dirt on, she didn't mind finding other ways to get at them.

Jeffers started to take a breath, and I shook my head. "Move on."

Ballard jumped in. "What about enemies?"

"Everybody. Anybody. Except maybe the staff. She paid them enough to buy their loyalty. There's not a lot of turnover in her household."

Ballard scribbled notes.

"The estate is unusual," Jeffers said.

"Is it?" I wasn't commenting. A lot of what was on the grounds was devoted to making me suffer.

"The rock climbing wall was unexpected," he said.

I couldn't figure out what he wanted me to say. I sure as hell wasn't going to tell him how the wall had actually been used. I glanced at the clock. "I've got a busy day. Is there anything else?"

Ballard exchanged an "I told you so" look with her partner.

"You haven't asked how your mother died," she said.

"You said she was murdered."

"Usually the families of victims want to know details."

I shrugged. "I'm just happy she's dead. I trust you wouldn't lie about that. But if her death was hideously embarrassing, that would make my day. Was it? Was bondage involved? A sex swing maybe?"

Jeffers gave a choked cough. "You do realize that statements like that make us wonder about your possible involvement."

"And gee, I thought honesty was the best policy. If you want to investigate me, go right ahead. You're barking up the wrong tree, but it's your time to waste. *My* time is valuable, however, and I've given you all I intend to." I reached into a drawer for a stack of folders on the upcoming estate sales.

"What about the beneficiaries of her estate?" Ballard asked.

"Not me. That's all I know."

"Do you know who her attorney was?"

"For all I know, she was repped by Judge Judy."

It made me ridiculously happy to see Jeffers rub his forehead like he was getting a headache. Or a tumor. So much for his confidence in handling me.

"Would you be willing to take us on a tour through the house? Tell us if anything is missing or where your mother might have stored her papers and valuables?"

"Ask Deirdre."

"We'd prefer you."

"Too bad." I stood. "It's not been a pleasure, and I have to say I hope whoever killed my mother gets away with it. Public service." I pointed to the doorway. "Don't let the door hit you in the ass on the way out."

Ballard and Jeffers both stood and set cards on my desk. I could swear Ballard smiled. Maybe because Jeffers looked so irritated. He definitely wasn't used to getting kicked to the curb.

"We'll be in touch," Jeffers said. "Call if you think of anything that might be helpful."

"Sure," I said and swept the cards into the trash as soon as they walked out the door.

# CHAPTER FOUR

Details of my mother's murder got into the paper the next day. She'd not been dressed in bondage gear, but it *was* decently embarrassing. The main house had a series of big, ugly gargoyles around the roof. Apparently one had been in need of repair, as well as the stonework where it perched. The creature had been left on a scaffolding to return it to its spot on the roof. My mother had been on the patio beneath when the scaffolding gave way and the stone beast had fallen on her, stabbing her with its huge penis and crushing her under its weight. Don't ask me why my mother had gargoyles with giant penises guarding her house. The paper called it a stone protrusion, but I knew the truth. According to the article, the scaffolding had been tampered with, making her death a murder. No wonder the detectives hadn't wanted to tell me. I'd never have stopped laughing.

I'd barely picked myself up off the floor when my cell rang. Jen.

"Oh my God! Can you believe it? Crushed by a gargoyle and impaled on its penis? Could it be any more perfect?

Didn't she know about safe sex?" She broke into laughter, sobbing with delight. I followed suit. Pretty soon I was back on the floor, holding my ribs and doing that silent laugh thing when you're out of breath and can't stop.

After a few minutes, I managed to collect myself. "Do me a favor and call Lorraine and Stacey. I've got a meeting in forty-five minutes."

"Of course. But we're having dinner tonight to celebrate. You cook. We'll bring all the fun."

I agreed and hung up then went to get dressed. I'd been up since five, going for my usual two-hour morning run. Even knowing mother was dead, I felt the need to speed faster with every step. I'd run sixteen miles practically at a sprint until I finally made myself stop. Finally made myself remember that I didn't need to run out of fear anymore. Maybe I could start running because I liked it. Maybe I could stop doing it altogether.

I put on a gray skirt and a soft green sweater with short sleeves. I picked out a matching pair of heels and added earrings and a necklace. I examined myself in the mirror and then flipped myself off in the mirror before collecting my purse and tote.

I didn't mind the clothes, but they weren't my style. I looked like the society types I tended to do business with. I looked like my mother. The uniform of the job. I preferred to dress for comfort.

I reached my appointment exactly at ten. I entered the lobby of the Marcross Hotel and crossed to its exclusive restaurant, The Bronze Raven. Garrett Hornsby the Fifth rose as I came in.

"I'm so very sorry to hear about your mother," he said, kissing my outstretched hand. He was old-school manners.

Not that he was particularly old. I guessed early thirties

with a spare build and a finely chiseled face. His dark hair was combed low over his forehead and across his eyes. His designer suit was black, with a crisp white shirt and a tie that matched my emerald green sweater. He was handsome in a reserved sort of way. He didn't wind my clock, but I bet he didn't have any trouble getting laid. No trouble at all.

I sat, setting my tote and purse beside him. "Don't be sorry," I said. "I'm not."

His brows rose, his dark eyes curious. "You have never spoken of her to me."

"And I don't mean to start today."

The waiter approached. "My usual, Andre," I said with a smile.

"Of course, Miss Wyatt. And you, Master Hornsby?" Andre had lived in the U.S. for years but still sported an English accent and some of the language foibles.

"The same." He glanced at me. "Better bring plenty of extra bacon. I'm not sharing this morning."

I stuck my tongue out at him and then shrugged. Bacon deserved its own level on the bottom of the food pyramid, if you asked me. Andre retreated after delivering coffee and orange juice.

"You'd think that you'd order extra bacon instead of stealing mine every time," Garrett said, stirring cream into his coffee.

"But when I'm ordering, I don't intend to steal. It's only when it arrives and smells so divine that I lose my self-control. My breakfast *does* come with bacon. It's not like I'm lying in wait for yours."

"And yet every time, yours is not enough. There should be a lesson there." He grinned at me.

"Business now or later?" I asked, already reaching for my tote. Neither one of us liked to wait.

"Are you sure you don't have personal business you need to be doing?" he asked gently.

"Nope."

He looked taken aback and a little bit hurt. Inwardly I sighed. I considered Garrett a friend. At least as much a friend as I allowed myself to have outside Jen, Stacey, and Lorraine. He and I had been doing business for a number of years, and he had shared a lot of bacon with me. I liked him and I didn't want to offend him.

I bent forward, looking at him earnestly. "Look, it's really okay. I wasn't close to my mom at all. I'd like to say I was, but she and I didn't get along. At all. It probably sounds horrible, but I really am more relieved she's gone than anything else."

He blinked at me and then reached out and took my hand between both of his, his dark eyes warm. "For your sake, I'm glad. I'm sorry that you and your mother didn't have a better relationship. Family is important."

I shrugged and drew back. "I wouldn't know. Now how about we change the subject? Please?" I smiled to take any sting out of the words.

Garrett smiled back, shaking his head. "Anything for you, my darling. But if I can do anything at all, please let me know. You always have my friendship and support."

I blinked, not quite knowing what to say to that. Garrett always seemed so reserved. His warmth surprised me. "Thanks," I said finally, smiling. "You're a gem."

I pulled a plastic file out of my bag and unlatched it, pulling the contents out. "Here are the pieces I've set aside for you, along with all the information on provenance, makers, and the like. There are some very interesting jewelry pieces and a collection of ivory dogs that appear to be at least three hundred years old. Then a list of furniture pieces. I loaded images onto a thumb drive." I passed it over to him.

He paged through the thick stack, asking questions and making notes on the sheets. Andre brought our breakfasts—crab eggs benedict for me, with four slices of bacon, and an apple German pancake topped with a thick basil cream for Garrett. When Andre set the plate of extra bacon in front of him, Garrett shoved it toward me with his fork.

"The better mood you're in, the better deal I get," he said.

Then he was going to take me to the cleaners because I'd just had the best twenty-four hours of my life. I was smart enough not to say that, and not just because I didn't want to talk about my mother.

"If you wanted a really good deal, you should have ordered me some sausage too." I flushed, hoping he wouldn't take that the wrong way. Luckily he didn't seem to read the penis parallel, so I didn't have to babble stupidly and apologize.

By the time our brunch was over, we'd negotiated on almost everything. A few pieces I refused to haggle on, and he decided he'd come see them for himself the next day.

"I won't make it until after seven," he said again. "You're sure it won't interfere with your Friday night plans?"

"No problem at all," I said. The girls wouldn't mind me running downstairs for a little while. In fact, as handsome as Garrett was, I wouldn't be surprised if they joined me to ogle him. Well, maybe not Lorraine. She'd been dating a hot accountant recently. I snorted inwardly. Who was I kidding? Even if she was off the market, that didn't mean she wouldn't want to admire the scenery. Garrett might not be my type, but he was easy on the eyes.

"Right. Your mother."

He took my hand and pulled me into a hug. He smelled amazing and totally edible. My mouth actually watered. His chest was more muscular than I expected. Maybe I could be into him.

He leaned back slightly, his pelvis rubbing into mine unexpectedly. I almost jumped out of my skin.

"I'm so very sorry for your loss."

Part of me wanted to just snuggle up to him like a kitten, but then he'd think I gave a shit about my mother, and he'd also think I was into him, and I wasn't going to blow a terrific business relationship for a little nookie. Anyhow, even if I was attracted to him, I wouldn't do anything about it. Another emotional crippling I could lay at the feet of my mother. I didn't date. I didn't get involved with anybody. Not with mom ready to eat them alive. The girls were different. We'd been friends since grade school and even when I tried to push them off to protect them, they'd clung to me like barnacles. Thank God. 'Course, maybe now that I was free, I could figure out how to get involved with someone.

But not with Garrett. I took one more breath of his delicious scent, then pushed away. I smiled. "Thank you, but honestly, I'm fine."

His hands lingered on my shoulders. "Are you sure? We can postpone all this for a few weeks. I was devastated when my mother died."

Because *his* mother wasn't a demon from hell. I frowned. "Oh my goodness, Garrett. I had no idea."

He shrugged but I could see old sorrow in his eyes. "It's been a few years. But, Beck, I'm not in any hurry."

I shook my head. "Trust me. I'm okay. I'll see you tomorrow night."

He smiled. "I look forward to it."

Wow. I'd never noticed his killer smile before. The girls were going to eat him alive and be irritated at me for keeping him a secret for so long.

Garrett left ahead of me. I retreated to the bathroom first and brushed my teeth. I had a couple of stops to make with new estate sale clients and didn't need to blow bacon breath in all their faces.

I'd parked in the underground garage instead of using the valet parking. I had a thing about other people driving my car. I went outside and down the steps to the second level. When I reached my car, it was blocked by a long black limo. A man leaned casually against the front end, arms crossed. He was dark blond with short hair on the sides and longer on top. He wore a leather jacket and jeans and a pair of boots.

He had a short beard, a brooding forehead, and a strong nose. Mostly he put off that sexy bad boy vibe that had women in a five-block radius wetting themselves and not knowing why.

As I approached, he straightened as if waiting for me.

"You're blocking me in," I said. "Do you mind?" I went past him without waiting for an answer.

"Miss Wyatt, I'm Damon Matrovani. My employer would like a word with you. You can ride with me and I'll return you here later, or I can have someone follow us in your car."

As if. Nobody drove my 1965 Thunderbird but me. Plus, I didn't take orders from strangers. Hell, I didn't take orders.

I opened the trunk, dropped in my tote and purse, and then shut it before turning back around to look at Mr. Sex on a Sandwich. He'd stopped barely a foot away. I could smell him—woodsy and musky and pure male. Better than

Garrett by far, except I didn't want to curl up on this hunk of man like a kitten. I wanted to tear his clothes off and claw his back.

"I'm sorry, Mr. Matrovani, was it? But I have several meetings that I can't miss. Have your employer contact my office, and I'll be happy to arrange a meeting."

"My employer is happy to compensate you for your trouble at whatever you should wish to charge."

I couldn't tell what color his eyes were in the gloom of the parking garage, but I could feel them boring through me. Not in any sort of sexual way, which oddly irritated me. It was more like I was being pinned to a foam board like a giant bug.

"Seriously? Throw money at a girl, and what? You expect her to just offer herself up? I've got news for you, Mr. Matrovani. I'm not a whore, and you can tell your employer he can stick his head up his ass and see if he can find a brain up there. Now move your car and let me out."

His nostrils flared. "I didn't suggest that you are a whore, Miss Wyatt."

"Sure you did. Now get out of my way."

I started to brush past him. He blocked my path.

"I did *not* suggest you are a whore," he repeated, his gaze furious. "As you say, you are a busy woman, and your time is valuable. I merely indicated that you would be compensated for your time."

Apparently I'd hit a nerve. I gave my best fake syrupy smile. "My valuable time is spoken for. Call for an appointment."

I started to pass him again, and once more he blocked me. "I'm afraid I must insist, Miss Wyatt," Damon Dickhead said in a completely nonapologetic tone that totally contradicted his words.

I let my gaze rove down his body and back up. I took my time, examining the broad sweep of his shoulders, the taut narrowing of his waist, and the roll of his muscular thighs inside his tight jeans. My mouth watered. He was sex on a sin stick. Just the type to get me hot and bothered in a way that polite and reserved Garrett never could. This guy exuded masculine animalism like Fukushima gave off radiation. He had that bad boy careless arrogance thing going on that made me want to rub on him like a cat in a bed of catnip.

God, I was a cliché. Why did women always want to screw the pricks? I bit back a smile. Oh yeah, screwing his prick could be loads of fun. Not that I'd know what to do with him.

My one and only sexual experience had been miserable at best. It had taken place in the backseat of a car with Marco Culver, a jock in my high school. He'd shoved his dick inside me once, and that had hurt like fuck. I hadn't hung around to see if it got better. The girls said I couldn't judge by a clumsy ass like him and that sex with someone who knew how to touch a woman was better than a refrigerator full of cheesecake, so I was ready and willing to try again. But not with Damon Dickweed, even if he did look like he was an expert at making a woman scream with pleasure.

"I admit, you're awfully pretty," I said finally, taking satisfaction in the red that had risen in his cheeks at my slow perusal. "But I'm not interested in anything you—or your *employer*—" (I put employer in air quotes) "—have to offer." I did my best to adopt the snotty-haughty tone my mother had perfected that always reduced people to squirming worms.

He scowled and then stepped forward, leaning into me,

his delicious scent curling around me. It was outdoorsy and male. Oh, so male. Dear lord, this ridiculous attraction had to be an aftereffect of mom's death. With her gone, my hormones were unleashed and had decided to make up for lost time and start slobbering over random men. If I wasn't careful, I'd end up humping his leg.

His tempting lips were just inches from mine, his stormy blue eyes piercing through me. His voice had dropped into a low growl that made my insides quiver. "Sweetheart, if *I* wanted you, I'd *have* you and you'd be begging on your knees for more."

He straightened, giving me a cool once-over. He clearly was not turned on. "The only thing I want from you is to come with me for a little while and meet my employer."

And a big bucket of ice water doused my lust. Thank goodness. I flipped my hair over my shoulder. "Insist all you want, but I've no intention of going off with a strange man to God knows where for God knows why."

"I have no intention of hurting you," he said, looking offended.

I couldn't help my smile. Another effect of saying bye bye to Mommy Dearest—I didn't feel like I had to keep myself shut down all the time. I could afford to smile. Laugh even. "I bet Ted Bundy said that to all the women he killed."

He cracked an appreciative smile, and it was devastating. My knees wobbled and my breath caught in my throat. God, I was way too easy.

He lifted his hands, palms up. "How can I convince you that I mean no harm?"

"Oh, I don't know. Don't lie in wait for me in a parking garage, for starters. You do realize how creepy that is, right?" I lifted an eyebrow.

He had the grace to look a little embarrassed. "This is too important to wait, and I wanted to speak to you in private."

"All right." I folded my arms. "I'll bite. What's so important?"

He grimaced. "I can't tell you. My employer wishes to speak with you himself."

"And we're back to the beginning. I can't imagine what your employer wants so badly from an estate sale coordinator, but he'll just have to make an appointment. In public," I added pointedly. "And during the day." I glanced at my watch. "I have places to be. You need to move."

I turned to unlock the Thunderbird, my back prickling with awareness of Damon Handsomepants.

He let out quiet sigh. "I really am sorry, but this really is for your own good."

A whirl of blue magic circled around me, pinning my arms to my sides. For a second, I was too shocked to react. Aside from my mother, I'd never encountered another person who could do magic. And now that I had, he was trying to kidnap me.

I twisted to look at him. "Are you serious?"

"Don't be afraid. I promise I won't hurt you."

He looked like he really wanted me to believe him. He even looked a little guilty. The asshole reached for me to drag me into the limo.

"I don't think so," I said stepping back and shimmying out of the magic binding. It fell to the ground like stretchy Jell-O.

I expected him to look surprised, but he didn't, which was more unnerving than his doing magic. He tensed, power crackling over his hands as he started to cast another spell at me.

Adrenaline and fear gave me the faster edge. Grasping my own magic in my hands, I whacked him in the chest. I clobbered him so hard, he rolled back over the hood of the limo and tumbled off the other side. That would leave bruises.

Before he could collect himself and come after me again, I looped magic under the front axle of the limo and flipped it backward onto its roof. The crashing sound echoed through the garage and made me jump.

I opened my car door and jumped inside then squealed backward out of the slot, swerving to miss Damon Asswipe, who'd already regained his feet. He staggered, shaking his head as if to clear it. I gunned the Thunderbird and screeched up the ramp and out of sight, leaving behind about half my tires on the pavement.

I pitched out into traffic, swerving to avoid a collision. I was running on instinct. Cars honked, but I put the pedal to the metal and roared down the street, turning quickly to make sure I was out of the line of sight of Damon Nutsack if he managed to pull his shit together and get to the sidewalk before I got away. I wouldn't put it past him to flatten all my tires with magic or maybe drop my drivetrain.

After I put a few miles behind me, I pulled into the parking lot of the Seventh Day Adventist Church and parked. My hands were shaking, and my heart was racing. I made myself breathe. What in the fuck had just happened? Who were Damon and his employer and what did they want with me? What should I do now?

I couldn't call the cops. What would I say? That he lassoed me with magic and tried to drag me off to his lair? They'd have me stashed in the looney bin before lunch, and from the way they questioned me, they already thought I killed my mother.

"Maybe he'll give up," I muttered. But he wouldn't. Nothing about the man suggested he was a quitter. He would be coming for me again. At home, in the shop, at a sale—I wasn't all that hard to find.

Well, let him. I could take care of myself. I'd survived my mother and all the hell she'd thrown at me over the years. Anyway, I'd fought off Mr. Damon Buttplug once. I could damned well do it again. If he wanted to come after me, let him try.

# CHAPTER FIVE

I made it to my appointments, checking over my shoulder most of the time. I was semi-surprised when I got back to the shop and I didn't see any sign of Damon HotStuff. Unless he could become invisible. Could he? I pulled thoughts away from that terrifying direction, or before long, I'd be thinking he could walk through walls and watch me through his crystal ball. Shit. What if he could?

I snorted. Well then, I'd better wear cute underwear. The idea of his spying on me mostly should have made me cringe, but I kept thinking of the wide plane of his muscular chest and gorgeous legs. Fuck. I needed to get laid for real. If only I did one-night stands ... but I didn't. Lust wasn't enough; I needed an emotional connection. Though the way I was going, my body might just start humping some strange guy before the rest of me knew what it was up to.

I spent the rest of the afternoon working on setting up a sale that would happen the following weekend, then running by the one happening on Saturday to make sure it was all ready. Monica, my right-hand Goddess of Organization, toured me through the house. I checked the prices and the displays, making a few changes.

"You did terrific," I said. "As usual. I'll be here by five on Saturday morning to help open."

"With or without coffee and doughnuts?" Monica asked.

"Are you serious? I always bring the goods, don't I?"

"I live in fear that you will forget," she said with a grin, looking around in satisfaction. "This is going to be a good one."

"I've already sold a lot of the stuff we held back," I said. "Met with Garrett this morning."

"How did it go?"

I thought of Damon Prancypants. Maybe that was exactly what he'd intended, but I couldn't help wondering just what his employer wanted from me. The magical connection made me think this had something to do with my mother and that both made me ultracurious and pissed me off. "Went fine," I said when I realized that Monica was staring at me.

"You all right?" she asked, frowning at me. "You look, I don't know, out of sorts."

I snorted. "Out of sorts? How old are you?"

"Stop deflecting. You know what I mean."

That was the problem with having a psych major for an employee. They were a lot more perceptive than everybody else.

"I had a run-in with someone this morning," I said, electing to go with part truth. "In the parking garage of the Marcross Hotel."

Her face went angry. She did not like people fucking with her family or friends. "What do you mean—*run-in*?"

"This guy cornered me in the parking garage. Said he wanted me to meet with his employer."

"There's more to it than that. What aren't you saying?"

Her gaze had narrowed, and I should have known better than to try to keep anything a secret. Somehow I didn't want her to think too badly of Damon Tightpants. He could have tried a lot more force. He'd been quite polite, as kidnappers go. He hadn't used a knife or gun. That had to count.

Finally I shrugged. "He tried to grab me."

Her eyes went wide. "Grab you? As in, kidnap? Rape? Tell me you called the cops."

I shook my head. "The cops aren't impressed with me right now, and anyway, nothing happened. I shoved him and got in my car and took off."

"Jesus, Beck. You need to tell someone. The hotel, at least. What if he goes after another woman?"

"Sure," I said, having no intention of calling anyone. Damon Dickhead had been after me, not making random attacks. The big question was why? The fact that, aside from my mother, he was the only other person I'd ever seen who could do magic suggested that his employer wasn't interested in my estate sales business. *Son of a bitch.* I wanted to kick myself. I'd revealed I could do magic just as casually as he had. Maybe that had been the point. I got away awfully easy, considering.

That's when it occurred to me to wonder if he or his so-called employer had had anything to do with my mother's death. I mean, it was really coincidental that Damon shows up right after she dies and is throwing magic lassos. Well, if either he or his employer had killed Mommy Dearest, I owed them both a gift basket. An expensive one with gold watches and a bottle of elderly single malt Scotch.

"Seriously, Beck. This isn't anything to take lightly," Monica urged.

"I'll think about it," I said. But now I was looking forward to seeing Damon again and finding out just what he and his boss had been up to.

Back at my apartment, I decided I needed to take a run. Despite my mother's using it as a torture device, I really liked it. Climbing and swimming too.

I got dressed and drove out to the river and parked at the Chemalok recreation area near the bathrooms. Trails ran up and down the river from the rec area. Upstream led to the bluffs and some of my favorite trails. They went for miles.

I got out, stretched, grabbed my water, then headed out.

I went slowly at first, savoring the sounds and smells of the water and the birds and the antics of the squirrels. I sped up as I went up the bluffs. There wasn't much to see on this leg of the trail. I cleared the top to the plateau and stopped to drink. I'd gone about three miles and had only just started to sweat. I looked back down onto the river. It was a ribbon of glittering gold in the sunlight. The breeze cooled my skin, and I fell into a ground-eating run.

I loved the feel of the power in my body. I liked knowing it was strong and capable. I liked knowing I could push myself to my limits and past and create new limits.

When it turned dusk, I headed back toward the parking lot. Dusk lasted a long time in the summer, and I figured I still had a good hour of decent light. All the same, tree shadows cast a gloom over the parking lot by the time I got there. I stopped to scan it before leaving the trail. A handful of cars and trucks were parked there, plus a van with a boat trailer. A couple of guys with kayaks loaded them into racks on top of their SUV. Nothing looked out of place.

I walked across to my car. I wouldn't have been surprised if Damon Jizzwizard popped out from nowhere.

Turns out I was right.

Just like in the garage, he came out of the shadows on the other side of my car. He stopped between me and it, arms folded, legs spread like one of those gunslingers about to grab for his gun. He had muscles on top of muscles and looked smoking hot, not to mention seriously irritated.

I stopped ten feet away. "Did you forget how to use a phone and make an appointment?"

He let his arms fall to his sides, hooking his thumbs into his pockets. He eyed me with scathing disgust. "Do you think you're invincible or something? Anybody could attack you. You'd be taken down before you knew you'd been hit. You may be good, but you're not *that* good."

His tone irritated the fuck out of me. Who was he to judge me? "Far as I can tell, you're the only one out attacking me today." After all, my mother was dead. I didn't have any other enemies. I smiled. "I figure I can handle you."

The fire of challenge lit his expression. "Can you, now?"

His gaze slid over me in the same measuring way I'd scrutinized him this morning. I wasn't wearing much. A sports bra under a loose tank top and a pair of colorful jogging capris. His expression turned appreciative. His eyes sparked with sudden hunger, and he slid his tongue over his bottom lip. Seeing that, my insides melted, and the rest of me nearly followed. The man was sinfully good looking, and I had a feeling he'd know how to play my body like a violin.

I swallowed against my suddenly dry throat. "Yes. I can." Dear God, I wanted to climb him like a tree.

He smiled lazily and moseyed forward. There was no other word for that slow, confident, loose-hipped walk. He stopped less than a foot away, and the heat radiating off his body warmed me like a fire. My nipples popped up into hard little pearls that I hoped the fading light hid. My sports bra and tank top certainly didn't. Luckily I was already panting from my run, so the fact that he made me breathless wasn't nearly so obvious. I fought the urge to squeeze my legs together to assuage the sudden ache there.

He lifted his hand and ran a finger feather-soft along my collar bone. I stiffened, feeling like a deer in the headlights. Half of me wanted to run, the other half wanted to lean into his touch and lick his chin.

"I might just let you try and prove it," he said, his taunting tone telling me he knew exactly what he was doing to me.

"Sure," I said, trying to remember what we were talking about. "Anytime you want your ass kicked, I'm available and very willing."

The last made his eyes flare with heat. He perused me again in that slow, possessive way, and I swear my panties went up in smoke. I was about ready to throw myself on the hood of my car, spread my legs, and beg him to shatter my world.

His eyes came back to mine, and if anything, they'd turned hotter. His fingers ran up the side of my neck, and his thumb brushed my lips.

"Have dinner with me."

That took me aback and doused me with ice water. I was having such fun with the angry-flirting thing. I was expecting him to double down on the sexual innuendo and ask just how willing I might be. So when he asked—or ordered—me to dinner, it caught me way off guard. It took a few seconds to recalibrate and focus. Disappointment washed through me, cold and black.

"Thanks for the offer," I said, my voice turning business crisp. "I'm off the clock for the night, though. Maybe you should have your employer call me during business hours, like I told you this morning."

I pulled away and took a couple of steps toward my Thunderbird. That's as far as I got when he grabbed my arm and spun me back around. He was glowering and confusion intensified the storminess of his blue eyes.

"I asked you to dinner with *me*."

"Actually, you *ordered* me. There was no question involved. But that doesn't matter. What does matter is that you have no earthly reason to want to have dinner with me, other than to get me cornered somewhere so that your employer can have a go at me. I'm not interested." Which wasn't entirely true. I was getting really curious about just what his employer wanted, but it's not like I was going to let Damon Dickjuice know that.

"Bullshit," he growled, his other hand coming up to clasp my arm. Then before I knew what was happening, he pulled me against him and was kissing me.

I don't know what I expected. I was pretty virginal on the kissing end of things too. I'd barely held hands with a guy. Damon's lips were softer than I'd expected. He took advantage of my startled *oh!* to slide his tongue sensually along my lower lip. I opened for more, and he obliged, slip-ping his tongue inside.

The intimacy of the touch shook me. I wanted more. I

tentatively touched my tongue to his. He tasted divine. Mint, a hint of garlic, and something incredibly him, incredibly male. And oh my God, but my insides were doing crazy things. I felt like I was free-falling from an airplane. Except his arms had come around me, one holding me tight around my waist while his other hand slid up my back. He fisted his hand in my hair and made a low sound of hunger. I lost track of thought in that moment as his kiss turned from delicate exploration to passionate hunger.

If he hadn't been holding me up, I'd have dropped to the ground. I heard myself moan, and I opened my mouth wider, inviting his hunger. I shivered all over at the sensation of his muscular body pressing against me, the heat of him throbbing through me, the smell of him making my head spin. I felt feminine and sexy and incredibly powerful at the eagerness of his touch. He was like a drug. Better than a drug. Better than anything I'd ever experienced before.

I don't know when I'd put my arms around him, but I had a death grip on his neck, like he was the only anchor in a whirling tornado. He just pulled me tighter. I was on fire. I ached so hard that I swear if he touched me just once in the right spot, the one between my legs that actually seemed to hurt with how bad I wanted him, I'd have exploded.

I rubbed my hips into his, feeling the hard column of his cock against me as I searched for relief. He groaned and widened his legs, thrusting against me. I whimpered as electric pleasure jolted through my clit and lit my whole body up like a firework.

His hand left my hair, and I whimpered protest, pressing myself against him as if he were trying to get away. I so didn't want to let this carnival ride end yet. But he wasn't leaving. His hand dropped to my hip and glided up my side. He stopped with his thumb just touching the underside of my breast. For a second I stiffened like the mostly untouched, mostly virginal woman I was.

Then his mouth lifted from mine and his hot mouth dropped to my neck. I stretched to give him room, my fingers digging into his shoulders for balance. At the same time, his hand closed over my breast, his thumb skimming over my nipple in a butterfly touch. I gasped and arched into him. His arm around my waist tightened, and he repeated his barely-there caress. I shuddered. Why had I thought sex was overrated?

He nibbled along my jaw and licked the edge of my ear before scraping his teeth across the lobe, sending delicious shivers reverberating all the way to my bones. Everything inside me tightened around a liquid ache in my belly. I needed more. I wanted to touch him, skin to skin.

He lifted his head, his eyelids heavy, his gaze lingering on my lips before meeting mine. "Do you still think I have no reason to want to have dinner with you?"

It took me a second to pull my fragmented brain together and sort out what he'd said. By the time I could put together a coherent thought, I was distracted by the ring of my phone through the cracked window of my car. It was Lorraine's ringtone.

I pushed against Damon, stepping back as he reluctantly let me go. I staggered to my car, unlocked the driver's door, and grabbed my phone.

"Hey," I said, not taking my eyes off Damon Hotpants. He stared at me broodingly, looking like a thunderstorm about to erupt in wild fury.

"I need you," Lorraine said, her voice strained. "I'll text

the address. Hurry. They want to kill him. We can't let it happen. I won't."

"Kill him?" I repeated, but she was gone.

My lust forgotten, I tossed my phone onto the seat along with my water bottle and slid behind the wheel. Damon grabbed the door to keep me from closing it.

"Kill him? Who? What's going on?" He looked like a panther about to spring on prey, all coiled up to leap, muscles bulging, face intense. He was a testosterone explosion held in place by a very fine body.

"That is none of your business." I slid the key home in the ignition and turned the engine over. It rumbled to life. I glanced up at him. "You should move."

He gripped the top of the door tighter. "I want to know what that meant. Who is killing who?" His deep voice was so hard, it could have cut diamonds.

"Whom," I corrected. I put the Thunderbird in reverse and started backing up.

"Rebecca, wait! You don't know the danger—"

I didn't hear any more. The big block V8 engine roared like a lion as I hit the gas and drowned out his words. Damon swore and the hand not holding the door started glowing blue.

Oh, no he didn't. I gunned the engine and he yelped, leaping aside as I twisted the wheel, my tires squealing protest. As soon as I had room, I jammed the car into drive and floored it. The door swung wide, and I grabbed the handle and yanked it shut. I think Damon might have screamed my name, but I didn't stop.

I made it to the driveway before a meteor of blue struck the trees on the left side of the entrance. They crashed into the road. I wasn't sure I even had time to brake. Good thing I didn't consider it. Instead I flung my own magic at the barrier. The tangled trees exploded into petals of pink light. I sped through them and out. I laughed out loud, wishing I could have seen Damon's face.

I forgot about him when my phone chirped with Lorraine's text. I fed the address into my cell's navigation app.

# CHAPTER SIX

Thank goodness I had the GPS app, or I never would have found the place. It was tucked way back in the hill hollows outside Sweetwater where there were still a bunch of little farms and homesteads that had been in the same families for generations. I drove past the lush, irrigated fields, smelling the damp earth and the green pastures and the sweet scents of summer that wafted through my open windows.

I turned down a narrow gravel lane called, of all things, No Name Lane. Nothing like truth in advertising. I passed driveways, the lights from the houses beyond sparking in the dark like fireflies. I went left when the lane split and over a wooden bridge with no rails then followed the gravel road around to a ranch-style house. Cool, blue-white mercury vapor flood lights lit up the area. I could see several outbuildings and a big barn. The entire place was swarming with cop cars, fire trucks, animal control, and even the forest service.

Lorraine's veterinarian truck was parked in front of the corral. I pulled up behind it.

"Ma'am, you can't be here," a uniformed officer said as he came trotting up. He had one hand on his holstered gun.

"I was called," I said, carefully keeping one hand on the wheel as I pointed to Lorraine's truck. "Dr. Tucker wanted me here."

"I'm sorry but she's not authorized to give anyone access. You need to turn around and leave immediately," he said. "The situation is far too dangerous."

"Wrong," I said. "My friend calls, I come. She needs me, I come through. So I'm going to get out of this car and go find her."

He drew himself up. He'd shaved his head into one of the coply crew cuts that looked good on about two people in the world. He wasn't one of them. His face was round and doughy, despite his lean build. He looked young, like just out of high school. Maybe that's why he'd gotten the haircut, so he'd look older and tougher. It hadn't worked.

"Ma'am, I *will* arrest you if you do not leave this area immediately."

I smiled. "I know." I opened my door, and he took a step back, his hand tightening on the butt of his gun. I probably should have been nervous. Cops these days tended toward the shoot-first-ask-questions-later philosophy, and really, with all the potential threats everywhere, I couldn't exactly blame them. On the other hand, Lorraine had sounded pretty desperate, and every minute I spent with Barney Fife here was a minute she wasn't getting my help.

I shut my door. The young officer pointed at me. His finger was actually shaking. That wasn't because of me. I flicked a glance toward the emergency vehicles. Something big was going down, something that had seriously freaked him out.

"Turn around and put your hands on the roof of the car."

I didn't bother telling him I wouldn't do it. Instead I leaped into motion. The element of surprise. I'm both a long-distance runner and a sprinter. So when I kicked into gear, I'd disappeared between a fire truck and an ambulance before the boy wonder could get out an astonished, "Hey!"

Nobody else paid much attention to me. Most looked grim. Radios crackled and there was a lot of traffic in and out of the house, but that wasn't where the tension was focused. Between the house and the barn was a big dog pen with a seven-foot chain link fence and a flat-topped square structure inside that served as a doghouse. The dog in question was chained to the house. He stood around four feet at the shoulder, with matted fur and what looked like swatches of blood where he'd been cut. He was thin, but even so, I guessed he weighed over a hundred pounds, probably closer to one fifty.

He prowled back and forth, dragging the heavy chain. Behind him, I could see two children huddled together inside of the doghouse. The dog growled low in his throat as he watched the emergency workers watching him.

"There's no way to get a shot on the dog without hitting the kids, sir," someone said.

"You don't need to shoot him. He's protecting them. We just have to get him to understand we're not the enemy," Lorraine said. She was standing in front of the pen's entrance, her feet set, her hands on her hips.

I pushed between people to get close. "I'm here," I said.

"Thank God." She looked at a man who appeared to be in charge. He wore a gray uniform. "Sheriff Anderson, this is my friend Beck. She's an animal whisperer, and no, I don't use that term lightly. I saw her calm a rabid cat once. I promise she can get Ajax to let us take the girls.

At the mention of his name, the dog growled again.

The sheriff started shaking his head. "I told you, Dr. Tucker, I won't put a civilian in that cage."

"It's safe enough," I said. "He's chained." Not for long. As soon as I could, I'd pull that off him. The poor thing. "It can't hurt to try."

The sheriff didn't speak for a moment then finally nodded and turned to the two officers beside him. Both carried rifles. "Maybe if she distracts him, you can get a bead on him. Take up positions and if you get a shot, take it."

"Sheriff! He doesn't deserve this. He's protecting those girls."

"Sorry, Doc, but I can't take chances. Those girls need medical help as soon as possible." He looked at me. "Do your best, ma'am."

I strode toward the gate, not waiting for a second invitation. I prayed I could get Ajax out before the shooters got their shot.

Lorraine grabbed my hand as another deputy unlatched the gate, pressing a metal syringe into my hand. "He's been starved and beaten, and the girls too. The father attacked the mother and she killed him, but then she decided she was going to send her girls off to heaven. She's in custody now. We've no idea how bad the girls might be hurt, but I can tell you that that dog protected them and kept them alive."

One didn't become a vet because one didn't love animals, and Lorraine had a particularly soft heart when it came to hard-luck stories. I didn't know how she'd come to be in the middle of this mess, but I was determined I wasn't going to fail her.

"I've got this," I told her with more confidence than I felt, my hand tightening on the syringe as I walked through the gate.

I have always had a weird calming effect on animals. For some reason they liked me and trusted me, even the wild ones and the rabid ones. I didn't even have to use magic. When Lorraine got problem cases, she called me in to help, which I was glad to do. Animals might just be God's greatest gift to the world, and I did whatever I could to look after them.

The bad thing was my animal whispering abilities took time. I usually started far away and crouching on the ground and slowly closed the gap between me and the animal until it let me touch it. That wasn't going to work here. I didn't have that kind of time.

The smell of dog shit was overwhelming. I almost threw up. The ground was practically paved with it. I'd be throwing away these shoes later. I strode toward the dog, covering the ground between us with a confident stride. I ignored the calls behind me to stop, that I was within the length of the chain. Ajax ducked his head and growled, his lips curling in an angry snarl as I drew closer. He tensed but made no move to attack, blocking my path to the girls.

I crouched so that I was at eye level with him. His eyes looked amber and intelligent. His fur was too dirty and matted to get any sense of what color he was, but his ears were like a German Shepherd, and his snout was long and pointed.

"My name is Beck," I told him. I always introduced

myself. "You've been guarding these girls, but your job is done. You need to let these people here take the girls somewhere warm and safe where they can get looked after." I spoke in a low voice as if he understood every word. I held out my hand, palm up. "These people want to kill you because they think you'll hurt these girls. I know you won't. But your job is done. They're going to be safe. I don't want to see you suffer anymore. If you let the girls go, I'll take care of you. I promise."

The dog tipped his head as if listening and following my meaning. I never was sure what reached out to the animals. I sometimes thought it must be magic, but I didn't use any. It was just me. I spoke to them, but they couldn't understand me. That would be ridiculous. Lorraine said it was something in my voice, in the way I held myself, in my aura. I didn't really care.

Ajax made a whining sound and inched backward. Damn. I didn't have time to build trust. I had to earn it faster than that. This was going to suck.

I dropped to my hands and knees, refusing to think about what my bare skin was touching. At least I didn't run in shorts. I crawled forward. In this position, I was shorter than he and definitely submissive. At the same time, I wasn't tentative. He growled again and his snarl grew bigger, if that was possible. His teeth shined bright white. If he decided to attack, he'd go for my neck. I wasn't about to hit him with magic, except as a last resort, and even then, I didn't know if I had the heart to do it. He was a warrior and a guardian. He'd been through hell, and he was protecting these girls with his life.

I got within three feet of him, then two, then he and I were pretty much face-to-face. He still hadn't tried to bite me. I breathed into his face, letting him get my smell. His smell was rank. I pushed closer and sat back on my heels right in front of him.

"All right," I said. "They're going to come in for the girls now. I'm going to stick with you." I reached out again, and he froze a moment then sniffed my hand. His lips still curled, but I could barely see the teeth now, and his growls were softer, almost questioning. Since I was terrified that he'd be shot at any moment, I decided to take that possibility off the table. I scootched closer to him and turned so I could slide my arm over his neck.

Ajax trembled but didn't move. I looked past him to the girls. The eldest couldn't have been more than ten. They had blood spattered all over them. I hoped to hell it was somebody else's. They were filthy and far too thin, with bruises flowering on their arms and faces. The younger one clung to her sister and stared at me like she was in shock.

"Hi. Do you think you two can walk to the gate while Ajax and I stay here?"

The elder girl frowned and shook her head.

"It's okay now. It's safe. Your father is dead, and your mother is in custody. That means they are going to take her somewhere where she can get help and she can't hurt anyone else."

A tension seemed to go out of the elder girl, but she still didn't move. "You really going to take care of Ajax?" she asked in a paper-thin voice.

I nodded. "I am. My friend over there is a veterinarian. You know what that is?"

The girl shook her head.

"She's a doctor for animals. She sent me in here to make sure that everybody would be safe, including Ajax." I was scratching lightly under his throat. I could feel wetness along the side where I leaned against him. I had a bad feeling it was blood. "I think he's hurt, though. My friend can't help him until the police make sure you're safe. Do you think you can go to the gate? So that my friend can come have a look at Ajax?"

The elder one nodded and pushed to her feet, pulling the younger one up with her. "Daddy was always mean to him," she said, tears rolling down her face. "He's a good dog."

"I know," I said. "I'll take care of him."

They walked away. I watched and then turned my attention back to the dog. I held up the syringe. "This pokes through your skin and the liquid inside makes you go to sleep. I don't want to use it, but if I don't, you're going to have to be calm. My friend and I are going to take care of you."

He looked at me, and I could have sworn he understood every word. He gave the inside of my wrist a lick. I took that as agreement. Just then, Lorraine came up. Ajax looked at her but didn't growl.

"And you work another miracle," she said. Tears were leaking out of the corners of her eyes. She dashed at them. "Come on. I want to get him out of here before they start thinking they want to put him down."

"Is it safe? Did the sheriff call off his shooters?"

She nodded.

I sat with my arm around Ajax as Lorraine wrestled with the chain. It turned out it was welded to a metal stake and she had to call for help to pull it out. The officer who'd tried to arrest me was the only one willing to approach.

"That's the damnedest thing I ever saw," he said as he strained to pull the stake up. "Wouldn't have believed it if I hadn't seen it myself. Sorry about trying to arrest you. Didn't know you could do that."

I didn't reply because I was talking to the dog. Sometimes I went for nonsense sounds, but he seemed to understand my words, so I told him how brave he'd been and how strong and what a hero he was. He leaned against me, nearly tipping me over, and then lay down.

"Lorraine? I think there's something wrong," I said as his breath shuddered inside his ribs.

"We've got to get him where I can see the damage," she said, and then the officer gave the chain a hard yank and it was free. It was two feet long.

"I'm not sure he can walk."

"Think he'll let me carry him?" the officer asked doubtfully.

I looked at him in surprise. "He will."

I told Ajax what was happening, but I wasn't sure he could hear me. His eyes had closed, and he was panting.

Officer Mock, as his named turned out to be, picked up him and carried him through the crowd. Everybody else was pretty much focused on the girls, and the rest just gaped at us. We got back to Lorraine's truck. I'd been right. The wetness on his side was blood, but it was impossible to see the wound through his matted fur.

"I need to get him to the clinic."

Except for the cab of her truck, there was no room to carry an animal Ajax's size, and even if there was, I wasn't going to be separated from him. I'd promised him I was going to take care of him. Officer Mock laid him on the seat between us, and I held his head and shoulders in my lap. I gave the officer my keys when he offered to return my car to me.

"I'll bring it to you as soon as I can. Is he going to be all right?"

"He will be if I have anything to say about it," Lorraine said.

# CHAPTER SEVEN

The rest of the night went by in a blur. I was allowed to stay with Ajax, but only after I'd showered twice with seriously nasty soap and put on scrubs. When I returned to the operating theater, they'd shaved Ajax and done an examination, plus x-rayed him.

He was still unconscious. I bit my lip, trying not to cry. Stupid. I barely knew the dog, and yet he already had a chunk of my heart.

They got him prepped for surgery and went to work. I stroked his head and talked to him, though he was under anesthesia. Lorraine worked quickly. At some point, Ajax had been kicked and a rib had penetrated his lung. That likely happened within the last few hours, Lorraine said. It's a wonder he hadn't died. He hadn't been shot. The wound on his side was from something sharp, though Lorraine didn't think it was a knife. The wound was more a tear than a cut and it was at least a few days old. The scab had broken open during the night.

He also was covered in bruises, flees, and ticks; had a

bad case of ringworm; and underneath the metal collar he wore, his skin was raw and infected.

"He's been through hell," Lorraine said when she was through. We sat on the floor and leaned against the wall, sipping coffee as we watched Ajax sleep on a large dog pillow in one of the recovery areas. "He's tough, though. He should recover just fine, though he's going to need good food, a lot of rest, and gentle care. Hopefully the county won't decide he needs to be put down."

"I'll take him home with me." I didn't even think about it. He and I belonged together. We'd both suffered terribly at the hands of people who were supposed to love us and protect us, and that made us family.

Lorraine looked at me in surprise. "What about your white couch and white carpets?"

"I'll can buy new stuff if I need to."

"He's a big dog. He's going to need a lot of exercise. He won't like being cooped up in your apartment all day, and he may not be good with other dogs or people."

"I'll figure it out. How much longer before he wakes up?"

"Soon. He'll be groggy, though."

"Can I take him home?"

She shook her head and grinned at me. "I always knew you were a soft touch. Yeah, he can go home later today. That should give you time to go shopping for the stuff you'll need." She got to her feet and left, returning a few minutes later with a pad of paper and a pen. She sat back down and made a list of things.

"He's probably never going to take a collar again. That's going to be a problem if you want to take him somewhere. Leash laws. He might take a harness, but I don't know. You'll want to give him a lamb and rice diet for a while—

mix of kibble and canned food. Feed him a half cup of each every three hours. He's been starved, and his stomach and intestines aren't going to be working properly. We've treated his worms, so you may see some ugly things coming out of him in the next week, but getting rid of all that is good. Once we're sure he's doing well, we'll increase his food intake. I'll want to see him every day, but I'll come over to check on him." She finished with writing out the medications and instructions on giving them.

It wasn't much longer before Ajax woke up. I explained all that had happened to him, where I was going, and that I'd be back to get him. He watched me, his eyes dull from the drugs they'd pumped into him.

"You sleep. I'll be back soon."

His eyes never left me as I walked out the door.

# CHAPTER EIGHT

I'd had to call Stacey to take me home. I was surprised to find my car parked out front of the store. It was barely five a.m. I hopped out and sent Stacey on her way after promising we were still on for girls' night at my apartment. I should have Ajax home by then.

My keys were under the mat, and Officer Mock had left a note on the bench along with his card. He asked me to call and let him know how Ajax was doing. Turns out the officer was a good guy.

I drove the Thunderbird around back to the garage, hitting the remote to open it. I could barely lift my hand to the visor where it was clipped, I was so tired. Plus, I still smelled, and I was starving.

The door rolled up, and I pulled inside behind the beat-up Ford pickup I used to use for hauling. Now that business had become so lucrative, I had a new model and a box truck parked in the next bay. Image was everything among the wealthy who had become my clients.

I pulled into my garage and parked, noticing a couple of paper grocery sacks just outside. I frowned and got out. I knew who'd left them the moment I touched them and felt a tingle of magic run through my hand. I unrolled the top of the first bag and found several steaming to-go boxes. The other one contained two large coffees, both just as hot as the food. Damon must have spelled them to stay hot. I pulled out a note. The words were scrawled in bold letters. *Enjoy your breakfast. I'll see you soon.*

No signature. I turned the note over, but it was just a white leaf from an ordinary notebook. I sighed and gathered up the bags. I could smell bacon and hash browns. My mouth watered. I climbed the stairs to my apartment. Damon had brought enough food for the both of us. He'd meant to share the meal. So why had he left? More important, why was I disappointed?

I slept until nine, stomach filled with an enormous breakfast, and my dreams tormented by dreams of Damon Hotpants. Safe to say, I didn't sleep well.

I made a pot of strong coffee and called Lorraine to see how Ajax was doing.

"Sleeping," she said. "We got him to eat a little and drink."

"When can I pick him up?"

"Let's keep him here most of the day. Come get him at five? Are we still on for tonight?"

"Like I'd cancel girls' night," I said. "I'll see you later."

I showered again, finally getting rid of my Eau de Dog Crap perfume, then dragged myself downstairs and worked for a few hours, trying to get the most pressing things covered before I abandoned ship for the afternoon. Luckily,

I hired good people and there weren't any wildfires to put out. I reminded myself that Garrett would be coming at seven so I needed to be back and ready by then. I'm not sure how much coffee I drank, but by the time I was ready to go pick up supplies for Ajax, I was crackling like a live wire.

I grabbed a sandwich on my way and then spent most of the afternoon shopping. I bought everything a dog might need along with everything he might want. I found several enormous cushiony beds and got them all. Can't have too many comfy places to sleep, after all. And what if he was picky?

I went home hauled all my loot upstairs. I checked my watch: four. I didn't have time to grocery shop or cook, so the girls would have to be happy with delivery. I could stop at the bakery for goodies, too, and then head to the clinic.

I picked up an assortment of brownies, cupcakes, cookies, and a couple of loaves of sourdough bread to share at the clinic. I already had a cheesecake in the fridge for cheesecake night.

It was close to five when I reached the clinic. I waved at Debbie and Mary, the two receptionists on duty and handed over the food before heading into the back. I came to visit the animals a lot, especially the hard cases, so I knew where I was going. Lorraine took on any animal that came in, regardless of an owner's ability to pay. To make it possible, I made the clinic my own personal charity, donating money to cover the costs of those animals. They deserved care and humans needed to be responsible enough to give it to them.

Given the number of animals that came in, Lorraine had had to add a shelter to the clinic, which was staffed mostly by volunteers, though she'd been increasing the paid positions. The community was pretty generous about donating, and we did fundraisers every year.

When I came in, Ajax saw me and struggled to sit up. I knelt down beside him and rubbed his ears and stroked his head.

"How are you doing, big guy? You want to come home with me?"

He nosed my chest and leaned into me. He was still groggy. Probably hopped up on painkillers, plus all kinds of vaccinations.

"Hey," Lorraine said as she stopped in the doorway. "I'll get Brian to help you out to your car with Ajax. He's walking a little but unsteady. I'll bring all his medications tonight along with instructions on his care. You might want to keep him downstairs for a while. Going up and down might be tough on him right now."

"I'm not sure he's going to let Brian anywhere near him," I said. I didn't know how he'd react to anybody besides me handling him.

"Brian took him outside a couple hours ago. Ajax hackled up and growled a little but let Brian steady him once he was clear of the chute."

For the difficult and scared cases, Lorraine had a walkway made of heavy-gauge wire that could be set up to allow animals to go outside without having to wear a leash. A lot of dogs refused to relieve themselves inside, and so the only way to keep them from rupturing something was to get them outdoors. Ajax was apparently one of those, and there was no way he could wear anything resembling a collar or harness with his injuries.

We cleared the parking lot of any other animals, and then I took Ajax to my car. He staggered and limped, his nose nearly dragging the ground. I stayed next to him.

supporting him as best I could. The battered beast refused to be helped into the car. He studied the opening a long moment then hopped up onto the backseat like he had rubber bands in his butt.

"Show-off," I said, petting him.

He stuffed his snout into my palm and parked it there.

"Great. Dog snot. My favorite." I wiped my hand on his head and slid behind the wheel.

I'd barely started the car and backed up when a furry body launched over the seat. Ajax's feet slid on the vinyl, and he half fell to the floor, yelping in pain.

"Crap!"

I put the car into park and reached to help him. Brian opened the passenger door and Ajax lunged toward him, snarling and snapping. Brian backpedaled and fell on his ass.

"Ajax, *no*," I said. "You do *not* attack people who are trying to help you."

He twisted and struggled, finally getting his feet under himself. He panted and made a distressed sound deep in his throat, his head dropping low. He still faced the door and Brian. He looked pathetic, his fur shaved and bandages quilting his body. All the same, he kept his attention fixed on Brian.

"Better close the door," I said. "We'll be all right."

Brian reached out and slowly pushed it closed. The moment it was shut, Ajax slumped to the floor. I rolled my window down.

"Brian, can you get Lorraine?"

She came out and I explained what had happened.

"All you can do is try to keep him still, and careful with who you let around him. He's definitely protective and he's been through a hell of a shitstorm. He's got PTSD and it'll take him a while to get comfortable with people, if he ever does. He might not. You know that, right?"

I knew what she was asking. If he was aggressive to people, would I be able to put him down? The answer was a flat *No*. I didn't need to say it, just like she didn't need to ask. We both already knew. I focused on my real concern. "You don't think he hurt himself jumping over the seat and falling?"

"It's possible but he's not in the mood to let me touch him right now. Take him home and get him settled. I'll drive my truck over so I have supplies on hand if there's a problem. In the meantime, keep an eye on him. If he struggles to breathe, gets lethargic, if his breathing sounds bubbly, if his stomach gets hard or distended, or if he won't eat or drink, then there's a problem."

"Should I leave him here, where he's got instant medical care?" I really didn't want to leave him. I was stunned at how attached I'd become to him. Like destiny or something.

Lorraine shook her head. "I think he's going to get better faster if he's with you. Healing requires an animal to feel safe and calm. You seem to do that for him. Not that I'm surprised. Wish I could bottle whatever it is you do with animals. Anyhow, being with you will be the best medicine. Now get out of here. I'll see you later tonight."

"Can you call Stacey and Jen? Let them know about Ajax?"

"Done and done." She waved and headed back inside.

# CHAPTER NINE

It took a couple of rest stops, but Ajax climbed up the stairs on his own. I tried to convince him to stay downstairs, but he wasn't having it. I took him into the kitchen and showed him his water dish and gave him some food. When he was done, I showed him his bed just outside the kitchen. He turned around three times and then collapsed. I thought he'd fall asleep, but as soon as I went to my bedroom, he got up and followed. Luckily I had another bed waiting for him.

I changed into professional clothing for my meeting with Garrett and checked the time. Quarter after six. I decided to go down to my office to get ready. Some of the items for Garrett to examine were in the vault. I'd need to get them out.

Ajax refused to be left behind and followed me down. I took him outside to relieve himself. The property was over three acres. A strip of grass and trees ran down both sides and curved together beyond the rear parking area into an overgrown meadow with a variety of old fruit trees, bushes, and tall grasses. A lot of deer like to dine there and who knew what else lived inside. I took Ajax to the side where it was mowed down and stood between him and the meadow. All I needed was for him to take off after a raccoon or a coyote.

Luckily he did his business, and I took him back inside. He flopped down on the pillow I'd put in the corner of my office. I dug out the paperwork and then went into the vault. I shut the door of my office to keep Ajax from following. In a matter of seconds, he started scraping at the door and whining and then skipped over barking to break into a full-throated howl. The fierce wildness of the sound sent a chill through me.

I went back and opened the door. "Listen, you. Take a chill pill. I'll be right back."

I shut the door, and the howl began again. Then I heard hard thud as he jumped against the door. I stopped, hoping he'd stop, but another thud and another. He was going to kill himself at this rate.

"Fine," I said, opening the door. "But you are going to have to get over this. You can't come with me everywhere."

He gave me an admonishing look and a woof and limped over to me, the tip of his tail wagging once. He was clearly hurting worse than before. I sighed. "Look. I'm not leaving. This is your home now. You don't have to worry about me disappearing on you. I promise." I scratched his ears and under his jaw. He leaned his head into the caress.

Since Garrett was due in just fifteen minutes, I needed to hurry. The vault was next door in a storage closet. At least the door was. I went inside and around behind the shelving unit on the right. Behind was another shelving unit on the wall, and between was the door going down into the ground. It was sealed by both ordinary locks and magic. The rest of the security on my place was the usual electronic stuff. It was a high-end system, and I didn't feel the need to bolster it with magic. Plus, I hadn't wanted my mother to know I was capable of using magic. She never got near the vault, and since I kept the most valuable pieces inside, I figured the extra security layer was a risk worth taking.

Concrete stairs led down inside, the lights coming on with the opening of the door. Inside, I kept jewelry, artwork, coins, and other valuable pieces. I carried up the three boxes I'd been holding for Garrett's perusal. Ajax ended up flopping just outside the storage closet so he could watch me go back and forth.

Once I was done, I sealed up the vault and emptied the first box onto my desk. I'd just finished arranging things for Garrett to see when the bell rang in front. I went to answer it, Ajax trailing at my heels.

Through the glass, I saw Garrett waiting. I unlocked the door and opened it about six inches. "Hi, Garrett. I've acquired a roommate, and he's kind of cranky."

Garrett's smile turned uncertain. "Roommate?"

"Yes. And he may not be very friendly."

"I'm sorry. I don't understand. Don't we have a meeting?" He glanced at his watch.

"Yes. Of course. But this was unexpected. I've got everything ready for you. I'm just not sure Ajax is going to be okay with you coming in. I'd lock him up, but he just hurts himself trying to get out and he's already been through so much."

Garrett blinked at me, trying to make sense of my verbal vomit. "Uh … I'm not sure what you want me to do. Should we postpone?" He looked at his watch again. "I'm leaving for overseas in the morning for a couple weeks or so. I could have my assistant set up something for us then."

"I'd rather not." I really didn't want to sit on the inventory that long. "I just wanted to prepare you. Come in, but don't get too close to me. He should be fine."

I stepped back and pulled the door open, putting my hand on Ajax's head. "Garrett's a friend," I said. "Behave."

Ajax made a chuffing sound and leaned into my leg. His hackles—what was left of them—rose. At least he didn't snarl.

Garrett bent down and picked up a satchel before stepping inside. Upon seeing Ajax, he froze. "You've got a wolf?"

"He's not a wolf."

"Yes, he is." Garrett looked at me. "Your new roommate is a wolf?" he asked, clearly questioning my sanity. "He looks like he's been beaten up pretty good."

I looked down at Ajax. He was gray-brown, but with his hair shaved, he just looked like a naked German Shepherd mix. Maybe a little bit bigger. "I don't know about a wolf," I said doubtfully. "He's had a rough time." Like me. "Come on into the back."

Garrett hesitated then stepped inside. Ajax kept his eyes glued to him, edging forward between us and making a rumbling sound deep in his throat.

"Look, maybe we should do this another time," Garrett said, stepping back.

"Hello. What's going on?" Damon appeared suddenly in the doorway. His glance swept over Garrett, Ajax, me, and back to Garrett. His expression was definitely not very friendly.

I glared. "What are you doing here?"

"I came to see how you were after last night." His intimate tone suggested that we'd spent the night naked together. He looked at Garrett and smiled, though his eyes were graveyard cold. "I'm Damon Matrovani. You are?" He thrust out his hand.

"Garrett Hornsby." He looked at me and back to Damon, shaking the other man's hand. He looked confused. "You're a friend of Beck's?"

Damon's hand closed on Garrett's in what was clearly one of those manly who-can-squeeze-harder sorts of shakes. A polite version of who has the bigger penis. Garrett winced. I gritted my teeth, suppressing the urge to punch Damon in the balls. That would definitely be unprofessional, though highly satisfying.

Damon's lips curved into a predatory smile as he cast a possessive look at me. "I'd say we are far more than friends," he drawled.

Seriously? Who the hell did he think he was? What if Garrett had been my date? Fury boiled inside me. "You need to leave," I said, fighting the urge to send him flying like I had in the parking garage. I was so angry, I thought my hair might catch fire. The only reason I didn't throw a punch was Ajax might decide to bite him. Not that he didn't deserve it. "Get out. Now."

"You're beautiful when you're angry. Do you know that?"

There are a few phrases you can say to a woman that will send her from zero to bitch in less than a second. The top two being: *you'd be prettier if you smiled*, and *you're beautiful when you're angry*.

"You're an asshole when you're being condescending. Do you know that?" I shot back. "In fact, you're pretty much an asshole all the time."

The fury of my words struck him hard enough to fade

his self-satisfied smirk, though it didn't go away completely. "For you, I'd be a pussycat," he purred.

The spark in his eyes told me he was just stirring the pot, twisting the knife, upsetting the apple cart. And it was working. I was ready to claw his eyes out. I grabbed his arm and shoved him outside, kicking the door shut behind myself. I kept pushing until we were on the other side of his truck, where hopefully Garrett wouldn't get an eyeful of our discussion.

"What the fuck do you think you're doing?" I kept my voice low, my arms straight at my sides, my hands balled into fists.

"I told you—"

"Shut up." I poked a finger into his chest. I'm pretty sure it hurt me more than it hurt him. "I don't want to hear any more of your fairy stories. Why are you acting like a dog peeing all over his territory?"

His eyes narrowed and he scowled. He looked pissed. He had no right to be, as far as I was concerned.

"Fairy stories?"

I rolled my eyes. "Make believe. Nonsense. Bullshit. You know, that crap you were selling about us being...." I shook my head, scrabbling for the right word. "Involved. Romantically. I mean, I'm beautiful when I'm angry? That's fucking asinine, not to mention condescending and insulting as hell."

His scowl softened as his lips curved in that wicked grin. I slapped his hand away as he reached out to touch my face. Or poke my eye out. I had no idea just what the hell he was up to.

"But you *are* beautiful when you're angry," he said, running his fingers up my arm instead. Streaks of heat followed in their wake. I hated that I was flattered, even though I knew it was stupid, knew that he'd probably said that to hundreds of women. It didn't mean anything. But the part of me who'd never been paid compliments by handsome men was eating it up.

"Do I look like a bimbo slut? Like throwing cliché lines at me is going to—" I stopped. He wasn't trying to get me into bed, which is what that sort of line was usually meant to lead to, so what *was* he up to? I pulled away from him, biting my lower lip hard. I folded my arms in front of me in an attempt at armoring myself. "What did you really come here for tonight?"

"I really came to see if you were okay. I saw some of the news about the shootings. They mentioned you. I was ... concerned."

The news? There hadn't been any TV crews or reporters around last night. And if the vultures knew about me, why weren't they here, banging on my door? In fact, what had happened to the camera jockeys who'd been scavenging for news about my mother's murder?

I filed the question away for later.

"Your concern is noted. You've seen me. I'm fine. Now leave."

"Um, Beck?" Garrett stood on the other side of Damon's truck, his blond hair glowing like a halo in the outdoor lights. He looked nervous and nauseated.

Shit.

Hoping to salvage the situation, I swung around and nearly ran over Ajax, whom I'd left inside. Alone with Garrett. Oh fuck. No wonder the poor man looked like he was about to vomit. "I'm so sorry, Garrett. Come back inside. Don't worry about Damon. He's leaving."

He shook his head. "Actually, I have to go. Something came up, and anyway, it looks like you've got your hands full with ... everything. I'll call when I get back from my trip. We'll get together to discuss those last items then. I left you something inside, though. I know you didn't care much for your mother, but she'd given me some pieces to sell, and I thought you might want them."

Before I could respond, he flicked a look at Damon, gave me a little wave, and practically sprinted over to his BMW, zipping out of the parking lot like a hive of bees was chasing him.

"Well, then. I guess it's just you and me," Damon said from behind me, not sounding the least bit repentant for chasing off my best buyer.

I turned. "No. It's just me and the dog. You can go to hell."

I stalked away before I could do something incredibly juvenile, like light his hair on fire. Or his pants. Let him get a few blisters on his fine ass, and he wouldn't be sitting down for a while.

"I don't like him."

I whirled. "Who the hell asked you? Garrett's sweet, smart, kind, and generous, and he's never once tried to kidnap me."

Damon prowled forward. I suddenly felt like that goat in the T-Rex pen in *Jurassic Park*. I thrust out my chin defiantly, planting my hands on my hips. I wasn't backing down. He loomed over me, his scowl deepening.

"So he *is* more than a business contact."

"Even if he was, my love life is none of your business."

"I'm making it my business," he growled, and then he was kissing me again.

I'd like to say I kicked him in the nuts and shoved him away, but he really was a good kisser and it felt amazing to be wrapped in his arms and pressed against his hard body. Plus, he smelled divine. Better than Garrett, even.

I hadn't risked any kind of romantic relationship since high school, and my lips and body wanted everything they'd been missing, which he was giving in spades.

His hands roved over my back and hips. He pressed me closer, his tongue delving expertly into my mouth, teasing and tasting and taking. I may have been an amateur at the romance game, but I was enthusiastic and gave as good as I got. My knees were syrup. I clutched him as if I were drowning and he was the only thing keeping me afloat. I may have momentarily lost my mind as my hormones took control and all my pleasure zones started throbbing and aching.

I was happily riding a frothing, whitewater river of pleasure when a half growl, half whine yanked me back to reality.

Ajax.

I shoved out of Damon's arms, wiping my mouth with the back of my hand. As if I could get rid of the taste and touch of him that easily. Ajax stood to the side, looking worried. He wrinkled his lips at Damon in a silent growl.

"Easy, now," I told him, petting his head and scratching lightly behind his ears. He leaned into me but kept his attention on Damon.

"I think you need to go."

"Rebecca—"

I looked at him. I felt flushed and my lips tingled and throbbed. So did other bits of me. All of them crying out for more. But Damon wasn't a good bet. In fact, he was a damned bad one.

"You came to see how I was. I'm perfectly fine. Now leave."

He looked confused and more than a little irritated. "A minute ago you were kissing me like you were dying and I was the only thing that could save you. Now you're the ice queen. Want to clue me in on your game? I don't mind playing, but I sure as hell would like to know the rules."

For a moment I was at a loss for words. That was a first for me.

My mouth dropped open then snapped shut. My teeth clenched so tight, I thought they might crumble. A *game*? He thought I was playing a *game*?

"There are no rules," I said very slowly, biting off each word. It took everything I had to keep my voice low and steady. I was half surprised that they didn't come out in chunks of ice. I wanted to tell him to fuck off and die. "Because there is no game. I do not play games. I've had my fill of those for a lifetime. A dozen lifetimes. My hormones got the best of me, but my brain is in charge now. I'm going inside. You are leaving. Do not come back. If your employer wants to see me—well, he can kiss my ass."

I went to turn around, but Damon caught my arm. Ajax leaped forward, snapping and growling.

Damon let go, hastily jumping back out of the way. Magic wreathed his hands.

I dropped to a crouch and pulled Ajax against me, crooning to him and stroking him between the bandages. He leaned into me, still growling low in his throat, his gaze fixed on Damon.

"Don't you even think about it. Ajax lives here. You don't. Go away. You aren't welcome here. Ajax has been through enough, and so have I."

I didn't wait to see if he was going. I stood and went to the door, calling Ajax.

"I'll go," Damon said behind me. "I'll be back. This conversation isn't over."

I made an annoyed sound. "Don't you know that no means no?"

He hesitated. "Are you talking about meeting my employer or you and me?"

"There is no you and me."

Another silence. "No. I reject that. There *is* something potent, and I'll be damned if I throw it away before I know what it is. You're angry and rightfully so. I screwed up in the garage, but you have to know I wasn't trying very hard to take you. I wanted to see how you'd react. You surprised me. You keep surprising me, and tonight—yeah, I fucked up. I'm sorry to blow your meeting. But I'd do it again. I thought it was a date, and I couldn't let you walk off with him without telling you I want a chance. I've been at the wrong end of too late, and I won't let it happen again if I can help it."

So many emotions exploded inside me that I didn't know what to feel or think. I wanted to turn around and see his face, see if he was playing me, but how would I know? Part of me didn't even want to know. That part wanted to believe without question. I'd never been pursued before, and it felt good. It didn't hurt that he was gorgeous and made my body turn to silk when he kissed me.

I touched my fingers to my lips. They felt hot and swollen. Behind me, I could feel him waiting for my response. Hoping, maybe. I didn't dare turn around. His sharp gaze would see more than I wanted to share. Not that I had any idea what I was feeling.

Deciding retreat was the smartest thing I could do, I grabbed the door handle of the shop and went inside, Ajax limping beside me. I shut the door without looking back.

I needed a lot more sleep and a lot of alcohol and cheesecake before I was ready to tackle the problem of Damon. That, and maybe a dozen appointments with a shrink. Because God help me, I was looking forward to his turning up again.

# CHAPTER TEN

I fled back through the warehouse, leaving Ajax to catch up. I put away everything I'd got out for Garrett to see and filed away my paperwork. Then I returned upstairs and got Ajax settled before getting into the shower.

I'd never understood what made my mother hate me, but there can be no doubt she did. Her schemes and tortures weren't tough love. They weren't any kind of love. It was all about making me suffer. All the same, it didn't keep me from wondering what I'd done to deserve it. Even though I knew I hadn't, I still wondered. I probably needed a therapist. I'd have to settle for the girls and some cheesecake.

Damon was interested in me. I couldn't see why, any more than I could see why my mother had hated me. I wasn't anything particularly special. In fact, I was temperamental, uptight, and slightly insane. If he liked me, could he be altogether sane?

Bigger question—why did I even care?

No duh! Because I liked him. I liked that he kept coming back no matter how difficult I was. I liked the way he seemed to want to look out for me. I liked the way he gave as good as he got when we were verbally sparring. I liked the way he looked at me, and I liked the way he kissed me.

"I'm such an idiot."

By the time the girls arrived, I'd ordered a bounty of Chinese food to be delivered and then sprawled on the couch with Ajax because he was glued to me. I have to say I couldn't mind it. It felt nice to be that kind of important to someone, even one of the furry persuasion.

Lorraine arrived first. She checked out Ajax, changed his dressings, helped me give him his medications, and went over what I needed to do for him. His jumping around and slamming into my office door didn't seem to have caused any lasting harm. A little of the knot in my stomach relaxed.

"I'll come back tomorrow night. He's definitely happier here than at the clinic."

"Someone told me he might be a wolf," I said.

"At least half," she agreed. "Maybe three-fourths, but the rest? Something big. Malamute maybe. Or possibly a Great Pyrenees." She looked at me. "Are you worried he'll be dangerous?"

"Funny," I said, seeing her smirk. "Bite her, Ajax. Bite her hard."

"Too late. He likes me already." She stroked his head, and he gave her a doggy smile.

"Traitor." He nosed my hand and swiped his tongue over my fingers.

I went to the refrigerator and pulled out orange juice, then started setting glasses, liquor, and mixers out on the counter, along with a blender and ice. When the doorbell rang, Lorraine ran down to let in Jen and Stacey, who came in with five bags of Chinese food, having encountered the delivery guy in the parking lot.

"Are you expecting a natural disaster?" Jen asked, setting her load on the table. "There's enough here to feed us for a week."

"I wanted to be sure we had everybody's favorites since I promised to cook and I totally blew that off."

"Yeah, we saw it on the news tonight," Stacey said, heading for the kitchen and then stopped cold. "Uh, Beck? There's a patchwork wolf in your kitchen. He doesn't look like he likes me."

"Oh, right. Everybody, this is Ajax. He's the dog from last night. He's okay but he doesn't really trust people very much." I went to kneel beside him. "Ajax, this is Stacey. She's my friend."

It was a sign of how much she trusted me that Stacey held out her hand. Ajax stretched out to sniff it and then pulled away but didn't growl or snarl. Progress. Next was Jen. He repeated his sniffing and then looked up at me as though he thought I was kidding.

"He totally doubts your taste in friends." Jen laughed. Stacey and Lorraine joined in.

Ajax pricked his ears and cocked his head at them. He took a step and listed to the side.

"Uh-oh. Drugs are kicking in. C'mon, boy."

I guided him to his bed outside the kitchen, and he collapsed awkwardly onto it.

"Daquiris, margaritas, or something else?" Stacey asked.

"Margaritas," came the unanimous vote.

Stacey set to work, and the rest of us unpacked the food.

Then something struck me. They'd echoed Damon.

"Wait a minute. I was on the news?"

They cracked up laughing. I flushed and then mentally kicked myself. These women were practically my sisters. Their laughter never bothered me, especially when I deserved it. I was feeling too damned raw and for no good reason.

"What did you think was going to happen?" Lorraine asked. "First the wife kills her bastard husband and then goes nuts and tries to kill the kids. Then there's a vicious dog protecting them, and you show up out of nowhere and talk the dog down. It's the biggest story ever around here. I'm surprised they aren't parked outside and ringing your phone dead."

"Actually, you know, the reporters bugging me about my mom's death are gone too. That's so weird." I couldn't help going to look out my windows, but the parking lot was dark. "What do you suppose happened to them all?"

"Maybe the coyote dropped an anvil on them," Jen suggested. "A big-ass anvil."

"Maybe they all got Ebola at the same time," Stacey said and then hit the blend button.

"What's this?" Stacey asked, nudging the leather bag on the counter when she'd finished blending and pouring out the margaritas.

"Garrett left it. Said it was stuff my mom had consigned to him. Or maybe sold to him." I shrugged. "He said I might want to see it now that she's pushing up daisies."

"What kind of stuff?" Stacey's blue eyes flashed. She did love to shop.

"No idea. Have a look."

She flipped it open and rummaged. Jen and Lorraine leaned in to get a closer look. Stacey pulled out a handful of jewelry, hair clips, jeweled boxes, and assorted expensive tchotchkes. All three women sorted the items, laying them out across the long counter.

Jen picked up a cuff bracelet, about two inches wide and inlaid with a design of opals, sapphires, rubies, and what looked like pink diamonds. "This is pretty."

"My mother had taste," I said, taking it from her and turning it over in my fingers. "I think this is platinum." I put it back down on the counter and looked at the rest of it. There were things that I'd wear—*if* they hadn't belonged to my mother.

"What are you going to do with them?" Lorraine asked.

"Give them back to Garrett." I shrugged. "I don't want anything to do with this crap. If anything looks good to you, grab it. She'd hate knowing you were wearing it."

"Well, when you put it that way...." Jen slid the cuff onto her arm while Stacey and Lorraine picked through the rest, selecting what they wanted.

When they were through, I reached for the leftovers to put them away.

"You know," Jen said, "she'd also hate it if you had anything of hers. Maybe you should take something too. Every time you'd wear it, it'd be a big *fuck you* to her."

She had a point. I looked over the collection, picking up each piece. I finally settled on an art deco–style ring. The center stone was a star sapphire in a lavender shade of blue, and baguette diamonds framed it on either side. I slipped it on the middle finger of my left hand. It fit perfectly. "Looks like this is the one. Put the other stuff away now and let's eat."

Stacey returned everything to the satchel. I set it aside to take downstairs to the vault until I could return it to Garrett.

We got through dinner with most of the conversation focusing on the night before. The ring on my hand felt cold and heavy. I yawned, feeling the lack of sleep catching up with me suddenly. At that moment, I could have crawled into bed and stayed there for a week. Not that the girls would have let me. Cheesecake nights were sacred.

I had taken a frozen cheesecake out earlier in the morning, and over dessert, we talked about my mother's murder investigation.

"The detectives really don't like me," I said.

"And people say the men in blue suck at their jobs," Jen said, clinking her glass with mine.

"Suits, actually, and one is a woman. That reminds me, I have to call that cop who brought my car back. He wanted to know how Ajax was doing. He turned out to be a good guy."

"Is he sexy?" Stacey asked, her brows lifting.

"Not for me," I said.

"Fucking hell, Beck. You're free. You can finally have a relationship," Jen said, slapping her hand on the table. "You can at least do some casual dating."

"Not with Officer Mock. He's nice enough but looks about ten years old. And no sparks." No, Damon was the one who caused sparks and a migraine and made me want to cut him in two with an ax, and with any luck, I'd never see him again. Right. He said he'd be back, and I believed him. The irritating thing was that as much as his return made me seethe, I also was looking forward to it, which made me want to stab my eye out with a fork.

I jumped up and started clearing the dishes. The girls followed suit, and Stacey mixed up another batch of margaritas before we all headed for the couch. We'd barely sat down when Ajax flung himself up and over, curling up beside me.

"Looks like you've got yourself a friend," Lorraine said, grinning.

"All the male I can handle," I agreed.

Silence descended and the other three women exchanged speaking looks. Then they all looked at me.

"All right," Jen said. "Your bitch of a mother is dead. Time to spill the beans."

"What beans?"

Stacey rolled her eyes. "Oh, please. We know your mother kept you under her thumb with threats, intimidation, and worse. We know you didn't tell us so you could protect us. But you don't have to anymore and you also don't have to carry the baggage alone. A burden shared is lighter."

"So talk to us," Lorraine said, patting my thigh.

I opened my mouth, and nothing came out. I didn't even know what I wanted to say. A tidal wave of emotion crashed over me, and all of a sudden, I was balling like a colicky baby.

Ajax got in my face and started licking me, the girls all clustered around, trying to hug me, much to the dog's increasing distress. Thank goodness he didn't snap.

By the time I got myself somewhat calmed down, my nose was full of cement, I'd gone through an entire box of tissue and was working through a second, my eyes were swollen, and my face felt blotchy and hot. I had slouched down on my side and curled my knees up to my chest. Ajax had burrowed in between to wedge his head against my stomach.

I hadn't cried since I could remember. Not once. Then suddenly I was a sprinkler turned on full blast. I couldn't blame my period. It was still weeks off. I groaned and hid my eyes in the crook of my elbow.

"I'm so stupid. Go away. All of you. Leave me with what few shreds of dignity I still have."

"Who are you kidding?" Jen said. "Your dignity got wadded up in a pile of Kleenex about a half hour ago."

Oh, God. My face heated and I flushed harder. I probably looked like a beet. "Have mercy on me and go away."

"Nope," Stacey said and settled a cold bottle of water into my hand. "We are utterly merciless. Drink that. I've got some ibuprofen for you too. Then you can start talking."

"At least we know she's human," Lorraine said when I didn't move. "She can both cry and wallow. I was beginning to think she was robo-Beck."

"Har-dee-har-har," I said, lifting my elbow just high enough to peek at her. "If you prick me, do I not bleed?"

"Shakespeare? And here I thought you only read the funny pages."

"Shakespeare in the Park," Jen clarified. "Last summer. Remember? *Merchant of Venice.* We were flirting with those guys from ErroTech. All except our girl Beck, who insisted on watching the play. Which brings us back to the question at hand. What did your mom do to you?"

They weren't going to let it go. I dropped my arm, twisting onto my back and staring up at the ceiling. I refused to look at them. "You really don't want to know. It's over and that's all that matters."

"It's not over for you," Stacey said. "We've let you shut us out all these years because we didn't want to make things worse for you, but we're done letting you hold on to this alone. We aren't leaving until you tell us. If we have to, we'll get you so drunk, you'll tell us all your deepest, darkest secrets. I've got two more bottles of tequila in my trunk, plus a fifth of vodka."

"My mother *is* my deepest, darkest secret," I said. Even though that wasn't entirely true. She was one but I was never going to let them know about the basement. And then there was my magic. I had never let them see it. "That and this whole crying thing. You guys didn't record it, did you? I don't want to see myself on YouTube."

"Too bad. Your exploits last night probably already got you up there," Jen said unsympathetically. "Stop stalling."

"Trust us," Lorraine said. "You need this. All those emotions you've kept bottled up tight, and now that your mother is gone, all your walls are coming apart. You need to talk, whether you know it or not."

"The detectives were right about one thing," I said after several breaths of silence. "I wanted her dead, so much. I thought of all kinds of plans to kill her, but I wasn't going to jail for her."

"That answers that," Jen said.

I lifted my head to look at her. "Answers what? You thought I actually killed her?"

"Wouldn't have blamed you if you did."

"None of us would have," Stacey said. "We'd have helped."

I inched upright and stretched my legs out in front of me. Ajax wriggled over so he lay across my thighs with his head on my shins. It looked hideously uncomfortable, but I was glad for the weight and the warmth, not to mention his concern and desire to protect me.

"I'll tell you some things," I said. "But I won't answer questions." I looked at them, and they each nodded. I uncapped my water and took a drink and then dived in.

I kept the details to a minimum, sticking to matter-of-fact descriptions. I described the water-wall torture. How she put me in the cage with the rock climbing wall and made me climb, all the while blasting water cannons at me to knock me off. Every time I fell, something would force me off the ground. Magic, but I couldn't tell them that. She'd send bees to sting me mercilessly or start beating me with invisible sticks. Eventually she figured out that all she really needed to do was start describing how she'd hurt my friends. She was vicious, and worse, I knew she'd follow through.

I'd get up and start climbing again and fall again and rinse and repeat. It would go on for hours. Giving up wasn't a choice. Failing wasn't a choice. When I made it to the top, I could drop down in the hollow on top of the wall. It was always full of water by then. I'd stay there until she got bored and left, and then I could climb down.

I never missed school. I never gave her the satisfaction. No matter how long I'd been up there, no matter how bad I hurt, I never let her win.

Then there was the running torture. The reason I still ran. She had a track. Made me run. Sometimes I could go slower, sometimes I had to sprint. When I went too slow or tried to stop, she'd hit me with electric shocks. Sometimes she'd drag out a pig and butcher it, showing me exactly what she'd do to my friends if I didn't do what she demanded.

I could go weeks and even months with her ignoring me, and then she'd focus her attention on me every day for a week. I started training so I stayed in shape for her sessions. I ran, I swam, I lifted weights, I climbed. I was fanatical about it. I still was.

I stopped talking after twenty minutes. My voice was thick and hoarse. My eyes were dry and gritty. I stared blindly at the opposite wall, lost in memories. Those were the least bad things she'd done to me. The other things—I didn't even want to think about them, much less talk about them.

"I need a drink," Stacey said.

I looked at her. She'd been crying. She climbed up over the couch and poured a shot of tequila. She drank it, then poured three more in quick succession, downing each. She lifted the bottle.

"Anybody else?"

"Fuck yes," Jen said, and it sounded like a prayer. She stared at me, face pale, eyes shadowed. "God, I wish we'd known."

"I don't," I said. "I never wanted you guys to know. You'd have tried to help, and she would have really gone to work on you. So long as I cooperated in her little torture sessions, she stuck to just harassment. Pissed her off, though, that you guys didn't walk away from me. She couldn't understand it. God, did I love you for that. You've no idea."

"She needed killing," Lorraine said in a shaken voice. "She was evil and someone should have put her in the ground a long time ago."

"If I ever find out who killed her, I'll give him a medal," I said then grinned. "I told the detectives if I figured out who did it, I'd suck his dick."

They laughed. It was a little too loud and a little too long, but it broke the tension.

"I'm pretty sure saying that didn't make you any less a suspect," Jen observed.

"I'm definitely sure you're right. Telling them I hated the bitch probably didn't either, but since I have an alibi, they'll have to set their sights on someone else."

"Have they?" Lorraine asked.

I shrugged. "Not so I've noticed. They want me to go to the estate and play tour guide for them."

"Take you back to the scene of the crime, as it were," Jen said, nodding. "Makes sense if all those episodes of *Law and Order* got anything right at all."

"Of course they did. TV and movies always show exactly what happens in the real world," Stacey said with a perfectly straight face. "I mean, *The Real Housewives*. Need I say more? By the way, if you believe any of that tripe, did I mention I have some beachfront property in Nebraska for sale?"

"Why was your mother so fucking twisted?" Jen asked. "I mean, as bad mothers go, she went off the charts straight into malignant psychopath territory. I wonder if she was always that way or if something flipped her switch. And why target you? Aren't mothers supposed to love their children? Isn't there some sort of maternal bonding thing that happens at birth? I mean, even monsters like Godzilla love their children."

"Godzilla isn't real, you know," Stacey pointed out.

Jen flipped her off. "You get my point. I wonder if she left anything that could tell you. Letters or a diary or something."

"I don't care. I don't want to know," I said, which was totally not true, but I didn't want to care why. There were no good reasons for anything she'd done to me. No justifications. No circumstances that could possibly make the way she treated me anything but pure evil.

"Don't you?" Lorraine nudged my leg with her foot. "Maybe not the why part, but what about her past? Your father? Any other family you might have?"

"If they'd given a shit, they'd have showed up and done something to help me," I said, not entirely reasonably.

Stacey made a face, tapping her lips with cranberry fingernails. "She might have driven them off. I wonder if any of her family or your father even knew about you."

"Doesn't matter. The only family I want or need is right here in this room. Everybody else can fuck off."

That declaration resulted in a group hug, more drinks, and eventually we got off onto other subjects.

Around one in the morning, I declared myself out. "I've got to be out at the sale by O-dark-thirty. You all know where everything is. I won't wake you when I leave." I had two extra bedrooms and the couch. No one would be uncomfortable as they slept off the booze.

I sat on the back of the rectangular couch and swung my legs over the other side. We all took Ajax outside and after giving him his medications, he and I went to bed. I set my alarm for four-thirty and crawled between the sheets. He ignored the dog bed on the floor and climbed up beside me and whuffled my ear before snuggling in to sleep.

If I ever got a love life, Ajax would probably put a crimp in it. Not that I ever would get one. I doubted I'd trust any man enough to let him spend the night, much less actually have a relationship with. Ajax was a much better bet. And *he* wasn't going to try to kidnap me.

On the other hand, Ajax wasn't nearly as good a kisser as Damon. For the first time since I walked away from him tonight, I thought about what he'd said. He wanted me. He was jealous of Garrett. I marveled at that. Did I want him?

My body sure as hell did. But the rest of me wasn't ready to trust him. I wasn't sure I even wanted to try.

Sleep swallowed me before I'd figured anything out. It pulled me down into a deep well of dreamlessness.

# CHAPTER ELEVEN

It was still dark when Ajax and I left the apartment. He was moving easier, though still very slowly.

"At least sleeping on a real bed is a lot better for your body than shit-crusted hard ground," I said, opening the front door of my Thunderbird to let him inside.

He hopped in and sat in the passenger side. I put my tote with my thermos in it on the floorboards along with my purse and got behind the wheel. I felt sluggish and tired. I'd have liked to crawl back into bed for the rest of the day, but there's no rest for the wicked or the owners of businesses.

The estate we were selling nestled in the hills above the river and had a wrought-iron gate. Thank goodness, because there were already early birds assembling. Not only early birds, but at least a dozen news vans and a bunch of other reporters were parked along the road and stood in front of the gates.

I scowled. They came here but not to the shop?

But as soon as I asked the question, I figured out the answer. Damon. He'd used his magic to keep them away. I wanted to resent it but I couldn't. I appreciated the gesture far too much. It almost made up for his wrecking my meeting with Garrett. Almost.

I drove up through the reporters, my doors locked and my windows up. I honked at them, and they didn't move. I gave a little *push* of magic to make sure all their pictures came out badly, and then I released a cloud of magical gnats. They swarmed, biting at every square inch of exposed fleshy real estate they could find. They flew into noses, ears, eyes, and mouths.

Within seconds, the horde started shrieking and dancing and flapping their arms and slapping themselves. The early birds watched their antics, amazed. The gates opened and I rolled through. I didn't call off my annoying little pests. What did I need Damon Dickweed for anyway?

I parked behind the house and went inside to find Monica. I'd stopped for coffee on the way and handed her a large cup.

"You're a goddess." She closed her eyes as she sipped.

"My trunk's full of pastries too."

"I knew I liked working for you. Terri! Grab Amy and go dig the food out of Beck's trunk and let everybody know there's breakfast."

"How's everything looking?" I asked.

"Perfect." She lifted a brow at me. "You, on the other hand, look like death warmed over. Not that I can blame you after what I saw on the news. You're going to have to tell me all about it later."

"It wasn't that big of a deal."

"Sure it wasn't."

Ajax chose that moment to step between us. Her gaze dropped. "That's the dog, isn't it?"

"I adopted him. His name is Ajax."

She eyed him doubtfully. "Should he be here? Is he friendly? Is he okay?"

"Jury's still out on his friendliness, but so far so good. Right now, he seems to want to be wherever I am."

"I've heard wolves bond like that."

"You too?"

"Me too what?"

"Except for his coloring, I just don't see the wolf. He looks more like a German Shepherd to me."

"Then you're blind. Anyway, I need to double-check the pricing of some things. I set up the smaller collectibles and antiques in the library and east salon."

I spent the rest of the morning until opening helping to price, organize, and fill whatever needs Monica had. She'd been running my estate sales for more than a year now. I'd taught her everything I knew, and then she zoomed past me, implementing methods and means that I'd never begun to think of.

We didn't do waitlists, so it was a first-come sort of thing. We did make sure only a few people entered at a time to keep from having stampedes. We also kept a big staff, both to help shoppers and to monitor for theft, with extra security to make sure nobody got robbed on the way out. It was expensive, but then, these sales were extremely lucrative and what we sold was valuable. I'd skimmed off the truly unique and important pieces to sell either at auction or to brokers such as Garrett, or to consign in my shop.

In an irony of epic proportions, my mother had done everything she could to make my business a success—recommending me to her clients and friends and talking me up on every occasion. It was all because she feared that I would fail on my own and my failure would humiliate her in the heady circles she traveled in. Now, between the shop, estate sales, and occasional auctions, Effortless Estates had cleared more than a million in profit last year and was on its way to doing better this year.

I'd retreated to a chair behind the cashier desk to keep Ajax from scaring people. I still couldn't seem to wake up, even with four shots of expresso in my coffee, and he refused to be peeled away from my side. I hoped he relaxed at some point. It could get awkward if I couldn't even go to the bathroom without the dog's company.

At the moment, he slept beside me with his head propped on my left boot. The bustle of people had unnerved him for a bit, but he'd calmed when I told him everything was all right and he didn't need to worry.

I glanced down at the star sapphire still on my finger. It wasn't nearly as pretty now as it had been the night before. The lavender blue had clouded, and I could barely see the star. The gold had darkened, turning almost gray. Even in death, my mother ruined things. I slipped the ring off and tossed it into a box of things that someone had left on hold while they continued shopping. It could be their bonus treasure.

For the next hour, I took money and chatted, though my brain was working slowly and I had a hard time focusing. I felt lethargic and drained. I was more than a little ready to go see if any beds hadn't yet been sold and take a nap.

All of a sudden, a microphone thrust in front of my face. "Are you a suspect in your mother's murder, Miss Wyatt?"

I blinked at the speaker, trying to process her rapid-fire words. The perky, black-haired reporter had pale skin and almond eyes. A square logo on the microphone read *KLON*. A scruffy man with a brown beard and shaved head held a camera on his shoulder just to the side as he recorded me.

"Have the police questioned you? Were you angry at your mother? Did she deserve to die?"

The questions were ludicrous and insulting. Well, except for the last one. My mother sure as hell deserved to die. Too bad she could do it only once. My mother would have hated this attention. One thing we had in common. I smiled tiredly and looked at the camera. Magic flowed from me, eating the pixels from the hard drive inside.

"I have spoken to the police Miss— I'm sorry. I don't think I've seen you before. What's your name?"

The reporter flushed, whether it was because she hadn't offered her name, or because I'd implied she wasn't famous or important enough to recognize, I didn't know.

"I'm Angela Cho, Channel Six News."

"Of course you are. I'm sure you meant to offer your condolences for my mother's violent passing, and I thank you for your obvious concern. She meant so much to so many people, to this city, and to me. Her loss is impossible to measure."

I let my voice catch and wiped invisible tears from under my eyes as I sniffed. "It's still so raw. I'm grateful for everybody's kindness and support through the terrible circumstances of her death." I covered my mouth and dropped my head, looking into my lap as if overcome with emotion. My shoulders shook, though from laughter, not grief.

A pool of silence fell around us. The waiting customers stared at the reporter in disgust. The lady in front of me wearing Chanel, her silver hair frosted white, bent and grasped my hand in hers and glared at Angela Cho.

"You ought to be ashamed, coming here and harassing this poor woman. I'm going to call your station and complain to your manager."

"No respect," someone added. "Harassing this poor woman right when she's grieving."

"You need to leave," a man declared, and everybody else echoed him.

Then a mob collected around Angela Cho and every other reporter who had sneaked inside and they were pushed out none too gently.

I decided that that was my cue to leave. I gave Monica a little wave, and then Ajax and I slipped out the back door. Angela Cho hadn't asked about him. Apparently his story wasn't as exciting as my mother's murder. Either that, or they hadn't figured out that the woman who'd talked the dog down and the daughter of Anne Wyatt were one and the same.

The estate had a back entrance, and I used it. I decided the day was nice enough that I'd take Ajax to the river, and given how crazy lethargic I felt, I needed a little R&R. And maybe another gallon or so of coffee.

I drove out of town and out along the south fork of the river. I parked at a fishing access and Ajax and I followed a deer track about fifty yards through close-growing trees and scrub bushes. I stepped carefully over the thick line of red-spotted, cream-colored mushrooms that crossed the track. As soon as my foot came down on the other side, the air shimmered crystal clean, like the morning after a rain.

The spot was like a little piece of Eden. It felt sacred and clean. I'd found it a few years ago during a particularly bad time and it had become my personal sanctuary, where none of the shit of my world could intrude. I was safe here. No one could find me here, and everything about the place rejuvenated me, heart, mind, and soul.

I went a little further, coming out in a verdant hollow just below a white roll of rapids. Miner's lettuce and grass covered the ground, with flame-bright poppies growing down the bank to the drop-off a few feet above the water.

A scalloped-out area in the wall of boulders below revealed a cupped hollow with a small pool, maybe twenty feet across. A hot spring fed into the chill waters of the river here, and even in winter, the water was delightfully warm. Nature's magic. The pool was about fifteen feet deep, with ledges in the rocks offering places to sit. It couldn't be seen from the river. It was my sanctuary and not even Stacey, Jen, or Lorraine knew about it.

I stopped long enough to strip. I was too tired to do more than leave my clothes in a pile on the ground. Normally I just hopped over the ledge and plunged into the pool, but with Ajax, I worried he'd try to follow. Instead I led him around a thrusting boulder and down an embankment to the water's edge.

A red sand beach filled the flat, six-foot-wide gap between the giant rocks and gave entrance to the pool.

"Stay here," I said, pointing to the sand.

Ajax sank down and put his head on his paws. He looked as tired as I felt. I stroked his head. "Poor baby. If I could kill the asshole who did this to you all over again, I would. Hopefully he's spinning slow on somebody's barbecue spit in hell."

I waded into the water and slid under. On the side where the spring flowed into the river, the water was practically steaming. On the other side, where the river washed through the rock tunnel entrance below, it was downright chilly. Since the morning was decently warm, I drifted closer to the river side. I let myself float, my head tilted toward the sky.

Tension ran out of my muscles and loosened the knots of emotion tangling my soul, the colder water doing little to cut through my thick exhaustion. Between a night without sleep to rescue Ajax and staying up too late drinking with the girls, I'd overdone it. I vowed that tonight, I'd go to bed early.

But it wasn't just lack of sleep. I was mentally and emotionally overloaded. With my mother's death, my whole world had changed. For the first time in my life, I was *free*. Free to do what I wanted; free to live where and how I wanted; free to make friends without fearing my mother's retaliation.

Freedom scared me.

I knew who I was when I was fighting my mother. I knew what gave meaning to my days. Every speck of my soul was defined by my mother, by my need to defy and withstand her. Who was I going to be now that she was gone? I had Lorraine and Jen and Stacey, and now Ajax. He needed me. Maybe that's why it had felt so right, so necessary, that I take him in. I hadn't even thought about it. His need gave me a purpose.

Pathetic.

What did other people live for? Their jobs? Lorraine saved lives. Stacey saved lives in her own way, too, as a bartender. She listened and gave broken people hope and friendship when they were at their lowest. Jen was a computer whiz, saving people and companies from technological hell. Me? I sold the belongings of dead people. Not exactly profound.

Sure, I gave a lot of money to the clinic to help animals. It was totally selfish. I did that entirely for me. To try to balance some of the evil my mother dumped into the world and to keep from hanging myself. The time I spent helping animals gave me solace and helped temper the bleak shadows that haunted me.

I sniffed and blinked. God, was I crying? I knuckled my eyes, sending a wave of water over my face. I *never* cried. What in the fuck is wrong with me? I didn't realize I said it out loud until a deep male voice answered.

"Doesn't look to me like anything's wrong with you."

I stiffened, an electric jolt of adrenaline shooting through me. What the fuck was Damon doing here? Anger ran over me in fiery flames, followed by an aching sense of loss. This place where I felt safe wasn't anymore. It didn't matter whether Damon meant me harm or not. It was enough that he'd found me. That feeling of loss quenched my anger and deadened the adrenaline. That emotionally flat feeling I'd had earlier returned, accompanied by a determination to escape.

Robotically I turned on my stomach and swam to the red sand. I stood and walked up out of the pool. Ajax followed me up the trail. I didn't look at Damon as I collected my clothing and dressed. I didn't bother pretending modesty. He'd seen all of me already. I didn't have anything left to hide. Had I really been looking forward to seeing him again? Just now, I couldn't imagine why.

"I wanted to talk to you about last night," he said.

I didn't answer. I'd already put on my bra and underwear. I hated putting clothes on when I was wet. If not for Damon, I'd have dried in the sun. I stepped into my skirt and zipped myself into it without tucking in my blouse and then slid my feet into my boots without putting on my socks.

"Rebecca? Is this the silent treatment?"

His voice was mocking, but I didn't care. I just wanted to leave him, leave this place. I wasn't ever coming back. Deep down in a place where words didn't exist, I knew I couldn't. The safety of the place, the precious serenity and peace of the hollow were shattered for me. The loss hurt more than I would have guessed.

I walked away, feeling like I was dragging a pile of cinderblocks behind me. I'd not yet reached the curve of the toadstool circle when Damon caught my arm. I didn't fight him. I didn't seem to have any fight in me. There was no prize to win. The prize was destroyed.

Why did I feel like I was destroyed too? Wow. That was over the top. Where had that come from? All the same, the sentiment felt accurate.

"Look, I want to talk to you about last night."

He waited for some kind of response. I didn't have any. Nothing he said mattered. I didn't even look at him. That would have required effort I didn't have the energy for.

He growled. "Come on, Rebecca. Cut the silent crap. You aren't ten. Talk to me."

Like he had any right to be frustrated. I couldn't stir up any anger at his expectations or assumption that he deserved anything from me. It took an unbearable amount of energy just to mumble a few words. "I don't have anything to say."

He pulled me around to face him. Water from my hair soaked through my silk blouse and trickled down my back. He scowled at me. "Why aren't you slicing strips off me with that razor tongue of yours?"

I wondered that too. Something had happened to me, like I'd been short circuited and all my wiring was fried. I just couldn't scrape up any anger or, really, any emotion at all. Mostly I felt like I'd been worn down to nothing. Surely a couple of nights of little sleep and a little bit of alcohol indulgence hadn't taken that much out of me? Maybe it was all of it—new freedom; confessing to the girls; the rescue of

Ajax; and dealing with the cops, Damon, and Garrett. Maybe I just needed a vacation.

"I'd like to leave now."

His big hands on my arms tightened, his fingers digging into my flesh. A muscle twitched in his jaw. "What's wrong with you?"

I didn't answer. I didn't really have one. Everything? Nothing? Beside me, Ajax growled deep in his throat as he eyed Damon balefully. I put a soothing hand on his head.

"It's okay," I told him.

"I see. You'll talk to the damned dog but not me. Is that it?"

"I don't have anything to say to you."

He gave me a little shake. "I have things to say to you."

"That isn't really my problem, is it?" With that, I stepped back.

He looked down at his hands in shock. He no longer held me. I wouldn't be able to tell him what had happened if he asked. The only answer I had for it was that it was magic, but nothing I could control or explain. It just happened sometimes. I turned into a ghost. Or something. Maybe that was my problem. Maybe I was really a ghost, with no soul and no heart. Just a shell of a person too stupid to know I was dead.

What a ridiculously maudlin thought. Self-pity much? I really needed to get over myself.

I settled back into a fully fleshed form and walked away again, stepping over the toadstools and continuing my way to my car with Ajax on my heels. I heard Damon swear and stalk after me. He overtook me again at the car. I'd already opened the door to let Ajax in. Damon grabbed my arm and pulled me around to face him before I could follow suit. He knocked the door shut with is foot and set his hands on either side of me, trapping me against the car.

"What the fuck was that?"

He was pissed. Ordinarily that would have amused me. Just at the moment, I couldn't bring myself to care. All I wanted was to crawl into bed and go to sleep.

"I want to leave," I said. My words slurred with exhaustion.

He scowled, shaking his head. "What is wrong with you? What happened to your glorious fire? All of a sudden, you're an ice statue."

The look I gave him was vaguely vacant, as if I were the village idiot or something. He started swearing. He probably thought I was doing it on purpose to annoy him. I would be, too, except I didn't care enough to make the effort. Maybe that's why Ajax wasn't smashing through the window to defend me, like I was pretty sure he would if he thought I were under attack. He must've been able to read my total lack of concern and decided if I wasn't scared, then I wasn't threatened. All the same, he wasn't all that pleased to be on the inside while I was on the outside. He whined and scraped his claws against the glass behind me.

"All right. I told you. I'm sorry about last night. Sincerely. Deeply. I didn't mean to fuck up your meeting."

A spark of something almost like curiosity. I considered whether or not I wanted to make the effort to ask the question. I almost decided not to. I didn't really care about the answer, after all. But I did want to take Ajax home. There was only one way to do that. I had to get rid of Damon.

"Why?"

"Why what?"

I had to debate again on whether I wanted to go to all the trouble of a full sentence. "Why are you interested in me?" There. That wasn't so exhausting. Six words and a little up inflection at the end. So why did I want to sink down to the ground as though I'd just run up the side of a mountain?

His bark of laughter hooked my attention for a fleeting moment, and then my interest faded.

"Damned if I know. You're all claws, teeth, thorns, and razorblades. If I had any sense, I wouldn't come anywhere near you."

I was pretty sure none of that was complimentary. I tried to summon up some irritation and smart-ass words. Nothing. Besides, the last thing I wanted to do was prolong this encounter. I thought longingly of my bed.

"Okay."

"Okay?"

I shrugged one shoulder, leaning back against my car.

His scowl deepened. "What does that mean?"

I shrugged again.

His gaze narrowed and all of a sudden it felt like he was looking at me through a microscope. I looked back without any emotion whatsoever.

"Something *is* wrong with you," he said finally. He actually looked worried.

"Probably. Mother always said so." Why had I answered? Kneejerk, I supposed. I was well trained to respond to attacks. "I want to go home now."

With that, I dematerialized and slipped through his arms and the door like smoke. I solidified and started the car. My head and body were on autopilot. It was all I could do not to tip over and take a nap.

Damon followed me home. Tailgated, really. I drove under the speed limit. Usually I liked to roll the windows down and practically break the sound barrier. Not today.

I parked in the garage, hitting the button to close it. Damon stepped inside before it got halfway down. I didn't pay any attention to him. I climbed up the stairs to my loft, stopping to rest every two steps. I didn't bother closing the back door. Damon would have just broken it down, not that I had the energy to lock it.

I dropped my things on the kitchen island, then got a glass out of the cupboard and filled it with ice water from the refrigerator door. I drank it, refilled it, and then carried it into my bedroom. I went to the bathroom, and when I came out, I stripped off my clothes and dropped them in a heap.

I was aware of Damon's watching, but it was like getting undressed in front of a lamp. Why be embarrassed? Or proud? Or anything else? I redressed in a tank top sans bra, wispy underwear, and a pair of cotton shorts and then crawled into bed. Ajax climbed up beside me, and I closed my eyes, forgetting all about Damon.

# CHAPTER TWELVE

I woke in the dark. Ajax sprawled across the bed beside me, his head on the other pillow. I stared up at the green light of the fire alarm on the ceiling. I had to pee. A shroud of debilitating emptiness folded over me, and it took a good five or ten minutes for me to make myself get out of bed and shuffle to the bathroom. When I came out, the nightstand light was on and Damon leaned against the wall across from me.

His gaze was hooded, his face like sculpted marble. Pretty. Ajax lay on the bed looking at me, his ears perked.

"Want to go outside, boy?" If I had had to pee, surely he did.

He gave a little bark and followed me out the bedroom door. Damon brought up the rear. We made an odd procession as we went outside to let Ajax do his business. It was night and the moon had set.

"What time is it?" I wondered out loud, not really expecting an answer.

"Three a.m."

I'd been in bed over fourteen hours. I didn't even feel

rested. "The pool should have made me feel better," I said. It always had before. It was like plugging in to the energy of life, somehow. I hadn't done that this time. Never again. Damon had broken it. That was sad. At least I was pretty sure it was sad, but I didn't feel it.

"Come on, Ajax."

Our little parade went back inside. This time I rested every step. I was late on Ajax's food and medications, which gave me a pang of guilt. I took care of both then started to check his dressings.

"I already changed them," Damon said in his smoky voice.

"That's nice."

He made a sound in his chest, halfway between a laugh and a something harder, angrier. "Nice?"

"Thanks." That was the proper response. He should be satisfied with that.

I drank some more water while he glowered at me, and when Ajax was done, I started back toward my bedroom without a word.

"Rebecca—Beck. Stop. Talk to me. What's going on with you?"

I didn't slow down. "I'm tired."

"Fucking son of a whore!" he swore and when I crawled into bed, he sat beside me, leaning over me and bracing his hands on either side of me. "What's *wrong*?"

"Nothing."

"The hell it's nothing. You're a zombie. What happened?"

I tried to sort out an answer so I could go to sleep. I was so *tired*. "I'm fine. You should go away."

"Like hell. I'm not leaving. Not until you're back to

yourself, so if you want me to leave you alone, you'd better start talking to me."

I stared up at him. I had no words and no interest in finding any. Anyway, I didn't believe he'd leave me alone. That was a lie.

"Rebecca?" He brushed the hair away from my forehead with a feather touch then ran his fingers down the side of my face and rubbed his thumb back and forth over my lower lip.

Something far beneath the layers of cotton encasing me shuddered and went still.

"You're not even giving me shit about your name," he said. "You hate the name Rebecca."

"It doesn't matter."

He swore again, pulling his hand from my face, clenching it and punching it into the bed. Ajax leaped to his feet and snarled, snapping his teeth at Damon. The man ignored the beast. "For God's sake, Beck! Something is terribly wrong. Help me help you. What the hell happened?"

"Nothing." Because that was perfectly true. "I'm just tired."

He rubbed a hand over his mouth and flung himself up, pacing beside the bed. I tried to watch, but my eyelids got heavy and I let them close.

# CHAPTER THIRTEEN

I was in water. It swirled over me and around me. I floated, boneless. A bar ran under my back, another under my butt. I opened my eyes then closed them against the brilliance of the sun. In that moment, I glimpsed Damon. His arms were the bars under me. We were in the river pool.

"Come on, Rebecca. Wake up. Do what you have to do."

What I had to do? I had nothing to do. I said so. I think.

"Yes, you do. You said this pool makes you feel better. That it didn't work before. I brought you back so you could make it work."

"It's broken," I mumbled.

"What do you mean?" His voice was gentle and raspy. Tired.

"No one else was supposed to come," I said.

"My being here broke something?" he asked. "What?"

"Who knows?"

"Yes, that's right. Who does know?"

When I didn't answer, he slid a hand around my face and under my head.

"Rebecca," he said urgently. "Who would know?"

"Where's Ajax?"

"On the sand. Who would know, Rebecca? Come on, tell me how to help you."

"She doesn't know." The voice was sharp, hot like cayenne pepper against my skin. I couldn't see who spoke. But then, my eyes had closed again and I couldn't bring myself to want to open them.

Damon's arms contracted, pulling me tight against the hard planes of his muscled chest. He was naked, or at least his top half was. So was I. Curious. Not enough to be interesting. Not enough to ask questions.

"Who are you?" Damon's accusing voice came out smoky dark and hard, all edgy and threatening.

"Who do I look like, boy?"

"Like an old cupid someone spray painted yellow."

"A cousin. Try again."

"This is stupid."

A crackling sound and Damon's arms tightened harder. He made a squeaking sound.

"Be polite. Have you not heard one catches more flies with honey?"

"I'm in no mood for—"

Another crackling sound and a twitching shudder ran through Damon's body. I smelled something acrid, like burned hair. I fought to raise my eyelids. They were so very heavy.

"Mind yourself, boy. Your mood is of as much concern to me as it is to the rocks and the river. My concern is for *her*. Now try again."

A beat of tight silence. Then Damon said "Buddha. The fat one."

"There you go."

"You're saying *you're* Buddha?"

"I'm *a* buddha. The famous one wasn't one of us. He merely borrowed our name."

"What does that matter? You said you were concerned about Beck. Can you help her?"

"She's correct. The power of the pool is broken. Or rather, it is invaded and overwhelmed."

"Told you so," I whispered, but I don't think either of them heard me. I wanted to see who Damon was talking to. I managed to get my eyes open a slit.

The roly-poly little guy sat cross-legged about two feet above the water. His face was round, his head bald, his body a mass of rolls. He was also naked, not that I could see any private real estate. Between his fat and his crossed legs, his bits were well covered. He practically glowed buttercup yellow.

"I did this? Following her here?" Horror colored Damon's voice.

"I do not think so. It matters not. She is dying."

"Why? How do I save her?"

"Bring back the light," the buddha said inscrutably.

That made me laugh. At least inside. I knew him enough to know that was exactly the sort of thing that would piss Damon off.

"What the hell is that supposed to mean? She's in serious trouble here. Quit wasting time and tell me how to help her."

He'd have made a great drill sergeant. One of those that turned newbie soldiers into giant puddles of piss.

"She has been cursed."

That sounded bad. Not that I knew anything about

curses except what I saw in horror flicks. At least I didn't have to ask who'd done it. The only candidate was my mother. She'd cursed me to sleep. Maybe some prince could come by and kiss me awake. But I didn't want to be awake. The prince could kiss my ass.

"I don't see one."

"Because it's a curse of blood, breath, and bone."

"Fuck."

"Her death will be a great loss. I will miss her."

He actually sounded like he meant it.

"She's not going to die."

The sound of Damon's words was…. I drifted away for a moment. My mind flickered. What? Oh. Vicious. He sounded vicious. Dangerous. That reminded me of Ajax. I struggled against the weight in my mind. Who would take care of him if I died? He wanted—he *needed*—me. We needed each other.

Wait—my dead bitch of a mother had left behind a curse to kill me? And I was letting it happen? She was so *not* getting the last word on my life. Plus, I didn't want to see her again. Not that I planned to go to hell, but that wasn't exactly up to me and God probably wasn't all that eager to have me on Team Heaven.

Damn but I could use a gallon of espresso. Mainline it right into my veins. At the moment, I could barely make myself keep breathing.

What was a curse, anyhow? Magic, duh. A lot more complex than anything I knew. I didn't think I could just bat it away the way I had Damon's attempt at kidnapping me. From what the buddha said, it was inside me. A virus. A cancer. How do you cure those? Death worked. Well, it stopped them cold, anyhow, but wouldn't be so good for me. Chemo, maybe. What was the equivalent of magical chemo? Or magical penicillin?

So what could I do? Because sure as the pimples on my ass, I wasn't going to let my mother beat me. Totally not going to happen.

Despite my inner bravado, no plan came to mind. I really had to do better than that. The trouble was, what I didn't know about magic— Scratch that. What I did know about magic wouldn't fill a shot glass. Maybe I should get Damon to teach me something if I survived.

Maybe I should try a different approach. My mother had spent my entire life torturing me. She'd never wanted me dead. Why would she want it now? Maybe she'd thought I'd be the one to kill her and had prepared a post-mortem revenge. That sounded just like her. So did cursing me so she could keep torturing me after death.

Why was Banana Buddha so certain I was dying? Had mom fucked up her curse? Maybe she didn't know shit about magic either. Or maybe it was me. I'd never let her know I could do magic. I'd done all I could to keep it a secret from her. I'd probably made it go haywire somehow. Plus, I'm pretty sure if Mommy Dearest had wanted me dead, she'd have found a horribly painful method, not death by coma.

Okay, then. She probably hadn't wanted me to die, but she'd accidentally sent me on the way to my coffin anyhow. She'd cursed me without knowing I could do magic and that could have caused a bad reaction. Sorry, Doctor Witch. I had a bad reaction to the curse. I'm allergic. Note that on my chart, would you? Can we try a different one? Maybe get me an anticursetamine? Benadrylahex? Benakillacurse? Calacurse lotion?

Oh, God. I was sliding off into the crazy swamp. Time to turn the train around.

Which brought me back to the fact that I still had no idea what to do. I couldn't let that stop me. So for starters, I should wake up. I couldn't do anything asleep, not to mention floating naked in a river pool. Well, not so much floating as reclining on top of a half-naked man's arms. I suddenly wondered what Damon looked like below the waist. Did he manscape? Was he loaded for bear or chihuahuas? What a disappointment if his equipment didn't match the glory of his muscled torso.

I was not 'scaped in any way, a fact he'd already discovered. Well, he shouldn't have been playing the Peeping Tom if he didn't want to see a full jungle. I wondered if naked me turned Damon on. I suspected I mostly made him question his sanity. His fault for stalking me and trying to kidnap me. Fuck him for thinking I wasn't sexy anyhow.

"I want to wake up now."

I hoped I said it aloud, but neither Banana Buddha nor Damon seemed to hear me. I'd checked out of their conversation and didn't bother trying to catch up. It all seemed like too much work at the moment anyhow.

Maybe a dip in the really cold water of the river would revive me. The frigid ice-melt ran right off the high peaks. But that would mean either climbing over the rocks blocking off the pool or swimming through the tunnel that let water pass between. Both seemed too enormous to contemplate, especially given the fact that I had as much strength right now as a dead octopus. Maybe less.

Of course, it wasn't exactly strength I was lacking. My muscles were fine. At least, I thought so. The problem was sheer fatigue. But I'd been tired before. Climbing the rock wall with water cannons shooting at me. Running ahead of the electric prods. Swimming for hours and hours in an endless pool so I didn't get chewed up by the steel jaws spinning just below me. I'd never given up. Never let my mother win. Today was not the day to start.

I drew seven deep breaths to oxygenate my blood.

"She breathing better," Damon said.

"Good for her, but you need a cursebreaker if you really want to help her. Voodoo witches are good for that. So are the native types, but not a lot of them around the area."

I didn't wait to hear Damon's answer. I wasn't waiting around for someone to come rescue me. I'd rescue my own damned self, thank you very much.

I twisted out of Damon's gentle hold. At some point he'd gone back to a relaxed grip. Good thing too. I'd have had to fight my way clear of him otherwise, and I wasn't exactly a kung fu master. I also didn't know how to do the turning into mist thing on purpose.

I managed to land facedown in the water, and I wriggled and kicked to go down. Even sluggish, I managed to dive. I scissor-kicked and knocked against Damon. He was trying to grab me. I made myself kick harder, pulling my arms around in a hard stroke. I couldn't let him stop me.

The temperature of the water dropped faster than I did. I followed the deepening chill to the eye-shaped entrance to the river access tunnel. I'd been through it before. I fit but it was a squeeze. More like a scrape. I grabbed a hold of the rocks and pulled myself inside and instantly whacked my head on the ceiling. I gave a little gasp and lost half my air.

I used my feet to push myself along, snaking my hands up under me and out in front to help pull myself. A protrusion scraped my forearm. The passage was longer than fifteen feet and made a little S curve near the end. I'd have to turn on my side for that.

My lungs ached. I was used to that, so it didn't worry me. Yet. I wriggled through the tunnel, still fighting exhaustion. Maybe if something about me screwed the curse up this much, I could kill it altogether somehow.

I felt the pull of the river current tugging on my fingers. I gripped the edges of the tunnel and dragged myself out.

Bad news.

The current was supersized, thanks to a recent hot spell in the mountains along with unexpected storms. It snatched me in its jaws and raced off with me. I didn't fight it. I could defy my mother, but Mother Nature was a whole other kettle of worms.

Who keeps kettles of worms around anyhow?

I could and did kick hard to get myself to the surface. I gasped and choked when my head broke the surface. I was facing the opposite side of the river. I twisted to look ahead just in time to see how I was going to die.

Devil's Jaw wasn't over near the right side of the river like it was supposed to be. The water had risen so high, it was nearly in the middle now, and I was shooting right for it. I didn't have time to do anything more than pull my legs against my chest and press my face into my knees while covering my head with my arms.

Ajax.

I screamed anger.

I separated from myself. It felt so weird. I was like thousands of starlings all flying together as they danced the salsa in the air. Or bees. Or maybe a horde of fish all darting in the same direction, turning and gathering and flowing and bunching. I was split apart into a million molecules, yet I could feel every part of me.

I'd never experienced this trick of mine like that before. Maybe because it usually was over within a few seconds. This time I didn't solidify. After Devil's Jaw came the Teeth. A mile-long stretch of white water with a narrow channel you had to follow if you wanted to go through safely. Most of the teeth were under water with the swelling of the river. They waited underneath like icebergs.

After that came the Tongue. It was a section around a half mile long that was just fast rapids channeled between great lumps of rock. In a raft, it wasn't too bad to navigate —not like the Teeth—but swimming wasn't advised. The current would churn you under and grind you into hamburger as it beat you against the rocks.

Past that, the river widened and normally slowed a little, though the high water meant the current would stay fast. I'd be safe there, though I'd have time to swim to shore.

It took a few seconds for me to realize that, all exploded as I was, I could actually see the curse. It didn't lose shape with me. It was a tangle of gray barbs, like razor wire or blackberry brambles. It was almost beautiful in its ugly complexity.

It had lost its grip on me because I wasn't tangible as smoke. I figured it would grab me again when I solidified. Not if I had anything to say about it. I smacked at it with my magic, and holy shit if it didn't spin away. Of course, it came right back like one of those paddle balls on a rubber band.

I grabbed it, only it was more like looping a little bit of my cloud around it. I blasted it with magical energy. I wanted it to burn. It flared orange, then went blue, then white, and I kept feeding magic into it. Abruptly it poofed away like ash.

I was so startled and pleased that my body turned solid again. A little too soon. I banged into a rock and pinballed into another before the rapids dumped me into the relative calm of the swift-running waters. My thigh slammed into a rock and my shoulder into another. Both hurt like hell. I screamed or yelped and got mouth and nose full of water. I sputtered and gulped and coughed as I rolled through the torrent. Finally I got myself right side up. The current was sweeping me along fast. I was close to the middle. I started swimming toward the left shore.

It's lucky I'm a very strong swimmer used to working against and through pain. The devastating fatigue was gone, but my right arm and left leg kept screaming at me to get some painkillers and fast. Every kick and every stroke of my arms was pure misery. Plus, I was cold as hell.

I must have drifted another mile or more before I found footing on the river's bed. I was still chin deep and feeling like a popsicle. I lurched forward, banging my shins and stepping on sharp stones. I swear I was going to need a wheelchair once I got out.

I didn't let myself think about how I was going to get back to the sanctuary pool or home. Instead, I wondered what Damon had done when I disappeared. He never would have fit through the tunnel. I couldn't imagine he'd climb over the rocks and jump in the river after me. That would be insane, and Damon certainly didn't seem to be crazy.

I remembered I was naked when I got halfway out and the breeze hit my skin. The sun was shining, but it didn't do anything to warm me. Who'd have thought there could be a windchill factor in summer? I didn't see anybody else around, which didn't really make a lot of sense for a Saturday in mid June. At least—I thought it was Saturday. I couldn't remember much since I went home and collapsed in bed.

I staggered out of the water and clawed my way up the rocky bank. I looked up at the twenty-foot wall I'd need to climb before I could go anywhere else and decided I needed to rest a while first.

There were bits of grass growing in pockets of soil and in the cracks of the rocks, but mostly I was exposed. I shivered and my teeth started to chatter. I went behind an outcropping to get out of the wind. The sun had warmed the stone, and I pressed against it, moaning gratefully at the heat it gave off.

I stayed like that, turning over when the sun had warmed my back. After a while, my shivering became less violent and my teeth stopped clacking together. I sighed, eyeing the rocky wall. Normally I could climb it in my sleep. Today was not normal. I supposed I could blast foot and toe holds in it with magic. When I tried, a pathetic little cloud of sparks danced on the surface of the stone. I made a face. I was out of juice.

Since I couldn't sit there forever, I started climbing, digging my fingers and toes into the cracks and niches. My shoulder and thigh kept giving up, and I'd end up dangling from one arm, or swinging with only a hand and foot holding on. All the same, I didn't have any choice, so I kept moving.

Once I pulled myself over the top, I sprawled in the grass, disturbing the bees and a couple of grasshoppers. My entire body throbbed, and exhaustion was creeping up on me. Not the mind-melting fatigue of before, but more     the     what-have-I-done-to-myself-am-I-insane variety.

At least I was alive, and I was back to being myself.



"Take that, you fucking bitch." I raised my middle finger toward the sky. I had no doubt that my mother had cursed me as her last act on earth.

# CHAPTER FOURTEEN

From where the sun hung in the sky, it was at least a couple of hours past noon. The road couldn't be far. If I went out to it, somebody was bound to pull over and either call the police or toss me in their trunk to pass around as a party favor later. More likely everybody would just keep driving past the bruised and—I lifted my head to look down at myself—very bloody, very battered naked woman wandering down the shoulder.

My head dropped back to the grass. Things were definitely starting to hurt. Who was I kidding? It had been hurting all along. I'd just been too cold then too busy to notice. But I was noticing now, and I really wanted some serious drugs to put me out of my misery.

After lying there for five minutes or so, I told myself to get up off the ground and to get walking. After another ten minutes, I managed to get myself up on my knees and then my feet.

I headed for the little rabbit track that cut through the grass and went up along the slope. The ground was reasonably smooth, but it didn't really matter. My feet were hashed with cuts and purple with bruises. They were going to hurt no matter what I walked on.

I went uphill. When the track forked, I went in the direction of upstream. I'm not even sure why. Down was closer to home, and up relied on Damon to be waiting for me. I was pretty sure that the Banana Buddha didn't have a phone or a car, though picturing him on the back of a Harley made me laugh. Which made my ribs ache and I started coughing, which only made things worse.

You'd think that a naked woman walking outside would automatically draw attention from everywhere. That satellites would shift in orbit and the whole world would get to see my humiliation. Weirdly, that didn't happen. In fact, I heard nobody and saw nobody. I didn't even hear the rush of cars on the road. Of course, if I *hadn't* wanted to be seen, then a hundred people would have popped up out of nowhere. Murphy's Law.

I came to a spot where a scree blocked my passage and I had to backtrack and hike up a steep ridge to go around it. That gave me a good view of the river. I'd gotten back up parallel to the Teeth. So I guessed I was around two miles from the sanctuary pool. The road was closer, but I'd have to finish hiking to the top of the ridge and then get down the other side. If I remembered, there was irrigated pasture-land between the bottom and the road, not to mention several barbed-wire fences to cross.

I decided to just start walking and concentrate on the next ten feet, and then the next ten feet, and then the next.

The mosquitoes in the pasture ate me alive. I don't even know why they bit me. They could have stuck their stupid straws into the leaking blood, but no, they had to make even more holes in me.

I got through the fences without raking myself too hard

with the barbs and then waded through an irrigation runoff ditch full of cattails. That left me a five-foot embankment to the road. That, too, was more work than it should have been. I was shaking, the bank was steep, the grass was slick, and I was like a sasquatch just learning to walk. I finally made it.

Standing there, I felt idiotic. I had to look like something out of a horror flick. Bloody Beck. Say my name three times, and I'd fall asleep on top of you.

The first couple of cars whizzed by like I was invisible. The third, a beat-up blue pickup truck, flashed past then hit the brakes and skidded to a stop. The driver thrust open the door and ran back to me, leaving his truck running in the middle of the road.

"Are you okay?" he asked, coming to a stop a few feet away and looking like he was afraid he'd scare me. "I mean, do you need help?"

"I'd take a ride to the hospital," I said.

"Come on."

He reached out to help me and then blushed bright red. He wasn't that old. Barely old enough to drink. He was wearing jeans covered in white plaster splatters and a blue button up shirt with the name "Liam" stitched in red on a white oval on his chest. He had hat hair, his brown curls stiff with dried sweat.

"Got something I could put on to wear?" I asked. "Or a blanket?"

"Oh, sure."

He ran back to the truck and dug behind the seat, returning with a gray T-shirt.

"Thanks," I said, taking it and pulling it over my head. It managed to just barely cover my crotch.

By this time, another couple of cars had stopped and

were gawking. A woman rolled her window down. "Do you need help? Should I call 911?"

"I'm gonna take her to the hospital," my rescuer said. He looked at me. "Did someone do this to you? Should we call the police?"

I shook my head. "I fell into the river. Went through Devil's Jaw and the Teeth."

Liam gaped, clearly awed that I'd lived. Lucky thing, too, because he didn't ask how I happened to fall in or why I was totally naked.

"Here. I've got a throw." The woman pulled a lap blanket out of her back seat and brought it over to me. I wrapped it around myself, feeling a bit less awkward.

"Thanks."

"You really should get to the hospital. You look pretty bad."

Liam glanced down at my feet. "Do you want me to carry you?"

"Thanks, but I think I'd be better off on my own." I smiled and from the look on my two helpers' faces, it was a scary expression.

I hobbled around to the passenger side of the truck, with both Liam and woman hovering in case I needed help.

I got up inside and settled back against the seat with a sigh. God but it was good to sit down.

"You want to put on the seat belt?" the woman asked.

I shook my head. "I'm good." I looked at her. "What's your name? How do I get this blanket back to you?"

"Cammie Pilts, and don't worry about it. Just get yourself better. God bless."

With that, she swung the door shut, and then my other savior hopped into the driver's seat.

"You're name's Liam?" I asked.

He startled like I'd pinched his ass. "How did you know that?"

"Your shirt."

He flushed and looked down at his name tag as though he'd never seen it before. "Right. Yeah. That's me. We'd better go."

The drive didn't take long. He pulled in to the emergency drive-up entrance and came around to help me out. I guess I looked pretty bad because I was barely out of the truck when an orderly in green scrubs whipped up with a wheelchair and gave me a ride inside.

After that, it was that annoying hospital game where they see how many times they can jab you with something sharp. I had an MRI and a CT, blood tests, shots, an IV with antibiotics and another with blood, seventy-three total stitches, and they made me stay overnight. They kept asking me what had happened and didn't seem to believe my story whatsoever. Through it all, I kept wondering about Ajax. I hoped Damon was taking care of him. What if he'd dumped the poor dog at the pound? What if Ajax had run off?

When I got the chance, I called Lorraine. I got her voicemail and left a message telling her where I was. I tried Stacey, but she didn't answer either. She was probably at work. Last I called Jen.

"What happened to you?" she asked. "I thought we were going to go hike Overland Trail today. I waited for you, like, two hours."

"I'm in the hospital."

A beat of silence. I could hear her grabbing control of herself and the carefully articulated, "What?"

Someone knocked on the door. I looked up. My two

favorite detectives stood in the doorway. Or rather, they knocked and walked in without any invitation at all.

"I've got company. Bring me some clothes, would you? Something loose. And maybe some slippers. They're keeping me overnight, but I don't have anything to wear home." I hung up. "What do you want?"

"The hospital called in a potential battered woman. When we heard your name, we figured we'd come check in on you," Jeffers said blandly.

His eyes were all over me, cataloging every stitch, bruise, scrape, and who knew what else. Ballard wasn't any better. She'd come around to the other side of the bed, so I was between them, and was giving me the same scrutiny. I felt like a bug under a microscope.

"What happened to you?" Ballard asked.

I grimaced. "Like you care. Here's what you really want to know. Nobody attacked me. This had nothing to do with my mother." Well, except for her curse. "I went to the river to lay out in the sun and fell in. Got banged up on the rocks. Then I managed to get out of the water and walk to the road for help."

Neither one of them appeared to have bought my story. Fuck them. Most of it was true, and they sure as hell wouldn't believe the part about me being cursed or the bit where I transformed into a cloud.

Ballard had whipped out her notebook and pen. "Go over that again. Start with where you went to sunbathe. Was anybody with you?"

I sighed and looked up at the ceiling as I relaxed back into my pillows. "You know what? I'm really tired. I'd like you to go away."

I hit the nurse-call button on my little remote control. She must have been eavesdropping because she popped into my room before either detective had a chance to answer. She bustled over to my side, elbowing Jeffers out of the way and offering him a brilliant smile. She was Latina or maybe Indian, with dark eyes, thick black hair, and dimples. She stood about five foot nothing and had the kind of curvy body that made men drool. Jeffers was no exception.

"How are you, Miss Wyatt?" she asked me, reaching over to shut off the call button and then check my IV and the machine it hung on. "I'm your nurse, Esme. How can I help you?"

"I'm really tired and hurting a lot." Both were true, though I could tolerate a lot more pain without more drugs. They'd told me not to let it get bad, though, or it would be harder for them to get it under control.

She grabbed my chart and looked at it, made a notation, and set it aside. "You're due for your medication. But first, let's get some readings."

She then took my blood pressure, temperature, my blood oxygen, and who knows what else.

"Hmm," she said as she wrote things down. "You've got a slight fever, and your blood pressure is low."

"And I'm hungry," I said. "I haven't eaten since—" I had no idea. "What time is it, anyway?"

She smiled. "Nearly eight p.m. I'll send for something for you. In the meantime, I can bring you some juice and your medication. What would you prefer?"

After hearing my choices, I picked orange juice.

She smiled. "I'll be right back." She gave the detectives a stern look. "Please remember that Miss Wyatt has been severely injured. Do not tire her."

"I'm already tired," I said, crossing my arms as best I could and giving them a defiant look. "Sick and tired of you.

If you're going to start calling me a liar and a murderer again, then just go away. Or better yet, I'll get myself a lawyer and you can talk to him."

"Now, Miss Wyatt," Jeffers began.

I cut him off. "No. I like Detective Ballard marginally better than you. She can ask questions."

Jeffers turned a little red, and his jaw clamped. He nodded to Ballard as if she needed his permission, which I doubt she did, but sometimes you played the game to get ahead. Cop work wasn't really welcoming of women was my bet. That was probably amplified in the elite world of the detectives.

"Miss Wyatt, if I understand correctly, you were not attacked. Was anybody else present at the time of your fall?"

I cocked my head, annoyance starting to peg into the red. "Exactly how would that matter? Why don't you get to the meat of your questions because I'm a gnat's ass away from telling you to fuck off again. Let's start with the fact that my adventure in the river has nothing to do with my mother's murder, nor was I attacked, so it's not police business. I'm done talking to you about it."

Ballard nodded and Jeffers made a noise and folded his arms over his chest. Ballard lowered her notebook and looked me in the eyes. She was probably around thirty with creamy smooth brown skin, straight black hair caught up behind her head in a ponytail, and wearing a blue suit with an ivory blouse. Her gun and badge hung on her hip.

"Frankly, Miss Wyatt, the mayor and governor are chewing our asses to make an arrest in your mother's case. We've got shit for leads. From what we can tell, the murder was carefully planned and carried out. The killer left no prints of any kind, no DNA, nothing at all. It's like he was a ghost. And yet your mother's place is practically a fortress. There's no way someone could sneak in and out without being seen unless they had inside help. We also think, given the circumstances, there might have been two perps, maybe three."

Her candor surprised me. Pissed off Jeffers, too, who looked ready to throttle his partner.

"What do you want from me?"

"Information. The kind only you can give. We need you to walk us through the crime scene and the grounds, tell us if anything is unusual or out of place. We'd like you to give us anything you can about your mother's last few weeks, her social and work lives, and anybody who might have had a grudge."

"When I told you we weren't close, I wasn't lying, Detective. I did not know my mother particularly well."

"All the same, you knew her better than anybody else except maybe some of the servants, and they refuse to say anything to us. They might be more forthcoming if you were present."

It was true I knew a lot of the staff, though in a distanced way. I had no idea exactly what they knew about my mother and what she did to me, or whether they knew she could work magic or not. I'd never done anything magical on the property, so it was a safe bet that they didn't know about my ability.

"We have yet to find a will, nor have her attorneys been able to provide any information concerning her heirs. Have you been contacted by the executor?"

I shook my head. "If my mother left me dirty toilet water, I'd faint. She wouldn't give me the time of day if it would save *her* life."

"Can you tell me exactly why your relationship was so poor?"

I shrugged and winced at the pain that ran through my banged-up shoulder. "If you figure it out, I'd like to know. I don't remember her ever liking me, much less loving me. Maybe I was a shitty baby. Maybe I crapped on her best shoes. Maybe I ruined her figure and made her breasts sag. Whatever crime I committed, I did it before I developed a memory, and she punished me for it my whole life."

That was met with startled silence. Even Jeffers had lost his just-ate-rotten-eggs look.

Ballard recovered quickly. "And your father?"

"No idea who he was. Never saw a picture or heard a name. If not for the fact that a woman needs sperm to get pregnant, I wouldn't even know he ever existed."

"So they weren't in touch?"

"Not that I know of, but like I said, I didn't know much about my mother."

"All right, then," Esme said as she bustled in with orange juice and a small plastic tray with a tiny plastic cup containing three pills. "Swallow these with water." She handed me the pills and then a plastic insulated cup with a bendy straw and *Doggett's Memorial Hospital* printed on the side.

I did as told and handed the water back. She gave me the juice.

"Your meal will be here shortly."

She turned a sunny smile on the detectives. "I'm afraid it's time for you to go now. Miss Wyatt needs rest, and visiting hours are over."

Nurse Esme didn't fool me or the cops one bit. She might be small and have a megawatt smile, but she expected to be obeyed or else. I kind of hoped Ballard and

Jeffers would refuse so I'd get to watch her mow them down. Sadly, they nodded and started for the door. Ballard turned around and came back, handing me her card. I think it was the third one she'd given me.

"Please call when you are ready to take us through your mother's home."

What she didn't say was, *and do it soon, or we'll be back to get you*, but I heard it anyway.

# CHAPTER FIFTEEN

Dinner proved to be an anemic ham and cheese sandwich with an apple and the ubiquitous hospital off-brand gelatin. Green. Accompanying those culinary nightmares were a small macaroni salad and a carton of milk. I ate the sandwich and the apple. The macaroni was swimming in mayo, and just say no to Jell-O. Always. I was still starving, so I decided to drink the milk. Thanks to the narcotics running through my system, I fell asleep before I could ask for anything more.

Pain woke me up to darkness. Well, as dark as it gets in a hospital, which isn't very. I knew instantly I wasn't alone.

"Jen? Is that you?"

Movement from beside me, and a tall figure rose and a warm, masculine hand slid over mine.

"It's Damon." His voice was hoarse. Maybe he was catching a cold.

"What are you doing here?" I rolled my eyes at myself. "Never mind. Your employer wants me, and you're stalking me, blah blah blah. How did you know where I was?" I struggled to sit up. "Is Ajax okay?"

He let go of my hand and pushed back on my shoulder. I yelped and fell back. The painkillers must've worn off because that little nudge hurt bad enough to make tears well up. I held myself still, panting as I waited for the pain to subside.

The dim evening light behind the bed popped on.

"What the—?" Damon pulled my hospital gown from my shoulder and then started swearing. Abruptly he cut off. "How bad are you hurt?" He reached out to touch my face but stopped before he made contact.

"Cuts and bruises. Lost some blood but they put some back, so I'm probably even. Curse is gone too. They say I'll be fine. How's Ajax? Where is he?"

"He's fine. Climbing walls and snarling. He's in my truck, actually, and probably chewing holes in my seats."

Relief made it hard to breathe. I put my palms over my eyes. "Thanks."

He slid his hands around my wrists and pulled them away from my face. He turned them over and rubbed his thumbs in my palms. "I thought you'd died."

The words held something I couldn't read.

"I was going to anyway," I said. "I had to try to do *something* to save myself."

"How?"

His gaze drilled into me and made me want to squirm. It felt like he was accusing me of something. "I wasn't trying to commit suicide, if that's what you're getting at," I snapped, trying to yank my hands away from him. He didn't let go, and he didn't say he hadn't thought it.

"Go away," I said. "I don't want you here."

"Too bad," he growled. "I'm not going anywhere."

I hurt too much to argue. I stopped struggling to get my

hands back and closed my eyes, taking a deep breath and blowing it out.

"Why do you have to be such an asshole?"

"Why do you have to bother me so much?"

My eyes popped open. "Bother you? Bother *you*? Are you serious? *You're* the one who tried to kidnap me. *You're* the one who keeps following *me* around. I haven't done anything to you."

"And that bothers me too."

I shook my head. A sound escaped me. My whole body throbbed. I didn't want to admit how bad the pain was in front of Damon.

"You're hurting."

"Duh. Prize to the idiot standing over the battered woman in the hospital bed. It's like you're a detective or something. What clued you in? The seventy-three stitches? Or all the black and blue?"

He sighed and let go of my hands. I knotted them together on my stomach.

"Call the nurse."

I had the childish urge to tell him to fuck off and the hell with me suffering. Pain won out. I'm no martyr. I hit the call button. "She's not going to like finding you here. She already chased off the cops."

His eyes narrowed when I mentioned the cops. "What did they want?"

"To ask if whoever killed my mother attacked me. When I told them it was an accident, they asked if I'd tried to commit suicide."

His long moment of silence reinforced that he'd wondered the same thing. I don't know why that pissed me off so much. I didn't give a flying fuck what he thought of me. Except that for no good reason I could think of, I didn't want him to think I'd tried to kill myself. I'd already told him so once, I wasn't going to say it again. If he didn't believe me, well, then I'd just have to deal with it, wouldn't I?

Except my mouth had other ideas. "If I really wanted to die, I could have stayed at the pool with you and Banana Buddha and just gone to sleep forever. Nice and comfortable. Instead, I swam into the frigid river, bashed myself on rocks, climbed up a rock wall, then hiked a few miles to find the road. Does that sound like someone who wanted to commit suicide? No, it doesn't. So fuck off and go away."

I was pissed enough to turn onto my side so I didn't have to look at him and he couldn't see my tears. Fucking hell. Why was a crying again? Overload, I supposed. And exhaustion. Maybe I was getting my period. That had to be it.

The door opened and Nurse Esme walked in. She turned off the call light. "What can I do for you, Miss Wyatt? Are you in pain?"

As she talked, she started checking all my vitals again. I had to roll on my back. Damon had disappeared. He must've slipped out the door when she came in. Well, good riddance. Maybe the bastard would stay the hell away. He'd damned well better take good care of Ajax, or I'd kick him in the nuts.

# CHAPTER SIXTEEN

I woke a couple more times in the night, always alone. At seven-thirty, my new nurse—Toby—brought me breakfast, and Jen came in hot on his heels. Lorraine and Stacey were right behind.

"What happened?" Jen demanded. "Christ, you look like you've been mauled by coyotes."

"I fell in the river and got banged up on the rocks. Then I had to walk out to the road and anyway, I'm going to be fine, but sore, or so they tell me."

"How did you fall?" Stacey asked. "And naked?"

Jen must've told them I needed clothes.

"It was stupid. I went to lay out and didn't want tan lines. I must have slipped when I got up and fell into the river."

I wanted to keep it vague. Details would only raise questions.

"Where's Ajax?" Lorraine asked. "I went by your place to check on him, and he wasn't there."

I hadn't thought about how to answer that one. They didn't know about Damon, and I didn't want them to find out. "I guess someone found him. That's what the cops said."

"Tell me where they have him, and I'll pick him up."

"I was going to call when I got home," I said, trying to deflect her. "Which is going to be as soon as I can get the doctor in here. I'm done with the hospital. I want to leave."

"Are you sure it's safe?" Stacey asked.

"I don't care. I want to go home." Now I really sounded like a teenager with an attitude problem. Which, to be fair, was true except the part about being a teen.

Right about then, the doctor and Nurse Toby came in and shooed the girls out. The doc rifled through my chart and then checked me over from head to toe.

"You certainly were thorough," he said. "You hardly left a square inch of yourself undamaged."

"I did my best. If you tell me where I missed, I'll try to get it later."

He chuckled. "It probably wouldn't hurt you to stay another night here, but it isn't necessary, as long as you take the antibiotics I'll prescribe and don't let the pain overwhelm you. That's important. Doing that will delay healing. You'll need to rest and stay off those feet for at least a week. Keep an eye out for inflammation or signs of infection, and take your full antibiotic prescription. Drink plenty of fluids too. You'll want to make an appointment with your regular doctor next week to get the stitches removed and double-check that you don't have any infections. You may also want to consult with a plastic surgeon. You're going to have some scars."

I nodded and listened, but he'd already answered my only question: When could I get the hell out of here?

"All right. I'll leave instructions for you and prescriptions. We should be able to get you checked out before noon."

He left and I immediately started struggling up out of the bed. "Where are my clothes?"

"Noon is still hours away," Stacey said.

"You should rest until then," said Jen.

"I should also go pee and get dressed," I said determinedly. Bullheadedly, some would say. Everybody in the room but me would say it, really.

I won the argument since I wasn't getting back into bed until I was dressed. Jen had brought me a maxi dress, a bra, and underwear. I opted out of the bra since it would put too much pressure on my wounds. She'd also brought me a brush and comb. My hair was sticky and stiff and raising my arms up hurt like hell. I persevered until I stopped looking like a freaked-out porcupine.

I took my next pain pill under protest. I was half afraid that I'd end up stuck in the hospital another night if my head wasn't clear enough to demand release. In fact, I wasn't allowed to escape until two in the afternoon. They wheeled me out in a wheelchair, and I climbed into the front seat of Jen's Mini.

Back at home, I desperately wanted to melt into a puddle of goo. I couldn't until I got Ajax back. The trouble was, I didn't know how to reach Damon.

"Okay, how do I get in touch with this guy who has Ajax?" Lorraine asked. "You're not going to relax until you have him here."

I bit my lips. "I don't know."

That confession earned me three stares.

"Excuse me?" Lorraine said. "What do you mean you don't know how to reach him? You said you were going to call him when you got home."

"I—" I couldn't find any words. They kept waiting and I looked like a gaping fish.

"All right," Stacey said. "I'm done."

"Stace," Jen said. "This isn't the time."

"The hell it's not." She glared at me, her pixie face set and determined. "We've held back long enough. Years and years. It's time you told us what you're hiding from us."

"Like who has Ajax. You and I both know that someone doesn't just find him and take care of him. That dog wouldn't put up with that kind of crap. And if you'd really fallen in the water, he'd have gone after you," Lorraine added.

"And you just fell into the river while sunbathing? What kind of stupid shit story is that?" Jen demanded, having clearly decided that now was, in fact, the time. "A five-year-old wouldn't fall for such a dumb explanation. It's insulting that you think we would."

"And we haven't," Stacey said. "Never. Not one single time you fed us a fairy story. But because of your mom, we didn't push. We figured you were dealing with things the way you needed to in order to survive. We always knew you were protecting us as much as you could. Now? It's time for you to start telling us the truth. We've got your back."

I decided I wasn't going to argue. It would only piss them off, and I'd end up confessing everything anyway. Well, "everything" covered a lot of ground, and I wasn't sure how fast they'd get over the whole magic thing.

"You might want to pour drinks," I said, sitting down at the kitchen island. "And I think there's cheesecake in the fridge."

Stacey made up a pitcher of something with cranberry, pomegranate, and pineapple juice in it, plus vodka, mint leaves, and who knew what else. I got a glass of iced tea with mint leaves. I made a face at it.

"You get the good drugs, so you can't drink," she said.

Jen cut generous slices of the turtle cheesecake and passed around the plates. I dug in because I was seriously hungry. Plus, there was the added benefit of delaying the inevitable.

"You going to tell us who has Ajax?" Lorraine asked.

God, but I loved her. Nothing mattered as much as the furbaby. "His name is Damon," I said, picking up a bite of cheesecake on my fork. "We met when he tried to kidnap me a couple days ago."

They squawked. Literally. Then they pelted me with questions. I kept eating until Jen banged the countertop with a flat hand. Stacey and Lorraine fell silent.

"Explain," Jen said, pointing a finger at me.

I couldn't get to Damon until I got to the magic. I made a light on the tip of my finger and flicked it onto the island. It bounced and spun. I did another and another. I kept going, changing the colors until there was a little cloud of spinning, dancing colored lights between us.

The girls stared wide eyed at the display, mouths gaping. I'd never seen them stuck for words before.

"I can do magic," I said. Then, "More cheesecake?"

Since they didn't respond, I reached across and slid the platter over and helped myself. I wondered how long it would be before they got themselves together. Because I was entertained, I decided to make the lights spin and swirl in a spiral and then create a waterfall effect with them rising in a little tube and bouncing down along the outside. I made a big smiley face out of them and spun it in a slow circle.

I started feeling tired again, and the hurt started flaring.

On top of that, the mosquito bites itched something fierce, and I couldn't do a damned thing about them. I pulled an invisible thread and the light bubbles popped and vanished.

"You can do magic," Lorraine repeated slowly.

"Magic," Jen echoed.

"'Fraid so."

"That's so cool," Stacey said. Then rounded on me. "You kept *that* a secret from us? All these years?" She jumped up and stomped around the island and snatched my plate away from me.

"Hey!"

"You so do not deserve cheesecake. How could you keep something like that a secret from us?"

"Seriously, Beck. What kind of friend hides something like that?" Jen asked.

"I was already freak," I said. "I didn't need to be more of one."

"Magic," Stacey said, frowning. "Like the real thing. Does that make you a witch?"

"What's a witch? I don't spend time coming up with spells or boiling newt eyes in cauldrons if that's what you're asking."

"I still don't get why you didn't tell us," Jen said.

I might as well tell the truth. I chewed my lower lip, looking away. "I thought you guys would finally figure out that being friends with me wasn't worth it. I was already trouble enough with my mom, and then suddenly I can do magic and turn people into frogs."

"You can turn people into frogs?" Stacey squawked.

I rolled my eyes. "No. Well, I don't think so. I've never tried."

"What *can* you do?" Lorraine asked.

I shrugged. "I don't really do stuff with it. I didn't want my mother finding out."

"Could she do magic?"

I hesitated. "Yeah."

"Wait a second," Jen said. "You were telling us about this guy Damon who tried to kidnap you and has Ajax. This magic thing is all interesting, but you're trying to distract us from the important stuff. So spill."

"Actually, I told you about the magic so I could tell you about him." I explained what had happened in the parking garage, then went on to tell how Damon kept showing up. "I guess Mom put a curse on me. Deathbed kind of thing and really potent. That's how I ended up in the water." I told them how Damon had taken me to the sanctuary pool and everything that happened after, including his visit to the hospital.

"How did the bastard get into your room? They made *us* stay in the waiting room," Jen complained.

I had to smile. Of all the things I'd just revealed, *that* was what she focused on. Trust her to be pragmatic. I could always count on her in an emergency. "Magic, probably. Or maybe he's just sneaky. The bitch is he has Ajax and I don't know how to get in touch with him." I didn't tell them he thought I'd tried to kill myself. That hurt too much. What if they thought the same thing?

"You aren't telling us something," Lorraine said, watching me.

I should have known I couldn't hide from them. Not if they didn't want to let me. All these years and I thought I'd been hiding really well. Turns out, they knew something was up and just didn't call me on it. I caught my top lip between my teeth and then looked down. "He thinks I tried to kill myself. So do the cops." I mumbled the last.

"Bullshit!"

"That's ridiculous."

"What an asshole!"

Not an ounce of suspicion in those responses. I lifted my head. "You don't think they're right?"

The three of them stared at me.

"You're kidding, right?" Jen asked. When I didn't reply, she scowled. "If your mother didn't make you kill yourself, then nothing ever will. Plus, you wouldn't do that to us."

"Or Ajax," Lorraine added.

"You're the least likely person to kill yourself," Stacey added. "You like living too much, and now that your mother is out of the picture, you've got more reasons to live than ever."

"This Damon guy is a total jerkwad," Jen said. "Who is he to judge you? Fuck, he tried to kidnap you! Why didn't you call the cops?"

"He's actually not that bad," I demurred, my cheeks flushing.

"Don't be ridiculous," Jen shot back, but Stacey put up her hand, interrupting before Jen could get on a rant.

"Wait a minute. You're not telling us something. What?"

Leave it to her to see right through me. "He kissed me," I mumbled.

"What was that?"

I made a face at her. "He kissed me. Twice."

"He what?"

"What a bastard!"

"Did you like it?"

Trust Stacey to ask the last question. Heat washed my face. "Uh...."

"You liked it!" Jen said, accusingly. "The bastard tried to kidnap you. What were you thinking?"

"He's really, really pretty," I said weakly.

Jen sighed. "There are a lot of pretty men out there, Beck. You're gorgeous and funny and smart. You can have your pick. You don't need to fall into the arms of some jerk."

"He's not that bad."

She just stared at me, brows raised.

"She's right," Lorraine said, reaching over to cover my hand. "Your mother stunted your sexuality. You might even think you don't deserve better than this scumbag but you do."

I found myself wanting to defend Damon. "I'm not saying he's perfect or anything like that—I mean, mostly he's an ass—but he *has* been trying to look out for me. He brought me breakfast after the night with Ajax, and he tried to save me from my mom's curse. I've never been afraid of him. He didn't force himself on me."

"That's the problem," Jen said, exasperated. "You think that just because he didn't force himself on you, that's good enough. But he's been *stalking* you."

Lorraine and Stacey nodded agreement, though Stacey looked reluctant. She liked a good Beauty and the Beast love story, and she believed in True Love and was always hoping that one of us would find it. Not that I was in love with Damon. And I wasn't sure which one of us qualified as the beast in this scenario. Maybe it was more a beast and a beast story, only with lust instead of love.

"You're right," I said, deciding that arguing wasn't worth it. Damon and I were never going to be an item, no matter how well he kissed. I didn't have time for a boyfriend, and even if I did, Damon wasn't exactly promising material. He was pushy, arrogant, and probably had herpes or something.

I yawned and shook my head a little, feeling twinges of pain all over. I needed sleep and more painkillers, but I wanted to see Ajax and reassure him that he could still count on me. Poor guy must be feeling so abandoned.

"I'm not planning on kissing Damon anymore. I just wish he would bring back Ajax."

"Maybe he's out there, waiting for us to leave," Stacey suggested.

I looked at them hopefully. "It's possible."

"Let's go look," Jen said, standing. She pointed at me. "You stay here."

The three of them went trooping out. I sat a long moment and then decided I wasn't an invalid and I could damned well go help.

I carefully slid my feet into a pair of ancient running shoes without lacing them up then hobbled down the front stairs. It was Sunday and the shop was closed. I unlocked the front door and walked out. Really, it was more of a Frankenstein stagger. Both feet hurt. More than I wanted to admit.

The girls had gone out the parking lot to the main road and started walking down the street looking in parked cars and up alleys. I didn't see any sign of Damon's truck. I contemplated going back inside, but if Ajax was out here, I wanted to find him.

When the girls brought me home, they'd parked out front. It would be just like Damon to go around back and hide in almost plain sight. I turned right and went down to the corner of the building. It was a good thirty yards, and by the time I got there, I was panting and leaning against the wall of the building. I turned. The side yard was empty.

I heaved a sigh and eyed the walk to the next corner. It was at least as far as I'd already come. I mentally kicked myself. I'd walked two or three miles on my hamburger feet. What was a few more yards? Plus, I was on painkillers. This should be as easy as falling off a bike by comparison.

I pushed myself away from the wall and started walking like I meant it. I clamped my teeth together and sucked hard breaths between them. God, but that hurt.

I refused to give in to the pain. I got to the next corner and came around back of the shop. Disappointment walloped me over the head. The big box delivery truck was parked in its spot, but otherwise, the area remained empty. I leaned against the wall and closed my eyes against the stupid rise of tears. This was getting so old. I'd never been a crybaby before. But somehow I'd become incredibly attached to Ajax, and everything in me just ached to see him.

I decided to go back out front again. This time my pace was slower, and I felt moisture in my left shoe. I'd probably opened up some stitches.

I'd just got to the corner when Damon's truck came squealing into the parking lot at NASCAR speeds. He shrieked to a stop in front of me and came lunging out.

"What the fuck are you doing? Do you want to cripple yourself forever?"

I ignored him in favor of Ajax, who jumped out behind him. I gracelessly dropped to my knees and got a couple more bruises for my trouble, but really, who was going to notice? I slid my arms around the wiggling dog. He licked my face and pressed against me, making little whimpering sounds, clearly happy to see me, his tail wagging fiercely.

"I'm happy to see you too," I whispered, and now I really was crying and I didn't even care.

Damon said something I didn't hear. Then he pulled me up to my feet. I protested and Ajax growled. Damon ignored us both. The next thing I knew, he'd swung me up in his arms and was marching back toward my apartment.

"Of all the stupid, ridiculous, braindead, stupid things you've done...."

"You said 'stupid' twice."

"I could say it a dozen more, and it still wouldn't begin to cover your idiocy."

I liked the sound of his growl and the way it rumbled through his chest, which was totally ridiculous if I thought about it for more than a millisecond, so I decided not to. I also liked the scent of him. Masculine and tangy. Kind of like cedar and smoke and something that was just him. I rested my head against his shoulder and took a deep breath of him. Tasty.

He climbed up the stairs and shouldered inside my loft and straight to my bedroom. He set me on the bed. Ajax bounded up beside me. If I didn't know better, I'd think he'd never been hurt. The damage around his neck was gone and the hair already growing in. The same for the cuts he'd had. He was still far too thin, but his eyes were bright, and he was wagging his tail ninety miles a minute as he licked me.

Damon pulled off my shoes and dropped them on the floor. I hadn't put on socks.

"You've split your stitches," he said in a rock-hard voice.

"I know."

His head jerked up, and he locked his gaze with mine. "What the hell did you think you were doing?"

"Looking for you. Ajax, really. I figured you were out there doing your stalking thing, so the girls and I went out to look for you."

His lips clamped together, and he shook his head in obvious disbelief. "You should have waited. You knew I'd be back."

"I knew Ajax had to be climbing walls. Anyway, the girls are taking care of me. You can go away."

"I'm not going anywhere." He folded his arms in the classic "make me" stance.

"What? Are you worried I'll climb in the bathtub and slice my wrists?" I asked bitterly.

"Who the fuck are you?" demanded Jen as she stormed in.

Lorraine and Stacey came in right behind.

"He's Damon," I said.

"The kidnapper," Lorraine said. "Get the fuck out, assbite. And stay away from our girl."

Damon flicked me a look of surprise, as if he hadn't expected me to tell them about him.

"Jesus Christ, Beck. What did you do?" Stacey asked, catching sight of my bleeding feet.

"Lorraine can fix them," I said and pulled Ajax closer. "And Ajax is home."

"You need to go see a human doctor," Lorraine replied.

"Nope. You or nobody. I'm done with hospitals."

"I don't have my truck here or any supplies."

"I'm not going anywhere. Go get them."

"And leave the three of you alone with him?" She pointed at Damon.

"Get used to it," he said. "I'm not leaving."

"Yes, you are," I said. "All of you are. Go away. I need to sleep." I sounded really crabby.

"Do you need a pain pill?" Jen asked. She checked her watch. "Shit, you're overdue by two hours." She zipped out of the bedroom without waiting for a reply and returned in less than a minute with my medication and a glass of water. "Here. You can't go forgetting. The doc was clear. You have to stay ahead of the pain and not wait until things start to really hurt. You'll heal slower if you don't."

I scooched upright and swallowed the pill. Now that I was lying down, I could admit—if only to myself—that I was in serious pain. I barely paid attention as Lorraine dug in my bathroom and came back with gauze, vet tape, and antibiotic ointment. Supplies I kept on hand for athletic injuries.

She wrapped my feet up as I lay there in quiet agony. "I need a shower," I mumbled against Ajax.

"Later," came Damon's obnoxiously high-and-mighty decree.

"Bite me."

"Don't threaten me with a good time," he said. "At least not until you're well enough to put your money where your mouth is."

I lifted my head and glared. "Not funny."

"Wasn't supposed to be."

The thought of his biting me—nibbling on my neck and lower—made me flush from head to do. I was burning up with embarrassment. I turned my face away so he wouldn't be able to read what I was thinking. Because thoughts of biting had progressed to thoughts of rolling around in the bed under and on top of him.

I took a deep, shuddering breath. I wasn't a one-night-stand sort of girl, and there wasn't a chance in hell that we'd ever be more than that. I didn't even like him. So why was my brain playing reruns of his holding me in the water, his bare chest wet and sculpted?

Lorraine finished her ministrations, and I rolled on my

side so I didn't have to look at any of them. "All of you go away now. I want to sleep." I sounded like a three-year-old.

I burrowed into my pillows and put an arm around Ajax. He whuffled my ear and snuggled closer, laying his head along the top of mine. After a moment of silence, my other four companions left, shutting the door. Outside I heard the murmur of voices. Then the door opened and shut again. Gentle hands pulled the covers over me. Probably Stacey. She was the one who looked out for the rest of us.

"Thanks," I said, my voice muffled in the pillows.

"You're welcome."

Damon's deep voice made me tense and want to fly up in the air like a startled cat. "I thought you left." In fact, I was shocked the girls hadn't kicked him out a window.

"You hoped I'd left," he corrected and didn't sound all that happy about it.

"Same thing. How did you get the girls to let you back in here?"

He didn't answer immediately. I twisted to look at him. "So help me, if you used magic on them, I will cut off your balls with a rusty knife."

"I didn't."

"Then how come you're here without them?"

He sighed. "I told them somebody was after you and I was the best person to protect you from another magical attack."

"Please. That curse came from my mother."

Another silence, pregnant with things he wasn't saying. I sat up, whimpering only a little bit at the pain. "That curse came from my mother," I repeated, my stomach curdling. If it hadn't been from her—

He shook his head. "I don't think so."

"Why not?"

"I can't say."

I clenched my fingers on the covers, tightening them into fists. "Why not?"

He sighed. "I want to, but it's not my story."

I flung myself back on the pillows and tossed my hands in the air. "And we're back to meeting your employer, who can't be bothered to make an appointment like a normal human being. What's his problem, anyway?"

"He sent me. Some would call that the personal touch."

"Personal my ass. You won't even tell me his name."

"You know mine."

"If that is your real name. It probably isn't. I bet your name is really something like Bubba Eugene or maybe Ted Bundy."

He chuckled. "Bubba Eugene is my superhero name."

"What's Bubba Eugene's power? Redneck beer bowling?"

"As fun as redneck beer bowling sounds, Bubba Eugene's superpower is catfish wrangling."

"Sounds unimpressive."

"It's very difficult."

"I wouldn't know."

"You're missing out."

"Why do you think the curse didn't from my mother?"

Damon sighed. "I can't say."

"What good are you, then? Go away." I turned on my side, facing away from him. My inner ten-year-old was in a snit, and she'd taken the rest of me with her.

The edge of the bed sank behind me. He brushed his fingers along my cheek, pushing the hair from my face. "Why would you think your mother cursed you?"

Oops. Didn't mean for him to ask *that*. "She was a

raving bitch and hated my guts." I told myself to scoot away from his fingers as they continued to stroke my cheek and hair, but I didn't listen. I didn't purr either, which, given how good it felt, I counted as a win.

"That doesn't mean she'd curse you to death."

I'd lost track of the conversation already, and it took me a second to refocus. I blamed it on the narcotics. "I'm just surprised the curse didn't hurt more. Totally out of character for her to just let me go to sleep. She was into the torture side of things."

His hand stilled. I managed to bite back my whimper of protest.

"Torture?"

What would he say if I told him the real story? He wouldn't believe it. Who would? The fact that my mother had been psychotic and enjoyed hurting me didn't match with her public persona. Maybe if he saw the wall, the pool, the track, or the basement— Thinking about the last made me shudder. I pushed those memories away. That was over and I wanted to forget what had happened there.

"You know, making me eat squash and broccoli and beets. Torture."

Damon didn't answer immediately. I could tell he didn't believe me but tough titties. He didn't need to know, and anyhow, he wasn't telling me about his employer. Why should I tell him about my mom?

"You need to go away," I mumbled through a yawn.

He drew his hand back. "I'm staying right here."

"That's right. You're still on the job. Get me to see your employer at all costs. Can't let me out of your sight. I might just kill myself if you're not looking."

I was surprised at how bitter I still felt about his thinking that I might commit suicide. No matter what, no matter how much shit my mother had thrown at me, I'd never even once thought about taking the easy way out. If I was going to die, I was going to make her work for it. Now that she was gone, I had everything to live for.

"We'll talk when you feel better," he said finally.

"I'm still going to tell you to go to hell. You and your stupid employer." Lazy bastard. Why couldn't he get off his ass and come meet me himself? Give me a call? Make an appointment? No, he had to send Damon Hotpants to annoy me and get me all hot and bothered. Well, it wasn't going to work. I could put up with a lot more and a lot worse shit than he knew how to dish out. Nobody topped my mother in that department.

Damon chuckled and startled me when he bent and pressed his lips against my cheek. "I wouldn't expect anything less."

# CHAPTER SEVENTEEN

I woke up sometime late in the night. Well, not so late, really. Close to midnight, so hardly late at all. But the Vicodin had worn off and I hurt. I groaned as I turned over to sit up and came face-to-face with Damon, who was sitting in a chair beside my bed. At least I didn't scream, though I did make a startled noise.

"What are you doing in here?" I demanded, a little too loudly. "Where are Lorraine, Stacey, and Jen?"

"Asleep. They won't be waking up anytime soon, so we have time."

I frowned. "Time for what? What did you do to them?"

"I made sure they'll stay asleep for the next few hours, while I take you to get better." He stood and reached out a hand to help me up. "Come on."

I stared at his hand and shook my head. "I'm staying right here and healing up on my own."

He sighed exasperatedly and planted his hands on his hips. "I just want to take you to your sanctuary and get you fixed up."

I started shaking my head as soon as he said *sanctuary*.

"I'm not going back there." The feeling of the place had shattered, and going there would be too hard to handle at the moment.

"But it could help you," he insisted.

"It's broken."

Deciding that making an exit would end this conversation, I stood and bit back my yelp as I hobbled around the end of the bed and to my bathroom. Inside, I found my medication bottles. I checked the prescription information then took what I was supposed to. I eyed my shower wishfully, but I wasn't going to shower with Damon standing outside.

*You were naked in his arms hardly more than twenty-four hours ago*, I reminded myself. I flicked a glance at the mirror and instantly looked away. No reason for him to be interested in me now. I looked like Edward Scissorhands had attacked me. Stir in a patchwork of bruises, and I had all the appeal of rotten hamburger.

I waved a hand and the mirror fogged white. I didn't need to see myself again anytime soon. I washed my hands and face then rebrushed my hair. I decided it was a good time to brush my teeth again, and so I did. When I couldn't find any other reason to dawdle, I went back out to my bedroom. Ajax lay just outside the bathroom door. I nearly tripped over him. He gave me a *how could you* look as he rose and returned to my bed, flopping down in the middle.

Damon leaned against my bedroom door. Did he think I was going to make a run for it? I flipped on the light and went to sit on the end of my bed, eyeing him with unconcealed annoyance.

His arms were folded over his chest. They were nice. Tanned and muscular. Like the rest of him, at least, what I remembered of him in the pool. I hadn't seen his legs, but his jeans couldn't hide the slope and curve of his hard muscles.

"You could be a nude model," I said without thinking.

"What?"

His startled response made me want to laugh. He wasn't the type who got thrown easily or often. It felt like an accomplishment to do it.

"You're handsome. Spanking-hot body. I bet artists would love to sculpt and paint you. And you wouldn't have to do anything but look good. Has to be a better gig than following me around."

His lips threatened a smile. "You think I've got a 'spanking-hot body'?"

I rolled me eyes. "Duh. I'm not blind. Jen, Stacey, and Lorraine would say the same. Plus, you seem to have a brain to go with the Norse god looks, which doesn't really matter for being a nude model but is useful for interacting with other humans."

"Thanks. I think."

"Truth is truth. No point lying about it. Anyhow, it still doesn't explain why you're still here."

"I've got a job."

That's when I figured out that he probably thought I needed to be on suicide watch. I might wake up and gnaw my wrists open or something equally dire. I practically grew sharp spikes all over me at the realization. He didn't know crap about me, and he'd decided I'd be such a coward that I'd kill myself.

Ajax must have felt the change in me. He sat up and nudged his nose under my arm. I stroked his head. Damon needed to leave. My loft, my building, my life. He needed to get the fuck out.

I didn't realize I'd said the words until he replied.

"Not going to happen."

I looked at him. I was starting to shake. It took everything I had to keep the tremble out of my voice. This time I didn't want to cry. I wanted to kill.

"I've had all I'm ever going to take of someone forcing me and torturing me. I will not let anybody else do that to me again. Not you, not your fucking employer, not God himself. Do you understand? I'm done."

He flinched as if the words were bullets. Abruptly he thrust away from the door and stalked over to me. He crouched, grabbing my arms painfully and giving me a little shake. "What did your mother do to you?"

His reaction startled me and inflamed my anger. Hadn't he paid attention to a word I'd said? I pushed his arms away. Or I tried. They were iron bars.

"What does it matter to you?"

His mouth worked. "It matters," he said finally.

It made no sense, and I didn't believe him. I lifted my knee and shoved my foot against his chest. Instead of letting go and falling back, he took me with him. I sprawled on top of him, crying out as pain slashed sharply across my stitched wounds. Ajax leaped down beside us, barking and snarling. He snapped at Damon, darting his head forward. The man beneath me twisted away.

"Don't you dare hurt him," I told Damon. With his magic, he could crush the dog. "Let me go!"

I tried to push off him, but it was like struggling with an iron octopus. His fingers dug into my hips, holding me fast against him. I lay between his legs, my chest on his. We were bumping uglies through our clothing, and I had to make myself not flush with embarrassment.

"What is wrong with you?" I demanded.

"God help me, you are," he said and then one hand

knotted in my hair, the other wrapped my back, though oddly gently as if he remembered I was hurt.

I was too stunned to do anything. He pulled me down until his lips touched mine. Despite his ragged breathing and the tight grip on my hair, his kiss was gentle. His mouth teased, his teeth nibbled. I should have fought him, but his kiss sent streaks of electricity through me, all the way to my toes.

I gasped at the shock of it, and he took advantage. He nudged my mouth wider and teased my tongue with his. I was still frozen in stunned surprise, and yet the heat in my belly had shifted from anger to something else. I tentatively slid the tip of my tongue over his lower lip. He made a pleased sound, and his hands moved to cup my cheeks, holding me as if I were delicate china.

I let it go on for long, delicious moments. Hell, who was I kidding? I reveled in it until some semblance of sanity returned and I pushed up against his chest. He let me pull away, his hands sliding down my body to rest on my hips. I shivered at the sensations that flickered through me. It was like skydiving over a live volcano. I felt his heat against me and the distinct hardness of arousal. I couldn't help but feel both proud and a little bit awed that I excited him, even all Frankensteined up as I was.

I met his smoky gaze, and my stomach did a flip. Then as though he couldn't resist, he tugged me down again. I closed my eyes so I could focus better on the feel of him, the smell of him, the taste. My head was starting to spin, and I couldn't tell if it was him or the Vicodin kicking in.

I lifted my head again. I was breathing as if I'd just sprinted a half mile. Beside us, Ajax whined and nosed my face. I reached out and petted him. "It's okay."

I frowned down at Damon. I could feel his heart thundering against my palm. With one hand, he rubbed the back of my neck, and with the other, he pushed my hair away from my face so he could see me better.

"Why do you keep kissing me? Is this just a ploy to make me stop being mad at you and agree to meet your employer?"

That earned me grimace and then a rueful laugh. "Jesus. What's there to understand? You fascinate me. I'm pulled to you like a fly to sugar, and dear lord, but you are scorching. I couldn't stay away from you if I tried. I tried to tell you the other night when I busted up your meeting."

I recognized the words, but they didn't make any sense at all. I wasn't the kind to inspire that kind of anything in any man. I was in the used goods business. I sold the possessions people didn't want or couldn't take with them wherever they went. I was about as ordinary as it got. I was definitely *not* fascinating. Plus, I looked like a quilt made by Hannibal Lecter.

"When was the last time you saw a psychiatrist? You might want to get an appointment. Like right now. You're having a seizure or something. You should probably have checked in to the mental ward when you were at the hospital instead of visiting me."

His chest jerked as he gave a quiet laugh. "You don't believe me."

"It's not that I don't believe you; it's that you're nuts. Though I've heard you should humor insane people. Otherwise they could get dangerous."

He gave me a lazy smile. "Yes. Humor me. Definitely do that."

He kissed me again. Thoroughly. By the time it ended, I was on fire and I could barely breathe.

"And you say *I'm* scorching."

His smile was smug. "It's good to know I'm not the only one who went up in flames."

"This is weird. I think I must be asleep. Or hallucinating. Narcotics do that, right? This isn't really happening." I let out a long sigh of relief as my world righted itself again. "That makes more sense. You aren't really here. You're just a figment of my imagination."

"The hell I am," he growled and then proceeded to kiss me breathless again.

"Wow," I said incredibly articulately when we came up for air.

"Do you still think I'm just a hallucination? I'll kiss you all night if that's what it takes for you to believe me. I want to be sure I get it through your thick head so I don't have to convince you again tomorrow." He smiled that lazy smile again, his gaze full of sensual promise as he rubbed his thumb over my swollen mouth. "Though I'm enjoying convincing you more than I can say."

He sobered. "For the record, I don't believe you tried to commit suicide. I did," he said, when I opened my mouth to challenge him. "I forgot how crazy independent you are. Nobody else I know would have up and flung themselves out into a nightmare of a river to break a curse. It shouldn't have worked. I don't even know why it did. The idea that you thought it would was more incredible than the idea that you tried to suicide. But I realized I was wrong. Very wrong. You just aren't the type to give up. You don't have any quit in you."

"And don't forget it," I said, somewhat mollified.

"That worries me too," he said cryptically. "Now can we get up off the floor? I'll take you to the sanctuary."

The man was tenacious and relentless. Well, so was I. I shook my head. "No. It's broken."

He sighed. "It's not. The buddha reset the protections."

"It's not the same." I couldn't explain that it wasn't the magic that was gone. It was the sense that it was my space, that I could close it around me and find peace. Maybe I'd feel differently later but not now.

He studied my face. "Okay. The hard way it is." He rolled me off him onto the floor and then got to his feet and helped me up. Ajax squeezed between us, still bristling.

"It's okay," I told him. "Damon's not going to hurt me." On the other hand, the river had done a hell of a job. My body was feeling achy, and pain flickered over me in little bursts. Rolling around on the floor with Damon hadn't helped, but the kisses had been worth it. I had to admit that much.

"I need to go back to bed," I said and then awkwardly hobbled around to crawl under the covers. Ajax hopped up beside me and nosed my face. I stroked him to reassure him that I was all right.

"He's healing a lot faster than he should," I said sleepily.

"He went into the pool when you disappeared. It appears to have done wonders for him."

"*I told you so's* are so childish."

"You only say that because you deserve it."

I flipped him off and flopped over on my side, putting an arm over Ajax as he curled up against me. The last thing I heard as Damon turned off the light was his quiet laughter.

# CHAPTER EIGHTEEN

Healing took longer than I'd have liked, but I still wasn't going to the river with Damon. Jen, Stacey, and Lorraine kept around-the-clock shifts staying with me. They didn't want to leave me alone with Damon, and I couldn't exactly blame them.

Not that I wanted them to leave. I still didn't know how to interpret his kisses or his professed interest in me. The more I thought about it, the more unbelievable it all was and the more likely it was a ploy, either to get into my pants or to get me to meet his employer, though what the hell the bastard wanted me so bad for that he'd a) try to kidnap me and b) have Damon stalk and live with me, was a total mystery.

Basically neither scenario made any sense to me at all, which left me feeling pretty sure Damon was playing some kind of trick on me. A con job of some kind. I've always hated pranks and practical jokes, and I hated being the butt of any of it, and I most especially hated someone messing with my head.

Having one of the girls around all the time buffered us. I followed the doctor's rules, which meant staying off my feet, and I tried not to be alone with Damon. I had plenty of work to do, so I spent a lot of my time with my head buried in that. Garrett hadn't called and I decided I needed to reach out to my other brokers to see if they were interested in the things I'd set aside. Sitting inventory only cost the shop money. I also spent a lot of time sleeping, per the doctor's rules, not to mention the fact that I couldn't stay awake.

Damon didn't seem bothered by my distance and set up a laptop on the kitchen table alongside stacked-up piles of folders and notebooks. He studied them and typed things into the computer and talked on the phone a lot. It wasn't nine to five either. More than once, I woke up in the middle of the night to hear the low rumble of his voice in the other room.

He also went grocery shopping for me. I could hardly imagine his wandering the aisles and selecting meat and vegetables. I didn't add anything like tampons to the list, though I was tempted.

I insisted on cooking since I couldn't get out to run. I was going a little stir crazy, cooped up all day and all night. Cooking helped calm my nerves, and I had to admit I preened under Damon's lavish praise and fluffed my feathers at his insulting surprise that, in fact, I could cook and with the skills of a five-star chef. Or at least four stars.

I had to take breaks and do a lot of the prep while sitting. Stacey got a phone call from her mom, which always took a half hour minimum, and left me alone in the kitchen. Not for long.

I was mincing onions when Damon came in and opened the refrigerator. He took out a bottle of water. He came to stand beside me, propping himself against the counter.

"What are you working on?"

"Pasta."

"Somehow I don't think it'll be quite that simple."

"I'm not sure if that's an insult or not."

"It's not. Your food is the best I've had. I'm getting fat."

I darted a look at his decidedly not-fat stomach, remembering its taut planes and rippling abs. I flushed and focused back on my onions. "Thanks."

"You've been avoiding me."

I considered arguing the point but opted for the truth. "Yep."

His brows rose, evidently not expecting agreement. He took a sip from his bottle, appearing to think. "Why?"

"Pretty much because it's easier than dealing with you."

"Dealing with me? Let me guess. You've decided that I have some ulterior motive for kissing you and staying here."

"I think we both know that you do."

He sighed. "Do we have to go through this again? Not that I mind. I've been aching to kiss you for days."

He turned to face me, still leaning against the counter. Good lord, but he was sexy. I turned back to my onions before I started drooling. Why couldn't I just run with it? The man said he wanted me. I would have to be braindead not to want him. It couldn't hurt to get hot and sweaty with him. Could it? The trouble was I didn't do casual, even if I wanted to. I needed a lot more commitment and trust than that.

He put his hand over mine, taking the knife and setting it on the counter. Then he turned me toward him. "Talk to me. Let's sort this out right now." He glanced toward the spare bedroom where Stacey had retreated. "Before we are interrupted. When are they leaving, anyhow?"

"When I'm well. Or when you leave. Probably the second."

"I'm not leaving. And I'm not sharing every minute of you with them forever."

For whatever reason, that hit me the wrong way. I stiffened and drew back.

He looked startled. "What?"

"I feel like this is a game. That you're playing me. I keep waiting for a joke to come bursting out. I don't want to be your fool."

His face tightened as he considered my words. Then he nodded. "I'll convince you."

"Why?" It popped out of my mouth before I could stop it.

"I already told you. I like you. I think you're beautiful and sexy and unexpected, and incredibly independent. You're also tenacious and you love dogs. That all turns me on like you wouldn't believe."

I kept looking at him, waiting for the punchline.

"Come on, you can't be surprised a man is interested in you," he scoffed.

"But you're not *a* man. You're the man who tried to kidnap me and then stalked me and now has invaded my house. You're gorgeous as hell. You're slick and say all the right things, and when you kiss me, my toes curl. But I don't know you, and I can't tell if you're lying to me and I just can't get over it."

His smug look made me want to smack him. "Your toes curl? I like that." He reached out and twisted a strand of my hair around his fingers. "You'll learn to trust me." He smiled and I felt like a dragon's lunch. "In fact, I'll enjoy the challenge."

He swooped in and kissed me fast. Too fast. Heat burst in my chest, and then he was gone, leaving my heart pounding and my entire body vibrating and my lips throbbing for more.

"Hey," I said, twisting to watch his ass as he returned to his computer. God's finest work, if anybody asked me. "What is all that you're doing?"

Damon slid into his seat. "Work," he said.

"Duh. What do you do?"

He looked at me and there was something unsettlingly secretive in his expression. "I'm an attorney."

I don't know what I was expecting. Something more exotic. Maybe a former Navy SEAL or a smoke jumper or a spy. He had the right body. A lawyer? That was a letdown.

"What kind of law?"

Maybe he was a criminal attorney.

"Contracts, mostly."

"That sounds ... boring, actually."

The corner of his mouth quirked. "You'd be surprised."

# CHAPTER NINETEEN

Damon disappeared that evening after dinner, leaving me alone with Stacey, Jen, and Lorraine.

"All right, dish," Jen said as we settled onto the couch. They drank wine and I drank hot cranberry juice with a cinnamon stick and an orange peel floated in it. "What's going on with the centerfold man?

"He kissed me again," I said.

"When?" Stacey asked.

"The night he brought Ajax back. When you guys were asleep." I paused. "Three times," I said.

Stacey said, clapping, "Maybe there's hope for you yet!"

Jen glared at her then tossed her hands. "I give up. It's true. Hallelujah! You're finally getting with the sex program."

My cheeks got hotter. "Not sex. Kisses. Three." Well, technically, that last time had been several, but I didn't figure the girls needed to know that.

"It's a start," Lorraine said. "He's handsome as sin too, and I bet he knows how to please a woman."

"Now you need to ride him like a pony," Stacey said, her eyes sparkling.

A vision of me straddling a naked Damon popped into my head, and my entire body turned into molten honey. I jumped up, refilled my iced tea, and sucked about half down, wishing for something a lot stronger.

"Is he a good kisser?"

I eyed Stacey in disbelief. "Of course he is. Because if he wasn't, it would be a whole lot easier for me to tell him to fuck off. I melt into a blob of goo when he touches me. You'd think I'd never been kissed before."

"Good," Jen declared. "You've never gone around the bases with any guy before and you really need to get your engine lubed."

Yippee. Baseball and auto repair, my two favorite metaphors for sex.

"I have too been around all the bases."

"Marco Culver doesn't count," Lorraine said. "You were eighteen, it was in the back of his car, and it hurt. He didn't even finish. It doesn't count. Your first time should be with someone who makes you explode."

"I beg to differ. The fact that Marco got his dick all the way inside me makes me not a virgin. That's the dictionary definition of losing your virginity, in fact. I'd have thought all of you would know that."

"One thrust does not make for sex," Jen said, agreeing with Lorraine. Stacey nodded vigorously. "Face it. You're so close to still being a virgin that you could be the poster child for abstinence. You need an orgasm. Several of them, all one after the other. With a man, not fingers or toys, though those are fun too."

Ew! I mean, I love Jen but I did not want those images in my head. I decided the smartest thing to do was keep my mouth shut on the subject and hope they'd drop it. Of course they didn't.

"You've been missing out, let me tell you," Stacey said. "Good sex is amazing. What I really like is when—"

Nope. Wasn't going to listen to specifics. "I get it. Orgasms good. Man-made orgasms really good. Yay. But that doesn't mean I'm getting down and dirty with Damon. Anyway, I thought you guys didn't like him."

"He's grown on us," Stacey said. "He may not be Mr. Forever, but he could definitely be Mr. For Right Now."

I rolled my eyes.

"If not him, we all know guys who'd would treat you right," Jen said.

"I'll start a list," Stacey said, going to a drawer and grabbing a pad of paper and pen. She immediately started scribbling down names.

"Wait. I didn't say I was going to go out with anybody. I'm not interested in a relationship."

"Sure you are. You just don't know it. Trust me, you *need* good sex," Stacey said blithely.

I sighed as the list quickly grew. "Nobody you've dated or slept with," I said, feeling all control slipping away. They were going to blind date me into hell. Though admittedly I was more than a little excited at the prospect of going out on my first real date. "And I'm not doing a one-night stand either."

Stacey crossed a couple of names off her already lengthy list. "Sure. You can try them all out of you want."

"I don't know if I even want to go out with one."

"Yes, you do. You need to have a man-induced orgasm. In order to do that, you actually have to have sex, which means finding a guy who you like and who turns you on and who treats you the way you deserve. That may take a few tries. You have to keep going until you get your world shattered."

I looked at Lorraine as she finished her little speech. "You too?"

"Sex has a lot of therapeutic effects. One night of good sex is like a week at the beach. Better than heroin or any other drug. You have to experience the good stuff at least once in your life, and since we can't trust you to do it for yourself, we need to help. It's our responsibility as your best friends. Scratch that. We're your sisters and it would be criminal to let you go on this way."

"Now that your bitch of a mother is out of the picture, you can open up to someone," Jen said, reaching out to grab my hand. "This isn't just about getting you laid. It's about embracing your freedom without fear that someone is going to hurt a lover or a friend or anybody else."

My heart swelled and my throat knotted. I didn't know how or why I deserved these women—sisters of my heart —but I was beyond grateful. Having them was a damned miracle.

"I love you guys," I said.

They all blinked at me in shock. I didn't do outpourings of emotion unless I got pissed. That was safe, but the other? Like exposing myself to nuclear waste. I knew I'd get burned. But not anymore. At least not with Lorraine, Stacey, and Jen.

All of a sudden, they got up and swept me up in a hug. Some of us cried. Okay, I definitely cried, but the tears were cleansing. Washing the bitter grime of my mother away.

After a few minutes, they went back to making the list. Within ten minutes, there had to be more than twenty names on there.

"That should keep you busy for a month or two," Stacey said with satisfaction.

"I'd say that will keep me busy for a couple of years."

"Oh no. You're not going to drag your feet. You're starting as soon as you heal up."

"Promise me we can double, triple, and quadruple date until I figure out how this whole thing works. You know I'll say inappropriate things and I won't even know it, and I'll get dumped before I can order a drink."

"If a guy can't handle the real you, then he's an idiot and his loss," said Lorraine with a shrug. "But we'll be your training wheels for a little while."

# CHAPTER TWENTY

Damon didn't return before I went to bed, which was little-old-lady early, but I couldn't keep my eyes open. I hated that about the Vicodin. I was ready to dump it in the toilet and switch to ibuprofen and just grit my teeth.

I got up just after dawn and showered then went to make espresso. Coffee wasn't going to cut it. I was just settling down with my tablet to check my e-mail when Damon came in. He was dressed in a cashmere sweater over a white shirt and dark jeans that hugged his ass like plastic wrap. In a word, he looked edible. Lord, but I wanted to take a bite of him. I took a big mouthful of espresso instead and burned my mouth and tongue.

"Good morning," he said. He took a bottle of water out of the refrigerator and set it down in front of me. "Drink that."

"I've got espresso, thanks."

"Drink it. You wouldn't go to the pool, so a bottle of the pool came to you."

"That's where you went last night?"

He shrugged. "Figured you might want to get better faster. Plus, I assume you didn't want me underfoot with your girlfriends around."

"Don't you have your own house? A wife? A family? Pets? Plants?"

His brows rose. "Are you trying to get rid of me?"

"I've been trying to get rid of you since I met you. I'm just curious about who's missing you. Or really, how you can manage to be here for days on end. Obviously you can work remotely, but then, watching me seems to be your side job, so I guess you can't be at your office and get your work done."

Damon propped himself against the stove, crossing his ankles and folding his arms over his chest. "All right. I'm not married. I don't have children or pets. Plants, yes, but I have someone take care of them when I'm not home. Now do I get a question?"

"Sure."

"What's that?" He nudged his chin toward the list of names the girls had left behind.

"Those are the men I will be going on blind dates with," I said, feeling a lot less excited about the prospect with daylight.

"Oh? Since when?"

He sounded as if he didn't care. That annoyed me after all his talk and the kisses. Clearly they'd meant nothing. I tried to dredge up some enthusiasm for the get-Beck-laid project so he wouldn't know his indifference stung.

"The girls think I need to find a boyfriend—actually they said I need to have great sex, and since I don't do one-night stands, they made a list of men I might be able to have a relationship with."

"I see. And how do you feel about it?"

"I've never really had much of a love life, and they aim to fix it. It should be fun, right? I mean, maybe I'll meet the love of my life."

"You believe in that? Love? The forever kind?"

I shrugged. "It happens to some people. Why not me? I mean, sure, I have no idea how to do a relationship thanks to my mother, but I can learn. I take it you don't believe in happily ever after and true love and all that."

"I haven't seen a lot of it."

"I've never seen the Grand Canyon, but word is that it exists."

I emptied my cup and started to get up to get more. Damon took it from me and pointed at the bottle.

"Drink."

I sighed. "What about giardia?"

"Don't be a baby."

I resisted the urge to stick my tongue out at him and took a drink. It tasted just like water. I don't know why I expected something different. Something to say it had healing properties. I drank more. Damon watched me finish it and then made coffee and poured me a cup.

"I was drinking espresso."

"Now you're drinking coffee."

"You're a pain in the ass," I grumbled.

He reached to take my cup back. "If you don't want it...."

"Back off, buddy, or I'll put you on the floor."

He smiled lazily. "Feel free to try. And speaking of that—"

He reached over and picked up the list. He looked at it then crumpled it up, and a puff of white smoke came out of his fist. He dropped the remaining ashes onto the counter.

"You didn't really need that, did you?"

"It would help me get my love life off the ground. I'm really bad at it. My future husband could've been on there. The father of my children, even."

"He's not."

I doubted it too. Hell, I didn't think I was destined to ever get married. And children? Completely out of the question. Just a boyfriend would be monumental. Almost unthinkable. All the same, I was hurt.

"Yeah, well. *Some* guy is bound to think I'm good enough to keep around. At least for a while. Anyhow, the girls aren't going to be happy about having to write another list."

"I'll burn that one too."

He came to stand over me, pushing my legs apart so he stood between them. He leaned down, one hand on the counter, one hand on the back of the barstool, his face inches from mine.

"If any man thinks you *aren't* good enough for him, he's got shit for brains. I, however, have all my gray matter intact, thank you very much, and the only list you need has one name on it: mine."

A shiver ran through me along with that kind of excited rush you get when you're sixteen and your crush notices you're alive for the first time. Not that I was crushing on Damon. That would be stupid. But all my female hormones purred with gooey gratification at his declaration. In that moment, I felt special. Chosen, like one of those fairy-tale princesses that never existed.

Looking into his stormy eyes, I thought he was going to kiss me again. Instead he straightened and whistled.

"Come on, Ajax. Let's get you outside."

The dog had been lying on the floor beneath me and now followed Damon. I watched them go, totally at a loss for words, smartass or otherwise.

"I'm in such deep trouble," I whispered when the back door closed. "If I don't get rid of him soon, I might actually fall for him."

# CHAPTER TWENTY-ONE

By the next morning, I was feeling a lot better. My bruises had faded quite a bit, and my cuts were a lot less red and painful. I drank the bottle of water Damon handed me without arguing. I'm stubborn but not stupid, and a little 'I told you so' action was a small price to pay for feeling so much better.

The next afternoon, he and Jen took me to the doctor who *oohed* and *ahhed* at the speed of my healing and then proceeded to start removing stitches right there. That took more than an hour, and when I left, I felt liked I'd been pecked by a flock of starving seagulls.

After that, we went out to dinner, where Jen grilled Damon. I ate my salmon and listened attentively. After Jen covered the basics, she moved on to more details.

"Who do you work for?"

"I own my own firm," he said. He was smiling but the way he tapped his finger against the stem of his wine glass made it clear he wasn't liking the interrogation.

"But you said you have an employer," I said.

"Perhaps I should have said client."

"Who is it?" Jen asked, leaning forward.

"I'm not permitted to say." He sounded regretful.

"Which is totally reassuring and makes me want to meet with him," I said, rolling my eyes. "Like going into a dark cellar when a serial killer is hanging around. Because that's always a good idea."

"It's attorney-client privilege. I can't reveal what I'm not permitted to."

"Aaaand back to square one." I really wished for a shot of something strong. "I'm getting so tired of the runaround."

"Maybe we should table that discussion for now," he said.

Jen pounced. "Why? So you can corner Beck to browbeat her? Don't you know that no means no?"

He sighed and rubbed his eyes with one hand then, ignoring Jen, turned his attention to me. "We need to talk. Alone and soon."

I snorted. "Does that mean you're going to actually say something for once?"

He didn't answer.

"I'll take that as a no." He was sitting to my left at the square table and I turned a little in my seat so I didn't have to look at him. He confused me. He said he wanted to—what? Date? Kiss? Fuck? I had no idea what he really wanted from me, and his unrelenting silence on the subject of his *employer* wasn't helping with my trust issues.

He remained quiet during the rest of our meal while Jen and I ignored him. Instead we talked about her job, her nutty boss, and her insane family. Then we started planning a rafting trip and considering a winter vacation to Cancun. I'd never left the country before. I'd never left the state. The idea of traveling in an actual plane made me almost giddy and made up a little for Damon's sucking silence.

Tomorrow I would go running, I decided as we walked to Jen's car. At least for a couple of miles. My feet were feeling back to normal, and I could use the chance to destress. I climbed in the back seat next to Ajax after letting him out to pee, and Damon sat next to Jen in the front.

I watched him from the back seat as I scratched Ajax, who was hogging most of the seat with his front paws and head across my thighs. Periodically he licked me and gave me a gleeful wag, squirming so I could reach itchy spots.

What exactly did Damon want from me? More important, what—if anything—did I want from him? I considered the idea of just jumping into bed with him and having a night of passion and pleasure. My body flamed and told me to go for it. My brain tossed out a giant anchor and said *whoa!*

Clearly I needed a therapist and maybe serious medication.

The trouble was he wasn't just handsome. Make that gorgeous. He was also funny and smart and, maybe the biggest draw of all, he was interested in me. Dear God, was I *that* easy? Maybe. He also smelled good and appreciated my cooking, though if he hadn't, that would have been an obvious sign he was batshit crazy and could be dropkicked off my balcony. If I had one.

Even the secrecy was kind of a turn-on—which clearly showed *I* was batshit crazy and that I had far too much in common with cats. It was kind of like being on a roller coaster and not being able to see where or when the next curve or corkscrew was coming. Exciting and scary, stomach dropping and heart pounding.

Damon also seemed to worry about me and want to take care of me, which also made me get all gooey for him. Basically, he was growing on me like mold on cheese, and I was liking it. I just didn't know what I wanted to do about it.

The drive from the restaurant wasn't long, and soon we turned up the driveway and into the parking lot. Since the place was set back from the road, I'd had flood lights installed up the drive and all around the parking lot and building. Our inventory was expensive, and I didn't want to give thieves a reason to think Elegant Estates was an easy target. I also had a state-of-the-art security system. If I'd have used magic for security, my mother would have known what I could do, so I stuck with high-end technology.

It was dusk and the lights should have been on, but everything was ominously dark.

"That's odd," I said.

Jen pulled up outside. "The front door is ajar," she said, the headlights illuminating the entrance. "Oh my God, Beck! The windows are all broken out. You've been vandalized!"

"You two stay here," Damon said tightly and got out. Every line of him radiated threat. He didn't seem remotely lawyerly. Maybe he'd been a soldier or cop in another life. Blue magic wreathed his hands up to his elbows.

Deciding I'd burn in hell before I got left behind, I followed him, making Ajax stay in the car. I didn't want him cutting his feet on the glass. Jen hopped out with me.

Damon reached the door first and bent to look at the lock before pushing it open. He reached around to flip on the lights, but they didn't come on.

I couldn't wait. I flicked bubbles of light from my fingertips. They rose up to hover just over our heads and revealed ... destruction.

As far as I could see, nothing was intact. No display shelves, not the counter, nor the registers. Every piece of furniture was broken and splashed with something that resembled black ink. Even the wood floor was wrecked.

The breath went out of me, and the world stopped. I couldn't make sense of what I was seeing. This—this was *me*. My heart and soul and sweat and tears filled this place. Not even my mother had made me feel as violated as I did at that moment.

I walked forward and my feet crunched over glass and splintered wood. Vaguely I heard Jen on the phone calling the police. Damon stopped me with a hand on my shoulder before I could go inside

"The bastards could still be here," he growled, his voice deep with anger.

I barely heard him. "Why would anyone do this?" My voice sounded thready.

He pulled me against him, turning me into his chest and rubbing up and down my back. "I don't know. But I sure as hell am going to find out."

Anger came to my rescue, stiffening the wilt in my bones. I sniffed and pushed away. "Thanks, but this is my shop. I can handle it."

His hands tightened on my arms. He waited until I looked up at him. His eyes were ferocious and burning with unrestrained fury and something else. Guilt? Did he know something about this?

"Stay here while I make sure it's clear."

My hackles went up. I did not take orders well. Damon seemed to realize his mistake almost instantly.

"Please, Beck." His grip on me softened. "You've already been through hell this week."

"I'm fine and I can handle myself, thank you very much." I glared, my body practically vibrating with rage. I didn't know if I was more pissed at him or the vandals. "I don't need anybody running interference for me."

"He's right," Jen said, grabbing my hand. "What if whoever did this is still inside?"

"Then I'll kill them," I snarled.

"Oh good, because the cops don't already suspect you of murdering your mom. Now they can get you for a different one."

"Not if the fucker is on my property and clearly violent. It's perfectly justifiable."

Jen changed tack. "All right. How about you let Damon go in and get himself killed and that way Ajax won't be without a mom?"

Damn it. She had me there. "Fine."

Damon didn't wait to see if I'd change my mind. He slipped inside. I'm not sure how long he was gone. I gripped Jen's hand and fumed. Who would do this? And why? Was it personal? This time it couldn't have been my mother, unless she were reaching out from the grave. Or to be more exact, urn.

Damon came back in a couple minutes. "They've cleared out."

"I want to see."

He gave me a heavy look. "It's bad."

I already knew that. Or I thought I did. Turns out I didn't know shit. We picked our way through the devastation. Everything had been torn apart. The back warehouse was as bad as the front. My office was worse, if anything. At least they hadn't found the vault. Thank goodness for small favors. And my loft? I started for the stairs and stopped when Jen caught my arm.

"Let me look," she said, her voice soft with sympathy and sorrow.

"I'll go," Damon said. He sounded hard, dangerous, like he wanted to hurt somebody. More than hurt. Eviscerate.

I nodded. My stomach and chest were so tight, I couldn't breathe. I sank down against the wall and pressed my head against my knees. What was I going to tell my clients? My employees? Jen bent down and hugged me.

"It's going to be okay," she said. "You have insurance. We'll make this okay."

I didn't know how. Given time, I could restore the business and keep going. But how was I going to fix the sense of violation I felt? The vandals had stolen my security, my feeling that I could retreat to this place and nobody and nothing could touch me here. This was a hundred times worse than losing my river sanctuary.

I looked at Jen. "Can you get my purse? I want to call my insurance agent. Leave a message."

She nodded and left. Damon came down the stairs. At the look on his face, I sucked in a sharp breath, a knife driving through my heart. My eyes burned but I couldn't cry. I couldn't think. He stopped in front of me.

"We'll fix this," he said, his voice stone.

"Sure." I didn't believe it.

He squatted down and caught my chin in his hand, turning my face to look at him. "We will *fix* this. I promise."

"How did they get in? I have an alarm system. Why didn't it summon the police?"

"The intruders melted the locks. I don't know about the alarm."

"*Melted* the locks?"

Jen returned at that moment, and I stood and took my purse. I dug inside it and found my cell and Detective Ballard's card. I looked at it. Homicide. There wasn't anything she could do. I put it back into my purse and dug for my wallet and my agent's contact info. My hands were shaking, and I could feel myself starting to lose it.

"I don't— I can't—"

My dinner lurched in my gut, and I ran for the back door. I reached it barely in time to spatter my stomach contents on the ground outside. I heaved long past the point I had anything left to throw up. Jen stroked my back and held my hair out of my face, all the while crooning soothingly.

Finally I straightened. I couldn't go back inside. Instead I walked around to the front, my hand tight in Jen's.

Out front, I sat in the back seat of Jen's car with the door open, hugging Ajax as we waited for the cops. I could hear sirens. It wouldn't be long.

"Where's Damon?" I asked.

"He's looking for some clue as to who did this."

I nodded. I doubted the perpetrators had left anything. They were professional enough to melt the door locks, put out all the lights, and cut the alarm system. They wouldn't be careless to leave anything that would point to their identities. "It should have worked, even with no power," I said. "It has its own generator backup and another backup for that."

"What does?"

"The alarm system."

Light suddenly erupted all around us, making me squint.

"Must have been the breakers," Jen said.

"A power outage wouldn't have hit the alarm either," I

said. "It's on an entirely separate circuit, and it's got a backup battery. But if they were professionals, why did they destroy everything? They could have stolen a small fortune. This is malicious. It makes no sense."

In another few minutes, a dozen cops arrived. More, probably, because of my mother's connections than had anything to do with me, but I was grateful to see them all the same. Twenty minutes into giving my statement, I saw Detectives Ballard and Jeffers drive in through the mass of reporters who'd come running again like sharks after blood.

"What happened?" Ballard asked as they strolled up.

I waved wearily toward the building. "See for yourself."

They left. Damon and Jen were each giving their statements. I stared off into nothing, too shaken to think clearly.

"I'm sorry," Ballard said, returning. Jeffers did not.

I shrugged. "It's fine." It wasn't and never would be, but what else was I supposed to say?

"You've got insurance?"

I nodded then looked at her. "The alarm didn't go off. Why didn't it?"

She shook her head. "We'll make sure to look at it carefully. This level of destruction seems personal. Do you know of anybody who might have a grudge against you?"

I almost laughed. She'd asked the same about my mother. "No. The only one is dead."

She made a notation in her ever-present notebook. "Have you considered this might be connected to your mother's murder?"

I blinked. "No. I mean, *no*. How would it? Why?"

My confusion and distress must have seemed as legitimate as it was. Her expression softened into sympathy.

"It's a coincidence and in my line of work, that's a red flag and a reason to be suspicious," she said. "How are you doing? Physically, I mean. After your fall into the river." The slight emphasis on fall indicated she still didn't believe my story. She was a smart detective, after all.

"Got my stitches out today."

"Already?"

"I guess I heal fast."

"I guess so. That's good. Maybe you can do that walk-through of your mother's place with us. The sooner the better if these two cases are connected."

"That's why you're here," I said as my brain cells started to move again.

"We heard the call, and like I said, there's not usually a lot that's coincidental about coincidences when it comes to murder. What do you say? Walk us through your mother's place?"

"Now?"

"In the morning."

I looked at my store, and my throat knotted so tight, I thought I might choke. Nothing in there needed my immediate attention. I nodded. "Sure. For a couple hours anyway."

She smiled and shut her notebook. "Good. We'll pick you up here at eight. If you don't mind, I'll go inside and have a look. See if I can spot anything."

"Sure." Not like I could stop her, even if I wanted to.

The next hours passed in a haze. Questions upon questions and Jen and Damon offering me coffee and snacks. I took the coffee, but I couldn't eat. Lorraine and Stacey showed up and we stood together. They talked and I just stared blankly at the building, my brain running in circles chasing the who and the why.

It was four in the morning before they were done with us. I still couldn't go inside. At the same time, I couldn't bring myself to leave, though Stacey, Jen, and Lorraine all offered to put me and Ajax up for as long as we needed.

"Beck?" Stacey said, putting her arm around my shoulders. "You can't stand out here all night."

She was right but I couldn't move either.

"What about my car?" I asked. I hadn't looked in the garage. Hope that it had survived died with Damon's next words.

"It can be fixed," he said.

I swallowed the ball of rock in my throat. There didn't seem to be an end to the bad news. "I'm going to stay here. It's home," I said and started to go inside.

This time it was Damon who stopped me with a hand on my arm. "You don't want to see."

I hadn't been back inside since we came home. "Of course I don't. But I have to sooner or later. No point waiting."

"Give me a chance to clean it up first."

"That's really nice, but I'm not made of glass. I'll deal with it."

Lorraine made a frustrated sound, and Jen started swearing. Stacey came around to stand in front of me.

"You don't always have to do things the hard way," she said, her crystal blue eyes shining with unshed tears. "Let us help you."

I smiled but inside I was numb. Well, part of me was. Underneath were feelings I couldn't let myself feel. If I did, I'd shatter. "I'm okay. Really. I can handle this."

I held the smile, which felt awkward and stretched, as if I'd hooked fingers into the corners of my mouth and pulled them upward. I didn't fool anybody.

Jen heaved a sigh. "All right. Let's go. But I'm going on

the record that this is stupid and unnecessary and masochistic."

At the door of the shop, I turned around. "I'd like to go alone."

"No way," Lorraine said.

"There's only so much stupid we'll let you get away with tonight," was Jen's response.

"If that's what you need." That came last from Stacey. She looked at the others. "We need to respect her wishes." She looked back at me. "I get it. You don't want an audience for this."

I squeezed her hand. "Thanks."

If anything, my loft was worse than the store. Like below, everything was broken or ripped or spilled, and graffiti covered every surface. But that hadn't been enough. The windows were broken, and the walls looked like they'd been hit with a battering ram. Much of the exposed brick was cracked and powdered. My refrigerator had been dragged out and all the wires pulled out of it. It looked as though a jackhammer had pounded on it. The stove and oven were the same.

The only sounds that left me as I went through were little animal sounds of agony. The destruction was thorough. Even my clothes were shredded and my bed had actually had a fire built in the center. It had smoldered but luckily hadn't caught. It had been thoroughly doused with a fire extinguisher or two. The acrid stench of it was enough to make my eyes water and my throat hurt.

I lost it when I came across Ajax's new bed. It was ripped into confetti. The feelings I'd managed to numb all night came thundering out and crashed through me with all the violence of a storm. They cut me to ribbons, a tornado of swords.

I slid down a wall in the corner of my bedroom and cried ugly, wrenching sobs. I couldn't stop. I couldn't control them; all I could do was feel the loss. Everything I'd built. Everything I owned.

But the worst of it was feeling so alone and betrayed. Unsafe. I don't even know. Of course, I wasn't alone. I had Jen and Lorraine and Stacey and Ajax. Even Damon. All the same, I felt like I were drifting off with nothing to anchor me to the ground.

# CHAPTER TWENTY-TWO

I woke to Damon carrying me down the stairs.

"Where are we going?" I asked groggily. My words rasped in my throat, and my head felt sticky and clogged.

"Somewhere else," he said in his best Grim Reaper voice, all hollow and angry.

I started to struggle. "I'm staying here."

Why I was so determined to torture myself, I don't know. I felt like a captain on a sinking ship. I couldn't leave. I needed to be here.

He tightened his grip. "No."

"You are not the boss of me," I said, struggling and kicking my legs and pushing against his chest as I twisted.

Damon grunted and twisted on the stairs, mashing me up against the wall. My head was trapped between his shoulder and the stairwell. His breath puffed against my hair.

"You are *not* staying here. I am taking you somewhere with a bed and a shower and, if you're very lucky, coffee.

Now either you hold still or I will have to take drastic measures."

"What are drastic measures?" I mumbled, my lips and nose crushed against his chest. He smelled delicious.

"You don't want to know. Are you going to behave?"

"Not likely but you never know."

His chest rumbled. "At least you're honest. I guess we do this the hard way."

He flipped me up and over his shoulder, holding my legs tightly with both arms. That put me nearly face-to-face with his ass. I swatted it. "You're kidnapping me again. I *will* fight back."

"But I'm not using magic, which means you can't either." He trotted down the stairs.

"Who says?"

"It's in the rules."

"Kidnapping has rules? What planet are you from anyway?"

"Magic has rules."

"You're full of shit." I lifted myself up straight, put my hands on his shoulders, and shoved.

He wasn't fazed. He grabbed the back waistband of my jeans and kept going. "You're strong. I'll give you that. Gives a man ideas."

Gave me ideas too, but I wasn't going there. I was actually grateful for the distraction from the devastation of the shop and my loft. I kicked my feet and kept pushing. I wasn't trying to hurt him; otherwise, he might worry about ever having children. To stop me, he shoved me up against the wall again and let me slide down, my body rubbing against his. The friction made my head spin. When my feet reached the floor, he wedged his leg between mine and pinned my hands to the wall.

I felt a wildness stirring inside me, a desperation I didn't understand, and a fear of fear growing like a cancer. I wanted to run. Right out the door and keep going until I outran everything biting at my heels. I wasn't a coward, and the entire urge to run disgusted me. The need to curl up in a ball and scream also disgusted me. I was stronger than that, yet I was shaken to my core and I didn't know how to find stable ground.

Damon looked at me, and something in his eyes said he knew how I was feeling, knew about the chaos swirling inside me. "You're looking for trouble, and if you're not careful, you're going to find it."

I squirmed and he pressed harder against me. "I don't belong to you," I said. "I don't answer to you or anyone."

He nibbled along the side of my neck and up to my ear. Heat swept through me, and the turbulence inside boiled hotter. "You answer to that damned dog," he said, continuing along the curve of my jaw. "And to your three friends. I sent them home, incidentally."

"They wouldn't have left me," I said, startled by the hurt his words caused.

"I may have used magic. Nothing harmful," he said before I could get angry.

"Why?"

"Because I can keep you safe and they can't."

"Fuck you. I can take care of my own damned self."

"Even if you can, do you want to drag trouble to them? Someone's out to get you. First the curse and now this. You want to see Jen, Stacey, or Lorraine becoming a target because you're with one of them?"

The brutal truth of his words cut through my anger. I deflated, my body sagging as I realized he was right. I was being a selfish bitch. I couldn't endanger my friends. "No."

He cupped my cheek, his gaze softening. "I'm not trying to cage you. I just want to take care of you. Let me do that. For tonight, at least."

I was supposed to take care of myself. I wasn't supposed to depend on anybody else. "I can—"

"Take care of yourself. I know. This is for me. Please."

It was that last word that melted my resistance. "Fine."

"I'll fix this," he repeated, stroking a hand over my hair.

I shook my head. "It's not your problem."

He gave a sharp laugh. "Isn't it?"

My brows furrowed. "What does that mean?"

"Haven't you figured it out? This wasn't an ordinary break-in. Magic killed your alarm and the lights and melted the locks. Magic did this destruction."

I stiffened. Something big loomed in front of me. I could feel it. That instinct to run and run fast returned with a vengeance. "What do you mean? How is this your problem? You didn't do it. You were with Jen and me when this happened. How does it have anything to do with you?"

"It's my fault. It wouldn't have happened if I'd been more vigilant. Hell, I probably led them right to you. I never imagined they'd do this."

"Who?"

He looked down at me. "I really wish you'd gone to meet my employer."

"Who did this to me?"

His mouth tightened and I could see the battle going on inside him. Finally he came to a decision. "Your family."

# CHAPTER TWENTY-THREE

"You'd better get over your stupid lawyer confidentiality shit and start talking to me. What do you mean my *family* is out to get me?" I slapped the table. "I *don't have* any. My mother is dead."

We sat in the back booth of an all-night diner. I was seething. Damon had refused to tell me anything else after he dropped his little nuclear bomb, except that I needed to speak with his client. It irritated the fuck out of me that he'd hooked me enough that I couldn't refuse.

I'd let him drive me here, only now I wanted to bolt, but not before I told the fucker just what I thought of him. But the words stuck to the roof of my mouth. Not because I was trying to be tactful or even because we were in a public place. What held me back was the knowledge that if I told him how pissed I was, I might also let on how much he'd hurt me and how scared I was. My mother was Satan's worst nightmare, and now it seemed I had more psychotic family members. Maybe one had killed my mother and now had me in his sights. Or hers.

I could have handled the fear okay, but the fact that Damon ShitForBrains knew things about me and had kept silent while kissing me and pretending he was into me made me sick. I was disgusted at my gullibility.

How could I have believed he actually might be into me? He was playing some twisted game, just like all my mother's games. I shouldn't have trusted him; I should have pushed harder to get answers. Instead I'd let him charm me into being stupid. The worst part was that my humiliation wasn't the worst of my pain. The worst was feeling like my heart had been skewered.

The man responsible shook his head. He looked regretful. I didn't believe it. "I've already said too much."

"You think so? Because *I* think you've got your lips sewn shut tighter than your ass, and I'm sick of you playing me. This is my life, and I swear to God, if you don't tell me what the hell is going on, I will wire your balls for sound and zap you into next week."

"I can't," he said. He reached across the table to take my hand. I snatched it away.

"Do not touch me!"

He winced and looked past me. "I can't tell you but he can. If he doesn't, then I will. I promise."

I sneered. "Your promise is worthless."

His lips twisted as he flinched. "All the same, I mean it." He stood and strode to the door of the diner.

There, Damon met a tall, lanky man. He wore a tailored suit that probably cost thousands of dollars and was hand sewn by naked women in Xanadu. His brown hair was slightly long and combed straight back from his face in a helmet sort of look. It fit him. Even the receding hairline with the widow's peak. His skin was pale, and he had a casually grim look as if he rarely smiled because the world was going to hell in a handbasket at any second and he didn't want to look too enthusiastic when it did.

He nodded to Damon but didn't shake his hand. Neither did Damon offer. Both turned to look at me. I just glared back, fighting the urge to flip them off. I was in no mood for any more games or lies. Deliberately I broke eye contact, turning my back and sipping my coffee. Footsteps approached and then they stood at the end of the booth. I looked up.

"Rebecca Wyatt, this is Mason Wyler Symms. Mason, this is Rebecca."

"Beck," I corrected. I leaned back and folded my arms. "You want to tell me why you sent this asshat to kidnap me? And who the hell destroyed my shop and home?"

Mason Wyler Symms's eyes were disks of tarnished silver. He examined me slowly, his gaze moving from my head down to where the table hid me from sight and back up. "You look like Elena," he said finally. His voice was light and warm. A contrast to the Mister Chill thing his face had going on.

"Who's Elena?"

"Your mother."

"My mother's name was Anne."

"That was your aunt, and her real name was Adriane. Adriane Wyler Symms."

I looked at Damon. "What kind of bullshit is this?"

"I'm afraid it's the truth, Rebecca," Mason said as he slid into the seat opposite me. He glanced at Damon and gave a little gesture with his head to tell him to go away. That Damon retreated to the opposite side of the diner without question or a glance at me said something, but I wasn't entirely sure what. Definitely that he jumped when Mason told him to.

"If you want me to believe you, then you'd better have solid proof," I said to the dour man opposite me. "Because right now I'm thinking you need to take an ambulance ride to the rubber room, STAT." I was tempted to get up and walk out. The whole conversation was ludicrous. Curiosity kept me there. That and the desire to find out who was behind the destruction of my shop.

He gave me a dry smile and reached into the breast pocket of his coat. He pulled out a small manila envelope. Opening it, he tipped its contents onto the table. A number of pictures fell out. He turned them over and faced them toward me.

He tapped one. "This is the woman you thought was your mother, yes?"

It was. She was young, maybe twenty, but her eyes held that unmistakable intensity that made most people cringe and do whatever she wanted. We looked a fair bit alike, though her hair was red-brown and her face rounder. Her features were delicate.

"That's her."

"This is your actual mother." He tapped another picture. This woman was older, probably nearing fifty. She was slender and petite, with blonde hair and a solemn air. Her eyes looked cold, colder than my mother's."

Mason looked at me, waiting for a response. I said nothing. I didn't see any point. The whole thing was too stupid to bother thinking about.

"Your mother has six siblings. Four who lived with the family, two who resided with their fathers." He pushed another picture toward me. The image was of a large group of people, probably taken at some sort of holiday. They were all dressed in elegant clothing. Everybody stood proud and stiff and none of them looked remotely happy. There wasn't a single smile on anybody's face.

In the back middle was an old couple with white hair. Beside them were four women and two men. They were younger, probably the couple's children. Then there was a bunch of younger adults, ranging from twenty on up to fifty, from what I could tell.

One was Mason. Another was the woman he called Elena. My mother—the one who'd spent her life torturing me—wasn't there. Maybe she'd been occupied plucking the wings off butterflies. Clustered in front were a bunch of children. I was willing to agree that I could see a resemblance to me in some of the people, but that's as far as I was willing to go.

"This is the entire living Wyler clan, as of twenty-five years ago, except, of course, you and your Aunt Adriane."

"Stop calling her that."

His brows rose and his broad forehead wrinkled. His gaze on mine wasn't particularly sympathetic. More like ... careful. "She was your aunt. My sister, in fact. Two years my elder. She took you within an hour of your birth and vanished. We could find no trace of her until I received this letter." He drew out another envelope, this one of heavy linen paper. He opened it and tipped it. A key fell out—an old-fashioned skeleton key. He drew out a paper and unfolded it then pushed it over to me.

I hesitated then dropped my gaze. I recognized my mother's elegant handwriting. The lines shimmered with a silver glow. Magic. I narrowed my eyes to help focus.

> *My dearest Mason:*
> *We have been apart far too long and I will always*
> *regret that my obligation to our family's blood and honor*

*required me to live apart and isolated from you. I swore on my soul never to allow Osterraven to claim his ill-begotten spawn, nor will I let his progeny scum ever know who or what she comes from. If Elena could have survived, I would have strangled the child in her cradle. She is an abomination and an eternal stain on our proud line. If you have received this letter, then I have gone from this plane. My death means that you must pick up the mantle of duty and carry it. I leave everything of mine to you, my dearest brother. I know that you alone will have the strength and determination to do what must be done. The key will give you passage to the heart of my home.*

    *Your dearest sister,*
    *Adriane*


I read the letter three times. I forced myself not to react to any of it, pushing my wildly erupting emotions down. Though I might get a T-shirt with YOU'RE LOOKING AT AN ETERNAL STAIN printed on it. I was not going to let this man—my uncle, if this letter was true—see how shaken I was.

Looking up, I shoved the letter back toward him. "All right. Supposing this is true, what do you want from me?"

"I've come to retrieve you and take you home."

"One," I held up a finger—not the middle one, for the record—"I am home. And two, I'm your family's eternal stain, so I can't imagine why you'd be interested in putting out a welcome sign for me."

"Not my family. *Our* family."

"Your sister sure didn't think so, which is okay by me because I hated being her daughter."

"Niece," he corrected. "Your mother would like to meet you."

"Tell her to get on a plane."

He frowned. "Youth defers to age in our family."

"Yeah? I guess I didn't get the memo."

"You are remarkably incurious about your history and how you came to be here," he said.

I leaned my elbows on the table. "In the last week, I have been accused of murdering my mother; got nearly kidnapped by a man hired by you; crawled through dog shit to save a dog; came close to dying of a curse; got turned into hamburger by the river; and now my home, my shop, and just about everything I own has been destroyed. The latter of which your buddy Damon seems to think was caused by my family. You can imagine how endearing I find that.

"So no, except for wanting to kill the assholes who attacked my home, I'm not interested in knowing about anybody related to the bitch who spent my entire life making me suffer in every way she could possibly think of. I especially don't want to rub elbows with the people who actually liked her. If you want to give me a list of who ripped my place apart, I'd appreciate that."

The truth was that I wanted to ask a couple thousand questions, but that would give him power over me and I wouldn't willingly do that. Been there, done that with Aunty Mommy or whatever the hell the bitch who raised me was.

Mason tapped his fingers thoughtfully on the letter then looked steadily at me. "I would like you to give me the opportunity to know you."

"I don't trust you. You sent your boy over there to kidnap me and then invade my life." I pointed to Damon. "If I cooperate with you, I might just end up someplace I don't want to be."

"I will give you my word that I will be nothing but a gentleman and will not make any moves against you."

There was a formality to the way he spoke that made me actually think I could trust his word. Or maybe just that if I doubted his word, he'd go rage-monkey on me.

"And if I say yes, just what would this getting-to-know-you business entail?"

"Meals. Outings perhaps. Do you play chess?"

"I play poker. And shoot pool."

"Not in my repertoire, I'm afraid. I could learn, however."

The guy reminded me of one of those velvet smoking jacket–clad men on PBS who sipped tea and read Shakespeare for fun. How could I possibly be related to him? He screamed elitism, privilege, and wealth. The very definition of upper crust.

I could move in that world, but I didn't like it. Whenever I swam in that pond, I wanted to come home and shower and scrub down with steel wool. That world was slimy, plastic, and fake. Everything was for show, and nothing mattered but what other people thought.

Mason must have read my doubts. He leaned forward. "You have been raised very differently from how you would have been had Adriane not taken you, but we are blood, and I'm not so old that I cannot learn new tricks."

I cracked a smile for the first time. "Was that a joke?"

He gave a faint shrug. "My sense of humor is dusty, perhaps, but not entirely dead."

"What do you really want from me?"

"You are a very direct young woman," he said, not answering. "You have very little artifice about you. It is refreshing."

"What you did there just now is called 'deflecting.' Or maybe you are an indirect man with a whole lot of artifice going on."

He actually chuckled then glanced at my coffee cup. "Is that swill any good?"

"Best you can get this time of the night or morning, whatever you want to call it. Beggars can't be choosers. Food's not bad either if you like grease and salt, which I've been known to indulge in from time to time."

"I think I'd like to fortify myself for the rest of this conversation," he said and gestured to the waiter, who had inexplicably ignored us up to that point.

Mason ordered French toast and bacon at my suggestion. I ordered the same, plus a pot of coffee. As soon as the waiter went off to the kitchen to put in our order, my new uncle began, and not with anything I expected, though I had no idea what exactly I thought he'd say.

"Your bloodline is coveted. You are a mixing of Osterraven and Wyler Symms genetics, which makes you very desirable for breeding."

"Say what? Breeding? What the fuck?"

"Our people are sorcerers. There are elite families with strong, pure powers, and then muddier lines whose powers have been diluted by mismanaged bloodlines. The Osterraven and Wyler Symms families both have strong magic genetics. They have chosen mates and created children to increase the strength of the line's magic. Families will contract for a pair to mate. Often there are twins and occasionally triplets produced. The releasing of eggs and fertilizing success are controlled by magic.

"Your sire, Ethan Osterraven, contracted with your mother and my sister, Elena, to produce two children. He wished to claim both children for his family, and the contract was therefore complex and quite valuable to both of sides. However, it seemed he sought to cheat us. Ethan is quite powerful and wields his power with great subtlety. During their lovemaking and without Elena's knowledge, he forced a third egg to be released and fertilized it. Because he held the pregnancy in such value, he lived with her through the entire ten months, which allowed him to successfully hide the extra child.

"But somehow Adriane realized something was amiss. She diverted Ethan away from the home and induced the birth early. Elena was unaware during this time. Carrying three babies is difficult for any woman, but she was somewhat frail and the magic Ethan deployed to hide your existence from her and soothe her fears made her mentally foggy. Add the magic Adriane used to induce labor, and Elena was out of her mind. She remembers very little of that day.

"Adriane was furious at Ethan's perfidy and treachery. The contract was written in such a way that he could claim all three children. Adriane refused to let that happen. She took you and vanished, and we never saw or heard from her again while she lived. She left a note telling us what Ethan had done, but of course, there was no way to prosecute him."

I took a few moments to digest that incredible story. I had a lot of questions, but one popped out ahead of the others. "Did anybody look for me and Aunty Mommy?"

Mason shook his head. "We were bitterly angry, and Elena was gravely ill for months and unable to have more children. If we retrieved you both, Ethan could claim you, and none of us were willing to reward his despicable, vile conniving and the harm he'd done to your mother."

All of this was incredibly bizarre, yet made sense in a weird way. If what he said wasn't a fairytale to fool me. "What did you think Adriane would do with me? Did you know she'd make me her personal voodoo doll? Torture me six ways from Sunday?"

Points to Mason for not looking away or soft-selling his reply. "We knew it was likely. You represented everything she'd had to give up as well as Ethan's trickery. Adriane was never one to forgive. She could hold a grudge into eternity, and she could be cruel."

"And that didn't bother you? To know your sister was going to be putting your niece through a living hell?"

"As I said, we were angry and in her action, we found justice." His thin lips pulled back in a grimace. "I am not proud of my behavior. I should have found you and protected you. I have often regretted that I didn't."

"Not so much that you came looking, though."

"A few years ago, I began a search and quickly aborted it."

"Why?"

"The circumstances were less than auspicious."

I rolled my eyes. "And here we go back to vague answers that tell me nothing. I thought you were going to actually give me some information."

"You aren't very patient, are you?"

"Not one of my virtues, no," I said.

A smile flickered across his mouth. "I began my search in a time of turmoil between some of the ruling families. I quickly realized that finding you could put you in grave danger. As I said, your heritage—your blood—makes you very desirable and also makes you dangerous. There are those who seek to claim you and, if they cannot, to kill you.

The fact that you are unprotected makes you easy prey, as you discovered tonight."

"Who did it? Who came after me? Who destroyed my home?" Anger overrode my growing fear. Not for me so much as for Lorraine, Jen, and Stacey, for my employees, all of whom wouldn't stand a chance against a magic attack. What if the same magic that had ripped apart the furniture and walls had been turned on human bodies?

The very thought of it made me sick and turned my fury up to high.

"I don't yet know. I have called in my people to help investigate and protect you."

"Why does Damon think my own family did this?"

"Because you are not technically a member of the Wyler Symms family. You are Osterraven and it's quite possible some of them perceive you as a threat."

"Me? A threat to them? I suppose your side feels the same way. I guess I won the criminally insane relatives lottery." I shook my head. "Whatever. I don't care. Family isn't about blood, anyhow. My family is made up of the people I love and would die for. They'd die for me. The woman who was actually blood tried to kill me, and now it looks like more of my blood relatives are trying to do the same. Far as I'm concerned, you're all just an accident of genetics and I don't want anything to do with you."

The last bit wasn't true. Not really. But right now, I wanted to drive them all off with a pitchfork until I could figure out who wasn't out to get me. If any of them fell into that category.

He frowned and bent forward. "We aren't monsters—not many of us, at any rate. I can help you repair what's been broken. You won't lose a thing. I promise."

He meant using magic. I shook my head. "Not a chance. The police are involved, and there's been news coverage. People will wonder if it's all turned back right like that." I snapped my fingers. "I'll fix things the good old-fashioned way. Insurance will cover the losses."

"The perpetrators will be back," he warned reluctantly. "You'll want to establish magical security. And once the news is out, others will come. Many will want to meet you. Not just family."

I liked that he didn't try to talk me out of it. I might be a pawn in this game, but he at least pretended he was going to respect my decisions.

"The news *is* out," I said. "How do they even know who or what I am or where to find me?" I asked. "Until you got that note from Aunty Mommy, *you* didn't even know."

"*That* is a question I'm going to get to the bottom of as well," he said, and the sharp edge of his voice said that he would make whoever had betrayed him pay and pay well.

Right about then is when our food was delivered. I dug in. If my mouth was full, I could think, and right now, I was so overloaded that I wasn't sure which way was up.

Mason ate slowly, cutting everything up in small squares with precise strokes. Even the bacon.

"I would like to see what the key unlocks," he said. "Will you take me to your mother's estate?"

"Get in line."

"I don't understand."

"I'm taking the cops on a tour in a couple hours. You could come, I suppose. They wanted to know who her heir was and that's you."

Mason gave me an inscrutable look. He was good at those. "I have no intention of taking any portion of my sister's belongings. I plan to turn all of it over to you."

"No thanks."

His brows rose. "She left behind a large fortune. You are entitled to it all."

"I don't want anything. Light it all on fire if you want."

His lips curved into a faint smile. "It is owed to you, at the very least, for the hurt she caused you. Understand that you will need that money to establish yourself in our society. Wealth, after all, is power in its way."

"Who said I'm interested in your society? Speaking of that, exactly where are you from? Because you said 'ruling families.' Do you have your own country somewhere?"

"Our country—our world—overlays the ordinary world. The ruling families have domain over the magic world, maintaining laws and justice and keeping renegades from unleashing magic on mundanes. I have homes in various countries. I spend much of my time in Milan, London, and New York. Have you ever been?"

"Never been out of California."

"No, I suppose Adriane wouldn't want to risk anybody accidentally discovering you."

"She said she couldn't kill me without trouble for Elena. Why is that?"

"Birth contracts are usually made with magical guarantees. To ensure the safety of the children and the parents, harm to one will result in equal harm to the other. The length of time that those constraints hold are agreed upon in the contract. In this case, the terms were a bit unusual. That death of any of the children would result in the agonizing death of both parents. Ethan dictated those terms, no doubt planning his deception and wishing to protect the third child, which made sense, given the tensions between factions of the families and the hard feelings that would rise when his treachery was discovered.

The particular contract clause was set to expire on your twenty-seventh birthday."

That was only seven months away.

"I wasn't going to survive to my twenty-eighth, was I? Not if my—" I caught myself before I called that sadistic bitch my mother again. "Not if Aunty Mommy had anything to do with it."

"Given what you've told me about your treatment, it's unlikely," Mason agreed.

"You have captured Damon's undivided attention," he noted suddenly. "He hasn't glanced away from you since I arrived."

Mr. Prettypants sat across the diner with a cup of coffee in front of him, watching me with undiluted intensity.

"He's a prick."

Mason's brows lifted as he studied me. "I've always found him to be a gentleman."

"Obviously he's got you fooled." Just like me. Or rather, I had closed my eyes to the signs. Such as trying to kidnap me.

"Surely he hasn't hurt you." Mason's eyes hardened and all of a sudden, a prickle of unease ran down my neck. In that moment, he bore too strong a resemblance to Aunty Mommy for comfort.

"He lied to me." His kisses were lies. Which *had* hurt me, but I wasn't going to admit that to anybody. "Anyway, he's staring because—" I broke off, a revolting thought occurring to me.

"You don't think he's got some bizarre idea about contracting a kid with me, do you? Because a) that contract business of yours is beyond disgusting, and b) if I ever have kids, which I highly doubt I will, I'm going to have them with someone who gets me all hot and bothered and isn't in it for the genetics." How's that for under the heading *things I never thought I'd hear myself say?*

Mason smiled. "I realize I'm not the proper demographic, but I always thought Damon attractive. You don't find him so?"

I flushed. "Oh, please. He's sex on a stick. He's also a snake in the grass, and now that I have a little better idea what's going on, I trust him less than before. For all I know, he's thinking about how sexy my DNA is and how he'd like to contract the hell out of me."

"I think you may be judging him unfairly. For what it's worth, I chose him to represent me with you because he's loyal, honest, and trustworthy."

"I got a different impression when he tried to kidnap me. Why send him anyway? Why not just contact me yourself?"

"To protect you. I didn't want to lead trouble to your door, though it appears that it came anyhow."

"Not your fault. The cops think whoever destroyed my place might have murdered Mommy Dearest, and if that's the case, they were here before you found out I was here too."

Mason considered that a moment. "I suppose it's possible, though unlikely. Adriane has been a ghost since she left. Her killer likely has nothing to do with whoever is coming after you. Rest assured, however, that I will find the culprit ... and whoever killed my sister." His smile gave me a cold shiver. "I would like to punish their temerity myself."

I had a feeling the perps would enjoy Mason's punishment a whole lot less than what they'd get from the good ol' American justice system. Given what they'd done to my place, I was in no mood to sympathize.

"I wouldn't mind getting a shot at them myself."

"Now then, the question is where will you stay while your home and shop are repaired?"

"I'll get a hotel that takes pets for a couple nights or so until my loft can be made livable, and then I'll go home."

My new uncle frowned. "Do you think that's wise? Besides, I understand the damage is extensive."

"I'll beef up security." I'd slap up a dozen magic walls, plus whatever else I could think of. "As for the damage, I just need a working bathroom, a coffee maker, a fridge, and a stove, and even the last two aren't all that necessary. I'll throw a mattress on the floor, and I'll be fine."

His eyes widened. "Certainly not. It sounds dreadful."

I had to laugh at his horror. "Maybe, but that's the way the cookie crumbles sometimes. A little discomfort won't kill me."

He shook his head. "No. You will be too vulnerable. You can't be allowed to live that way."

That brought me up short. Anger crackled through me. "Excuse me? I *can't be allowed?*"

"It is much too dangerous. You have no idea who you're up against or what they are capable of. If I know my sister, you aren't even trained."

He spoke like the decision was made and I would cave to his orders. I had news for him.

My lip curled. "I know enough. Anyhow, it's my choice, not yours."

He scowled. "Please be reasonable, Rebecca—"

"My name's Beck," I snapped. I stood up and dug in my purse, tossing a twenty-dollar bill on the table. Without another word, I wheeled and marched away, ignoring his attempts to summon me back. I thrust through the door and stopped. Ajax sat in the driver's seat of Damon's truck, his nose poked out the three-inch crack we'd left at the top.

I was tired and pissed and beyond out of patience. I strode to the locked truck and thrust a strand of magic in the door. It popped open and Ajax nosed my ear.

"Let's go," I said, patting my leg. He jumped down.

"Where are you going?"

Damon stood behind me. He looked tense and worried. I don't know what the hell he had to be worried about. Fucked-up assholes hadn't torn apart *his* home and business. Fucked-up relatives hadn't crawled out of the woodwork thinking they could run *his* life for him.

The glass door of the diner pushed open, and Mason stepped out.

"That's none of your damned business. Either one of you."

Damon took a step toward me, the tendons in his neck tightening, his arms knotting with tension. "You're wrong."

"Then I'm wrong but that's my problem, isn't it? I don't need anybody telling me how or where to live. I've had enough of that bullshit to last me twelve lifetimes, and I'm not putting up with that kind of crap again. Understand?"

I whirled and strode off out of the parking lot, Ajax trotting at my knee. I turned and headed toward downtown. It was stupid. I had nowhere to go. No clothing stores were open at this hour, and I needed to get home anyway to meet with the detectives in a few hours. It was at least a five-mile walk. Actually, that was good. I needed the exercise to work off my anger.

I swung into a ground-eating pace, my brain tumbling with all that had happened. I wasn't particularly surprised when Damon's truck pulled up beside me a few minutes later.

"What do you think you're doing?"

Luckily his tone was casual and not combative. Lucky

for him, anyway. "I think I'm walking. I think I'm breathing. I think I'm using my lips and tongue to form words to answer a really dumbass question."

I have to admit his laugh went a long way toward filing the sharpest edge off my anger.

"You've had a long day and night. You sure you want to walk all the way home? I can take you to my hotel. You can shower and I'll taxi you back to your place."

The fact that he didn't try to bully me into anything made me waver. That and the shower. That sounded like heaven. Nevertheless, I wasn't going to be bribed.

"No point in showering. I don't have clean clothes to change into and it's disgusting to put dirty underwear back on after getting clean."

"I'll find clothes."

I snorted. "Where? And don't say Walmart. I'd rather wait until the shops open."

"Trust me." He grinned, eyes gleaming, fully aware I had a problem trusting him and daring me to do it anyway.

I resisted the urge to stick my tongue out at him. Barely.

"Think of Ajax," he coaxed. "He's got to be hungry. And thirsty."

Guilt assailed me. When had I fed him last? I thought it might have been yesterday morning, almost twenty hours ago. I looked down at him, stricken by my carelessness. He depended on me. He had nobody else.

"Don't go there," Damon said quickly. "You haven't neglected him. He's fine. He adores you. Plus, I brought him a snack." He held up a to-go box from the diner. "You can give it to him now or climb in and feed him on the way."

I was too tired to argue, and Ajax deserved a place to sleep tonight. What was left of it. We climbed in. I snarled at Damon's smug grin, taking the box from him and opening it. Inside were mostly cold scrambled eggs and several sausage patties from the diner. Ajax whined and perked his ears, pawing my leg. I held the box so he could reach it, and he bolted the food as if starving. Even though the reasonable side of me knew that he always ate his food that way, the sappy, guilty side of me recoiled at his obvious hunger and my failure to properly care for him.

Damon pulled up to the valet stand in front of a very fancy, very expensive, and very exclusive boutique hotel. He got out and came around to my side. I'd opened the door, and he offered his hand to help me balance. I took it but when I went to let go, his fingers tightened on mine, holding me fast. His eyes dared me to make a scene. I was tempted but I was also tired, so I didn't fight.

"C'mon, Ajax," I called.

Damon gave his keys to the valet and started inside. I thought someone would get in our faces about Ajax, but nobody paid us any attention as we crossed the lobby to the elevator and took it up to the ninth floor. Damon guided me to his suite, waving his key in front of the lock to open it.

Inside, it was just as grand as the lobby. We walked into a sitting room with plush leather furniture and steel, marble-topped tables. It looked very modern yet comfortable and warm. There was a small kitchenette off to the side and a half bath. On the other side was the bedroom.

Damon took me inside. A king-sized bed dominated the room. Ajax jumped up on it and lay down like he owned the place. Good dog.

"Shower's in there," Damon said, pointing. "There's a robe for you to put on when you're done. Take your time."

I glanced at the clock on the nightstand. Six o'clock. "I have to be back at the shop in two hours to meet the detectives." I bit my lower lip as a tide of anger and loss and hurt crested over me. I was tired and my defenses were down.

I hadn't felt this low in a long time. This helpless, this wounded. I'd learned to armor myself against my mother's —Aunty Mommy's—attacks. I knew where she'd strike, and I was always prepared.

Having Lorraine, Stacey, and Jen in my corner helped, even when I had to protect them. But the attack on my home and business? I'd been blindsided. I'd been floating on a high of success and freedom, and I didn't even know that this kind of vicious and malicious attack was even a possibility. It struck me hard and deep, and I felt like I was bleeding and didn't know how to make it stop.

I wanted to blame Damon or Mason, but they hadn't ripped apart everything I owned. Someone else had and I dearly wanted to make whoever it was pay.

"I'll get you there; don't worry."

"Okay."

I waited for him to leave. He looked undecided then went to the dresser and drew out a gray short-sleeved shirt and handed it to me. It was soft, almost like silk.

"You can put that on for now if you want more than a robe." His voice had developed a gruff edge.

"You may not get it back." I rubbed it against my cheek. "I might never take it off."

"I can live with that."

The harshness in his voice made me look up. He was staring at my lips. If he hadn't been, I wouldn't have noticed they were dry and licked them, but he was and I did. His gaze rose to mine. His eyes burned.

"I should go."

I nodded. "I should shower."

Neither one of us moved. Then slowly and ever so

gently, he bent and touched his lips to mine. The brush of his tongue was feather light. Gradually he pressed closer. The only place we touched was our mouths, and between us the air heated, wrapping me in aching flames. I tipped my head to give him better access, and his tongue swept against mine, worshipping and then teasing, then demanding.

Little pops of desire burst all over my skin, and I wanted to rub against his hard warmth and let him stroke me and soothe the ache his kiss caused. I refused to think about why he was kissing me. At the moment I didn't care. I just wanted that connection, that sense of being wanted. I wanted not to feel so alone.

He pulled back. I bit back a sound of complaint, glad to see I wasn't the only one breathing hard.

"If I don't go now, you aren't showering alone."

It wasn't a question, but it felt like one. Part of me wanted to tell him to stay, wanted him to fulfill the delicious promises his mouth and eyes made. But I wasn't a casual sort of girl, and what I knew about him would fit in a tuna can. Plus, I still didn't trust him. Plus, he worked for Mason, and that was bound to put us at odds.

I gave a faint shake of my head. Damon heaved a sigh and nodded.

"I'll see you soon."

Regret filled me as I watched him go. I didn't call him back.

# CHAPTER TWENTY-FOUR

The shower loosened my muscles and woke me up. If I cried a little for the loss of everything I'd worked for in my life, nobody would ever know.

I borrowed a comb and a hair dryer after wrapping myself in the fluffy robe. When I came out of the bathroom, Ajax sat up on the bed and chuffed at me. I petted him, scratching his chest and then his belly when he flopped over and twisted onto his back and waved his legs in the air.

"Turns out you're a creampuff," I said. "I hope the people that who hurt you burn in hell."

I put Damon's shirt on. It came down to just above the middle of my thighs. It felt like kitten fur against my skin, and I decided right then and there I wasn't ever giving it back.

It was only six-thirty, and since I had nothing better to do, I climbed on the bed with Ajax. I snuggled up with him and fell asleep.

Damon woke me with a light hand on my shoulder. "Wake up, Beck," he said softly. "We need to get going."

I blinked, my eyes gritty. "Do I smell coffee?"

"With five shots of espresso," he confirmed.

"I think I love you," I said, sitting up.

He chuckled. "That was easy. I brought some clothes for you. I think they should fit."

I sat up and swung my legs over the side of the bed. "Where did you get them at this hour?"

"I'm going to plead the fifth on that one."

I eyed him narrowly. "What does that mean?"

"It means I may have broken and entered, but I did leave a note and cash to cover the clothes and my unconventional means of shopping."

"Wow. You made that sound almost like you didn't just commit a felony."

"It was for a good cause, though I could stand you walking around in my shirts all day. You look a hell of a lot better in that one than I do."

A shiver of heat ran through me, and my stomach turned to syrup. I was acutely reminded I was not wearing any underwear. I didn't know what he was up to with the flirting and the kissing, but there was no doubt it made me feel good. Special. Wanted. I'd never felt those things before, and I hugged the feelings to me, refusing to think about the fact that he had to be manipulating me.

I got up to examine the clothes he'd found. He'd covered all the bases. Jeans, dresses, skirts, underwear, bras, and a variety of tops, plus shorts. I looked at him. "All this? From one store? How did you know my sizes, anyway?"

"I may have visited a couple places, and I stopped at the loft to look at labels." He pointed to a paper sack. "There's also a toothbrush, hairbrush, and some other toiletries you might need."

I shook my head as I looked over the bounty. "This is amazing. Thank you. I mean, wow."

"My pleasure," and he actually sounded sincere. "Get dressed. No coffee until you do."

"Tyrant!" I called as he shut the door behind himself.

He laughed, totally uncowed.

He'd chosen lacy underwear with matching bras. Though I hated bra shopping with a holy passion, he'd managed to find several that fit pretty well. I pulled on a pair of bootcut jeans and a tank top, and then because I couldn't resist, I put Damon's shirt on over it. I told myself it was because of how soft it was and had nothing to do with the fact that it was his.

Damon had Ajax's breakfast ready. The dog pounced on it as soon as I opened the bedroom door. Damon pushed a box of danishes toward me as I came into the little kitchen. "I know you only ate a couple hours ago, but you might want to top off."

I picked out a cheese danish, nibbling at it as I sucked down my coffee. He watched me, amusement dancing in his eyes. I set aside the cup. He went to the refrigerator and pulled out a bottle of orange juice and poured me a glass, setting it in front of me.

"I'd have bought you two of those, but I didn't want you bouncing off the walls."

I scoffed. "I'll have you know that I am perfectly able to handle far more high-octane coffee than that little baby cup."

"It was an extra large."

"It was barely a sip."

"You have no blood in your veins, do you? It's strictly coffee, isn't it?"

I grinned. "Yep. We should stop for more on the way, don't you think?"

"Better get going, then, or we'll be late." He frowned. "Didn't the shirts fit?"

"I like this one. It's soft."

He gave a lazy smile that was entirely too sexy for my comfort. "My closet is always open."

I flushed. "Everything else fits okay. Next time I need clothes, I'm sending you out to get them."

"I thought you women loved shopping for clothing."

"*We* women might. *This* woman realizes they are necessary and enjoys wearing them but isn't a big fan of the hunt to find them."

"I knew there was a reason I liked you," he said.

I wished I thought he meant it.

# CHAPTER TWENTY-FIVE

Ballard and Jeffers beat us to the shop. They got out of their sedan when Damon pulled up. About thirty seconds later, a gray BMW pulled in. Mason parked and unfolded himself from the driver's seat and approached me, coming to a stop a couple of feet away. Ajax's hackles rose and I didn't know if it was because he didn't like Mason or because I didn't.

Mason ignored the dog. "I want to apologize."

"Go ahead."

His mouth quirked in appreciation. "I'm sorry for my earlier behavior. I am not entitled to give you decrees."

"And yet why do I get the feeling you'll keep doing it?"

His smile widened. "Because I like you and I want to know you better. I can't do that if you're dead."

"Dead?" Jeffers interjected, stepping forward.

Mason turned to face the two detectives. "Yes. Did you not tell my niece that the destruction here could have been caused by the same person who murdered my sister?"

Jeffers shot me a suspicious look. "You said you didn't have any other family."

"I didn't, until what, four-thirty this morning?"

I glanced at Damon, who nodded.

"Yes, I'm afraid I surprised Rebecca," Mason said smoothly. "My sister had left the family and cut all ties. My niece tells me that you wished to know who will inherit my sister's estate. It seems she left everything to me."

"You've got proof of that?" Jeffers asked.

"I do."

"We'll need to see it."

Mason's brows rose. "I don't think so. My sister's correspondence with me is private."

"I can get a subpoena."

"Can you? Well, then. I'll wait with bated breath for you to serve it."

Clearly Mason didn't mind mocking Jeffers, whose face turned red as a hot pepper. Next to Mason's elegance, he looked rumpled, which didn't help his Goodwill appearance. I couldn't judge. He'd been up all night working on my case. I even felt slightly bad for him. Not so much that I didn't enjoy his embarrassment. He'd been offensive as all hell when questioning me, after all.

"Are you ready to go?" he asked curtly, then without waiting for an answer, "get in the back seat."

"She's riding with me," Mason said.

Before I could tell both of them to fuck off, Damon held out his keys. "Want to borrow my truck?"

"Hell, yes," I said, snatching them. "I could kiss you for this."

He brows rose in challenge. "I wouldn't refuse."

Why the fuck not? I stepped up close and threaded my fingers through his hair and pulled his mouth down to mine. I didn't go for the peck either. Kissing Damon was right up there with chocolate and bacon. Maybe even higher on the makes-Beck-happy scale, but I wasn't going to think about it too hard. At the moment I could live without Damon. I couldn't live without chocolate and bacon. And garlic. If he were any higher on the ladder, I might start believing I couldn't live without him, and that would be disaster.

I barely noticed him wrapping his arms around me and snugging me tight against him. I got lost in him. I started the kiss, but he took over, taking his time and worshipping me with his lips, tongue, and teeth. I ignored the loudly cleared throats of our audience. Damon didn't seem all that interested in their irritation either. His hands roamed over my back, and I wanted to purr.

A tap on my shoulder. "Miss Wyatt." Detective Ballard's amused voice broke through my haze of delight.

I pulled away, gaze locked with Damon's. To my utter satisfaction, he looked a little shaken. As in, the earth moved. Maybe he wasn't indifferent to me after all. The sane voice in my head suggested that if I didn't want to encourage him, I shouldn't kiss him anymore. The rest of me told my stick-in-the-mud sane self to shove it.

"Right," I said, a little bit breathless. My heart was thudding as if I'd run up a steep hill. God but Damon knew how to kiss. "Gotta go take a tour of the Wicked Witch's lair."

I stepped out of Damon's embrace and went to let Ajax into the back seat of the crew cab. I climbed up behind the wheel and started the truck. Damon hadn't moved. I frowned and rolled down the window.

"Are you coming?"

"If I'm invited," he said.

I grinned. "Talk like that turns me on. Are you trying to get me to kiss you again?"

"I can only hope."

He went around and climbed into the front seat. Ajax stood with his front feet on the console, and before Damon could buckle in, the dog hopped into the front seat, turning around on Damon's lap and flopping down with his forelegs and head dripping into my lap and the rest of him sprawled over the console and onto Damon.

"You seem to be getting a whole lot more comfortable around people," I said to him, scratching his stomach. He twisted to give me better access. "You also appear to be a bit of an attention whore."

His doggie smile was entirely unrepentant.

"I don't think he's a big fan of the detectives and Mason," Damon said.

"Neither do I. What does Mason want from me? Wait, no, don't answer. You'll either say you don't know or you'll give me the party line, and right now I like you so let's keep it that way for at least a few minutes."

He waited until I'd pulled onto the road before he spoke. "Mason will protect his family with every last drop of blood in his body." He paused. "This doesn't necessarily make him trustworthy."

I glanced at him. "I wasn't planning on trusting him."

He nodded as if to say that was a good idea.

"What do you know about my mother and when I was born?"

"Most of it, as far as I know. Mason wanted me to have the background before I met you."

I lifted my brows. "Met? That's rewriting history a bit, don't you think?"

"It's accurate."

"Right, like Lee Harvey Oswald just *meeting* JFK." I made air quotes around "meeting."

"Bad comparison. They never met."

I rolled my eyes. "You get my point. Did Mason— Never mind. More of the cone of confidentiality."

"He did not tell me to kidnap you, though he impressed on me that he thought you could be in danger. I took it upon myself to take you by force. I thought the sooner you were warned, the better."

"So you tried to kidnap me to help me? That's ... kind of ridiculous."

"I thought the ends justified the means and—"

"And?"

"Once I saw you, I didn't want to see harm come to you."

"Good thing I didn't have warts all over my face, then."

He chuckled. "Good thing."

"What about moving in with me?"

"He wanted you watched, and I wanted to know you. Moving in was the perfect solution."

"Why didn't you take me to him when I got so sick with that curse?"

"You'd told me you didn't want to see him."

I considered that bit of information. He'd attempted to kidnap me in order to protect me, and then when I was on the verge of dying, he'd not called on Mason, who might have resources to help me. That made about as much sense as scuba diving on horseback. I said so.

He sighed. "It was my next stop if the pool didn't work. I regretted my decision every second after you vanished into the river."

"That still doesn't explain why you didn't call Mason. Unless—"

I looked at him again. "Did you think he was the one who'd cursed me?"

"No. The possibility occurred to me, but it's highly unlikely."

"I can tell you're a lawyer. You answer everything but the question. Why didn't you call him?"

"You didn't want me to, and I didn't want to betray your trust any more than I already was by keeping secrets."

"You'd only known me for what, a couple days or so. I'm supposed to believe I charmed you into defying your employer? That's ridiculous. Nothing about me is charming, and I can't imagine a couple kisses got you that hot and bothered."

"For the record, they did. Also for the record, I'd made up my mind in the first five minutes I knew you."

"Before or after I knocked you on your ass?"

He smiled. "I'll never tell."

"So where do we stand now?"

He hesitated. "I still work for Mason."

"Gotcha. Thanks for the heads-up." I was more disappointed than I should have been, but at least he'd told the truth.

"Look, Rebecca—"

"How many times do I have to tell you my name is Beck? I loathe Rebecca with every fiber of my being."

"Why?"

"None of your business." I tightened my grip on the steering wheel, my knuckles turning white. I could hear my mother—my aunt—screaming that name, drawing it out, mocking. I got to where I refused to answer to it at all, which pissed her off even more. And all because she didn't like the way I was conceived.

Well, you don't blame the children of rape; they're victims too. I was just as much a victim of my father's shenanigans as my mother, and really, all he did was give her a litter instead of twins. I was simply a business deal gone bad. Aunty Mommy had nothing to do with any of it. What right did she have to be so pissed at me?

"I will get it right from now on," Damon promised.

I could feel his gaze on me, heavy and probing. Like he was trying to get a peek inside of me.

"What?" I asked finally. "Just ask already."

"I don't even know where to start."

"How about answer one for me, then?"

"Shoot."

"How did you—a contracts lawyer—end up being the one to contact me?"

"I've proven trustworthy to Mason, and I've wanted an opportunity to move deeper into his inner circle. Hell, into his inner circle at all."

"So kidnapping me was to impress him with how well you did your job?"

"Stupid, I know."

"Yeah, but I get the ambition thing. I mean, short of kidnapping."

"Mason had emphasized that you were in danger."

"Doesn't make it right."

"No, but I'd kidnap you in a heartbeat if I thought it would save your life."

"So nothing's changed."

"Everything's changed," he said flatly. Then before I could follow up on that particular little bomb, he switched subjects. "How much training have you had in using your magic?"

"Nothing."

"None at all?" he asked in disbelief.

"Trial and error. Oh, and what I could figure out from watching Aunty Mommy."

Damon rubbed his hands over his face. "That woman was criminally negligent."

"It wasn't negligence. It was entirely deliberate. She hated me and she did everything she could to show me just how much. Anyhow, I never let on that I could do magic. It would have made things worse."

"Didn't you try to leave?"

I wanted to tell him where he could stick that question. I settled for a terse, "No."

"Why not?"

I gave him a saccharine smile, my blood starting to boil. I didn't need him or anybody else judging me. What the hell did he know? Aunty Mommy had threatened Jen, Lorraine, and Stacey if I stepped out of line. Given she hadn't been shy about fucking with them while I *was* toeing her line, I never had an urge to test her.

"Maybe I'm just sadomasochistic."

I ignored him after that as every mile brought us closer to Aunty Mommy's hellhole. Several times Damon tried to speak to me, but I couldn't even think about him anymore. I'd half promised myself that I would never go back to this place. Every molecule of my being wanted to run in the other direction, which, because I never liked letting my mother—make that Aunty Mommy—win, it also made me want to walk in there and strut around. I'd lived through her curse and now I was in her house. Maybe I'd even pee on the carpet.

I pulled up at the elaborate gate. Joseph came out of the guardhouse. The brown skin of his bald head gleamed in the morning light. His gray uniform was crisp and ironed, the creases down the front of his legs sharp as a knife blade, just the way Aunty Mommy liked it.

I rolled down my window.

"Good morning, Miss Wyatt."

"Hi, Joseph. I need to go inside. Behind me are the detectives investigating my mother's death. The guy in the Beemer is the new owner of the place."

That last news made him blink but didn't crack his impassive facade. "Yes, Miss Wyatt. I'll let the house know you're on your way." Which meant there would be refreshments ready.

The estate encompassed more than three hundred acres. The house sat up on a hill with two broad wings on either side of the grand entry. It looked like a castle with four turrets on the ends and gargoyles along the roofline, hanging off the corners, and spewing water into and out of downspouts. The fortress contained twelve bedrooms and seventeen bathrooms and was surrounded by manicured formal gardens and lush emerald lawns.

I went right around the central fountain and pulled up in front. Ajax followed on my heels. He shook himself and sniffed around, lifting his leg on one of the fluted pillars holding up the stately entrance portico.

"Good boy," I murmured as he trotted over to another likely spot and repeated his territorial marking.

"Nice place," Damon said, joining me.

"If you say so." My stomach was knotting almost the way it had when she was alive, and I knew I was walking into hell. Maybe this little tour would teach my subconscious that the Wicked Bitch really was dead and I was safe now.

A few minutes later, the detectives and Mason joined us.

I led the way up the sweep of steps to the front door. It was opened before I could knock.

"Thanks, Linus," I said to the man who answered. He wore pinstriped slacks, a charcoal jacket, and a snow-white dress shirt.

"Miss Wyatt. It's good to see you."

I raised my brows but didn't challenge him. The entire staff knew Aunty Mommy and I had hated each other. They'd always been as kind as they were allowed to me, but they'd also been loyal to her. Not that I blamed them. Who knew what she'd have done if they weren't? Plus, she paid them well, and it was never a good idea to bite the hand that fed you. To say it was good to see me was a little over the top, though. Or maybe Linus had heard about the shop or my time in the river and was glad to see me upright and breathing.

The entry was beyond grand. It rose up three stories to a vaulted ceiling. A crystal-encrusted chandelier sparkled about midway down. An alabaster stairway swirled elegantly up to the second floor. Priceless modern art covered the walls in complete contrast to the medieval look of the outside. Light poured in from the domed frosted glass far above.

"I have to get back to talk to my employees and call my insurance company," I said to the detectives. "Let's get this over with quick."

"Let's start out back," Ballard said and clearly she'd already been in the house because she needed no guide to find her way.

Mostly the house seemed deserted, though I knew the house staff numbered at least six, and the grounds crew was probably double that. Dierdre, the housekeeper, overtook us as we entered the long garden room. It had always been my favorite place in the house. The rear wall was nothing but glass, giving a lovely view of the back patio and gardens.

"Miss Wyatt, I have had the chef prepare refreshments for you. Would you like them served here or in the breakfast room?"

Dierdre was a small, birdlike woman with dark skin, walnut eyes, and sleek black hair. I wasn't sure how old she was. She didn't look any different now than when I was a child. Everything about her was enigmatic. I never knew what she was thinking or feeling. She'd never been particularly unkind to me, making her relatively safe in my world.

"Thank you, Dierdre. Put it in here, why don't you? The detectives have some questions for me, but I'm sure that after, they would appreciate your hospitality." I gestured at Mason. "This, by the way, is—" She wouldn't get it if I called the woman formerly known as my mother Aunty Mommy. I settled for, "My uncle. He's the new owner of the place."

She cast him an inscrutable look. "Good morning, sir."

"Good morning," he replied.

"If you'll excuse me, I'll bring out the refreshments," she said before vanishing through the door leading into the kitchen area.

Ballard opened a set of French doors and stepped out onto the broad patio. The edges were scalloped like seashells, with steps all the way around. We went along the left wing of the house. The patio narrowed before widening to spread out in a large apron around one of the turrets. Crime scene tape wrapped a temporary chain-link fence around most of it. Inside was a cracked fountain and a scaffolding that now lay tipped on its side.

One of the gargoyles lay nearby. Like all of those standing guard in niches on top of the exterior walls, this one had—or used to have anyway—a large, protruding penis and cantaloupe-sized balls. The rest of the stone creature was vaguely bat-shaped with bear claws on its feet and arms and a leopard head, but with longer ears. A tail wrapped its feet, and its wings folded tight against its back.

All that was left of its three-foot penis was a little stub. That was the worst of the damage, but the creature's nose and one ear had also been chipped off. Three of the curved claws on its left paw had snapped away as well.

"So it's true," I said, unable to help the smile that spread across my face. "Aunty Mommy was stabbed by a gargoyle penis." I looked at the detectives. "Tell me I can have copies of the pictures. Please. I'll pay you whatever you want."

Jeffers scowled at me. Ballard jumped in before he could spew whatever was bubbling up in his craw.

"Miss Wyatt—I'm sorry, did you say Aunty Mommy? What does that mean?"

She was sharp, I'd give her that.

"According to my uncle here," I gestured at Mason, "the bitch was my aunt, not my mother. She stole me from her sister right after I was born."

Ballard scribbled notes after a startled glance at me and Mason.

"She kidnapped you?" Jeffers asked, letting go of his annoyance with me and sliding into detective mode.

"Yes," Mason replied. "Until I received a letter following her death, no one in the family knew of her whereabouts. She vanished without leaving any trace we could follow, and we made every attempt."

"Are you sure? Is it possible Miss Wyatt's biological mother or father learned of Anne Wyatt's location and came to confront her?"

"Her real name is Adriane." He didn't correct the last name. "I haven't informed anyone else of Adriane's and Rebecca's whereabouts. You can bet that if her parents knew where to find Rebecca, nothing could stop them from being here."

I don't know why, but that startled me. Okay, I did know why. As far as my so-called father goes, he was little more than a sperm donor and an egg thief. Sure, he'd plotted to get an extra kid out of the birthing contract, but that was twenty-six years ago, and I couldn't believe he'd be all that eager to find me now. As for my actual mother, she'd never intended to keep the other two kids from the litter, so she wasn't all that likely to be excited that I'd invaded her uterus.

Damon had been looking through the fence and now turned to the detectives. "It appears that the scaffolding collapsed and dropped the gargoyle on her. What makes you think it was intentional?"

Good question. Gold star for him. I looked at the detectives expectantly.

Jeffers motioned us to follow him.

He unlocked the gate and ushered us through. "Try not to touch anything. The techs have been over everything, but it's still an active crime scene."

He took us over to the scaffolding and showed us where the supports fixing the gargoyle in place had torn free. "Our techs tell us that the statue's weight wouldn't have caused damage in this fashion. The screws simultaneously released, which isn't possible unless they were tampered with."

"That doesn't mean Adriane was the target," Mason said. "Or even that anybody was. It could be someone was playing a malicious trick that ended up accidentally killing my sister."

"Even so, it's still manslaughter," Jeffers said. "But that's not all. We found a camera up along the wall that allowed the perpetrator to watch for his intended victim. If you look on the bottom of the scaffolding, you'll see where the side struts melted away completely, causing the scaffolding to topple and the gargoyle to fall. We've not found any evidence for how it was done yet, but once the tests come back, we're sure to find there was an exterior force at play. It was all well planned and choreographed."

I could see Damon and Mason arriving at the same conclusion with all the speed of a runaway freight train. Magic had played a hand in it. Melted struts here and melted locks at my place. I wasn't ready to say that magic was involved or that the same people had done it. Anyway, why go to such elaborate lenghts? Why not just pick up the gargoyle and drop it on her? Why leave any evidence of foul play?

"What could do that?" I asked. "Melt the steel, I mean."

"We're looking into it," Jeffers said vaguely.

Meaning, none of your business, if we wanted you to know, we'd tell you. Or else he didn't want to let on that they didn't have a clue. I was leaning toward the latter.

"Doesn't this strike you as a ridiculous way to murder someone?" I asked. "I mean, a gun, knife, or poison would be a lot more efficient. Hell, running her over with a car or shoving her down the stairs. This seems really involved and kind of stupid. So many things could have gone wrong."

"Which is why we think it must be personal," Ballard said. "Someone went to a lot of trouble to kill your ... aunt ... in this most unusual fashion. It has to mean something. Did the gargoyles have any particular significance to Adriane?"

"Where we grew up, they were believed to be house-hold guardians," Mason said before I could answer. "It's quite traditional and they continue to be used in modern building even today. They are common decorations on most family buildings. An homage to the past."

"Where was this?" Ballard asked, scribbling in her notebook.

"Europe, mostly," Mason said. "Italy, France, Germany, Ireland—we had homes in various places."

That earned him a sharp look from the detectives. Money was always a good motive, and clearly the family was swimming in it. Plus, Mason had just inherited another big pile. I didn't know if I was ready to believe he was capable of murder, but I didn't know that he wasn't either.

"How extensive is her estate?" Jeffers asked.

"Millions," Mason said as though he were talking about the change you found in the couch cushions. "It's difficult to know. I wasn't in charge of managing her funds in her absence, and of course, she's clearly accumulated a small sum in her new life."

*Small?* I winced. I considered myself comfortable. I made a good living, I bought the clothes I liked, drove the car I liked, ate out, and entertained myself without worrying a lot about the costs, and I put money away for retirement and more for a rainy day. Aunty Mommy was stinking rich, and that didn't include whatever she had left stashed in her former life. That Mason was entirely unim-pressed by such an enormous addition to his finances spoke volumes for how much he was worth and how different his entire existence was from mine.

"'Small?'" Jeffers repeated with raised brows and then shook his head. "'Small,' he says, and I'm scraping to pay the mortgage on my salary. Where can I get a small sum like this so I never have to work again?"

"Lottery," Ballard suggested.

"That's throwing money away."

"Can't win if you don't play."

"Guess I'll have to stick with good, old-fashioned nine-to-five."

"More like twenty-four/seven."

Their easy back-and-forth told me they were comfortable with each other—friends as well as partners. It made me like Jeffers a tiny bit. He wasn't all gruff annoyance and rudeness.

"Are you aware of anyone who might mean you sister harm?" Ballard asked Mason.

"No."

I wondered if the fact he was lying was as obvious to everyone else as it was to me. My unknown father definitely had an ax to grind with Aunty Mommy, and so did my biological mother, for her snatching me away. *If* that bothered my biomom, which I had doubts about. The whole business of contracting children was so foreign to me that I couldn't imagine she wanted me or my siblings. Holy crap. I had brothers or sisters or one of each.

"How do I find my brothers? Or are they sisters?" I demanded, spinning to confront Mason.

"One of each," he said. "I'll be happy to tell you about them." He glanced at the two detectives. "Later might be more appropriate."

He was right but it still irritated me. Twenty-six years old. Twenty-six years and I had a brother and a sister I'd never met. We were triplets. I wanted to know about them *now*.

"Do they know about me?"

Mason scratched his forehead. "I couldn't say."

I frowned. "How well do you know them?"

"We have met from time to time."

"So not real close."

He hesitated, considering his words. "Their father didn't want them spending much time with our side of the family."

"Divorce?" Ballard asked.

Mason nodded in a total lie. I guess he thought telling the cops about the whole contracted-babies thing might sound a little repulsive. Or just plain horrifying, not to mention unbelievable.

"How long since they divorced?"

"Just after the birth of the children."

The detectives nodded and I realized they assumed that my kidnapping had something to do with their parting ways. I wanted to laugh.

I checked my watch. "I've got about a half hour left before I have to go."

"The estate has tight security, so it's likely whoever did this either had access on his own or was working with someone on the inside. We've seen nothing on the surveillance videos from that night. Is there anybody on the staff who might have been nursing a grudge against Adriane?" Ballard asked.

"I'm not all that familiar with most of them."

Jeffers gave me a doubting look. "You lived here a long time."

"We moved here when I was around five. I moved out after I finished my business program. I was twenty-one. I never bonded with any of the staff. Aunty Mommy would have fired them if I did." I'd already given her enough weapons against me in Jen, Lorraine, and Stacey. I wasn't about to give her any more.

I did know all their names and a lot about their lives. I used to sneak around the house and listen, trying to get information on Aunty Mommy so that I'd know her plans and could prepare.

"Do you know where your aunt kept her records?"

"Her office, I guess."

Jeffers shook his head. "We've gone over it. There isn't much there."

I thought about the key in Mason's possession. Undoubtedly it led to a treasure trove of that kind of thing.

"She didn't confide in me. Like I've been telling you, she hated me. She didn't trust anybody. She might have kept things in a vault in a bank for all I know."

She wouldn't have. That would have meant letting go of control, and there's no way Aunty Mommy would ever have done that. The truth was, there probably was a vault somewhere in the house, and it was probably disguised and protected with magic. The cops didn't have a snowball's chance in hell of finding it without magical help.

Ballard tapped her pencil against her notebook, eyeing me thoughtfully. I couldn't tell what was going through her mind. She had one of those inscrutable faces that some black women have. As if she were sculpted from stone rather than made of flesh and bone. She looked better than the first day she'd interviewed me. Rested and her skin was no longer ashy. The circles under her eyes were gone too. She was actually kind of lovely.

"Why don't we go inside?" she said.

Jeffers locked up the crime scene cage, and we started back along the patio. Ajax barked right before I felt an invisible *thrust* in the air. Bits of gravel and dust pattered on top of us and against the patio surface. Stone grated. I looked up to see the gargoyles above tipping off their foundations.

"Run!" I shouted as I shoved Ballard.

Damon looped his arm around my waist and jerked me along, thrusting me ahead of him down the stairs onto the lawn just as the morning stillness shattered apart. Falling gargoyles smashed against the patio. Bits of masonry spun through the air. Amazingly, none hit us. Or maybe not so amazingly. I could feel magic in the air. I had a feeling it came from Mason or Damon.

"What the hell happened?" Jeffers twisted around to look at the destruction. He looked shaken. Windows had shattered all along the promenade. The dozen or so gargoyles on this side of the patio had smashed into pieces. Bits of gargoyle penis had flown everywhere. That almost made me laugh. It wasn't funny. This wasn't natural. I'd felt a sweep of magic just before they fell. Someone had tried to kill us.

Damon had pulled me close against him, his body held in front of mine like a shield. He exchanged a look with Mason. It wasn't any too friendly and all too knowing for my comfort. They knew who was behind this. Or at least, they suspected. That pissed me off. I was tired of their acting as if I needed to be taken care of. Tired of keeping secrets about me.

I elbowed out of Damon's grasp and took several steps away. I crouched and put my arms around Ajax. He stood stiffly, hackles raised. A growl rumbled below hearing. I felt it against my chest. "Well. That was terrifying," I said.

"That was damned sure not natural," Jeffers said.

"On it," Ballard said and started tapping numbers into her phone. A minute later, she'd summoned a CSU team and backup.

"I think it's time for me to leave," I said. "There's no reason for me to be here anymore, is there?"

Ballard shook her head before Jeffers could protest about my being a witness. "Not now. We'll want to get a statement later."

I smiled my gratitude. "You know where to find me. I'm getting pretty good at them by now." I looked again at the destruction, which looked almost like a bomb had gone off. The doors we'd come out of were shattered, and glass shards hung in the opening. "I think I'll just walk around the outside of the house. It'll be safer."

They all fell in behind me as I followed the path out through the gardens and a small orchard and turned right without even thinking. My mistake. The path passed through a tunnel of vines and sweet-scented orange bugle flowers and came out on a small, grassy lawn with a single bench. It faced one of my torture chambers: the rock wall Jeffers had asked me about after Aunty Mommy had died. I was shaking from the near miss of gargoyle bombs and wasn't thinking clearly, or I'd have gone around the opposite way. But my feet followed the familiar path like sparrows returning to Capistrano.

My footsteps hitched and I sucked in a sharp breath before striding past in quick, sharp steps.

"Miss Wyatt," Jeffers called as I knew he would. Stupid cop curiosity. "I've been wondering—this is rather an odd setup. Could you explain how it was used?"

I felt all their eyes on me. I turned to face my nemesis. It was a climbing wall. Standing three stories tall, the gray hulk was contained inside a metal-mesh cage. All around it, on pillars and along the top of the wall itself, were water cannons. Their pressure could be adjusted from a fairly-light spray to close to firehose strength, and the release could be adjusted so that it ranged from intermittent bursts to unrelenting spray.

"That's where I learned to rock climb," I said, my fingers curling into Ajax's ruff. It was almost fully grown in now, thanks to the water of the sanctuary pool. I never knew how Aunty Mommy had come up with this deranged torture method. It was creative, I had to give her that.

"I used to climb," Jeffers said, puzzled. "I've never seen a training wall like this one. What's up with the cage? And are those water nozzles?"

Something inside me broke open. Maybe it was wanting to tell Mason what I'd suffered at the hands of his sister. Maybe it was just the relief of telling someone how I'd suffered and how I'd survived. Maybe it was the dawning look of something too much like pity in Damon's eyes.

"It's actually pretty straightforward," I said, keeping my voice even and matter-of-fact. "You only come out if you win." My lips stretched into what they meant to be a smile and was anything but. "See, I would have to go inside and the gate would be locked. Then I'd have to get to the top. There's a little hollow up there. The difficulty came with the cannons."

I stepped over to the front of the bench and flipped the marble top off the wrought-iron table in front of it. Inside was a control panel with buttons and dials. I flipped everything to the *on* position then dialed the cannons up to about half power. I flipped their patterns to automatic. Jets of water zigzagged, circled, and wiggled, blasting the climbing surface, all the way around.

"You tend to fall a lot," I said. "Even after you get pretty good at it. The grips get slippery, and if the water hits you in the face, it's rough. Luckily the ground below gets soft pretty quick, so usually you don't break anything. Once you get to the top, the hollow protects you from the jets. Then it's just a matter of waiting until the water shuts off. After that—climb down. I don't recommend shoes, though. They get super slippery."

Everybody had looked over at the wall as I talked, and now their heads swiveled back to stare at me. Jeffers's jaw hung open, and Ballard looked a little sick.

"Why?" she asked.

"I told you. Aunty Mommy didn't like me much. It's all good, though. I learned a skill. And that's not the only one. She taught me about swimming and running too."

"How?" Damon ground out.

I didn't look at him. I didn't want to see the pity or the anger or whatever would be there. I didn't know what I wanted from him.

"Pretty much the same sort of deal. She gave me incentives not to give up, and I tried not to get mutilated. Fun times."

I turned off the water and flipped the tabletop closed and walked away. Despite the fact that my stomach was knotted and I wanted to throw up, I felt lighter. I didn't have to keep the secrets anymore. I had no reason to be embarrassed. It was all on the bitch who'd raised me. She hadn't wanted outsiders to know what she was up to. That was part of the bargain we'd come to. I'd willingly suffer her tortures and keep them secret, and she'd leave Lorraine, Stacey, and Jen alone. Plus, I got to live in my own place and run my own business.

By the time we got around front, I wanted a stiff drink. Already today, my business and home had been destroyed, I'd found out my mother wasn't my mother and that I had a family, one or more of which might have destroyed my home. I'd been bombed by gargoyles with giant penises, and I'd ripped open one of my most painful secrets for strangers to enjoy. What I really needed was a gallon bottle of tequila and a quiet place to drink myself into forgetfulness.

Maybe later.

I yanked open Damon's truck door, ignoring everybody else and their pitying silence. Maybe I shouldn't have told them. They couldn't handle the truth. I chuckled, imagining myself as Jack Nicholson yelling at Tom Cruise: *"You can't handle the truth!"*

"Come on, Ajax. Let's go see what else the day has to throw at us."

He jumped in and curled up on the passenger seat. I climbed up after him. I started to pull the door shut, only to find it blocked by Damon.

I looked at his throat, avoiding eye contact.

"I have to stay here for a little while," he said. "Are you going to be okay?"

"Why wouldn't I be?"

"Come on, Re—" He caught himself. "Beck. You've had a hell of a day. You don't have to pretend it hasn't been a steaming pile of shit."

The corner of my mouth twitched, and I couldn't help meeting his gaze. They burned with intensity, but the pity I thought I'd find wasn't there. Instead there was admiration, pride, and possessiveness.

"I've got to go," I said, but I didn't move. His gaze pinned me in place. Sparks spiraled slowly to life in my chest.

"I'll come as soon as I can," he promised.

"Take your time. I'm going to be talking to my insurance company and taking pictures. Thinking I might go for a run. I need to blow off steam."

"Not without me," he said, folding my hand in his. "Please."

"Why?"

"Someone killed your aunt and came after you. Then this business with the gargoyles. You shouldn't go anywhere by yourself right now."

I shook my head. "Whoever is doing this is a coward. A sneak. Nobody's going to jump me out in the open. Anyway, I've got Ajax."

Damon's mouth pinched into a flat line. "Humor me."

"Fine. But I'm not slowing down because you can't keep up. And I'm not cutting my run short either. So you'll have to suck it up."

He was smart enough to believe me. "How far do you run?"

"Depends. But I'd count on at least ten miles if I were you. Probably more like fifteen." Whether or not my body wanted to. My spirit needed it.

With that, I pulled my hand from his and reached for the door. He stepped back. I smirked at the faltering look on his face.

# CHAPTER TWENTY-SIX

I made it back to the store well before Kenny or anybody else arrived for work. Once inside, I took a moment to survey the damage. I told myself to see it and accept it and then start fixing it.

My chest ached and my stomach burned, but after a few minutes, I pulled myself together and hardened my resolve. I couldn't change what had happened, so I'd better deal with it and move on. Life sucked sometimes and I just took the good and overcame the bad in whatever way I could. Aunty Mommy had taught me that much. Well, she and the girls. They gave me the good and Aunty Mommy gave me the bad and somewhere in there I discovered I'd rather fight than not, even if I was just pissing into the wind.

I rigged up a makeshift counter. The cordless phone had been knocked on the floor along with the base, but it hadn't broken.

I started by calling Kenny and telling him what happened. After he recovered from his shock, I asked him to start calling the employees to tell them not to come in today and that we'd have a meeting in the morning.

"Can you set something up at Rosie's? They've got the big back room, and I'll buy breakfast. Make sure everybody knows their jobs are safe too," I said. "And that they aren't getting temporarily laid off." Nobody was going to miss bill payments because of what had happened. "When you get done, come in and we'll start going through the inventory to see if anything can be salvaged."

Next I called my insurance agent. I probably should have called him first. He'd received last night's phone message and promised to get there within the hour. I called Jen, Lorraine, and Stacey to let them know I was okay. I didn't go into the business about Mason and my family. I'd tell them when we had more time and plenty of cheesecake. I promised to call them all later.

Next on the list was finding someone who could replace the shattered windows. I explained what had happened and that this was both a rush job and a large job, and the receptionist transferred me to the shop's owner after a flood of sympathy. He declared he'd be there just after lunch, and I thanked him.

I had a billion other calls to make, but I couldn't make myself make any of those yet. I needed to steady myself before contacting my clients. They weren't going to be happy, though I'd pay them for all the consigned pieces.

I thought about putting up some magical protections, but since I didn't have anything left of value to steal, it seemed like a waste of energy. I was already dead tired, even though my body was wired with unsettled energy. I needed to be doing something physical.

I found some empty boxes up the street at the liquor store and started going through the shop. I picked up everything I could salvage. I'd filled four boxes when John, my insurance agent, arrived. Ajax noticed him first, standing up to growl softly in warning.

John was dressed in slacks and a striped button-up shirt. He stepped inside the door and stopped to take in the destruction.

"Tell me I'm covered," I said as I greeted him.

"You are, except for the deductible. I'm so sorry. Who did this?"

"No idea. Cops are investigating."

He shook his head, disgusted. "What's wrong with people? I'll get on the phone and get the adjuster out as soon as possible. He'll need the police report, so I'll need their contact information. Do you have your inventory list?"

"Luckily it's in the cloud," I said. "They wrecked all the computers. I'll get it printed as soon as I can. They didn't get in the vault."

"Good. I'm just going to snap some pictures to send along when I call the adjuster."

"My loft and all the vehicles have to be evaluated too."

I still hadn't looked at my Thunderbird. I didn't want to. I'd bought that car with my first savings. It didn't have air conditioning and it sucked gas like a hooker, but it was fast and I loved driving in a vintage vehicle. The fact that the interior was red with white stitching was the cherry on top. I couldn't imagine what the vandals had done to it. I didn't want to imagine, and I sure as hell didn't want to know. But tantrums weren't going to help and neither was sticking my head in the sand.

Maybe it could be repaired. Maybe pigs could fly.

John toured the shop, snapping pictures and taking notes. When he disappeared into the warehouse, I decided I should go buy a laptop and a printer. I told John where I was going, and then drove out to the office store, picking up coffee on the way and a couple of hamburgers for Ajax. I found what I needed with the help of a tech and loaded it all into the back seat of Damon's truck. I also got a folding table to set it up on, a chair, and some other necessities.

All the way back, I told myself this break-in was a good excuse to remodel and redecorate. Not to mention declutter. I'd been wanting to put in some faux walls to create different room ambiences. Now I could. So I was lucky this had happened.

Even *I* couldn't make myself believe *that*.

I spent the trip back home planning some changes. I pulled in to find Damon pacing in front. He yanked open my door.

"Where the hell have you been?"

"Shopping," I said.

In the same moment, Ajax snarled and lunged into my lap, snapping at him.

Damon jerked back.

"Didn't I tell you it's not safe for you to go around by yourself? Do you have any idea what would have happened to you if you'd been here last night? You'd have been chopped up like that furniture ... or worse. It was a fucking magic attack, Rebecca. And the gargoyles today? It was no coincidence you were there when they fell."

"But I wasn't hurt, and throwing stone statues is a really stupid way to murder someone, don't you think?"

"Don't pretend you didn't feel the spell that brought them down on top of us."

"I felt it."

"Then you know I'm right."

"What I know is that I have work to do and I'm not going to cower while some asshole tries to destroy my life."

"Rebecca—"

"Beck," I corrected, dropping the truck's keys into his hand. I stroked Ajax to convince him I was all right and then slid off the driver's seat.

Damon didn't budge. I glared at him.

"Are you going to move?"

"I'm thinking about strangling you."

I lifted my brows. "Do the gargoyle bomber's dirty work for him?"

"I'm seriously tempted."

"Ajax would have something to say about that."

My furry shadow stood on the seat behind me, his breath warm against my neck. He made a low, threatening sound that rumbled up from his chest.

"How the hell am I supposed to protect you if you won't listen to reason?" Damon demanded.

"Who made you my bodyguard? And if you say Mason, you can both fuck off. I've had enough of someone trying to run my life. I'll live and die on my own terms, thank you very much."

He shut his eyes and drew a deep breath and let it out slowly. "I'm not backing off."

"So the stalking thing is back on? Well then, at least you can be useful. Help me unload this stuff."

I ducked under his arm and opened the rear door. I grabbed the laptop and left him to sherpa in the rest. John's car was still out front, but I didn't see any sign of him. I cleared a space in a recessed nook to set up. Damon helped move out the broken bits of furniture, and I found a broom that was still in one piece to sweep it out. We got the table unfolded, and I set up the printer and laptop while Damon put together the chair.

I downloaded my business software and installed it and then pulled my documents off the cloud. By the time I'd started printing my inventory list, John found us. I introduced him to Damon and handed him the thick stack of papers.

"This is what we had in on consignment and our own stock with assessed values."

"Very good. Mary Carphon, the adjuster, will be out this afternoon around three. Will that be all right?"

I hugged him. "You're my hero."

"Don't get too excited. Once she gets done, she'll have to make her report. I'll do my best to hustle it through. There's no doubt this was vandalism, so I don't see any obstacles. You should see checks from each of your policies by the beginning of next month at the absolute latest."

Four weeks. I had money in savings, and I was willing to use it in the interim. It was for a rainy day, and there was a damned hurricane running through my life.

"Thanks."

"I'll need an inventory of your personal belongings for the homeowner's policy. I've got all your vehicle information at the office— Say, how the hell did they manage to do that to your Thunderbird?"

I frowned. "Do what?"

He blinked in surprise. "You haven't seen it?"

My cheeks colored. "I haven't had the heart. I love that car."

He shook his head and squeezed my shoulder. "I know. I'm really sorry, but there's no way to salvage her."

I widened my eyes so I wouldn't start blubbering all over him and remembered that I was going to buy a new, shiny car with lots of bells and whistles and air conditioning. Or maybe I'd get a new Corvette or Camaro.

Once John left, I decided I'd better suck it up and check out the vehicle damage and then go upstairs and see what I could salvage up there.

"Don't you have some lawyering to do?" I asked Damon when he followed me.

"You're more important."

As annoying as having him hovering around was, the words made a lump rise in my throat. I'd never had a man say that to me before. Then my bubble burst, and I mentally kicked myself.

"Right. I forgot I was your job there for a minute. I hope Mason's paying you overtime."

He grabbed my arm and swung me around. "I'm here because I care about you."

I studied his face. That intensity was back in his eyes. A shiver ran through me. I couldn't hide it.

"What's wrong?" His scowl deepened.

Abruptly he let go of me and stepped back, and I realized he thought I was scared of him. My first instinct was to give him an earful. It would take a lot more to scare me. But then I stopped myself.

The truth was, on some level, I *was* scared of him. Scared of his kisses and the way he made me feel. Scared that the only reason he was here at all was because he was being paid. Scared how much I wanted him to be there with me and scared how much I wanted to wrap my arms around him and start kissing him again.

Distance between us was a good idea.

I shrugged in answer to his question and walked away. He stalked after me, his silence like a lead cloud.

The box truck should have warned me. It looked as though someone had taken an enormous scythe to it and sheered off pieces. I walked through to the Thunderbird's bay in the garage and froze, my mouth hanging open.

*This* was very personal.

A wedge had cut through the car lengthwise. Oil, coolant, gas, and other liquids spilled across the floor like blood. The smell of it coated my nasal passages and washed over my tongue. Like licking an engine.

I could see why John said there was no hope. The body was bent inward, following the thrust of the giant ax that had cut through the car. The engine was chopped in two. The axles, the gas tank, the transmission— That one single strike had severed just about every important component.

I doubled over like I'd been punched, gasping for breath. Then fury boiled through me.

"When I find out who did this, I'm going to tear them apart with my bare hands."

I flexed my fingers and balled them into fists. I desperately wanted to hit something. I wanted to scream and kick and raise hell.

Instead I made myself relax. I wrapped a blanket of cool calm around myself. Old habit. Or maybe it was a skill. Another thing Aunty Mommy had taught me. Don't let your anger get the best of you.

"I'm going upstairs. I'm surprised the steps hadn't been destroyed."

"I fixed them," Damon explained, his voice tight.

"When?"

"This morning when we got here and found this mess."

He'd used magic, of course. I'd pictured him with a hammer and nails, muscles bunching and rolling as he worked. I set that image aside to enjoy later when I was taking a bubble bath, maybe.

I sighed. My bathtub had a dozen cracks through it.

I walked through my loft, making myself inventory the damage. It was like a food processor had wandered through, chopping at the walls, the furniture—everything. I found some jewelry that remained intact, and a few knick-knacks. My bedroom smelled like the perfume department in some store. All of my bottles had been shattered.

After I toured through all the destruction, I returned to the living room. My arms were crossed over my chest. I felt as if I was about to explode, but I didn't know if I was going to go into a rage or drop to the floor crying.

Fresh start, I told myself. Reinvention if you want it. You've got a blank slate to change anything you didn't like when you built this place.

The building had started as a granary, and later a feed store had been added. When the owner died, he didn't leave a will, and eventually the place came on the market. I didn't have much competition for it, but it was perfect for what I wanted. I'd loved its charm.

I'd turned the bottom floor into my showroom and warehouse and the upstairs into my home. The structure had ended up being in pretty good shape. I'd added some windows then brought in plumbers and electricians, added insulation and a new HVAC system, and then built out the spaces the way I wanted.

It had been a few years, and over time, I'd realized where I could have done better. Putting in little faux room spaces in the shop to better display the furniture was one way. I also wanted to do a featured artist area where they could display and sell their works with a small commission to the store. I'd also considered putting in a little coffee kiosk with a seating area. I had the room. Just the bottom floor was more than six thousand square feet, and that didn't include the garage.

My loft took up half of the top floor, and the other half was empty for the most part. I'd been debating adding another apartment or two to rent out, or else turn it into showroom space. Now was the time to decide.

"Oh, hell," I said. "The water. We need to shut it off. And the gas. There could be leaks."

"The police took care of it," Damon said. "They found a broken pipe in the bathroom and shut off the water and then shut off the gas for good measure.

I took a deep breath to steady myself. "Good. That's really good."

What else was I forgetting to do? There was so much, I hardly knew where to start. I had to start phoning clients. And the window guy was coming soon. And the adjuster.

"I'd better get downstairs," I said. "I've got a lot of work to do."

"Are you okay?"

"I'm upright and breathing, and that's always counted as a win in my book."

"Your aunt was a psychopath."

Damon's comment came out of left field and invited me to confide in him. Not going to happen.

"What do Ballard and Jeffers think caused the gargoyles to fall?" I asked as I descended the back steps. I was going to put in a better entry, I decided. For both the front of my loft and the back. Maybe I should call and architect and see what sort of creative options I had.

If I could afford them. Insurance would pay out, but I still had to cover the deductibles, which weren't pocket change. All the upgrades would be on me. I also needed to cover employee expenses without any income for a while. At least the estate sales part of the business would march on, thank goodness. And I could send my shop employees to Monica. She'd appreciate that, especially since she'd been bugging me to expand and pick up sales in a wider radius.

I needed the interior of the shop to look as high end as the merchandise, which was going to cost money, but the renovations could be deducted off my taxes, which might balance things out enough to make an extensive remodel the smart move. And if I turned the other half of the upstairs into two apartments, the added income would really help. If I put in quality finishes and appliances, I could charge top dollar.

"How can I help?" Damon asked when I sat back down at my makeshift office.

"Do you think you can rig the phone to work in here? I have to make a lot of calls. And maybe you could show the insurance adjuster around when she gets here. There's a guy coming to look at replacing the windows too."

"You might want to call the gas company and a plumber too."

I grabbed a piece of paper and started scribbling my to-do list. Damon continued to hover, and I looked up at him. He was scowling at me.

"What's wrong?"

"This was never supposed to happen," he said. "I was supposed to protect you."

"It's not like you knew it was going to happen," I said. "Anyway, what could you do? They beat my security system, and it's top of the line."

"I should have set wards. I know the world of your heritage. You don't. Its politics are ugly and personal. You have the potential to be an important player. Like it or not, you are now a walking target. Some are going to want to get their hands on you and use you; others are going to want you dead. I should have done more to protect you. You sure as hell weren't doing much."

The obvious condemnation in his last words stung. Part of me wanted to demonstrate just how capable I was of protecting my own damned self, but the other part was curious. Since I could always kick his ass later, I let the curiosity win out.

"All right. I'll bite. Enlighten me about the world you come from. What makes me so interesting?"

He smiled mockingly but I didn't think it was aimed at me. Then he planted his hands on the top of the folding desk and leaned down to look me straight in the eyes.

"Your family—both paternal and maternal—are like royalty in the world of magic. In the mundane world, they would be the equivalent of leaders of countries. That makes them targets for all kinds of opportunists and people who would harm them. They can't trust their friends any more than they can trust their enemies. The game is power—both political and magical. The more you have of the latter, the better you rate in the former. Your family is swimming in an ocean of power where everybody is a shark, even the least capable sorcerer. I'd say it was far more than you could possibly imagine, but you've been kept in the dark, so you can't even begin to imagine anything.

"You are a rare prize, if only for the sake of the blood running through your veins. Your magic is largely untried. You barely know what you are even capable of. Just the ability to turn yourself into smoke makes you unique. That feat isn't even possible as far as the magic world knows. There are many who would take you and use you, and in all truth, you don't really have the tools to protect yourself. Yes, I know—"

He waved away my protest even as I opened my mouth.

"Sure, you protected yourself from me when I tried to take you. But I wasn't trying very hard, and I didn't want to hurt you. Trust me when I say that nobody else is going to underestimate you. If anything, they'll overestimate. Your bloodlines carry that much magic. You will not be able to save yourself when they come for you again ... and they will." He gestured behind himself, toward the destruction. "That's just a surface scratch."

My first reaction was to tell him to fuck off. I could damned well take care of myself. But I also liked to be reasonable on occasion, and I knew better than anybody that I wasn't invincible. Someone could control me and make me do things against my will. All they needed was the right leverage. In my case, threaten my friends or my employees. Or Ajax.

He'd curled up on the floor under the table. An unhappy, high-pitched whine periodically emerged from him. He didn't like the heat in our voices, but for whatever reason, he didn't find Damon a threat at the moment. Maybe it was the table between us. Looking up at the man, I thought the dog was nuts. Damon radiated threat and the table would be no better than wet toilet paper if he wanted to come after me.

His body vibrated with dangerous intensity. He might look like a civilized lawyer on the outside, but inside hid someone much less tame, a warrior, maybe, or a knight ready to chop an enemy to bits. And his eyes—they promised both violence and safety, the first for his enemies, the second for me.

In that moment, I almost believed it was because he wanted to protect me and not because Mason had told him to.

His voice softened and he ran his fingers along the side of my face in a feather-light caress. "Your life has been hit by a freight train. Like it or not, everything's going to change. It already has. If you don't take better precautions, then you're either going to end up dead or at the mercy of someone else."

My eyes narrowed and I pushed his hand away. "What's the difference between you running my life, Mason, or somebody else?"

He straightened. "I'm not trying to run your life."

I snorted. "Sure you are. You're always telling me what I should be doing or not doing or where I should go or how I should take care of myself. It's like you think I'm the village idiot."

"You damned well seem to need a keeper half the time," he retorted.

"I'm perfectly capable of taking care of myself."

"Oh yes, I can totally see that," he said sarcastically. "You have no idea what sort of shit is about to hit your fan. You may be decently powerful, but if you don't know what you're doing or who your enemies are, then yeah, you need a fucking keeper."

I flushed hot, my fingers curling tight on the arms of my chair. "Kiss my ass. I'll handle whatever and whoever I have to on my own."

He snarled and slapped his hand on the table, making the printer and laptop jump. "How the hell do you think you'll stop them?"

Ajax had been growing more and more uneasy as our argument grew angrier. At the sound of the slap, he launched himself at Damon. The dog clamped his jaws around Damon's arm, his head twisting and jerking as he growled furiously.

Damon swore as he'd grabbed Ajax's muzzle. A flash of blue light. Ajax dropped to the ground and staggered drunkenly back, shaking his head.

I didn't know who to go to first. Damon's arm was torn and mangled. Blood streamed from it in miniature rivers. Ajax collapsed and went still. That's when I stopped thinking and went straight to action.

I stripped off my shirt and wrapped it around Damon's arm. His shirt, actually. His arm was shredded. I was sure Ajax had bitten him to the bone. A welter of emotions churned inside me. I didn't even know what I was feeling. Horror. Panic. Terror for both dog and man. Clawing guilt. If not for me, Ajax wouldn't have bitten Damon. Neither would be hurt. Dear God, let Ajax only be hurt.

"You need to get to the hospital. We need to get you in the truck before you pass out." I could hear the tremor in my voice. What if Ajax had torn through an artery? What if Damon died?

My shirt was already soaked through. He could be bleeding to death right in front of me. Panic sent my heart into overdrive. "I have to find something to bind your wound better and slow the bleeding. I'll be back. Wait here." As if he could even walk.

I pushed Damon down into the chair and raced desperately up the stairs to my loft. I grabbed shredded sheets off the floor where they'd landed after the vandalism. I found a paring knife in the kitchen and fled back downstairs. The entire time I berated myself: Why hadn't I called an ambulance? Why hadn't I called 911? I dug in my pocket for my phone then remembered it was still on my desk.

I raced back, half expecting to find Damon passed out or worse. Instead he remained slumped in the chair, his eyes closed, his mouth pulled wide in a pained grimace. My shirt lay sodden on the floor. The hand on his undamaged arm wrapped the wounds. A blue nimbus lit it, sheathing his fingers and his arm in an icy glow. I stopped in the doorway, watching as the wounds closed up. Relief made me dizzy. My legs sagged and tears burned my eyes. I blinked fast and carefully didn't think about how shaken I was to see Damon wounded. I'd rather it had been me.

It took several minutes for the healing to finish. Finally the glow faded and Damon slumped.

I dropped the sheets and knife and went to his side. I touched his shoulder gently. "Are you okay?"

His face was pale and grooves cut deeply around his nose and mouth. "I'll be fine. Check the dog."

I hesitated but then dropped to my knees beside Ajax. He lay awkwardly twisted, his eyes closed. Blood stained his lips and muzzle, and I had to swallow nausea. This was my fault. I'd assumed my knack for calming animals would keep him from hurting anyone. I'd pretended he was an ordinary dog but he wasn't. He was abused and half wild. And maybe a wolf. Clearly he was dangerous. I also loved him with all my heart. He'd only been protecting me. How could I fault him for that?

I stroked his head. He was too still. I couldn't see any evidence of a wound. I bent down. He was still breathing, but his breaths were shallow and sluggish.

"Oh no," I whispered and tears ran down my cheeks. "No, no, no. C'mon Ajax, you've got to wake up."

I pulled him across my lap and hugged him, nuzzling my face in his fur.

"Wake up. Please wake up." My voice broke and my chest felt so tight, I could barely breathe.

Then Damon dropped down in front of me, his legs straddling mine. He rested his bloodstained hands on Ajax.

That icy blue burst of light again. It rolled over Ajax's limp body, enveloping him. The dog kicked and whimpered, his body tensing. His eyes fluttered, showing the whites.

All of a sudden, he went boneless. The light of Damon's magic went out. He sat back on his heels, breathing hard, his head hanging down.

"Are you all right?"

He gave a slight nod but didn't look up. "Tired," he rasped. "He'll be okay."

I'd already given up hope when Ajax's body went limp. I held him tight against me as if that would keep his soul trapped in his body. It took me a second to process Damon's words.

"Okay?" I echoed and now I felt the rise and fall of the dog's ribs, slow and steady.

"Needs rest," Damon said. He gripped the table to help himself up, but he'd only gotten into a crouch before his legs gave out. He dropped back on top of my legs and then slowly pitched over in a dead faint.

At least I hoped it was a faint.

I laid Ajax back down and turned to Damon, pushing his legs out straight. I put a hand on his chest. His heart thumped fast against my palm. The answering surge of relief made me dizzy.

I grabbed the phone and dialed. Jen answered.

"How are you?" she asked, her voice worried.

"I need help," I said. "How fast can you get to the shop?"

She didn't hesitate, even though she was probably knee deep in a project. "Twenty minutes."

"Bring Stacey and Lorraine if you can. Hurry."

I hung up and tossed the phone back on the table. I gathered the torn sheets and folded them into something resembling a pillow and put that under Damon's head.

With the water shut off, I had no way to wash his arm or hands. Or mine. They were smeared with his blood from trying to stanch the wounds.

I didn't know what to do with myself. I didn't know what to do to help.

Without thinking, I reached out to brush Damon's hair away from his face. I traced my fingers down along his cheekbone and over the soft bristles of his carefully trimmed beard. Funny, I hadn't paid any attention to it when he kissed me. Now I stroked my fingers over it.

Abruptly I yanked my hand back. His blood was literally on my hands and I was petting him? God, I was insane. Psychotic.

It seemed to take forever for the girls to arrive. Jen rushed in first.

"Beck? Beck?" she called.

"In here."

She stopped in the doorway. "What the hell happened? Jesus, you're covered with blood. And Damon too!"

She dropped her purse and came to pull me to my feet. "Are you hurt?"

I shook my head. "The blood's Damon's. Ajax bit him."

"With all that blood, it was a hell of a bite. Did you call an ambulance?"

"Damon healed himself."

She gaped.

"With magic," I explained.

She ran her fingers through her straight, black hair. "You've got to be kidding me."

"There's no water here. We need to get him back to his hotel so I can get him cleaned up and he can rest."

"What happened to the wolf?"

"He's a dog."

"Sure he is. What happened?"

"Damon hit him with some sort of magic and it hurt him. Then Damon healed him. That's what he said before he passed out. I've got a feeling neither one of them are going to wake up any time soon."

# CHAPTER TWENTY-SEVEN

We managed to haul Damon and Ajax back to Damon's hotel. The clerk at the desk eyed us suspiciously as we carried Damon in. Stacey and I had his arms over our shoulders. Lorraine and Jen carried his legs. Stacey beamed a brilliant smile at the clerk and gave a flirty giggle. "We wore him out. Now he needs to sleep off the fun."

The clerk rolled his eyes at us and went back to doing whatever he'd been doing. We'd stopped for bottled water and paper towels and cleaned the blood off Damon and me before we came in. I didn't need anyone calling the police. It would not soothe the detectives' suspicions of me.

We dug in his pockets for the key, and once inside, we laid Damon on his bed. Stacey pulled off his shoes. I pulled off his bloody shirt, pausing a scant moment to admire the scenery as I tugged it off. Jen and Lorraine went back for Ajax and laid him on the couch.

"We came in the side entrance," Lorraine said when I wondered how the clerk had reacted to the dog. "Now tell us what happened."

I'd explained already to Jen, who'd driven me and Damon in his truck. Lorraine and Stacey had put Ajax in Stacey's Prius and followed.

I started to tell the story again and then stopped, shuddering. "I can't do this. I've got to clean up with soap and water."

I retreated to take a fast shower. I turned up the heat to nearly scalding and scrubbed. There was blood under my nails that didn't want to come out. When I finally felt clean enough, I got out and dried off and put on a change of clothes. I checked on Damon before returning to the living room. He hadn't moved. I touched my hand to his forehead. His skin was hot with fever.

I summoned Lorraine—the closest thing I had to a medical expert. Stacey and Jen came in with her.

"Should we be worried?" I asked.

"I don't know," she said. "He's definitely hot, but that could be normal for this sort of situation."

"Let's give him a few hours and see how he's doing," Jen said. "Maybe it's just something to do with using magic."

I had to shake my head. The three of them just accepted the fact of magic without batting an eyelash. I was so incredibly lucky to have them in my life.

"What if he's really sick?" I asked. "What if Ajax gave him rabies? Maybe we should have taken him to the hospital."

I twisted my hands together, remembering the torn flesh of his arm and the wash of blood. My stomach knotted with worry. He looked so helpless. Lifeless. It felt so wrong to see him this way.

"I tested Ajax. He doesn't have rabies," Lorraine said, rubbing between my shoulder blades. "I also vaccinated him. But as much as I hate to say it, he's dangerous."

"He was protecting me," I protested, whirling around. "He's been well behaved since I got him except for today."

"Today is a big exception," Lorraine pointed out.

"You want me to put him down?" The idea made me want to throw up.

"I don't want him to hurt you or anyone else."

"I don't— I just can't." I stalked away into the living room. I sat on the couch, scooching under Ajax so his head was in my lap. The girls followed.

I stroked Ajax. What was I going to do? Lorraine was right. He was dangerous. He'd been trying to protect me, but that really wasn't an excuse. Now that it had happened once, it would happen again. That's what everybody said. But there was no way I could put Ajax down. Maybe a muzzle would work. I hated that idea. It felt cruel but it was better than euthanizing him. I snorted inwardly. *Euthanize* made it sound clean and clinical. Putting him down was killing him, plain and simple.

I wouldn't do it. People do violent things all the time and get second and third and more chances. Why should Ajax have just one strike and he's out? Especially when he was trying to protect me.

"You don't have to figure it out now," Jen said, sitting on the arm of the couch and eyeing me sympathetically.

Stacey sank cross-legged into the chair opposite to me. "Any news? Do the police have any idea who hit your place?"

"No. But Damon said it was done with magic." I hesitated. I needed a drumroll for the next bit. Sadly, I had to do without. "Also, good news. My mother was really my aunt. She kidnapped me when I was a baby."

That dropped all three of their jaws, and they hit me with a flurry of questions. I told them about meeting

Mason and what he'd said about Aunty Mommy and my real mother.

"Those people are seriously fucked up," Jen said. "Contract babies? That's medieval."

"Apparently it's also twenty-first century," I said drily.

Lorraine just shrugged. "Eugenics really isn't that big of a deal—if people are willing. I mean, farmers and ranchers have been selectively breeding since they first started growing their own food."

"But people?" Stacey gave Lorraine a wide-eyed look of disbelief. "I mean, that's what slavers did."

"Like I said, if the people are willing, I don't see the problem."

"Question is, how willing are they really?" I asked, interrupting before it could turn into a major philosophical argument. "The pressure from the families must be intense."

"I sure wouldn't want to get mixed up in that world," Stacey said fervently.

"Me either," Jen echoed.

"Beck already is," Lorraine said, eyeing me.

I scowled. "I'm not."

She smiled crookedly. "I'm not saying you're going to be contracting babies, but you have a family now—a mother and father and uncle, siblings, and who knows how many others? They'll becoming to see you, is my bet, and that pressure is going to end up on you too."

I snorted. Not that she wasn't right.

"You don't think...." Stacey's voice trailed away, and she ducked her head, avoiding my look.

"Don't think what?"

She grimaced. "Well. I mean, not that you aren't amazing and gorgeous and what sane guy *wouldn't* be into you, but Damon *does* come from that world too. Are you sure he's not just trying to get into your ovaries?"

I'd asked the same thing of Mason. I tipped my head back, closing my eyes. Would Damon really be that kind of a dick?

Despite my lack of trust in his kisses, I couldn't make myself believe it. The kind of man who'd trick me into pregnancy wouldn't have stuck so hard to his attorney-client commitment to Mason. He'd also have tried a lot harder to get me between the sheets when he was living at my apartment. With that ass and those abs, not to mention the humiliating way my brain dissolved when he kissed me, he probably would have succeeded.

I opened my eyes and looked at the girls.

"I don't think he's after a kid, but even if he is, there's always the morning-after pill."

I didn't let myself think too hard about whether or not I'd actually take it. The talk of having children unnerved me to no end, but it also gave me a weird little jolt under my ribs. Right. I'd never so much as changed a diaper, much less been responsible for another human being. Ajax was more than enough to keep me on my toes.

Deciding to change the subject, I told them of meeting the cops and going to Aunty Mommy's murder scene.

"You were bombed with gargoyles?" Jen said at the end, eyes wide. "That's ... ridiculous."

"I think Damon might be right," Lorraine said thoughtfully. "At least about you needing protection. Maybe having Ajax around and ready to fight *is* a good idea."

I latched on to that. "That's true. He obviously won't let anything bad happen to me."

She smiled wryly. She knew I was only agreeing with her to have a good reason to keep Ajax unmuzzled. I scratched behind his ears and made a face at her.

"So if somebody in your family destroyed your shop, then who did it and why?" Stacey asked. "Didn't your uncle say that he hadn't told anybody else about you? If he's not lying, then that means that Damon's either wrong or your uncle did it."

"If that was the case, then why come out of the woodwork?" Jen asked. "He could have attacked without Beck even knowing he existed."

"And why kill your—" Stacey broke off and tossed her hands. "What do we call the bitch now?"

"I've been calling her Aunty Mommy, but The Bitch works."

"Or the Wicked Bitch," Jen offered.

"Okay, the Wicked Bitch works for me," Stacey said. "Why kill her?"

"Maybe she stole his favorite firetruck when he was a kid," Lorraine offered.

"I got the impression that family bonds really matter to him," I said. "And anyway, even if he did want to kill her, he doesn't seem the type to drop gargoyles on people."

"What type of killer does he seem like?" Stacey asked.

"I don't know. Something sneakier, more elegant."

"Murder can be elegant?"

"More than dropping gargoyles with giant penises on his victims."

"Okay, I'll give you that much," Stacey said. "But it still doesn't answer who would have gone after your shop or killed the Wicked Bitch. And it's just as possible they weren't done by the same person."

"Awfully coincidental timing, though," Lorraine said.

"But the whole conversation is pointless since you have no idea who really knows about you and how these new relatives feel about you. Mason and Damon could both be lying, or someone overheard a conversation or who knows? Maybe their computers got hacked or someone's following them or they talk in their sleep. What's really important is that you stay safe."

"Not that easy when you're being targeted," Jen said. "Especially since they're using magic. Can you do something like set up a magical bubble around you that no evil can penetrate?"

I smiled. "If I knew how—maybe. But I don't. What I can do is pretty basic. Well, except for the smoke trick, and I don't know how to do that one on purpose."

I had to explain what that meant.

"If only you could have done that when the Witch Bitch came after you," Jen said.

I shook my head. "I didn't want her knowing I could do magic, and besides, disappearing wouldn't have helped. She'd still have gone after you three. Better to suck it up and let her do her thing."

"If you say so," Lorraine said doubtfully.

"Back to the problem. It looks like someone with magical abilities is targeting you and may have killed the Wicked Bitch," Jen said. "That means that the police aren't likely to find the culprit since he or she can just *poof!* away the evidence. The question is, how are we going to keep you safe and stop this guy?"

"You could hire security for the shop," Stacey offered.

Memory hit me. "Oh shit! Kenny's coming in. He could already be there and all that blood. He's going to freak when he sees it. The claims adjuster is coming in too, and the window guy. I can't afford to cancel."

I looked down at Ajax. "I don't want to leave him. If he wakes up while I'm gone, it could be very bad."

"No worries," Jen said, standing up. "I'll go clean up the blood and hang out at the shop. I'll get caught up later tonight." She was a freelance Web designer and all-around computer geek, which made her schedule very flexible.

"I'll go too," Stacey said. "My shift doesn't start until five."

Lorraine glanced at her watch. "I've got to head back to the clinic," she said regretfully. "I'll call when I get off."

"Call us when they both wake up," Stacey said, hugging me. "Or if you need anything, but that goes without saying."

Once they were gone, the silence caved in on me. My eyes felt gritty, and my head was full of sludge. All my adrenaline abandoned me, leaving me to feel as exhausted as I was. I wondered how I could reach Mason. Maybe he could help Damon. But I had no idea where to find him. I turned and lay on my side with Ajax's back against my stomach. His warmth and steady breathing lulled me to sleep.

# CHAPTER TWENTY-EIGHT

I woke to feel Damon's hand stroking my hair.

"Wake up, Beck. Rise and shine."

I groaned and blinked. My eyes felt as if they'd been rolled in sand. Damon crouched in front of the couch at eye level. He'd showered. His hair clung wetly to his forehead. Ajax still slept, his head on the couch between us.

"Are you okay?" I asked.

His hand came to a rest, though his thumb continued to stroke back and forth along my cheekbone.

"I'm fine."

"I'm sorry Ajax bit you."

The corner of Damon's mouth quirked up. "He was trying to protect you."

I sat up. "That's exactly it. He was abused by the people that had him, and he's not a vicious dog—"

Damon's finger pressed against my lips.

"I know. I saw the news footage when you rescued him and the little girls. I'm glad you have him." He pushed to his feet. "I'd rather he didn't bite me again, though."

"That was—"

I swallowed. I didn't even know what I wanted to say. The memory of his arm ripped open and blood streaming down twisted my stomach. "That was awful. I'm really so sorry." I swallowed. "Does it hurt?"

He lifted his arm and flexed it, twisting it to let me see. "It's good as new."

"Does it hurt?" I repeated.

"Not anymore."

I nodded solemnly. "Thank you for healing Ajax. Especially after he bit you so bad."

"He was trying to protect you, so I can't fault him. I didn't mean to hit him so hard either."

"When will he wake up?" I frowned. "What time is it?"

"Almost six. He'll probably wake soon. His body was a little overloaded. He can't tolerate magic like we can."

"We as in humans? Or we as in people who do magic?"

"The second one. Ordinary humans would react just like him."

"You passed out too. How come?" I was fascinated. I knew almost as much about magic as I knew about shaving goats.

"Healing yourself is harder than healing others, and I'm not good at it in the first place," Damon said. "It also makes me hungry. I need to eat, and then I've got something I need to show you."

"Okay," I said. "I'll be here when you get back."

He frowned. "Aren't you hungry?"

"Starved."

"Then why aren't you moving?"

"I can't leave Ajax alone."

Damon nodded and didn't disagree, which added a big checkmark on my imaginary list of reasons to like him. That list was getting longer and longer, but the big question was, did I trust him?

"I can order pizza." He didn't sound remotely enthusiastic.

"Don't you like pizza?" My tone sounded like I'd just accused him of not washing his hands after using the bathroom.

He smiled. "I'm not a food snob, but I was hoping for steak or prime rib."

"There's room service."

He made a face. "I'd rather have pizza."

"Why don't you go out, then? There's a good steakhouse not far from here. You could bring back a couple of doggie bags for Ajax and me."

He started shaking his head before I got all the words out. "I'm not leaving you."

"Why not?"

"Because I don't want to," he said, totally spoiling my reply. I'd been expecting something about me being in danger.

"Just how long do you expect to glue yourself to my side? Because I don't see this as a viable plan."

"I'll do it until we find whoever came after your shop." His tone said he wasn't going to listen to any arguments. Not that that would stop me.

"And if we never find the person?" I rolled my eyes. "Having you hanging around will put a serious crimp in my sex life ... when I get around to having one."

His gaze sharpened, pinning me in place and sending shivers through my lungs. The air between us heated. Even though he stood two feet away, I felt the intensity all the way down to my bones. In that moment, it felt like I was his entire world.

"Maybe I'll be the one to get you into bed and then just keep you there so you can't get into trouble."

It took a few seconds for his words to sink in. I really hadn't let myself go there before. I hadn't mentally undressed Damon or considered how his skin would feel against mine, or what it would be like to have him kiss more than my lips, much less how it would be to have his weight on top of me and his dick inside me. Now my mind hitched an express ride to Orgasm Town, and all of that flashed through my head, with memories of his naked chest in the river, the play of his muscles, and the touch of his tongue on mine.

I think I drenched my panties. My nipples actually hurt, they wanted his touch so bad. My brain, however, was trying to stand up against the torrent of desire sweeping over me.

Whatever Damon had expected for a comeback, it wasn't silence. And something on my face must have revealed how hot he'd made me. He smiled a lazy, smug smile, his eyes practically glowing with the fire of hunger.

"Better answer quick," he rasped softly. "Because in ten seconds, I'm going to take you into the bedroom and this time I'm not stopping with kisses."

The flames inside me roared higher. My naughty places all ached, and I nearly tossed Ajax aside and flung myself into Damon's muscled arms.

Then a bucket of cold water.

A loud knock sounded against the door. I started and Damon swore. Receding desire left me shaking, my heart racing. Damon stomped to the door and yanked it open. Mason waited on the other side.

"I've been looking for you," he said then glanced past Damon at me. "You too."

"I needed a nap," I snapped because my entire body was swimming with cock-blocked hormones and because I didn't trust Mason in the least. The two combined with an empty stomach and too little sleep took me a long way up the cranky meter. Plus, I didn't want Damon blurting out what had happened with Ajax. It was none of Mason's business. Of course, he was bound to notice the dog was unconscious and not asleep since Ajax hadn't acknowledged the knock at the door, much less the man standing in the hallway.

Mason walked in to Damon's suite without waiting to be asked.

"I hope you're rested now?" he asked me, and I couldn't tell if his concern was genuine or a slick veneer. In fact, that was the whole problem with him. I couldn't tell anything for sure about him. I could ask him what his favorite color was, and I wouldn't know if he was lying.

"Better than I was."

He nodded and looked at Damon. "We need to gather the supplies."

"I was about to order up dinner," Damon replied.

"We'll eat on the way."

I guess I didn't get to have an opinion. I still didn't move. I kept praying Ajax would start waking up before Mason noticed him, which he did when I didn't move.

"What's wrong with the dog?"

I looked at Damon, pleading with my eyes for him not to tell Mason. He must've got the message.

"He fell off the stairs when we were at the shop," he said smoothly. "I hadn't had a chance to stabilize them yet. He broke a rib and did some other damage. I healed him. He's sleeping it off."

Mason nodded as if that made sense, which to be fair, it did, but at the same time, I couldn't help but notice how easily Damon lied and that he faked truth really well.

"Then you and I will take your truck and pick up what we need. We'll bring back dinner for Rebecca."

Would they never get it through their thick skulls that my name was Beck? At least Damon got it right *part* of the time.

"Ahem," I said loudly. "Do you know how rude it is to keep calling someone a name she's especially asked you not to call her? I'll tell you how rude it is. Very. Insultingly so, in fact. Enough that a person could be forgiven for assuming the insult is deliberate. Like my opinion of my own name doesn't even matter. Do you think that's a fair assessment? Uncle?"

Mason had the grace to look a little taken aback. "I'm very sorry ... Beck. I won't forget again."

"That would be a pleasant surprise."

I wasn't expecting his smile.

"Point taken." He looked at Damon. "Are you ready to go?"

Damon scowled at me. "I don't like leaving Beck alone."

Mason nodded. "I understand, but it'll take both of us to load the supplies. We have to do it tonight."

"Do what?" I asked.

"We're going to put the gargoyles back together," Mason said as if it were a perfectly reasonable thing to do.

"Why?"

"That's what I was going to show you after dinner," Damon said, rubbing a hand over the back of his neck.

"I'm confused. What exactly were you going to show

me? And why on earth are you two planning to piece the gargoyles back together? I'd have thought you'd just buy new ones if you wanted to put them back up, though I have no idea why you'd want to. Aunty Mommy generally had very good taste in decorating, but those things are hideous."

Mason chuckled. "Gargoyles are supposed to be hideous."

"If you say so, but that's no reason to put them on her house, and why pick ones with giant penises?"

Mason made a choking sound, and now it was Damon's turn to chuckle. I guess my new uncle wasn't used to hearing words like giant. Or maybe he'd taken issue with penises. So hard to say.

"There's an explanation," Damon said.

"But now isn't the time," Mason said. We need to pick up supplies before the stores close, and I have to gather two more spell ingredients. There's no moon tonight, which will help a great deal. If we wait until next month, pieces will disappear. I want to be ready when full night descends."

Damon nodded as if all that made sense.

"What spell?" I asked, completely confused.

"I'll explain later," Mason said. "Let's go." He opened the door and stepped out into the hallway.

"We'll be back as soon as we can," Damon said, following reluctantly. "Lock the deadbolt when we leave."

"Sure." I couldn't help the acerbity in my voice. I was feeling a whole lot like a mushroom—kept in the dark and fed a lot of shit.

Damon paused in the doorway. "Order up room service. We'll be back sooner if we don't stop for food. Be sure to check the peephole before you open the door for them. Charge it to the room."

I waited until they left then I slid out from under Ajax, bolted the door, and called down to the kitchen. I ordered three cheeseburgers, one for me, two for Ajax. After a moment's thought, I added a green salad and a strawberry milkshake.

I waited with Ajax until the food arrived about forty-five minutes later. I dutifully checked the peephole, took the tray from the server, then signed the bill, adding a generous tip.

I set the tray on the little dining table. That's when Ajax woke up. He lifted his head, sniffing, ears perked.

"So that was the trick to waking you up? Food?" I shook my head. "Men are so easy sometimes. But you only get to eat if you promise not to bite Damon again. Or anybody else, for that matter." I considered. "Only if someone actually hits me. Then you can tear them to shreds."

Ajax staggered a little as he came over to me. I was sure he had to go outside for a nature call, but he still needed to steady up. Maybe by the time he ate his dinner, he'd be up to it.

I needed a run. A long one along the river. I needed to push myself and fall into the rhythm of my muscles stretching and clenching. Unfortunately, I didn't have running shoes. Or leggings. Or shorts.

I cut Ajax's two hamburgers into quarters and removed the vegetable matter, then scraped the fries onto the tray before setting the plate on the floor for him. He bolted his burgers as though he hadn't eaten in days. Then he sat back on his haunches and looked longingly at mine, licking his chops.

"I know you ate," I told him. "I fed you this morning. I'm not sharing mine with you."

In the end, I gave him half my hamburger because I'm a sucker. The salad, milkshake, and fries were more than enough to fill me up.

I hadn't put a leash on Ajax before. I didn't know if he'd put up with one. Or a collar. So far he tended to stick by my side, but after the incident with Damon, I didn't know if I could trust him in public. Not that I had any sort of leash.

"All right," I said after making sure the water bowl Damon had put down on the floor at some point was full and Ajax had lapped up all he wanted. "Let's go outside but you'd better behave yourself."

I didn't have a key to the room. I debated whether or not to close the door, and decided that I'd better. I didn't want to be responsible for Damon's getting robbed. Ajax and I would wait in the lobby for him and Mason to return. But first, a walk.

# CHAPTER TWENTY-NINE

The evening wrapped me in a balmy hug. This time of year, the sun wouldn't go down until nearly nine o'clock. I decided I'd take Ajax to a nearby park.

On the way, I called Jen, who assured me that everything at the shop was fine. The adjuster had come and gone and left her card for me. The window guy had taken measurements and would have a bid to me within a few days. Kenny had called an employee meeting for ten the next morning and then had started cataloging the destroyed pieces, taking pictures and tagging them with their assigned number in the ledger.

The man was a gem.

The park was only a mile from the hotel. It covered around forty acres and held within it a baseball complex, basketball and tennis courts, and a bunch of walking trails beneath a mix of oak, maple, and ash. Mosquitoes swarmed near the creek, so I took Ajax around the opposite side of the park, where the grass grew taller. Much to my relief,

Ajax refused to go far from me, staying within a fifteen-foot radius.

He made the people around us a little nervous since he wasn't on a leash and had such a wolfish appearance, so I decided not to stay very long. We'd cross the back end of the park and then head back toward the hotel. He wasn't interested in any of the other dogs except to give them a perk of the ears and an assessing look. He was on guard duty. He wasn't even distracted by the taunting squirrels.

I headed for the rose garden in the corner of the park where I planned to exit. I took the bark path circling around its border, breathing deep of the flowers' rich perfume. That was one thing I still wanted to do: plant flowers and maybe put in a vegetable garden on the land behind the shop.

I'd nearly reached the parking lot on the other side of the rose garden when a young man stopped in the center of the path, looking around himself as if lost.

He turned when he saw me. I could see the confusion on his face turn to certainty.

"You're her," he said, taking a step toward me.

Ajax stepped into the path between us, a low growl rumbling in his chest, his head dropping low in wolflike fashion. The man stopped in his tracks.

"Do I know you?" I asked.

He shook his head, making a face as if that were a ridiculous question. "No. Of course not. You'd remember me. I make an impression." He flashed a cocky smile, and I realized he probably wasn't quite out of his teens.

He looked me over. "What happened to you? Did you fall into a garbage disposal?"

I glanced down at my arms. The cuts were mostly red welts, and the bruises were an ugly shade of yellow. I was remarkably healed, but I still looked pretty awful. I looked back up at the kid. "I had trouble using the can opener." I didn't crack a smile.

For a second he just stared, half believing me, and then he laughed.

"For an Osterraven, you're funny. They don't usually have a sense of humor."

That caught me up short. I'd heard that name only once —earlier this morning when Mason had told me about my family.

"What did you say?"

"I said—"

"I heard you. How do you know who I am? Or where to find me?"

"The e-mail today. Once I got into town, it was easy to track you. You're not even shielding."

"What e-mail?"

"The one to the Proclamation Server. Early today. You know."

I had no idea what he was talking about. "What did it say?"

"It said that a third child from the contract between Elena Wyler Symms and Ethan Osterraven had been located here. I go to college only an hour or so away, so I decided to come and find you."

"Why?"

He clearly thought that was the dumbest question he'd ever heard. "Because you're Osterraven–Wyler Symms and nobody knows anything about you. I wanted to get here first and get the scoop."

I understood then. He wanted to be the one who'd met me and got to be the center of attention because he knew things others didn't. I'd gone to high school with kids like that. They earned their glory by gossiping.

"Who are you?" I asked.

"Ben Sharpentier."

Clearly he thought his name should mean something to me.

"Okay, well nice meeting you, but I've got to get back." I veered off onto the grass to go around him, Ajax trotting at my side. I put my hand on the dog's back, maybe to grab him if he tried to lunge, maybe to reassure myself I wasn't vulnerable. I'd told Damon I could protect myself, but the truth was, I didn't know. I'd never had a reason to try to use my magic that way. Ben had found me because I wasn't shielded. Who else was looking? Is that how the vandals had found the shop?

Too many questions and too few answers.

"Where are you going?" he asked, turning to parallel me, though giving Ajax a healthy cushion of personal space.

"And that's your business how?"

"It's not," he said cheerfully. "But you don't get answers if you don't ask."

He had a good point. "This Proclamation Server—what is it?"

Ben gave me a startled look. "You don't know?"

"Of course I do. I'm also an idiot and ask questions I already know the answers to."

He flushed and then grinned. "You're funny. Okay. The PS is a way for all the families to contact the rest of the families."

"So all the families know about me now?" This didn't sound good.

"Whoever reads their e-mails. Well, texts too. You can get notified however you want. But yeah. Everybody's buzzing about it."

"Who sent the e-mail?"

"Said it came from Adriane Wyler Symms. That was weird because she's been gone so long, I didn't think she even had access to the PS."

"She's dead."

"Really?"

"So if that e-mail came this morning, somebody else sent it."

He nodded then shrugged. "Whatever. The thing is you exist."

"Why's that a big deal?"

He stopped and stared. "Are you kidding? You're Osterraven and Wyler Symms."

This conversation was beginning to give me a headache. It's like we didn't quite speak the same language. "So?"

"You're of breeding age. Everybody wants a contract with the Osterraven and Wyler Symms clans."

"They're shit out of luck, then, because I'm not having anybody's babies."

He gave me a *don't be ridiculous* look. "It's not like you get to decide."

"Excuse me?"

He shrugged. "You either contract or the family withdraws protection and whoever's strong enough to capture you does and you end up doing it for free. Well, there's a minimum payment for any child produced from any family, but it's not that much, so if you're going to have to do it anyway, it's better to let the family negotiate and split the profits."

By this time, I was both too shocked to speak and livid beyond words.

"That's barbaric," I said finally when I could find my voice.

"You're not the only girl who thinks so, but what can you do? It's the way things work, the way they've always worked. My family would love to get a baby on you," he said as if all this weren't disturbingly disgusting, though I suppose by definition, disgusting *was* disturbing. "But of course, we don't have the money or other considerations to compete. You're way out of the Sharpentier league."

I stopped and faced him. "I am not somebody's incubator and genetic WalMart. If and when I ever have a child, it's going to be because *I* want one and because I love the father. Understand? Feel free to e-mail blast that out. In fact, give me your phone and I'll do it myself."

He laughed and dug in his pocket, tapping on his phone. "You're one tough chick, you know? I think I'm going to like you a lot."

"So long as you keep your dick to yourself, I might let you hang out."

He laughed again and passed me his phone. The e-mail was open, and the cursor blinked in the subject line. I typed in *Urgent* and then tabbed into the body.

I hesitated. Did I go polite or get straight to telling them all to go fuck themselves? I elected to go the middle ground.

> *To Whom It May Concern:*
> *I have less than no interest in having anybody's children. Try to get into my uterus and I will castrate you and stuff your balls up your nose.*
> *With all due respect,*
> *Beck Wyatt*

I hit the send button and handed the phone back to Ben. He read my e-mail and his mouth fell open, and then he started laughing again, having a hard time catching his breath.

"Oh my God," he said. "The prim and propers are going to shit bricks."

"Prim and propers?" I asked, but my thoughts went instantly to Mason and Aunty Mommy. That pretty much covered both of them.

"Generation moldy," he said. "The ones who run everything." He made a face.

"Why do you let them?" I asked as I started walking again.

He frowned then shrugged. "Nothing I can do about it."

"Just say no?" I asked.

"They'd cut me off."

"So what?"

That made him think a moment. "I don't know. Probably wouldn't be so bad. I mean, once I get out of college and get a job. But your friends would have to pretty much shun you. Same with the rest of the family. Plus, they would probably have some magical punishments."

"Does anybody ever say no?"

"Not really. I mean, not and goes through with it. Like I said, it's what we do."

I snorted. "*You* don't. The girls do. All *you* men do is get your rocks off. I'm surprised the women in your families haven't revolted. I sure as hell would have."

He sobered. "There's a lot of pressure put on them. All of us. To strengthen the bloodlines so we're prepared."

"Prepared for what?"

"The histories talk about a split that happened centuries ago, where the ruling families got into a fight, and just when war was about to break out, one side managed to destroy many of their opponents. Some lost their magic; others, their lives. The losers who survived were cursed never to be able to have more children. Their lines would end with them. The winners went back to business as usual. But then, on her deathbed, Olirya Siddiqui had a vision. She was a powerful seer. She said that in the future, those we thought we destroyed would rise again and with them would come pain and destruction."

"So everybody believed her, and all the leftover families got together and decided to breed for magical strength so when the other team shows up, you can overwhelm them before they cause all sorts of mayhem," I said, seeing where he was going.

"Pretty much."

"And your whole life, you're told that the fate of the world rests on your cooperation and participation."

He nodded. "Especially since a magic war would bleed over into the mundane world and cause all sorts of disasters. The cursed-bloods never cared about ordinary people and didn't mind slaughtering them."

"Did it not occur to anybody that this Olirya might have had a tumor or a stroke or Alzheimer's?"

"The writings of everybody who was there say she was coherent to the last."

"All the same, you people are seriously fucked up," I said. "Now I know where Aunty Mommy got it from. You're all demented."

"Aunty Mommy?"

"The bitch who stole me and tortured me all my life," I said. "Adriane Wyler Symms is her real name, I guess. She told me she was my mother, but turns out she was my aunt. Hence, Aunty Mommy."

He nodded. "The e-mail this morning said something about that. Up until then, nobody knew you existed or that Adriane had taken you when she disappeared."

I wondered what my sperm donor had said when he found out I was gone. Or even if he asked. Since I was his special secret, how could he demand they produce me?

We walked a little bit with neither of us speaking.

"Listen," Ben said. "I don't mean to be rude or anything, but you should really think about shielding yourself if you don't want everybody descending on you like, well, like me."

"I'm in the phonebook," I said dryly. "It's not like I'm that difficult to find. And anyway, I don't know how to shield."

His eyes popped wide. "Seriously? You don't know how? But that's the first thing any of us learn, practically before we're out of the cradle."

I shrugged, not wanting to explain that I'd hidden my magic from Aunty Mommy and that even if she'd known about it, she wouldn't have taught me anything. Not if she could help it.

"Can you show me this shielding thing?" I asked.

"Sure. I guess."

I stopped again, sitting down on a bench in front of a little bistro. Ajax flopped down beneath me. "Show me now."

"Okay. Well, there's no one way to do it. The best way is to cast a spell and anchor it to something you carry around. A necklace or a bracelet or a ring or something. That way it keeps working and you don't have to pay much attention to it except to recharge it every so often."

"I don't know how to cast spells. What's another way?"

He blinked his surprise at my confession but didn't freak out, which saved him from having me kick him in the shins. I got the point. I was a magical mutant. Get over it already.

"You make a bubble of magic around yourself and then tell it to keep you hidden from a magical search."

"Just like that." I snapped my fingers.

He shrugged. "Mostly magic is in the intent—you know, focusing your desires and excluding all your other thoughts. That's really tough to do. I mean, have you ever tried meditating? Your mind is always running off in interesting directions and you have to drag yourself back to clearing your head. Magic is the same way."

"Oh." In fact, most of the time I just decided what I wanted to do and made it happen and didn't really think about how or why it worked. I guessed I had good natural focus.

"Now there are two things to remember. You have to make sure that your magic encloses all of you. A lot of beginners just stop at the ground and forget the bottoms of their feet. Second, you have to keep feeding the shield with magic or it will vanish on you."

"I can chew gum and walk at the same time."

"Don't worry if you don't get it at first. It can take weeks to master. Most of us learn young so our parents or minders can't find us when we don't want them to."

"Minders?"

"You know—nannies, tutors, babysitters—that sort of thing."

"Oh. Sure."

I was beginning to be less annoyed that I'd been kidnapped from his world. At least I'd had a reasonably normal childhood ... if you didn't count the torture stuff.

"Try it," he said. "Wait."

He looked around. Pedestrians strolled the sidewalks, and the little courtyard of the bistro behind us was full. "You should wait until you're in private. You don't want people to see you doing it. They tend to freak."

I frowned. "What's to see?"

I let magic flow out around my feet, and in a gesture that looked a little bit like a ballerina, I dropped my hands down to my sides and raised them up until my fingers met. The magic rose with it and swirled together. I dropped my arms and lifted my feet one at a time to close the bubble.

Okay, then. One part down. I narrowed my gaze, concentrating on the notion of shielding myself from other magic. Ben was right. Once you wanted to concentrate, you started thinking of everything else, such as the itch on the bottom of your foot and how exciting it was going to be to try to put back together a bunch of gargoyle penises.

I made myself focus again. It took me a minute or two, but I finally felt something sort of snick into place. The bubble around me expanded and then contracted against my skin.

"Wow!" Ben leaned back, wide eyed. "That's really cool. Your magic is invisible."

"Yeah, well, everybody knows that now you've practically shouted it to the world," I said. A couple walking toward us was giving us a wary look, probably looking for errant pentacles and a tattooed 666 on my forehead.

"Oh, right. Sorry," he said, flushing. "But wow. It worked too. I can't pick you up anymore. You're pretty talented, but then you'd have to be with your bloodlines."

I was starting to feel a lot like a broodmare. Not going to happen. "How close do you have to be to someone to find them with magic if they aren't shielding?"

"Depends on the practitioner. I can be a few miles away. Other people have to be within a hundred feet, and others could be a hundred miles away."

"So I keep feeding it. Do I have to keep telling it what to do?"

"Shouldn't. Not so long as you don't let it collapse. If you do that, you have to start all over again. It will disappear on you when you go to sleep or pass out. That's one reason to use a spell. Those don't shut off when you sleep."

"Good to know." I stood. "Thanks for the help, but I have to get back."

He looked disappointed. "Already? But we've only just met."

I had to wonder why he was so interested in me. Probably he wanted more juicy details to relay to friends and family.

It had only been an hour and a half or so since Mason and Damon had gone shopping. I doubted they were back yet. It was still quite some time before sundown.

"I could use some coffee," I said finally.

We walked up to a little coffee cart and then ambled along with Ajax in between us. He really didn't like Ben being too close.

"You're going to college?" I asked.

"Pre-med," he said. "If I can make the grades, anyhow. Then I want to get into neurosurgery."

"Wow. Impressive."

"Not if you ask my grandmother and mother. I don't need the money and anything I can do with a scalpel I can do with magic, so why bother?"

I glanced at him. "Is that true? I mean, healing with magic being just as good as using a scalpel."

"No. Healing is hard and takes a lot out of you. I couldn't do that for too many people before I'd be in a coma myself. Plus, I'm pretty sure if I knew what I was doing medically, I'd be able to use magic more effectively. I think I could pair magic with surgical skills and really do some good work."

His enthusiasm was obvious. "But your mother and grandmother don't think it's worthwhile?"

Ben's face fell. "They don't see the point. We all share the world with mundane people, and we protect them from magic, but other than that, nobody thinks they're worth anything. I like people and I really want to help them. If I can save people, make their lives better, and keep their families from heartbreak, I want to do it."

I smiled at him and patted his shoulder. "You're a good man, Charlie Brown."

He flushed. "You don't think it's stupid?"

"I think it's pretty damned awesome. The world needs more people like you. Your family ought to be proud of you. I've only known you less than an hour, and I know I'm proud of you."

"Thanks," he said and looked away, and I swear he was tearing up. Poor kid. His mother and grandmother needed a come-to-Jesus meeting.

"Have you got any more family? Besides your grandmother and mother?"

His father was also a sperm donor, and he had five sisters and brothers, all with different fathers. He also had half a dozen aunts and uncles and a bunch of cousins, plus some nephews and nieces. "Of course, that doesn't include anybody who was contracted out to another family," he said. "I grew up mostly in Connecticut, but the family has houses in other places. I live in the City. I go to school at UCSF."

In northern California, 'the City' always referred to San Francisco, as if it were the only one. I was willing to bet that in New York, the City was always New York City. Likewise with Chicago in Illinois and Seattle in Washington.

"Tough school," I said.

"One of the best. But so far I've pulled straight A's, except for a B in Latin."

"Latin?"

"A lot of medical terminology is Latin based, so I figured it would be useful."

"Why the B and not an A?" I ask curiously.

He sighed. "I missed the midterm when my mom called with an emergency."

From the sound of his voice, I could tell he was angry about it.

"What was the emergency?"

"Meeting a potential contract."

"Shit."

"Yeah."

"How did that go?"

"She's eight years older than me, and this would be her fifth kid. It would belong to my family."

"You'd have to leave school to raise the kid?"

He shook his head. "Not according to my mom, but if I'm going to have a kid, I'm going to raise it."

"Good for you."

I had to admire him. He was absolutely dedicated and clearly not an ounce of meanness in his body. He also wasn't selfish, and he clearly had a big heart.

"I'm glad you came to meet me," I said. "You're all right."

He flashed a smile at me. "I'm glad too."

We wandered back toward the hotel. By the time we got there, I was pretty sure he and I were going to be good friends.

We stopped outside the hotel.

"This is my stop."

"When can I see you again?"

"What the hell is going on?" Damon came bursting out of the doors. "Where have you been? I thought you—" He glared at Ben. "Who the hell are you?"

"I'm a Sharpentier," Ben said, not backing down from Damon's dominating presence. "Who are you?"

"Matrovani." Damon turned to me. His face was tight with emotion, his eyes churning. "I told you not to leave."

"Ajax needed a walk." I had a hand knotted in his ruff in case he decided to attack Damon again.

"You should have let him pee in the damned suite. How can you be so stupid?"

The last was nearly shouted. Despite the fact that the question burned through me like a bullet, I didn't flinch.

Ben started to step between us. Damon planted a hand in the center of his chest and shoved.

"Get the hell away from her."

People were stopping to rubberneck. I was so angry, I could barely see straight. Ingrained habit pulled it inside and shaped it into walls.

I wrapped my heart around the pain of his words and the bitterness of my anger and let them strengthen me the way they'd always carried me through Aunty Mommy's tortures.

I turned to Ben. "It was good to meet you, and thank you for the lesson."

With that, I turned around and walked away. Damon caught my arm to pull me around, and Ajax lunged, snapping and growling. I pulled him back before he could bite.

"No, Ajax," I said and I felt magic roll off me. He stilled but stared at Damon, warning in his eyes. I'd stopped him, but I knew if Damon came at me again in anger, Ajax would attack and I wouldn't be able to do anything about it.

"I'm leaving," I said. "You can go to hell."

I started walking again. I had no idea where exactly I planned to go. I had my phone, though. Stacey was working, but Jen and Lorraine would both come and get me.

Damon dodged around me and blocked my path. "Beck. Stop." His anger had mixed with something else. Concern maybe. Didn't justify anything.

"I've got nothing left to say to you." My voice sounded dead. It was the same one I'd always used with Aunty Mommy. If I didn't have emotions, she couldn't read what hurt and what didn't; she couldn't figure out when her attacks were successful and not.

"I was worried," Damon said. "All of a sudden you vanished off the radar, and I couldn't find you. I didn't know if someone had taken you or if you'd been killed."

The shield. That had to be what he was talking about. Still didn't justify anything.

"Okay," I said. "I've got to go." I started to step around him again. He sidestepped but was smart enough not to touch me.

"Please listen to me. Please try to understand."

"You know, I get that you think I'm helpless and that the Big Bad Wolf is lying in wait around every corner. I get that you think you know better than I do how to live my life. That I'm too stupid to survive in the big bad world of magic. I don't agree, but I get it.

But you seem to think all that entitles you to actually run my life for me, and you don't give a shit how I feel about it. For you, the end justifies the means no matter the cost. I'm tired of being the cost. I'm done with it. Get out of my life, and stay out of it."

The words hurt to say. I *liked* Damon. I liked him a lot. Maybe more than I wanted to admit. But I wasn't going to be a pawn in the genetic contracts game, and I didn't need another bully shoving me around. I understood there was danger. I really would be stupid if I didn't believe that, not after Aunty Mommy's curse, the destruction of my shop, and the avalanche of gargoyles. That didn't mean I was going to spend the rest of my life jumping at every shadow and hiding in a hotel room. When I'd taken Ajax out, I'd considered the danger and decided with a lot of people around and during the daylight, I was reasonably safe. Especially with Ajax at my side and my own magic to defend myself.

"Why can't you just believe in me a little bit?" I burst out, losing the war with my emotions. "Why can't you give me the slightest benefit of the doubt when it comes to keeping myself safe? You know, *I* broke that curse. Me. All by myself. And sure, maybe something bad would have happened to me if I'd been home when the vandals hit, but there's just as good a chance I'd have sent them straight to hell in a handbasket. Same with the gargoyles. I was perfectly capable of getting clear.

"Ever since I met you, you've treated me like the village idiot. I can't think for myself, I can't protect myself, and I sure as hell can't be allowed to live my own damned life the way I want. I'm sick and tired of it."

He looked a little sick at my outburst. Maybe I'd hit a nerve. Good. Now he could be the one feeling stupid and upset. He angled his face away from me and visibly collected himself, keeping his head averted as he replied in a low, tense voice.

"I *know* you're powerful. Probably more than either side of your family realizes. I *know* you're smart, tenacious, stubborn, brave, and capable. I *know* it."

He tapped the side of his head to emphasize it. Then he turned to look at me, and his gaze was so hot, I nearly incinerated on the spot.

"I do know it," he said softly. "But here—" He knocked his fist against his chest. "Here I'm terrified for you. Jesus, Beck, I've had to watch you nearly die. I've seen you hooked up to a transfusion in a hospital bed, and I've sat by your bed, listening to you breathe and praying you didn't stop. It doesn't matter what I know here." He knuckled his forehead again. "I can't— If anything happened to you—"

He broke off again. I just stared at him with my mouth hanging open, trying to make sense of his words, but I couldn't compute them. Not even a little bit.

He reached out, cupping my cheek and brushing my lips butterfly gentle with his thumb. "God damn it. You don't have to look so surprised. I haven't exactly made my attraction to you a secret."

"Attraction," I parroted. "Sex. That's all."

He scowled and his hand yanked back as if scorched. "Is that what you think?" he demanded, sounding as though I'd just called him the worst name on the planet.

Yes. I thought the better of saying it. Instead I went with the big question. "Then what do you want?"

He hunched his shoulders and shoved his hands into his front pockets as if he didn't trust himself not shake me.

"You really want to know? Because I don't know if you can handle it."

I recoiled. "Handle it?"

Was I some child incapable of the hard truths? He did *not* just say that.

"There's nothing you can dish out I can't take, big boy. So why don't you get over your bad self and just lay it out for me."

"All right," he said, jaw thrusting out, blue eyes locked on mine, not letting me look away. "I'm in love with you."

I blinked, feeling about as shocked as George Clooney finding out he's pregnant. "Say what now?"

He snorted and rolled his eyes as if I'd just confirmed his low opinion of my ability to deal with his confession. I felt about two inches tall. He stepped closer so I had to look up at him, his eyes lasering into mine with all the intensity of a sun going nova.

"I love you, Beck," he rasped in that voice you use to tell somebody to fuck off and die. "Maybe I'm too protective. Hell, I *am* too protective." He gripped my upper arms, ignoring Ajax's baleful growl. "Don't wall me out. Give me a chance. Teach me how to make you happy. I swear on all that's holy that I will earn your trust."

I think the feeling in my chest was the kind you get when you're kicked by a mule. The breath went out of me, and all I could do was stare. He *loved* me? He loved *me*?

My head spun as I tried to make sense of my emotions. I was still pissed. But wonder pushed back against it. Wonder and shock and maybe a little panic. Okay, a whole lot of panic. Love? Seriously? The raw fear and hope on his face said that he was deadly serious.

Did I love him? I didn't even know what it was. Except —I loved the girls. I loved Ajax. And Damon—

"I really like it when you kiss me," I said, perfectly inanely, giving a great deal of credence to his accusation of stupidity.

He stepped closer so that only a few inches separated us. "I really like kissing you." One hand came up to stroke the hair from my face. "Don't go. Don't walk away."

"I don't know if—"

He pressed his fingers to my mouth to block the words. "You don't have to," he said. "You never have to."

Then his lips replaced his fingers. He didn't hurry as he explored with his tongue. His touch was tender and possessive. His arms slid around me and nestled me against him. My body melded to his. I could feel the thunder of his heart. The smell of him—spicy and earthy—swept over me, spinning me out of control. I slid my arms around his neck and stood on tiptoe, pressing into him.

He made a sound in his throat and deepened the kiss. His touch was seductive, with an edge of desperation that melted any resistance I had, which wasn't much. I didn't hold anything back.

I wasn't thinking. I wasn't doubting or questioning or anything else. All I was doing was feeling. Ripples of heat and desire rolled through me, and want settled heavy in my belly. My breasts ached to be touched and held. The hard plane of his chest only teased them, making them ache more.

He stroked my back as if to be sure I was real, and then his arms crushed me tighter and tighter. I could barely breathe, and I didn't care. I was lost. My blood throbbed in my veins. I wanted his touch. I craved it. I ached to feel the slide of his skin against mine. I longed to explore his body, slide my tongue along his neck, down the seam of his stomach, along the inside of his thighs.

We might have started stripping clothes off each other except for the loud cough that broke through our delirium.

"I hate to be a wet blanket, but you two do realize this is a public sidewalk, do you not?"

Mason.

I stiffened. Well, as much as limp spaghetti can stiffen. Damon lifted his head.

"Don't regret it," he said. His eyes pleaded.

I still couldn't wrap my head around his declaration of love. It's not that I didn't believe it. Or that I did. But more that it had happened. That this was even real.

"I don't."

And I didn't. Not the kiss. Not his words. I held them inside like blown glass snowflakes. I wanted to examine them, understand them, cherish them. I wanted to believe that they were real and wouldn't melt away into nothingness the moment I trusted them.

"It's getting dark," Mason prodded.

I twisted my head to look at him. Ben stood smiling broadly at me just behind him. I flushed then realized I was already so overheated that nobody would be able to tell the difference.

"We've got to get going," Mason said, prompting us when we just stood there in a daze.

At his words, I nodded. I started to step away from Damon. He tightened his grip on me and then slowly he loosened his arms. He slid a hand down my arm and threaded his fingers through mine. I stroked Ajax's head, soothing away his confusion and ire.

"Do you need anything upstairs?" Damon asked, his thumb turning seductive circles on my palm.

"Not that I know of."

"Then let's go. The truck's across the street."

Mason turned to lead the way. Ben looked uncertain.

"Do you want to come with us?" I asked.

Mason turned to frown at me, but I ignored him. Ben didn't. He glanced at Mason and then Damon and then back at me.

"Are you sure?"

"I wouldn't have asked if I wasn't. Though it isn't going to be much fun. We're going to repair gargoyle statues and it involves piecing their giant penises back together, along with everything else that broke off."

He stared at me as if waiting for the punchline. Another look at Mason and Damon and then back to me. "Statues or the real thing?" he asked.

"Real," Damon said.

My head jerked up. "What do you mean?"

He sighed. "I mean that your aunt imprisoned real gargoyles and what we're doing tonight is more like healing than repair." He hesitated, weighing his words. "In order to completely fix them, we have break the bonds your mother put on them. They're probably going to be pretty wild with anger. They might be violent."

"Gargoyles don't know what a good mood is most of the time anyway," Ben said. "I'll help if I'm welcome."

"You are," I said and glared first at Mason and then Damon, daring them to contradict me.

Damon just tightened his grip on my hand. Mason grimaced and started for the truck.

# CHAPTER THIRTY

V vAs the eccentric new owner of Aunty Mommy's house, Mason had sent the staff away for the night. We unloaded the adhesives and quick-drying cement and a dozen other materials, along with buckets and a drill with a stirring rod, scrapers and a broad assortment of tools.

"We have to get the pieces together long enough to cast the spell to let them animate," Damon explained. "Once we do, they'll heal on their own, as long as all the pieces are in place."

I looked at the pile of rubble and the gargoyles. "We have to do this all in one night?"

"Yes," Mason said. "The moonless night is when gargoyle power is strongest. It will give them the best chance of completely healing."

"We need help," I said and called Jen and then Lorraine. Stacey was at work. Both promised to be there as soon as possible.

Damon and Ben set up the bright work lights while Mason used magic to set all the gargoyles upright in a circle around the rubble, including the one that had fallen on my mother.

When I asked what the police would think, he said he'd cleared it with them.

"Just like that? I'm surprised."

"I can be persuasive." The look he gave me was inscrutable. I don't know if he was saying he'd used magic to influence them or if he'd talked them into it. I hoped it wasn't magic. The idea made me feel slimy.

The whole project was insanely impossible, but I wasn't going to say it. "If we can't find all the pieces, can new pieces be made for them?"

"Sure. But not just anybody can make them. Has to be someone with stone magic. They aren't that easy to find, and most stone practitioners don't get along with gargoyles," Mason said. "Better if we can put them together."

We dug in. It was actually easier at first than I'd expected. We sorted out various parts—wings, claws, ears, tails, snouts, penises, and some balls.

"Are they really this well endowed? And why on earth are they all at full mast?"

Damon gusted a breath. "Yes to the first. Normally their equipment would be tucked up inside. There's a pouch. The only reason they'd be waving proudly like this is if your aunt forced them."

"The more I hear about her, the less I like her," Ben said.

"You have no idea," Damon replied, flicking a look at me.

Neither of them had any real idea, and I was good with that.

"Why imprison them at all? Just for decoration?"

"It's a good question," Mason said grimly. "I wish I knew the answer."

Lorraine and Jen showed up about a half hour in. After introducing them to Ben and Mason, I explained what we were doing and why. Mason and Damon took on the job of sticking things back together while the rest of us worked on figuring out the puzzle pieces.

"How bad do you think it will be if the wrong pieces end up on a gargoyle? I mean, a piece of penis here, a wrong wingtip there," Jen said, turning over a chunk of stone in her fingers.

"They aren't very friendly apparently," I said. "They already have a reason to be seriously pissed with being imprisoned with boners. I imagine getting the wrong pieces wouldn't improve their moods."

"Do you think they can hear us?" Lorraine asked, her face a comical mask of horror.

"No idea," Ben said. He kept glancing at Jen with a faintly shell-shocked look on his face.

"It's possible." Mason used extra-thick mortar to push the nose onto one of the gargoyles. "Gargoyles are a secretive species in general, so we know little about them."

"But they are sentient?" Lorraine asked, finishing a penis she'd been working on.

"They are."

Luckily, instead of shattering, most of the creatures had broken into just a few pieces. There were a fair number of smaller chunks that were difficult to fit, but eventually we felt pretty confident that all the right parts had been reattached to the correct gargoyle. The results weren't pretty. In fact, the statues looked like they'd been attacked by rabid grade-schoolers wielding wet clay, papier-mâché, mud, and a lot of bandages. Damon and Mason had used anything and everything to help fix the pieces on. So long as the reconstruction held until the beasties reanimated, we were golden.

"Glad the ones on the front of the house didn't fall off," Jen said, using her forearm to rub the sweat from her face. She glanced at her watch and groaned. "Almost three. I've got a client meeting at ten. I'm going to be dragging tomorrow. Today. Whatever."

"Chocolate-covered espresso beans," I told her. "Those will perk you up like nothing else."

"Except a night in bed," Lorraine said.

"Only if I'm alone," Jen said airily. "Otherwise it's a lot of exercise. Very nice exercise."

Ben blushed.

"We don't need you to finish if you'd like to go rest," Mason said.

"Oh, hell no," Jen said. "I want to be here for the fireworks and to see these guys start moving."

"Me too," Lorraine said, grabbing a patio chair and pulling it around to sit.

Ben quickly fetched a chair for Jen and then me. Mason took out a marble cutting board and set it down in the middle of the gargoyle ring.

Using a red felt-tip pen, he drew a series of designs across it. Next he drizzled fine black sand over the lines. They glinted in the light. Damon had come to stand behind me, rubbing my neck and shoulders. I leaned back into him, breathing him in. He practically made my mouth water.

"What's in the sand?" I asked.

He smoothed his thumbs up my neck, digging in to loosen the muscles. "Gold. The sand is volcanic."

I wanted to ask more questions, but between exhaustion and the gentle kneading of Damon's hands, I melted into goo.

When Mason finished the pattern, he took a pouch out of his bag of party tricks. He spilled the contents into his hand. They included a variety of stones. None were polished. He picked each one out carefully and placed it on the cutting board. I couldn't see any rhyme or reason to any of it. Watching only made me aware of how little I knew about magic. As fascinated as I was by what Mason was doing, I wasn't sure I wanted to learn.

Once each of the stones was in place, he took out a roll of thin copper wire and started cutting ten-foot lengths of it. Once he had fourteen of them—one for each of the gargoyles—he twisted the ends together. A spark of scarlet magic welded them together.

He then took out a bottle and a clear crystal bowl. He set the bowl in the middle of the board and poured the contents of the bottle into it. The liquid flowed viscous and green. Even from several feet away, I could smell it. Astringent and sweet and something else I didn't recognize.

He wrapped the end of one wire around a protruding bit of each gargoyle. Once he completed that, he set the welded end that connected them all together in the bowl of liquid.

Mason dug in his pocket and took out a pocket knife. He flicked it open and sliced through the pad of his thumb. Blood welled. He held it over the bowl and dripped fourteen drops into it.

Taking out a handkerchief, he wrapped his thumb, then wiped the blade of his knife clean and pocketed it again.

"It would be best if you all stood back," he said. "Damon, Ben, shield the girls in case the gargoyles become violent. I'd prefer if you only attacked if absolutely necessary. Their anger will be deserved, and they've suffered far too long already."

We retreated twenty or so feet away on the lawn. I called Ajax, who'd spent most of the evening exploring the yard and sleeping. He rose from where he'd sprawled on the grass and trotted to my side.

Damon formed a blue bubble around us. Ben's magic was also blue, but pale, like a summer's sky. He made another bubble inside of Damon's then pushed it out until the two merged. I could feel the current of magic in the air. It lifted the hair on my arms and the back of my neck.

Jen elbowed me in the side and leaned over. "What's up with you and Damon?" she whispered loud enough for everybody to hear. "You two seem awfully cozy."

I flushed. Before I could say anything, Damon twisted around.

"I'm in love with her," he said, folding his arms over his chest as if daring her to challenge him.

I was saved from interrogation by a flash outside the bubble shields. Magic vibrated through the air and ground, sending shivers quaking through me.

"Whoa," Lorraine said, grabbing Jen to steady herself.

Mason stood with his back to us. The blue of Ben's and Damon's shields turned Mason's scarlet magic purple. He stretched out his hands to either side and tipped his head back to the sky. He was saying something, but I couldn't make out anything. His hands glowed and all of a sudden, streaks of magic leaped out of the ground, targeting his hands. More and more rose up. The glow of power ran up to his shoulders.

The air around us tightened. It felt like a violent storm was about to burst, yet the night sky was clear, stars glimmering like diamonds. Jen and Lorraine took each of my hands and crowded close. Neither spoke, eyes fixed on the mesmerizing demonstration in front of us.

Ajax came to sit between my feet, though he didn't appear to be all that concerned. He was taking this magic stuff all in stride.

"He's gathering power," Ben said from behind us.

I wasn't the only one who started at the sound of his voice.

"When he's ready, he'll trigger the spell," Damon explained. "After that, everything depends on how well he constructed it, how powerful your aunt's magic was, and how good the repairs are."

The seconds ticked past, and I kept waiting for Mason to do something, but he just kept pulling up power.

"How much does he need?" Jen muttered, clearly feeling as edgy as I was.

"The spell that binds the gargoyles is strong," Damon said most unhelpfully.

I looked at him. "But not stronger than Mason?"

"He doesn't think so."

"What happens if he's wrong?" Nuclear annihilation? Everybody grows a tail? We all turn into hobbits? Bueller?

"Then I'll step in to help," came Damon's quietly determined answer.

I wanted to ask if *he* was strong enough, but clearly he didn't know. The only thing *I* knew for certain was that if something *did* go wrong, Damon wasn't "stepping in" alone. I'd be going with him. I didn't think about why.

Suddenly the jagged streamers of power shut off. Mason's entire upper body glowed like radioactive waste in a Saturday morning cartoon. As we watched, the glow condensed, sliding down his arms to bundle around his hands before shrinking to the size of a bowling ball. He let go of the mass of power.

The magic ball floated like a soap bubble. When it landed in the nest of wire, crystal, green liquid, and blood, it went out like a blown candle. For a second, nothing happened. We watched, breathless. Mason backed away from his handiwork.

Light bloomed in the bowl. And heat. I was already warm, but I went to sweating to broiling in the oven in a couple of seconds. It was hard to catch my breath. I panted. So did Lorraine and Jen. Their fingers tightened on mine. I wanted to reassure them, but what could I say? It will be all right? The hell if I knew.

The magic burned white. Even with the blue of the shields, I could tell. Light sucked back into the bowl. The contents—now white as pearls—overflowed onto the sand and red marker patterns. The liquid traced along the writing. Where it touched, light gleamed like a stroke of sunshine.

When all the board was outlined and the bowl emptied, the light winked out again. Sort of. More like it evolved into black not-quite-light with a slight shine. I thought it was the volcanic sand and gold flecks, but those had been transformed into something else like molten glass. The rocks in the spell pattern started to burn. They turned orange like hot coals.

At some point, the outer edges of the spell pattern began to draw inward. Everything massed together and collected around the base of the bowl, then ran upward to pour inside it. Instead of filling the crystal, however, the power of the spell ran out along the strands of copper. When it reached the gargoyles, it spread, coating them in a thin layer of gold-specked black.

I held my breath, my hands tightening on Lorraine's and Jen's.

Nothing happened.

We waited.

Still nothing.

"How do you know it worked?" I whispered.

"They've been stuck in stone form for many years. It could take a while," Damon said.

I had an urge to stomp my foot. My first big magic spell, and it was a big wait and see?

"Did you see that?" Jen asked.

"What?" Lorraine and I said at the same time.

"Check out their eyes."

They glowed orange like the stones Mason had set into the pattern. Only these weren't just inanimate rocks. I could feel the intelligence staring out at us. I shivered. The rage inside them was palpable.

A *crack!* shattered the heavy silence. The black spell skin of one of the beasts zigzagged with fissures, and then it shattered, falling to the patio with the clink of broken glass. The beast inside shuddered and shook itself. His penis retracted and disappeared so fast, I didn't even see where it went.

He had looked big as a statue. Now he was enormous. He stood and spread his wings and suddenly became eight feet tall with muscles boiling inside his massive gray body. Then the whole bunch started moving as the spell shells all cracked apart.

They'd looked strange and ugly before with animal faces, tails, claws, and powerful legs and arms halfway between human and cat. They spoke to one another in oddly soft voices, stretching and flapping wings. One launched up into the sky and flew upward and streaked away. Who'd have thought a rock could fly? And so fast?

It didn't take them long to look around for us. The first one who'd broken free seemed to be the leader. His face reminded me of an Egyptian jackal with a long, squared-off snout and tall, pointed ears. His gaze swept over us before settling on Mason.

He leaped forward, almost too fast to see. He hulked over Mason, his tail lashing as he bent over the slender man. He drew a deep breath and then growled.

"One of the families," he said with pure disgust.

His hand shot out and wrapped Mason's neck. Mason didn't move a muscle.

"We want our mates back."

"Mates?" I repeated, my stomach hollowing as I started leaping to the obvious conclusions.

"Oh, shit," Ben said. "This is bad."

"We invoke blood pact. Give us our mates now, or we will raze every stone of every house we guard. We will bury every member of the families. We will destroy you."

I let go of Lorraine's and Jen's hands and strode out of the shielding. Behind me, Damon swore and followed hard on my heels. The girls and Ben weren't far behind.

"Stop!" I called and came to stop by the angry gargoyle. He twisted his head to look at me. He had whiskers, which struck me as odd for a creature made of rock.

I looked up at him. "The bitch who imprisoned you did awful things to me too," I said. "She's dead. In fact, you'll be glad to hear that one of you crushed her."

"I know," the gargoyle said, his hand or paw still wrapped around Mason's neck. His fingers were long and surprisingly supple. His claws extended a good three inches past the fingertips.

His reply answered the question about whether the gargoyles knew what was going on around them when they were imprisoned. Which meant they probably knew who killed the Wicked Bitch. I wasn't sure I wanted to know. From their perches on the roof, they also would have been able to see my adventures on the rock wall and maybe the track. Plus a lot more than that. They'd witnessed my suffering and humiliation, just like I'd witnessed theirs every single time I looked at the roofline.

"What happened? How did the Wicked Bitch imprison you? Did she do something to your mates?"

I didn't just *want* to know. I *had* to know. I needed to fix this. Put right something Aunty Mommy messed up. Heal a hurt. Maybe if I did, I wouldn't have to regret my whole childhood. I'd have won something good out of it.

His lips and the top of his nose wrinkled into a snarl, exposing daggerlike black teeth. His tongue flicked out. It was oddly blue.

"She summoned us, every adult in our warren. She trapped us and took the females. She forced us to swear blood pact on this house and its land. If we did not, she would slaughter our mates. We could do nothing but agree. It wasn't enough. It amused her to humiliate us. She forced our erections, and when we shifted to stone, she put a spell on us so that we could not shift back unless the place was attacked, and when we were done battling, we must return to stone."

Behind me, Lorraine and Jen gasped. I didn't. This was nothing new. It wasn't even the worst thing Aunty Mommy had ever done.

"What did she do with your mates?"

"We do not know. She would not tell us."

He turned back to Mason. "This one smells of her blood."

"He's her brother," I said. "But until she died, he had no idea where she was or what harm she was doing. He performed the spell to free you. I wouldn't have known how."

The gargoyle glared another long moment then slowly released Mason's throat one finger at a time. He had seven and a thumb.

"Thank you," Mason said, stepping back. "It means little, I know, but I apologize for my sister's behavior. Had we known, we would have stopped her. We wish no enmity with the Halvard people. My family owes great reparation. But first, we must discover your mates. This cannot be allowed to stand."

I could see the steel in Mason, the thing that made him a leader and made men such as Damon serve him. He carried a nobility around him, like a king. Ruling family, I reminded myself. I was seeing it in action.

"How do we find them?" Lorraine asked the question.

The big gargoyle looked at her and sniffed, taking in her scent. I wondered what he learned about her from it. His eyes flamed nearly red.

"We cannot sense them," he said, answering her question.

"Oh, shit," Ben said.

Damon muttered something. Abruptly he walked away, striding into the house. I wanted to follow, but I couldn't leave Mason to deal with the gargoyles alone.

"What does it mean that they can't sense them?" I asked.

Mason kept his eyes on the gargoyle leader. "So long as they are on the earth, they should be able to sense their existence, if not their location. Mated pairs always can. Often members of a warren can as well.

"And since they can't?" I wasn't going to jump to any conclusions.

"They may have been destroyed," Ben said. He sounded as young as he really was. Young and lost.

"No. Aunty Mommy wouldn't have done that."

"How can you know that?" Mason asked, looking hopeful.

My smile was bitter. "Because she wouldn't throw away leverage, and she wouldn't lose the chance to make others suffer. They're somewhere, they're alive, and they need us to find them and rescue them." I knew I was right.

"Where did Damon go?"

"Searching is my guess," Mason said. "Looking for a lock that the key Adriane left me fits into. Maybe she left something to tell us where the female gargoyles are imprisoned."

I ran into the house like my ass was on fire. Lorraine and Jen came with me.

"It's probably disguised with magic."

"So what should we look for?" Jen asked.

"No idea." I stopped and turned around in a circle in the garden room. "But she has to have a hiding place somewhere. Her letter to Mason said it was the heart of her home."

"Does that mean it has to be in the house? Or could it be somewhere else on the property?"

I looked at Lorraine. "I don't know. Why?"

"It's just—anybody who got inside here would go looking for her hidey hole. She had to know that they'd search with magic, and if it could be found that way, then it's too easy. The Wicked Bitch was sly, and she would hide it so well, magic couldn't find it."

"That's true," Jen said, and I nodded.

"Maybe it's not hidden with magic at all," I said. "Maybe what makes it hard to find is that it's so cleverly disguised."

"So we just start pulling books off shelves and twisting sconces and hoping a fireplace spins around into another room or a secret door opens?" Lorraine said doubtfully. "I think that only happens in the movies."

"They've got to get their ideas from somewhere," Jen said.

"Let's give it a shot," I said. "What do we have to lose? Look for places where maybe the wall doesn't go as far as it should, or the outside of the house extends farther than the inside."

"Why don't the two of you start at the top and work your way down. I'll start in the basement," I said, even as goose bumps prickled all over my skin. The last place I wanted to go was the basement. But even more, I didn't want them down there. I didn't want *anybody* down there. I'd rather just seal it up. Better yet, burn the whole place down and walk away.

"What about us?" Ben asked as he, Mason, and the gargoyle came in. The gargoyle's bulk splintered the wood jamb of the French doors.

"Can you have your people start searching the grounds?" I said to him. "They'll be faster since they can fly."

His head snaked back and forth, eyeing the room, and then he nodded. "We will do it." He retreated outside.

"Damon and I poked around this morning and found nothing," Mason said.

"Then we look harder. Go upstairs. Help the girls search the upper floors," I told him and Ben and then hustled away before anybody besides Ajax could join me.

I didn't see Damon, and I was glad. I needed to do this next bit alone.

I went through the kitchen and library and out into the far wing. The basement had a number of entrances. One led down into the opulent wine cellar that had a wet bar and a grand entertaining space packed with couches and chairs. Another led down into a theater room that seated thirty people with an enormous screen. The entrance I was looking for was known only to Aunty Mommy and me. This was the place she liked to conduct punishments when she was more angry with me than usual.

For a torture chamber, it was remarkably well lit, with a high ceiling. Though I knew from experience just how dark it was when the lights went out. I closed the door as Ajax and I went inside. The entry was disguised as a bookshelf, just like in the movies, except once it opened, there were two more doors behind, one after the other. Aunty Mommy was more than a little paranoid.

Once inside, I stood at the top of the stairs as my heart shifted into high gear. Pavlovian response. But I was in control now, I told myself. The Wicked Bitch was dead.

I mustered up the courage to go down the stairs. Ajax stayed at my side, leaning into me as if sensing my distress. Under the stairway was a little cell. Only four feet by four feet, it was made of flat steel bars with a thick steel plate on the floor and another for the roof. There was nothing inside except a steel toilet in the corner. All the luxury my prison afforded.

In the middle of the wall opposite the stairs hung a giant hook about nine feet up. From it dangled two chains attached to a horizontal metal bar, about three feet wide. Manacles hung on the end. A drain on the floor beneath guaranteed a quick cleanup after the floor show.

I stared at the wall for a long minute, my breathing speeding as adrenaline flooded my system. I'd ended up here a lot as a kid. I was always talking back and breaking rules. When I got older, Aunty Mommy had moved me outside to the wall and the track and the pool. She still liked to bring me down here sometimes. She liked to remind me that no matter how strong I was, she could break me.

She always did.

I sucked in a breath and let it out slowly, trying to settle my pounding pulse. This place was just a room and nothing else. Memories couldn't hurt me, no matter how awful. I relaxed my hands. I'd balled them into fists so hard, my nails were getting ready to cut through my skin. I stroked my fingers over Ajax's head to soothe myself.

I knew in my heart that if the bitch had a hiding place in the house, this was where she'd hide it. Nobody but she and I ever came down here, and it was her favorite place. Like a small country where she ruled with absolute authority.

Against the left wall from the steps stood an oak cabinet, five feet tall and six feet wide. Tools filled it. The things she'd use on me. I made myself turn away from the cabinet and the chain wall and moved to my cell. Beyond it was a narrow space. It was the first place I'd thought to look for her hiding spot.

The niche was only six or seven feet deep and barely wide enough to walk down. It dead-ended into an empty wall, painted gray like everything else in the room. I ran my hands over it, searching for a crack or a keyhole—something to indicate it was more than a wall. I tapped, hoping to hear hollow sounds.

After five minutes, I stood back, wondering if I should break it down with magic to see what was on the other side. Instead I turned and examined the two walls on either side. Both searches proved fruitless.

I retreated out of the niche and scanned the room. Nothing looked unusual. Nothing looked like it could be hiding a door. I opened the cabinet, pushing aside the tools of torture and pretending I wasn't about to vomit. I couldn't ignore the chills running through me and giving me goose bumps. Even so, I made a thorough search for hidden levers or buttons. Nada.

Frustrated, I ran my fingers through my hair, holding them on top of my head as I turned in a circle. What was I missing? Or was I just wrong about its being here?

"You got any ideas, Ajax?"

He looked up at me, perking up his ears. Clearly he didn't. I dropped my hands with a sigh.

It *had* to be here. Everything I knew about the bitch who'd raised me convinced me that I was right. I just had to be smart enough to find it.

I examined each of the stair treads, thinking maybe one lifted up or had a spring lever hidden somewhere in it. I checked the railing and examined every square inch of the floors and walls.

Still nothing.

Even though it made no sense for the secret heart of the home to have anything to do with my cell, I checked it too, shuddering and sweating as I went inside. It was bolted to the floor, so moving it wasn't possible.

Even more nothing.

I'd been in here for at least forty-five minutes, and I was just about to give up. I took one more look around, trying to see what I missed. My gaze hooked on the drain.

I crossed to it and squatted down. I put my fingers through the slots and lifted the cover off. Inside was a pipe leading off to the sewers. But about six inches down was a toggle switch. Time and the waste down the drain had turned it nearly black. If I hadn't been looking for it, I never would have seen the switch. I put my hand down inside the pipe and flicked it. A momentary soft whirring sound and then silence.

I scowled as I twisted to look around. Something had changed. I was sure of it. Setting the drain cover back down, I began another search of the space. I gravitated quickly to the little hallway behind my cell. *Bingo*. The dull gray wall now contained a large keyhole, right in the middle. It looked like the kind to take the big skeleton key Aunty Mommy had sent to Mason.

Triumph ran through me. I wanted to shout and pump my fists in the air. Instead I ran back up the steps with Ajax bounding at my heels. I opened the doors into the house. Instantly I heard my name being shouted by several voices.

"Here! I found it! Bring the key!"

I ran back toward the garden room and bumped into Ben coming into the kitchen, followed closely by Jen and Lorraine.

"Where have you been? We've been looking everywhere for you!"

The girls grabbed hold of me, and Lorraine hugged me hard.

I was too excited to pay attention to their concern. "Where's Mason?"

Just then he and Damon came bursting in. Damon looked a little wild. Make that wildly angry.

"I found it," I declared triumphantly.

The Wicked Bitch hadn't been able to hide it from me. I'd beaten her at her own damned game.

"Jesus, we thought something happened to you," Jen said.

I frowned. "What do you mean?"

"You disappeared. Nobody could find you," Lorraine said.

"I was here," I said. "I was just down—"

That's when I realized that they were all about to find out the worst Aunty Mommy had done to me. How could I prepare them?

I glanced at Damon. He'd lost the wild look. In fact, he'd transformed into an inscrutable ice statue. Not the first time I'd seen that—just before he erupted like Mount Vesuvius. I should apologize. I would apologize when we were alone. I'd been thoughtless. No—it was more like I'd forgotten I didn't have to do things alone anymore. It's not like they weren't all going to find out what was down in the basement once I found the keyhole. Pride was a shitty reason to make people worry about me. I'd already put Damon through a lot.

That thought caught me up short. Did I care? That was stupid. Of course I did. I liked him. A lot. He pissed me off to no end sometimes, but I still liked him. Was it love? Could it be? I had no idea. I wasn't sure I wanted to know. I'd just gained independence for the first time in my life. Falling love would mean a relationship. It would mean answering to someone else again. Someone a lot less agreeable than a dog.

"I found the keyhole," I said. I looked at Mason. "Do you have the key?"

He held it up. "Right here."

"Come on, then."

I turned to guide the way. Every step twisted my stomach tighter. I berated myself for feeling nervous. What was I worried about? Pity. I hated pity and I didn't want it. Ajax nosed my hand. I looked down at him. He licked my fingers.

He'd suffered. He'd been through hell. I'd felt sorry for him. So had Lorraine and Jen and Damon too. Did Ajax hate that? No, he was smart enough to be grateful that people cared enough to be angry on his behalf and to be sorry for what had happened. What made me any better than he?

Stupidity. Pride. More stupidity.

I resolved that I had no reason to be embarrassed. That I would not reject the sympathy and sorrow of my friends. I would have a little grace.

Easier said than done.

I opened the first door to the basement, and my chest thickened. With the second, I had to clamp my teeth hard against a weird tremble. With the third, I wanted to throw up. I opened it, blocking the passage. I took a breath and turned around.

"There's a little narrow hallway under the stairs. That's where the lock is."

I stepped back and gestured them all inside. My heart hammered in my chest. I drew a couple of deep breaths as they each went in. Damon went last. He paused on the threshold.

"You going to be okay?" he asked.

For a second, all I could do was marvel. Despite being wall-to-wall pissed, he was thinking of me. He was reaching out to take care of me.

I didn't need anybody taking care of me. I was perfectly capable of taking care of myself, and I liked being independent. But damn, it felt nice all the same. I blinked back tears that had no business falling.

I considered his question. My go-to response was always "I'm fine." I didn't want to be weak in front of anybody. This time I wanted to offer him something real, something more than being flippant.

"Honestly? I'm not entirely sure. I think I'm holding my own."

His brows rose at my candor. He reached out and squeezed my hand and then started through the door. I held on a second, wanting to warn him. But what could I say that would prepare him? There wasn't any way to soften the truth. I let go of his hand and listened to his footsteps on the stairs. They stopped partway down. I could picture him surveying the space and fixing on the shackles hanging on the opposite wall. He wouldn't be able to see the cage yet, but the others would have.

I straightened my shoulders. Well, then. No more looking back at the shadows. I was going to keep my face to the sun, and Aunty Mommy didn't get to have a hold on me.

I stepped through the doorway.

# CHAPTER THIRTY-ONE

Everybody froze as I entered. I almost laughed but they wouldn't have understood that reaction. Somehow that moment with Damon had broken Aunty Mommy's mental grasp on me. I finally realized down in my DNA that she was really out of my life forever.

"All right," I said. "Now you all know the worst of it. I'm not saying that what happened down here was no big deal, but I survived and the Wicked Bitch didn't. I'm ready to move on. More importantly, I want to find the gargoyles' mates and start dismantling Aunty Mommy's evil legacy."

Ben was positively white. "This is barbaric," he said, his voice barely above a whisper. "How could she…?"

Jen started pacing around. Stomping really. She angrily brushed away tears. Lorraine's rolled down her cheeks, and she didn't try to wipe them away. She looked at me and shook her head, unable to find words.

Mason stood grim faced, more so than when he'd confronted the big gargoyle leader. His eyes had narrowed to glittering slits, and he looked dangerous. In that moment, I could see the resemblance to Aunty Mommy. In that moment, he seemed capable of anything.

"I'm beginning to understand the extent of my sister's derangement," he said. "She should not have been allowed to live free."

"This isn't sick," Jen said, whirling on him and getting up in his face. She needed to vent her anger, and he had given her a target. "This is psychopathic. Evil. She shouldn't have been allowed to live at all!"

Mason's gaze rested on her. She didn't look away, didn't back down. Her pale cheeks held spots of bright red. She held her hands clenched at her sides, her body tensed as if she were about to throw down. If Mason didn't use magic, I'd put my money on her to win.

Finally he gave a short little nod. "I can't disagree."

Jen made a *hmph*ing sound and began pacing again, casting angry glances at the cage and the manacles.

Leave it to Ben to stir the flames. "What's in the cabinet?"

"I'd suggest you all not look in there right now," I said. "It's only bound to piss you off more."

I don't know who reached it first—Jen or Damon. They wrenched open doors. Inside, there were three shelves on the top and then a large, open area with pegs along the cabinet sides and the inside of the doors.

Damon slammed his hand down on the top of the cabinet, cracking it and probably shattering his knuckles. Idiot. If I didn't know he could heal himself, I'd have been worried.

Jen started swearing, calling Aunty Mommy every filthy name she could think of and more she made up. Lorraine stopped crying. The professional mask came out, the one she used when dealing with abused animals. Good. I hated seeing her cry.

Mason came to look. Shock and horror flickered over his expression and then he masked up too. Ben looked ready to faint. I ran down the steps and put an arm around him.

"Hey now, breathe. Come on. Sit down." I guided him over to the stairs and sat him down. I pushed his head between his knees. "Deep breaths. Focus on happy thoughts. You're going to be fine."

I turned around and the others stood in a semicircle, watching me. Damon looked agonized and I didn't think it was his rapidly swelling hand.

"That was stupid," I told him. "But at least you didn't pick the wall to argue with."

I was hoping to relieve the tension a little, but it didn't work. I decided that I'd keep talking until they got a grip. Better than this grim silence.

"She started on me before I really remember. As I got older, she wanted more privacy and a more specialized space. She'd had the mansion built and I guess was already planning this particular fun zone. I started getting mouthier and more rebellious, and I ended up down here fairly often. Luckily I had school, so I had a regular escape during the year. When I hit my high school years, she started in with the climbing, running, and swimming, and I was in here less and less often. In the past few years, it's been only once or twice a month for the most part."

Nothing I said seemed to be helping. Maybe if I reminded them why were down here.

"Did you try the key?"

Mason jaw muscles flexed. "No."

"It's just around there behind my—" Oops. "Behind the

cage." I edged past them. "I found a toggle switch in the drain. It triggered the keyhole somehow." I pointed down the little stub of a hall. "There. See?"

Mason went past and inserted the key. He twisted it and the wall dissolved. A wave rippled outward from the lock and the wall morphed into silver dust that faded away like sparks from a fire.

I couldn't see what lay beyond. I followed as Mason stepped inside Aunty Mommy's hidden lair. Within was a bigger room than I had imagined. Elegantly appointed, it contained modern furniture with squared-off lines in blacks, whites, and grays, making the brilliant colors of the abstract paintings pop. I felt a distinct letdown. I couldn't see any signs of storage. It was just a sitting room.

I turned in a circle. Damon stood in the doorway, the girls and Ben behind him.

"There's nothing here," I said, my earlier triumph mutating into disappointment. It was a punch to the stomach. I grabbed hold of myself. No. I wasn't falling down that rabbit hole. The gargoyles' mates needed to be found. If there were no clues here, then we had to start looking elsewhere.

"The heart of the home," Mason murmured, tossing the key in his fingers. "Adriane was paranoid. More than most of us, which is saying something. One lock wouldn't have been good enough for her."

"So we need another keyhole?"

"Maybe."

"Maybe you're the key," Damon said. "She could have tied another lock to you so that only you could open it."

Mason nodded and I couldn't tell if he agreed or was just accepting the suggestion. He walked around the walls, studying the paintings and the furniture. A medallion rug sat in the center of a group of chairs and a love seat. He paused in the middle. My heart jumped but steadied when he returned to the center of the room. He looked up.

A chandelier cast a soft glow over the room. Ornate and crusted with hundreds of crystals, it looked seventeenth-century French.

"That's odd," I said.

"What?" Mason and Damon asked at the same time.

"The room is modern. The chandelier is anything but. It belongs in a room full of Louis XIV furniture. This sort of mismatching is a decorating faux pas of epic proportions for someone as finicky as Aunty Mommy."

Mason nodded. "I agree."

"Does that help us?"

He gave an absent sort of smile. "Possibly."

He walked around the hanging fixture, studying it from every angle. I backed out of his way. I wanted to check Damon's hand, but I didn't think he'd be happy about it. He'd gone back to robo-mode. All business. Yet under that steel exterior burned passion. What would it be like to unleash it?

I shivered and returned my attention to Mason. Now was not the time to think about getting hot and sweaty with Damon. I wasn't sure when that time would come.

"Was there some sort of secret that you and Aunty Mommy shared?" I asked. "Something that she'd count on you to think of and nobody else?"

Mason gave me a startled look. "We were close as children, separated by only a few years. Adriane was younger. She and I...." He trailed away as he looked up again at the light. "Could it be?" he whispered to himself.

He gestured and scarlet magic whirled in his palm. He tossed it upward, and it broke into a cloud of fluttering butterflies. Each settled on one of the chandelier's many crystals. As they touched down, a gold light flashed and the butterfly vanished. The crystals continued to shine. By the time they'd all lit up, the chandelier resembled a small sun. It began to spin. It went slowly at first and then faster, the crystals chiming softly.

All at once the chandelier burst apart. The crystals flew into the air and stopped, a sprinkling of gold stars against the high ceiling. They fell slowly, like feathers, trailing sparks that hung in the air behind them. When the last one fell, the sparks contracted into a shining oval. Mason stepped toward it and placed his hand flat against it. For a second, the world froze. Then everything around us whirled and melted. Instantly I felt seasick. I closed my eyes. My body swayed and I braced myself.

I smelled jasmine.

I blinked and opened my eyes. The room had changed. More than changed. It was half grotto, half sitting room. The modern furniture had disappeared, replaced by walls of stone with niches and hollows full of pillows. The floor rippled up, providing natural chaises mounded with plump cushions. Light came from cupped areas in the walls, dozens of them. A waterfall splashed from a rock wall. Verdant moss grew all around it, and where the moss gave way, white jasmine hung in perfumed curtains.

I turned. A wood-paneled room opened on the wall opposite the waterfall. The walls glowed honey gold. Shelves and cabinets crowded inside, with a desk fitted into the corner.

I started toward the room, but Mason stopped me with a hand on my arm.

"Now's not the time to forget Adriane was paranoid."

I itched to go inside and rifle through her secrets, but he was right. Just because we'd gotten through two locks didn't mean there weren't a dozen more.

I glanced toward Damon. He wasn't there. Neither was the doorway into the torture room. Shit. I bet he was climbing walls with both me and Mason vanishing.

"Where are we?" I asked. "Are we still in the house even?"

"We didn't travel anywhere, if that's what you're asking," Mason said. "We're in bubble that overlays and shares the same space as the room, but in a different dimension. Building that is a rare talent indeed and requires a great deal of power. Adriane didn't have the former and not nearly enough of the latter. Someone must have helped her." He frowned.

"Why do I feel as if I just landed in Oz?" I muttered.

He looked around. "It looks very much like a place we used to go in Ireland, though that spot was not underground." He shook his head. "She spent her magic lavishly here. I suppose she was limited in the real world, afraid that she'd call attention to herself and someone would find her."

He'd paused outside the entry to the secret room. Now he stepped inside. A film of magic wrapped him as though it had been waiting in the doorway like a giant web. It wound around him, turning him into a golden mummy. Thirty seconds later, it melted away into nothingness.

Mason smoothed his hands over his hair and then down his arms. "That was unpleasant," he said.

"That was her hallmark. Do you see anything useful? A binder labeled *Gargoyles* or something?"

He started opening cabinets and examining the

contents of the shelves. After ten minutes, he stepped back into the grotto room.

"I'm afraid this is going to take a while. I want to return you to Damon and the others. Speak to the gargoyles and let them know what we've discovered. I'll continue to search here."

Tired of feeling useless, I agreed.

The return trip proved just as unsettling as the discovery one. Mason repeated the butterfly trick, and even though the chandelier wasn't there, the magic brought us back to the room. The door to the hallway had closed. Mason put the key in the lock and turned it. Outside, Damon whirled around. Ajax jumped up, landing with his paws on my shoulders. He licked my chin. I laughed and scratched behind his ears before pushing him down.

"Where did you go?" Jen demanded, shoving past Damon, who reluctantly backed out of the way. Lorraine crowded in behind her.

"I have no idea. There's another place there or something. Hidden behind magic." I felt the space behind me firm into a solid wall again. "Mason is going to see what he can find."

"So what do we do now?" Lorraine asked.

I shrugged helplessly. "The best thing to do is go home and get some sleep. You two need to go to work. Once Mason finds something, we can figure out the next step."

"I hate to leave without being able to offer the gargoyles more than just crossed fingers," Lorraine said.

"Me too," I said. "But we've been up all night. We're all exhausted and there's nothing else we can do right now. I'll talk to them and let them know we aren't giving up until we find their mates."

"Okay, but...." Lorraine chewed her lower lip.

"What?"

"We want to talk about what happened down here," Jen said.

I nodded. "I know."

"Soon."

"Whenever you want."

# CHAPTER THIRTY-TWO

We trouped back upstairs. Ben had got hold of himself but had lost that happy-go-lucky puppy thing he'd had going on. He appeared to have grown older.

"Do you have anyplace to go?" I asked him as we walked into the kitchen.

"I've got to grab my car and get into the City."

"Are you okay to drive? Maybe you should get a hotel room. I'd put you up, but I'm already crashing with Damon," I said, sliding a look at Mister Stoic.

He'd not said a word since I'd come out of Aunty Mommy's secret lair. His face was shuttered, and he gazed out the window as if we weren't there.

"No, I've got a lab tomorrow." He hesitated. "You need me, though, just call. I want to help with finding the gargoyles' mates. And—"

"And?" I prompted when he didn't continue.

"Our families don't interact much. Sharpentiers are down the ranks quite a bit, but I like you, you know, and we could stay in touch maybe."

I groaned. "I don't care what my DNA is. You and I are friends now. Of course we'll be in touch. I'd have to kick your ass if you didn't call and visit." I dug in my pocket for my phone and passed it to him. "Put your digits into my contacts."

His expression brightened and he practically snatched my cell away. He input his information then called his phone. Once I popped up on his caller ID, he hung up and passed my phone back.

In the meantime, Jen and Lorraine had been casting meaningful looks between Damon and me. If I didn't know better, I'd say they were talking telepathically.

"Why don't we give you a ride, Ben?" Jen asked, linking her arm through his. "These guys still have to talk to the gargoyles. If we hurry, we can grab breakfast before you hit the road.

In all of a few seconds, I was hugged by all three and they took off, leaving me with Damon.

I wanted to ask if he was okay, but who was? And then I wanted to ask if something was wrong, but the answer to that was too obvious for words. I considered asking what exactly was bothering him, but we'd just been hanging out in a place where I'd spent a lot of time getting tortured. Not to mention he was just as frustrated we hadn't found any clues about the gargoyles' mates as I was.

"I'm going outside," I said after a minute of uncomfortable silence and headed out of the kitchen through the garden room and back out to the patio. Ajax padded beside me. I'd begun to really feel my exhaustion. My head felt stuffed full of sawdust.

Half the gargoyles had returned from scouting. The sun would be up soon. I wondered if they'd all return and take up their former positions on the roof or if searchers would turn back to rock wherever they were or if the sun even mattered.

My question was answered a couple of minutes later when several more dropped out of the sky, including the one who seemed to be their leader. He dived for me, landing heavily.

"What do you know?" he asked without preamble.

I shook my head. "Nothing yet. We found a place where there might be information. Mason is checking it out now."

The creature snarled and hissed. The others, listening in, muttered and growled. One punched the wall of the house. The sound was explosive. A hollow appeared as brick turned to powder.

"We demand them back!" the leader declared. "We will not tolerate you holding them captive. We will not serve a house that betrays us." Threat and malice rolled away from him, and his eyes flamed.

"Yeah, about that," I said. "What will it take to free you from this bondage?" I waved at the house.

The gargoyle looked taken aback, which was kind of funny, given how scary looking he was.

"It is not possible," he said finally, and he seemed to deflate a little. "We are bound to protect this house and grounds for all eternity."

Now it was my turn to be surprised. "Eternity? No way."

"It was the oath the witch required. We had no choice."

"Because she took your mates," Damon said.

I hadn't heard him come out. I looked over my shoulder. He stood a little behind me. Talking about watching my back, literally.

"Yes," the lead gargoyle said.

"There has to be some way to free you," I said. "I'll find it. In the meantime, we're still going to be searching for your mates. I won't give up until I find them and bring them back to you."

The gargoyle eyed me for a long moment. I met his gaze, hoping he could see my sincerity.

"We must trust you," he said at last. "We have no choice."

That was not the most ringing endorsement but understandable. "I'll update you on how our search is coming tomorrow night. I'm Beck Wyatt, by the way." I stuck out my hand to shake.

The gargoyle looked at it and then stretched out a giant clawed paw and wrapped my hand in it. His skin felt dry and oddly warm and softer than I'd expected. I thought he would feel like a rock. I could feel the strength in his grip, though, and if he wanted, I was pretty sure he could not only crush my hand, he could break it off without straining.

"Beck Wyatt, I am Torastan, Speaker for clan Mearow."

"I promise I will never stop looking until I find your mates, Torastan," I said.

"Do you keep your promises, Beck Wyatt?"

"Every last one."

"Then I will be glad to see you tomorrow night and hear your news."

He let go of my hand and said something to his fellow gargoyles that I couldn't understand at all, and then they leaped into the air and settled onto their perches. Their poses changed to be more menacing, and this time they weren't flying their penises at full mast. As I watched, they hardened into solid stone, the orange flames of their eyes fading away to nothing.

I sighed and turned. Damon had vanished.

I went into the house and called his name. No answer. I went out the front door.

"Damon?"

He had his shoulder propped against one of the fluted marble columns with his back to me. I held the door for Ajax and then shut it behind myself then went to lean back against the other column, facing him. Neither of us spoke right away.

"Thanks," I said finally.

He didn't look at me. "For what?"

"Letting me handle that."

The corner of his mouth twitched. "Pretty sure you would have kicked my ass if I got in your way."

I smiled. "Maybe. All the same, I know that had to be killing you."

"I wish I'd known," he said. "I would have come sooner."

He was talking about Aunty Mommy and the basement. "I know."

"I wish I could take away all that pain. Take away the memories and the horror you must have suffered. I feel so god-damned helpless! I can't—" His hands clenched as emotion overwhelmed him. He spit off into the bushes.

"I can't say it doesn't matter. I can't say it didn't hurt and that there weren't days I wished I was dead. But I fought back and I survived. I'm not going to let the Wicked Bitch have any more of me than she's already taken."

"What can I do?"

"Feed me. And Ajax. I could use a shower and some sleep before I have to meet with my employees."

"All right. Let's go."

He stepped down and walked to the truck, pulling open the passenger door before going around to get in. He still wasn't looking at me and carefully didn't touch me. I wasn't sure what to make of either.

"Dine in or drive through?" he asked as he pulled out onto the road.

I rolled my window down a couple of inches. "Drive through. I'm ready to collapse."

He took us through a local fast-food breakfast drive-through that served actual food, ordering enough to feed six of us. He passed me the takeout bags full of styrofoam boxes, and I set them on the floor, pushing Ajax's interested nose away.

"You'll get yours," I promised him.

Damon wasn't talking and I was too tired to do much of my own, so it was a silent ride back to the hotel. We took the food upstairs and sat at the small table and ate. Damon had ordered a batch of scrambled eggs and ham for Ajax.

I eyed his swollen hand. "Is there any more water from Banana Buddha's pool? You should drink some."

He shook his head. "All gone."

That was the extent of our conversation. When we were through eating, we stashed the leftovers in the refrigerator.

I showered first and when he went in to take his, I grabbed an extra blanket out of the closet and stole a pillow off the bed. I stretched out on the couch. Ajax hopped up and curled up on my feet. I heard Damon come out of the shower.

"Beck?" He sounded irritated.

"What?"

"Get your ass into the bed. You aren't sleeping out here." He came to stand in front of the couch. The light from the bedroom outlined his bare shoulders and chest, highlighting the curves of his biceps and the way his powerful chest narrowed to a taut waist. My mouth went dry.

"It's your bed. You get to have it."

"Fuck that."

He bent and swung me up into his arms. Ajax jumped down after us but didn't get feisty. Or violent for that matter.

I didn't get much of a chance to savor the satin heat of his skin before Damon dropped me on the bed. I caught sight of his hand. It was swollen and purple with bruises.

"Jesus. You need to ice your hand. Or heal it up."

"I'll heal it later, when I've got time to crash that long."

"You mean when you don't have to worry about me while you're asleep."

"That's exactly what I mean," he agreed, leaning over me to yank back the covers and then shoved me over onto the sheets. He flipped the covers back over me.

I couldn't tear my eyes away from his rippled abs and the way his silk pajama pants hung low on his hips. They looked as if could slide off at any moment. I silently encouraged them to do so.

"Stop looking at me like that," he ordered roughly.

"Like what?"

"Like you want me to do to you what I've been dreaming about since I first laid eyes on you."

"What's that?"

He gave a choked laugh. "If you don't know, then you're an idiot, and one thing I know for a fact is that you are anything but stupid. Go to sleep."

He shut the light off and got into bed—or rather, he got on top of it so that we had the separation of the covers—and turned so his back was toward me. I scowled. That was it? Not even one of those spectacular toe-curling kisses? Maybe a little pillow talk?

I lay there, waiting for him to turn over and give me what I ached for. He didn't move. Instead, Ajax leaped up onto the bed and curled up at my feet.

It took a long time to fall asleep. I tossed restlessly while Damon remained relentlessly silent and still.

A few hours later, I woke with my head on Damon's arm, his leg slung over mine, his other arm draped over my waist. His large hand cupped my breast, thumb circling slow torture over my nipple. I caught my breath and squeezed my legs together, trying not to moan as my insides turned to honey and sharp pleasure spread from where he stroked.

Was he awake? His chest rose and fell with slow, even breaths. Oh, God. He wasn't. That was good, even though my body totally disagreed. I wasn't going to be able to take much more of this. I put my hand over his and pushed it down. I lay there, my body humming like a plucked guitar string. I wanted so much to just turn over and lose myself in the heat of his touch. I took deep breaths to slow my racing pulse.

What time was it? Feeling as I did, I had a snowball's chance in hell of falling asleep again. Maybe I should try to slip out of bed and move back to the couch. Holding my breath, I lifted my head and shifted forward, drawing my leg out from under Damon's. As I leaned away from his chest, he made a sound of protest and gathered me close again. Once again his hand covered my breast, and an agony of delight surged through me. I had to either get some distance or give in to my craving for him.

I went to push his hand down again. I'd got it off my breast when I heard his breath hiss between his teeth. His body tensed. I froze.

"Beck?" Damon's voice was midnight rough, and it sent shivers over my skin.

"Yes." I sounded as breathless as I was.

His hand flexed under mine and then pushed upward

again to cover my breast. He cupped and massaged it gently. I made a sound in the back of my throat and arched my back, pushing into his grasp. His arm tightened over my ribs as his fingers teased my nipple. He strung kisses down my neck and along the top of my shoulder, the heat of his chest like a fire against my back. I shuddered and wiggled my ass into him, feeling his hard length pressing into me.

Abruptly he flung himself back, rolled over, and swung up to his feet, leaving me cold and aching. He was panting like he'd been sprinting.

"I'm sorry. That was— I shouldn't have done that."

"It's not like I wasn't enjoying myself," I said crankily, feeling like my emotions were pinballing around inside me. I was glad of the darkness so he couldn't see how flushed I was.

"I want you, Beck. More than I've ever wanted any woman in my life. But I don't want you doing something in the heat of the moment that you'll regret later. I'm not sure I could survive that. I want a real shot with you. I know you're attracted to me, but I also know I fucked up when I tried to grab you that first day and then kept secrets about your family. You have every reason not to trust me. I need to earn your trust. I need to know that if and when we make love, it'll be because you chose me and that our first time won't be the last."

My mouth had gone dry as I listened to his impassioned speech. I pulled myself up and faced him. I drew my knees up to my chest, wrapping my arms around my knees.

"In your world—the magic world where you and Mason come from—do any of you get happily ever afters? Or is it all contracts and negotiations?" I wondered what Damon's childhood and home had been like. I realized I didn't know a lot about him. Well, except for the fact that he was thoughtful, kind, and protective, not to mention hot as hell.

My question startled him, and he stood silent a long moment. "Over the years, line management has taken priority in the ruling families."

"So that's a no? What about your family? Are your parents together, or are you a contract baby too?"

"Contract. I was raised with my father's line. Wait—" He switched on the nightstand light and faced me ferociously. "You don't think that's what I want from you, do you? Babies to strengthen the power of my line?"

"I didn't," I said. "But now that you mention it...." I trailed off. I didn't think so at all, but I wanted to tease him. His faced darkened with fury and more than a little hurt. Uh-oh. I should probably put him out of his misery.

"Okay, I've thought about it. No."

He shook his head as though he'd been slugged in the jaw and his head was reeling. I smiled. I liked being able to throw him off balance.

"Do you mean it?"

He really was worried about my thinking that.

"You wouldn't trick me like that. If you wanted a baby from me, you'd say so."

Something crossed his expression, something like shell shock.

"What?"

"You having my baby," he choked out and then nothing else.

I frowned confusion. "What about it?"

"It's sexy as hell."

"You have a very odd idea of sexy," I said. "A hormonal woman with swollen everything and a beer gut the size of a base drum. Though I've heard that the swelling includes giant breasts, so I can see how that part might be a turn-on."

This was such a surreal conversation. The idea of my ever getting pregnant had never occurred to me. Hell, I'd barely lost my virginity. Though looking at him right now in the soft glow of the light, I wouldn't mind practicing making one. He was mouthwatering. I wanted to explore every ripple and swell of his hard muscles with my fingers and tongue.

"If you keep looking at me like that, I'm going to have to come over there," he said in a low, smoky voice.

"That's the second time this morning that you've threatened me with a good time."

He dragged his fingers through his hair. "You're killing me."

I would have said I was sorry but I wasn't. Not even a little bit. But if we went down this road, it wouldn't be casual. Not for either of us. Did I want that? Did I want to try a relationship with Damon? I'd never dated anybody before, and this would be jumping in with both feet. We hadn't even gone out on a basic date.

I did like him—a lot. He was smart, funny, brave, dependable, sexy, and thoughtful. Plus, I wanted to lick him from head to toe like a lollipop. If I could fall in love with any man, he'd be my top choice. But I wasn't ready to say he was the one for me. I needed time and maybe some normal dating.

"Maybe you should ask me out," I said.

He blinked at me, clearly trying to collect his scattered wits. "You want to go out on a date?"

"I don't know what your experience with women is," I said, "but I've never actually been on a real date. I kind of lost my virginity in the back of a car when I was seventeen, which was not such a great experience, by the way. Until you started kissing and touching me, I thought sex was pretty overrated. Anyhow, that backseat fumbling around is about the entire extent of my love life.

"I've never wanted to get involved with anybody. It wasn't fair. Not with Aunty Mommy hanging over my head. It was bad enough she went after the girls. I wasn't dragging anybody else into my shit storm of a life. My point is I need to start in the kiddie pool before jumping into the ocean."

He closed his eyes and took a deep breath, letting it out slowly. Was that disappointment? Irritation? Then in one fluid motion, he opened his eyes and crawled back onto the bed. He settled with his knees on either side of my ankles, my upraised knees between us. He leaned forward, grasping my head in both hands.

"We'll go as slow as you need to. I know you don't need me to tell you, but any time I cross lines, kick my ass. I'll back off."

With that, he captured my lips in a slow, sweet kiss that melted my bones. When he pulled away, I was gripping his arms to keep from flying away.

"*That's* your idea of the kiddie pool?" I sounded as shaken as I was.

He grinned. "Maybe you should kick my ass."

"I can't. You turned me into marshmallow fluff."

"I'll have to remember that for future reference."

"This doesn't do anything to solve our sleeping problem."

"I'll take the couch."

"That doesn't seem very fair. If you hadn't gone all caveman and dragged me in here, then you'd be cozy warm and asleep right now with Ajax and me out on the couch."

"Trust me. I wouldn't be sleeping. You'd have been keeping awake."

"You slept fine until you started sleep-pawing me," I pointed out.

He chuckled. "I'd better get to the couch, or I might start again."

"What time is it?"

He turned and looked at his watch on his nightstand. "Nearly seven."

"I'm not sure I'm going to be able to go back to sleep," I said. "Maybe you should stay here and I'll go—"

"What?"

I shrugged. "Watch TV? Or go outside. Ajax is going to need a walk." I'd love to go running, but I still had to get some clothes and shoes for that. Maybe tomorrow. Today, really.

Damon just nodded. His lack of protest surprised me.

"You're not going to tell me not to go walking by myself? Not that I would be. Ajax is pretty ferocious."

"He is. So am I. We'll both go with you."

I rolled my eyes. "I don't need a keeper."

He picked up one of my hands and kissed my wrist. "Humor me."

"You're not exactly humoring me."

He sobered and studied my palm as if he couldn't bring himself to meet my gaze. "I'm doing my best here, Beck," he said gruffly. "Everything I am wants to lock you safe inside until I can find the bastards who went after your shop. I'm scared shitless of you getting hurt. I know that's not reasonable. Even if it was, I know you'd start hating me pretty quick if I tried it. But I need to do something to protect you, especially after seeing that hellhole last night. I'll go nuts if I can't." He lifted his gaze again. His eyes held a primal fire. "So please let me be a pain-in-the-ass bodyguard."

He was asking and that meant a lot. I had a feeling if I said no, he'd be stalking me from afar and keeping an eye on me that way. A few days ago, that probably would have infuriated me. Now it felt more like we were a team. He was trying to find a compromise that would make both of us happy. Could I do less?

Well, yes. But I since I wasn't actually a bitch, I wasn't going to.

"Okay."

"Okay?" he repeated. "Just like that. No arguments?"

"You sound disappointed."

"No. Not at all. I may be a little surprised. Shocked. Floored."

"I get it."

He leaned in and pressed a fast kiss to my lips and then stood. "I'll get dressed. Maybe I'll grab a cold shower while I'm at it."

Once the bathroom door closed, I fell back onto the bed. My heart was thumping. My head reeled.

The bathroom door opened, and Damon stepped back into the room. He had a towel around his waist and nothing else. My gaze ran up his muscular legs and stopped where they vanished beneath the white terrycloth. All my hormones kicked up into a whirling storm of desire. I squeezed my eyes shut before I jumped up and ripped away the towel with my teeth.

"About that date," he said. "Can we start this morning with breakfast? Coffee? Both?"

His eagerness turned my insides warm and gooey. I felt feminine. Desirable.

"Sure," I said, my voice sounding strangled. "Can you go cover yourself up now? I'm dying here."

He laughed and stepped back inside. His towel landed on my legs as the door clicked shut.

Wicked man.

# CHAPTER THIRTY-THREE

"I probably should tell you something," I said as I sipped my coffee.

Damon and I sat in a little hole-in-the-wall restaurant owned by two extraordinary chefs who'd left the hustle and bustle of San Francisco to settle here. I'd ordered crème brûlée French toast with bacon, of course, and Damon had a lobster hash with eggs over easy. We'd taken a square table in a corner, our knees touching. Every so often, he ran his hand along my thigh.

"That sounds ominous."

"You'd know better than I would. When I met Ben, he told me about this thing called the Proclamation Server. Somebody sent an e-mail announcing my existence and where I live. It came from Aunty Mommy's e-mail address. That's how Ben knew where to come find me."

"I wondered," Damon said darkly. He pulled out his cell and started check his e-mail. He scowled and then snorted. "Nice reply."

"I thought so. Ben also taught me to shield myself so people couldn't find me."

"I should have done that," he said grimly.

"Why didn't you? No, wait, I know. You've been shielding me, haven't you? So I didn't need to know how."

"It seemed prudent and you didn't exactly seem willing to let me teach you anything."

I grinned and leaned toward him. "I'm willing to let you teach me now," I said. "Where do you want to start?"

His eyes flamed and he clenched his fingers on his fork. Lucky for him, he'd punched the cabinet with his off hand, or he'd have had trouble eating. "You're an evil woman. You know that?"

I smiled and ran my tongue over my lower lip. "I don't know what you mean," I said innocently.

Without warning, he pulled me close and kissed me. It was hot, quick, and devastating. If I'd been standing, I'm pretty sure I'd have fallen over.

He pulled back, his eyes locking with mine. The desire in his eyes made me shake.

"I think you might be the evil one," I said huskily.

"Just giving as good as I get."

It took me a couple of minutes to cool off enough to remember what we'd been talking about. "Who would have sent that message? And why announce my existence?"

"I wish I knew. Whoever it was, they wanted to stay anonymous."

"Could it be the same person who destroyed my shop?"

"The timing's highly coincidental. I just don't know what the game could be. If they just wanted to out you to the magical world, why attack your place? And why go after your aunt?"

"You're saying you think Aunty Mommy's murder, the vandalism, and the e-mail are all connected?"

He nodded.

"Okay. The cop shows always ask who benefits from the crimes. Is there anybody you can think of who does?"

"Too many."

That took me aback. "Seriously?"

He set down his fork and focused just on me. "Think about it. You and Mason benefit from Adriane's death. He inherits and you get free of her. Then there are your parents. Her death brings you back into the fold. Until you are twenty-seven, your life is critical to their survival. Then there are Adriane's enemies. Who knows how many people she'd angered enough to want revenge? There are at least a half dozen that I know of littering her old life. Then there are her business dealings. If she's dead, do those fall through? Did competitors knock her out of the way?"

My head had begun to throb. "I get it. That avenue of investigation isn't going to help us much." Something occurred to me. "Who benefits from vandalizing my place? I don't have a lot of competitors, and it's not a cutthroat business. The whole thing seemed more angry—like a tantrum. Why?"

Damon gave a little shrug.

"You still think whoever it was came for me and, when I wasn't home, they got pissed and tore the place apart."

He grimaced. "I did say that someone might be after you."

"Aunty Mommy's killer. That didn't seem real likely."

"And now?"

"It's a definitely possibility—depending on why someone killed her. The dumping of the gargoyle on her seems personal. There has to be a thousand better ways to kill someone. This one is symbolic. But of what?"

We poked at the question for a while but couldn't come to any concrete conclusions. Hell, we couldn't come to any semisolid conclusions. I changed subjects.

"Where could Aunty Mommy have hidden the gargoyle females? She had to have put them somewhere. She never would have crushed them up into gravel. Not if she might have a use for them at some point. Speaking of which, why not use them for guarding somewhere like the males?"

I felt like I was practically speaking a foreign language. The whole conversation was completely unreal. Gargoyles, for fuck's sake.

"It's risky to force gargoyles into service and requires a great deal of magic. But that magic needs constant renewal —even with a blood binding."

"What is that anyway?" I asked, interrupting.

"It's a ritual that binds their service for a hundred years. It's rarely given because it could destroy an entire warren. The females can't breed without males and may choose to join other warrens. Though gargoyles generally mate for life, a blood binding will take priority, and some females can't live with that. In this case, it sounds as if the males took the binding to protect the warren."

"For eternity. Not a hundred years, either. The females don't make that sort of binding?"

He shook his head. "Never. They are the heart of a warren. Its health and safety is their only priority, save for their own children. A blood binding wouldn't take because they'd never put anything above those two things."

"Coercing their males by holding the females hostage wouldn't sit well with the ladies," I said. "Especially since that threatens the well-being of the warren. The Wicked Bitch would have had to do something serious to keep them from rioting and fighting back. At the same time, she'd want to preserve them in case they became useful. She'd probably be thinking she could use the males to force the females into temporary service. In the end, she'd have had to neutralize them somehow or find herself at the mercy of a pack of angry gargoyle females."

"That's my guess," Damon agreed.

"So where would she put them?"

"There are couple key requirements. First, natural elements erode magic. So she couldn't put them outside or drop them in the river. She also wouldn't put them underground or surrounded by earth. It amplifies their strength. Second, she'd need to recharge her containment spells fairly regularly. Female gargoyles have magical abilities and will fight those spells. Remember, the males said they couldn't feel their mates, so however they are being held, it involves quite a lot of power."

I thought about that. "All right. She needed somewhere out of the weather that she could access regularly. I'm not sure that helps a whole lot." Or did it? "She'd want total control of the space, which means she'd have to own it. Then she could install security and keep others out."

I looked excitedly at Damon. "Maybe she's got another property we don't know about. If so, then there has to be records at the courthouse. We should go down there and —" Damn. "It'll have to be after my employee meeting," I said, deflating a little.

"I can go check while you're at your meeting. It shouldn't take me long."

My brows rose. "I thought you wanted to stay glued to my side?"

"I do, but you should be safe enough surrounded by your employees in a diner."

"You'll have to take Ajax with you," I said. "He won't be

able to come inside with me." Right now the big dog was in Damon's truck with the windows rolled down.

"We'll be fine. I won't make him bite me again."

"Make him?"

"I was getting loud and angry. He thought I was threatening you. It was my fault."

"I don't think that's the way it's supposed to work," I said. "You weren't actually threatening me."

"After what that poor guy has been through, I can't blame him. Can you?"

"Obviously not."

He checked his watch then signaled for the waiter to bring the bill. "It's almost nine-thirty. We should go."

We tussled a moment over who should pay the bill.

"First, this is a date, so I want to pay," Damon said.

"Why can't I?"

"I asked you out. That's the way it works. Anyhow, you need to be putting your money into fixing your place. Unless you're going to let me help you out on that front?"

I gave an adamant shake of my head.

"I didn't think so. I can contribute in this tiny way, so let me."

I didn't argue anymore. On the way out, I realized I should apologize.

"That wasn't exactly much of a date. All we did was talk murder and vandalism. Not exactly romantic."

"You can make it up to me at dinner."

"Are you asking me on a second date?"

"I'd ask you for a couple hundred right now, but you'd probably think I was being presumptuous."

"How's your hand?" I asked. It had turned purple and was swollen, though he was using it a little.

"Hurts."

"If I agree to go out to dinner, will you heal yourself after?"

"If you promise not to go wandering off alone."

"Deal."

# CHAPTER THIRTY-FOUR

The diner where I'd asked Kenny to arrange the meeting was about twenty minutes away. Damon pulled up in the parking lot. I petted Ajax and told him to behave then reached for the door handle.

"Hey," Damon said huskily then pulled me back to kiss me. One of those toe-curlers.

When he pulled away, I was breathless again. He smiled with smug satisfaction at my response.

"You're entirely too pleased with yourself," I complained, wishing he'd kiss me again.

"I won't lie. It's sweet as hell to see how I affect you. Gives me hope."

"Makes you cocky, is what it does."

"That too."

He kissed me again and then gently pushed me away. "You've got a meeting, and I need to do some research. I'll be back in an hour or so. If I'm late, wait."

"Yessir," I said with a little salute as I swung open the door. I figured the meeting was going to take more than an hour.

He pulled away as I went inside the glassed-in outer entry. Another set of doors led into the main lobby. I reached for one of the inner doors and it opened. I found myself face-to-face with Garrett.

"Beck!" He pulled me into a hug. "I just heard what happened. I wanted to tell you how sorry I am. Why would anyone do something so horrendous to you?" He held me away from himself to look at me then frowned. "What happened to you?"

My cuts and bruises from my trip on the river had faded quite a bit, but the welts from the cuts were still red. "I took a tumble into the river. I'm fine."

"You've been through hell since I've been gone. I'm so very sorry."

I smiled. "Thanks. That means a lot." And it did. While Garrett and I weren't super close like Jen, Lorraine, and Stacey, I still considered him a friend.

He smiled. "That's not the only reason I'm here. I've got a check for you. I wanted to bring it right away. You might need some liquid funds right about now."

"You're so sweet. Thank you. I definitely could use it."

He reached into the inside pocket of his suit and then frowned. "I left my wallet in my briefcase. It's in the car. I spoke to Kenny. I know you have a meeting." He checked his watch as if he were late. "I can run and fetch it. Unless—do you have a moment to come get it?"

"Sure."

We followed the sidewalk along the front of the restaurant around to the side. He was parked in the first slot of the rear parking lot, where the sidewalk dead-ended.

"How was your trip?" I asked.

"Quite successful. In fact, I wrapped up so quickly, I returned a few days early."

We reached his car. It was a low-slung sedan with dark-tinted windows and four doors. He opened the door of the back seat then bent in to rummage in his briefcase. I glanced up at a couple of crows squawking in the crepe myrtle beside us. Garrett straightened and I turned to look at him—just in time to get a face full of powder.

I coughed, inhaling the little gray cloud. Instantly my body turned to pudding. Garrett caught me as I sagged. He opened the front door and put me inside, reclining the seat to help keep me from sliding to the floor. He shut the door and came around to the driver's side.

Once inside, he took out a pair of handcuffs and put them on my wrists. I could do nothing to stop him. None of my muscles responded to my commands. I tried to speak, but all I could manage was a little breath of sound.

"Don't worry. I'm not going to hurt you," he said, patting my leg. "Just relax." He took my purse and dug inside for my cell phone. He shut it off and then popped out the battery. "There. That will make it harder for anybody to find us."

He started the car and slowly drove out of the parking lot. Inside, panic rolled through me. What was he *doing*? I struggled to make myself speak, to move, anything. I drew on my magic. Nothing happened.

I was helpless.

"You probably want to know what's happening," he said. "It actually won't make a lot of sense, but I'll try. You see, I've been looking for you most of my life. Much of my family has. This is the part you won't understand." He glanced toward me. "Or maybe you will. Maybe Matrovani and your uncle explained.

"Your aunt, who pretended to be your mother for your whole life, kidnapped you as a child and disappeared. She left a huge mess behind. My family—the Sandrinis—have long been on the bottom of the ruling families. It wasn't always that way. But after some devastating illnesses and other unfortunate events, we dropped in the ranks. We'd worked for years to raise our status but hadn't been able to negotiate business deals or child contracts with anyone in the upper tier. We weren't able to offer enough advantages and considerations in those contracts.

"That all changed when my father managed to convince your family—the Wyler Symms—to join us in an investment opportunity. It would have been worth more money than I can say, but more importantly, it would have established the Sandrinis as the only major source of Inua in the world. That's a substance used in many spells that is difficult to make. We were working on a process of refining it, and with the Wyler Symms's money and access to their library, we would have succeeded."

His lip curled on his next words, his voice dripping bitter venom. "But then you came along and ruined everything." His hands tightened on the wheel, knuckles gleaming white.

"When Adriane disappeared, she left behind letters accusing several families—including mine—of colluding with Osterraven in his deceit. We hadn't, but they believed that malignant bitch. The pending contract was dissolved and Wyler Symms closed their doors to us. So did Osterraven and every other upper-tier family. We fell to the gutter of society. Few would talk to us; fewer would share their line genes with us. Not at the risk of being ostracized.

"Our only choice was to search for you and Adriane and bring you both back. We hoped it would demonstrate we'd had no part in the whole mess. Years passed and no one could pick up her trail. Then five years ago, I found her. I couldn't believe she'd totally cut herself off from the magical world. I decided that the best place for her to remain hidden while still obtaining information was the Proclamation Server. I was right. She'd been logging in every so often since she disappeared. Nobody monitors logins. From there, it was just a matter of tracking her. Thank God for modern technology."

He fell silent for a few minutes as he negotiated the downtown traffic. His story hadn't told me anything about what he was up to, but whatever it was, he'd been planning it for years. How long? I tried to remember when we first met. Aunty Mommy had introduced us at some sort of charity event. Apparently she hadn't recognized a man from the family she'd destroyed—if Garrett's story was true, which I thought was likely. He had no reason to lie, and the Wicked Bitch reveled in being vindictive. That had been when I was just starting Effortless Estates.

"My grandfather believed that bringing you back would restore our position in society. I knew better. Your line families would never let it be known they were wrong. I wanted to make the Wyler Symms and Osterraven families pay. I had originally planned to kill your aunt and then you, and through you, your parents. I even put a curse on the jewelry I gave to you after I killed your aunt. I don't know how you escaped it. The curse was quite potent."

*He'd* cursed me? Not the Wicked Bitch? If I could have, I'd have hammered him in the balls for that. And another time for kidnapping me. Who was I kidding? I wouldn't have stopped there. I wanted to hang him up and use his ball sack for a punching bag.

"I planned to kill you one night at the shop, but you weren't there. I'm afraid I lost my temper. That's when I realized that killing you would be a waste of first-tier bloodlines. I should be breeding you. Not just me—all the males in my family. Every year you could produce twins or triplets. In just ten years, we could have twenty or thirty children, all bearing Wyler Symms–Osterraven DNA. In less than thirty years, we'd have the blood talents to wedge our way back into the ruling tier. No one could stop us."

Thirty children? Who the fuck was he kidding? But if he kept me helpless like this, how would I object? How could I even hope to stop him?

Fear thundered through my veins like nothing I'd ever felt before. Even the Wicked Bitch hadn't caused such terror as this. With her, I'd still been me. I'd still had a life. But with Garrett, I'd be nothing more than a uterus. I'd be kept incapacitated, unable to fight or run. I couldn't pull up any magic either. I was truly helpless with no chance at freedom or rescue in sight.

Panic overwhelmed me. For a few minutes, my vision went black as my blood pressure hiked up off the charts. I started to pant as I fought against the weight of my fear. It noosed my throat and squeezed my heart. Finally I sort of passed out. Everything around me moved in and out of focus. Garrett's voice was far away and tinny, as if he spoke from the bottom of a deep hole.

I came out of the fog slowly. He was still talking. He wanted to brag, I realized. He wanted me to know how clever he'd been.

"...brilliant stroke of genius. Don't you think? I'm betting they'll be here before the end of the day. I figure they fueled their jets the second my e-mail came through about you. Now I won't have to kill you to get at them. I've already set the trap. I have to just sit back and wait for them to walk in."

He giggled merrily. It was so out of character for the

elegant, urbane man I thought I'd known. He was giddy with triumph. "I can't wait to see their faces." He glanced toward me again. "Well, their eyes, anyhow. The mesmer dust immobilizes most muscles." He shrugged. "I suppose I can't have everything. At least they'll know *I'm* the one killing them. *I'm* the one who outwitted them. *I'm* the one getting the last laugh. I was so disappointed I had to get your aunt from a distance. She didn't know I'd killed her. It's really such a shame." He shook his head but then his mood brightened.

"After I take care of them, you and I will go start making babies. I have to tell you, I'm looking forward to it. I've always found you quite attractive."

He scowled at me. "I saw you kissing Matrovani in the parking lot. You didn't fuck him, did you? Well, no matter. I can abort the pregnancy for you and make sure my seed takes. The first time, anyhow. The second time I'll offer you to my Uncle Thomas. I think children with him will have a lot of potential."

Everything he said horrified me, and yet I could do nothing. I again tried to summon magic, but nothing happened. My body was nothing more than a wet rag.

I was startled when he headed toward Aunty Mommy's estate. Hope burst like a star in my chest. The gargoyles! They could help me if I could make them aware I needed help. Or Mason. He could come out of the secret room at any moment. He'd sent away house staff and grounds crew last night. For how long?

Garrett seemed entirely too confident as he pulled in.

He clicked open the garage door and pulled inside. So much for the gargoyles even seeing me.

He carried me inside the house. There was no sign of any staff. He took me into a small sitting room where Aunty Mommy had liked to serve tea when she had visitors. He sat me in an armchair and propped me upright with the help of throw pillows. I felt like a life-sized doll. What little hope I had of rescue drained when I saw Mason lying opposite on the couch, his legs and arms bound. His stared, unblinking and unmoving.

Garrett pulled him upright so we could look at each other. I could see horror flicker in Mason's eyes, and fear. Or maybe that was just a reflection of mine.

"There now," Garrett said. "We're all ready for company. Let's hope they arrive soon. I'd like to get this party started."

Time drifted slowly past. Garrett fiddled and paced, walking in and out of the room impatiently. He kept checking his watch and then started playing with his phone. Every so often, he'd stand by the window facing the front of the house and just stare out at the driveway.

I was fast arriving at one conclusion: the world of magic and these ruling families was cancerous. It produced psychopaths. I wanted nothing to do with it. Not that Garrett planned to give me a choice.

Fuck him. I was going to find a way out of this if it killed me. I'd rather it did than let him turn me into a brood mare.

About a half hour into waiting, Garrett began to chatter again. He seemed almost manic and so very different from the man I'd come to know over the years. Only I'd never known him. I'd been completely conned. I wondered if any part of the man he'd showed me was real.

"You know, I haven't shown you my goodies," he said to

us. He picked up a leather duffel bag from behind the door and set it on the coffee table. One by one, he began pulling out weapons. The first was a combat knife. He held it up, turning it to watch the light flashing across the blade.

"I haven't decided how to kill everyone yet," he said. "With this, I could slice an artery or throat, or go right for the heart. I've never stabbed anyone, though, and I'm not sure if it's the best option."

Next he pulled out an ice pick. It was longer and more heavy duty than any I'd seen. "This is used for chipping ice on a river or lake so people can ice fish. I like that it's smaller than the knife. More elegant. I wonder if it would be easier to stab into the heart. Or I read a mystery one time where the murderer shoved an ice pick through the victim's ear. There wouldn't be a lot of blood that way. That's always a positive."

Next came a gun. "Shooting's probably the easiest method. It's a little impersonal, though. I think I might like to strike a killing blow myself."

He set the gun beside the other two weapons and drew out several jars, each stoppered with a large cork covered in different-colored melted wax—green, pink, and yellow.

"I really like the idea of a good poison. Then it's still a personal kill and the target dies painfully, which is perfect justice. I brought several kinds." He held up the green one. "This is tetrodotoxin made from puffer fish. It's a slower death, depending on dosage. I think I might enjoy watching that." He set it down and picked up the pink jar.

"Now this one is good old cyanide, the workhorse of poisons. It's painful but fairly quick. This last one is wood alcohol. It works fast and is also painful." He set the yellow jar next to the others and considered all his weapons.

"I just don't know. I considered strangulation, but

that's just so crude. Like beating someone over the head. No style."

As I listened, it began to sink in that he was really going to go through with his plans to kill people and make me his incubator. I guess I hadn't really believed it. It was too James Bond villain to be believable. Only it wasn't. The certainty sank down into my heart and jabbed me full of terror. I was helpless. Mason was helpless. Anybody who might rescue us would end up just as helpless. We were so screwed.

It was close to another hour later when Garrett perked up. "They're here," he sang.

Disappointment crushed his excitement a moment later. "Oh, it's just that bastard Matrovani. He's got your girlfriends with him. That's unfortunate." He shook his head. "It can't be helped. I can't leave witnesses."

My panic and terror shot up like Old Faithful as Garrett grabbed the handgun and scurried out of the room. On some level, my brain put together the fact that he didn't need to feel the personal kill with the girls and Damon. A gun would suit him fine. Once they were hit with the dust, he could just put the barrel against their heads and they'd be gone.

Thought abandoned me and I exploded into smoke. The mesmer dust hung in the air like tiny black stars. As I had with the curse, I knocked the particles away from me. They sifted onto the woven silk rug.

I bolted after Garrett. I didn't solidify. I couldn't go through the wall, so I flowed out the door and streaked along the corridor toward the front vestibule. I reached it just as Garrett did. He'd stopped outside some kind of spell circle he'd drawn along the outer edge of the entryway. It bisected the threshold between where he'd stopped and the doorway. He took a glass ball full of mesmer dust out of his pocket, cocking his arm up to smash it inside the circle.

I could hear voices on the other side of the door. The handle turned and the door thrust open. Damon and the girls rushed inside. The symbols of the spell flared, and Garrett's arm thrust downward, the glass ball rushing to smash against the floor.

In rapid-fire thoughts, I understood immediately that the spell would contain the dust to keep Garrett from falling under its power. I also understood that that's all it would do.

I lashed out with a tentacle of magic and snatched the ball before it could hit the floor. In the same moment, I slammed Garrett against the wall. I smashed him against it three times, putting body-shaped impressions into the sheetrock. He cried out the first time, and by the third, he'd slumped, his eyes closing. Blood ran down his neck from where his scalp had split.

I dropped him to the floor and then carefully settled the glass ball into Damon's hand. All at once the desperation left, and I coalesced into flesh. I fell to the floor, landing facedown, my head thumping on the polished marble. Pain exploded in my forehead, cheek, and nose. Blood streamed out my nostrils as I fought to catch my breath. It had been entirely knocked out of me.

Hands grabbed me and pulled me over to sit me up. The girls gabbled words I couldn't make sense of. My head spun from the shock of hitting the floor. I was having a tough time making myself focus.

Damon picked me up and carried me to a nearby couch and laid me down. He disappeared and Jen stroked the hair out of my face.

"Are you okay? Beck, come on, talk to us."

I grabbed her hand and held it tight. "Garrett was going to kill you."

Silence. I started wriggling to sit up, and then Stacey was there with some ice wrapped in a dishtowel. Lorraine pressed a damp towel against my nose.

"We need to go to the emergency room," she said. "She might have broken her cheek bone or the orbital bone. Her nose is definitely broken."

I groaned.

"She said that Garrett was trying to kill us," Jen said in a taut voice.

"Garrett? But he's always so sweet," Stacey said.

"So's antifreeze but drinking it will kill you," Lorraine said, sounding shaken.

"Has a gun," I managed. "Mason needs help too."

"Damon's making sure Garrett's not going to be a problem," Stacey said. "He's out cold. You can do the poltergeist thing?"

I choked out a laugh. I loved that she was always curious and rarely fazed by much of anything. "Not on purpose."

I heard Damon's quick, heavy footsteps. He leaned above the others, his face black with anger and worry.

"Are you okay? What's the matter with Mason?"

I translated that to mean: What did Garrett do to you, and are you both going to die?

"That glass ball has this stuff Garrett called mesmer dust. He's a Sandrini," I said, going off on a short tangent trip.

At that name, Damon swore something in what sounded like Italian. I didn't know he spoke another language. It sounded so pretty, even when I was pretty sure the words themselves were vile.

"It paralyzes you. You can hear but not move."

"How long did it take to wear off?" Damon asked.

"It didn't. I changed and was able to sweep it out of me."

"She needs to get to the hospital," Lorraine told Damon firmly. "Now."

He hesitated then I heard the chink of keys as he passed them to her. "I'd better stay here. See what else the bastard might have done."

"He said someone was coming. He wanted to kill them. Revenge. I think it might be my parents." In fact, I was sure of it. Who else would come running?

The pain was starting to overcome the shock, and my face was throbbing. My whole head pounded in time with the pulsing throb.

"Can you help Mason?" I asked as the girls helped me to my feet. I swayed and Jen and Stacey braced me, pulling my arms over their shoulders. I could see out of only my right eye. My left had swelled shut. My front teeth felt odd. I ran my tongue along them and discovered a ragged edge. I'd chipped it. Yippee. When I fell, I went all out.

The rest of me ached too. I'd pretty much belly flopped like a rag doll onto the marble floor from a good five feet above. My ribs hurt every time I breathed. I wondered if I'd cracked them. I wouldn't put it past me.

"Will Mason be all right?" I asked Damon.

"Yes."

I wasn't sure he wasn't lying to make me feel better. The girls started to maneuver me out of the house. I staggered along, finding more and more aches and pains with every step.

"Call me," Damon said. "I'll get to the hospital as soon as I can."

"You got it, Sunshine," Jen said. "Are you going to call the cops?"

"He killed the Wicked Bitch," I said and then made a whimpering sound as I bit my tongue. Talk about adding insult to injury.

They loaded me up into the truck. Apparently they'd all driven together. Ajax made little snuffling noises as I collapsed across the backseat. He sat on the floor and licked my hands and arms. I wanted to tell him to stop, but he seemed to need to do it, so I didn't object.

Lorraine drove like a bat out of hell, and we got there in less than twenty minutes. I was surprised we weren't being chased by a dozen cops with all the laws she had to have broken.

I recognized a few of the ER staff as they took me inside. It must've been a slow day because they got me back into a cubicle in just ten minutes. The doctor who'd treated me the first time came in and started examining me.

"Did you take another fall in the river, Miss Wyatt?" he asked dryly.

"Business client kidnapped me and my uncle," I said, pleased by the startled look on his face. He'd probably thought I was getting beaten by my boyfriend or something and that I was going to protect him.

"Did you call the police?" he asked.

"Boyfriend was going to. Stayed to talk to them."

"How did you get these injuries?"

I couldn't tell him the truth, so I went for something close. "Tried to run away. He tackled me. Marble floors."

I was beginning to shiver. Reaction setting in. Shock or something. My whole face ached and talking was getting to be really painful. The doc seemed to notice and stopped asking questions beyond, "Does this hurt? How about here? On a scale of one to ten, ten being unbearable ...?"

I whined about being cold, and they covered me with blankets that had come out of a toaster oven. Then they cleaned me up and shoved me into a CT doughnut. Neither my eye socket nor cheek had broken. Just my nose. After that, I got chest X-rays.

"Your nasal septum seems to be fine, but all the same, you'll want to follow up with an ENT within a day or two. You don't want to have to break your nose again to fix it, so don't wait more than a week. Ten days and I promise you there *will* be breaking," the doc told me sternly after the tests were all completed.

"Yessir," I said.

"Your ribs don't appear to be fractured, but you may have separated or torn the cartilage. Not much to do about that but ice, rest, and take it easy on yourself for the next few weeks. It would be a good idea to arrange an MRI to see the extent of any damage. I'll give you a referral. I'll send you home with something to take care of the pain for the first week. After that, over-the-counter pain medications should work just fine."

I got wheeled out of the ER about four hours after I went in. All I wanted to do was crawl into bed and sleep for a week. Damon still hadn't shown up. That surprised me. Worried me more. Had something happened?

"He's fine," Jen said. "The police made him hang around. They want to talk to you too. They came by the hospital."

"Where are they?"

"They took our statements, but we made a fuss about how much you'd been through, and they said tomorrow would be all right for you to talk to them."

"Oh, thank God."

"What now?" Stacey asked. "Where do you want to go? You're welcome to stay at any of our houses."

I didn't even consider it. I wanted to go back to the hotel. I didn't examine that desire too much. I wasn't sure why I'd rather be in Damon's bed than with my best friends.

"Could we get a milkshake on the way?" I asked plaintively as we loaded back into the car.

"Rockin' Rogers?" Lorraine asked.

"Where else?"

We also went to a drive-through pharmacy to fill my prescription. I explained everything Garrett had told me. They were all gratifyingly outraged for me and proud of my escape and the way I'd stopped Garrett.

"You're pretty badass," Jen said. "For an antique dealer."

I slid into one of Damon's super-soft shirts and crawled into bed after downing one of the painkillers. Ajax curled up against my stomach and propped his head on my hip. The girls closed the bedroom door and settled in the living room to wait for Damon's return. I didn't argue about their staying. I wasn't going to win.

I woke up later, my body throbbing and my bladder demanding that I get moving. I pushed myself up, and the nightstand light went on. Damon sat in a chair beside the bed.

"This scene is awfully familiar," I said, wincing at the ache in my face.

He looked haggard. "Too familiar. I wouldn't complain if you didn't get hurt again for another decade or two."

My stomach warmed. He planned to be around that long. Or longer.

"Me either. What happened to Garrett? Is Mason okay?"

"The police took Sandrini. I notified the Law Council. They've dispatched a team."

"What does that mean?"

"He can't stay in prison. At least, not in one that isn't prepared to deal with holding a sorcerer. They'll take custody of him and decide his fate."

"His fate?"

"He may be put to death. He may be imprisoned. Given the power of your families, I'd guess the former."

I wasn't sure how I felt about that. Sure, he'd killed the Wicked Bitch, but that was more of a public service than not. But then, if I hadn't stopped him, he'd have killed Stacey, Lorraine, Jen, Damon, and Mason, as well as my parents, plus turned me into a baby factory. Oh, hell.

"Did my parents show up?"

Damon nodded. "They both want to see you."

"Yippee." I probably could have sounded less enthusiastic, but I was in pain. "When is this supposed to happen?"

His mouth quirked. "That's up to you."

"Somehow I doubt it."

"I'm not going to let them anywhere near you if you don't want to see them."

"Can you stop them? Aren't they super magicians or something?"

His smile was steely. "It's possible that I am far stronger than anybody knows. It's also possible that I am highly motivated to protect you." His expression turned dark and self-disgusted. "I let that bastard get close to you. I should have stayed and gone into the diner with you."

"If you'd gone in with me, he'd have dusted you too."

He rubbed his hands over his face and then dragged his fingers through his hair. "When I think of what he wanted to do—what he nearly managed to do—I'd never have forgiven myself if he'd taken you." He leaned forward, propping his elbows on his knees, his eyes intent. "I want you to know that I would have come to find you, no matter how well hidden or guarded you were. I wouldn't have given up until you were free."

"I know."

He kept looking at me as if he didn't believe my answer and then nodded. "Good."

"Now I need to use the bathroom," I said.

I maneuvered myself up onto my feet and went to do my business. As I washed, I got a good look at my face in the mirror. I could have been Quasimodo's dream date. My left eye was eggplant purple and swollen. My nose was also swollen, and I had a ping pong ball on my chin where apparently I'd bounced after hitting the floor with my face.

No fixing any of *that* with makeup.

I came back out. Damon still sat in the chair. He stood as I returned.

"Can I get you anything?"

"Water. I need to take another pain killer."

He nodded and left, returning a moment later with a bottle. He twisted off the cap and handed it to me.

"Is this from the sanctuary pool?" I asked, hoping it was. I'd healed so much faster the last time with it.

He shook his head. "I'll go get some tomorrow. Unless you want to go with me and take a swim?"

"No. I'm not— No."

"I get it. No problem."

He didn't really get it, but then, I wasn't sure I did either. I looked at the bed and back at him. "Aren't you going to get some sleep?"

"I didn't want to disturb you. I wanted to heal you," he said and a guilty look suffused his expression.

"Not a good plan. Not with the police wanting to talk to me. They'd want to know if I'd been hit with a miracle."

"I thought so too."

"Your hand could still use fixing up."

He shook his head, looking at it. "The detectives noticed the damage. I've got to leave it for now."

"As for disturbing me, I think I can handle sharing the bed with you. And Ajax."

I made a face. Or tried. It's surprisingly difficult to do that when your face is a giant puffer fish. The big wolf-dog thumped his tail at the mention of his name and made a little woofing sound at me. I stepped over and scratched his ears.

"He probably needs to go out," I said.

"The girls walked him before they left," Damon said. "He'll be fine for a few more hours."

"Okay, so why don't you put on your pajamas and come to bed?"

Something was bothering him. I noticed the nightstand had a bottle of scotch on it with an empty glass beside it. It appeared Damon had drunk a healthy quarter of a bottle. His face looked haunted. He had a hyper-responsibility complex. He'd probably decided this whole mess was his fault.

"Why don't you just tell me what the problem is?" I suggested. "Then I can tell you you're an idiot and to get over yourself, and then we can go to bed. If it wouldn't hurt like hell, I'd suggest a little light nookie."

That earned me a slight smile that vanished like a flash of light across water. "Nookie?"

"Kissing, hugging, maybe a little petting."

"I didn't find any other properties that your aunt owned," he said, veering abruptly off the subject. Both subjects. It worked.

"None at all?"

"We could check in the surrounding counties. She might have purchased something there." He didn't sound all that hopeful.

"Maybe Mason found some records," I said. "A rental or something." I didn't sound hopeful either. "I still believe Aunty Mommy would want and need them to be close by and would want total control of wherever she stashed them."

"But where? You already said there's no place on the estate."

"I said I couldn't think of any. I could be wrong. We should at least search. Maybe she used magic to hide a shed or something."

"Worth a try but not for at least a few days. Right now, you should get back into bed. You look like you're about to drop."

I'd started to sway as the Vicodin kicked in, but I wasn't ready to head to oblivion again. Not yet. "Something's bugging you. Are you going to tell me?"

"No."

"You're just going to drink in the dark."

"Seems like."

I was beginning to get seriously annoyed with his stonewalling. "Fine. Whatever. Enjoy."

I crawled into bed, making a point of leaving plenty of room for him, though I pointedly called Ajax up to lie next to me. I turned on my side with my back to Damon and closed my eyes. Most of me was hurting pretty bad, and it took a good fifteen minutes or more for the painkillers to overwhelm the pain and sink me into unconsciousness.

I was still feeling pretty irritated when I got up the next morning. Damon had taken Ajax for a walk. I sat up slowly, taking shallow breaths as my ribs seemed to move around in my chest. Ow.

I glanced at the nightstand. The bottle was still there. It didn't look substantially more empty than in the night. Maybe it was a second one. Had Damon gotten any sleep at all?

The first order of business was a shower and then to get dressed, all more easily said than done. The spray of the shower hit like nails. I adjusted it and found something almost like a fog setting. It wasn't all that great for washing hair, but it didn't feel like someone beating me with a sack of oranges either.

I looked worse than at the hospital. The purple around my eye had darkened, and my ping-pong ball chin had turned purplish. The eye bruise had crawled over the bridge of my enormous nose and curved under my other eye. My lips swelled huge and pouty. I probably should have liked that look. All the Hollywood starlets were getting marshmallow lips left and right. I thought I looked ridiculous.

Getting dressed involved sliding on underwear and pulling a maxi dress over my head. I couldn't have managed to put on a bra if I tried, and even if I had, the pressure around my ribs probably would have made me curl up on the floor and whimper.

The dress covered the bruises on my knees and more on my hips. It did nothing to help with my arms. But then, with the whole rotten-prune face going on, who was going to notice?

I didn't have my phone. I wondered if anybody had found it in Garrett's car. It was probably evidence and I wouldn't get it back 'til hell froze over.

I combed my hair out but didn't dry it then went out to the bedroom. Ajax lay on the bed, facing the bathroom door. He sat up as I came out, wagging his tail as if he hadn't seen me in weeks.

I petted him, bending to rub my undamaged cheek against the soft fur of his head. He licked every bit of exposed skin he could. I straightened and headed into the other half of the suite. Damon sat at the table talking to Ballard and Jeffers. They stood as I entered. Jeffers actually winced in sympathy.

"That looks painful," he said.

"Only when I'm awake. I take it it's question time?"

"We'd like to get your account of what happened to you yesterday," Ballard said. I sank into a chair.

Damon went to the phone and dialed. I could hear him ordering coffee and breakfast. Three empty takeout cups from a nearby coffee shop littered the table. My mouth watered as I eyed them.

"Tell us what happened. Start from when Hornsby accosted you," Jeffers said.

I explained that I'd been going to an employee meeting and that he'd lured me to his car with a promise of a check. I told them he'd blown some sort of powder in my face and that I pretty much could do nothing but listen to his crazy chatter.

"He told me he killed Aunty Mommy," I said. "He was going to take me off somewhere and rape me." There was no explaining the contract baby stuff, so I didn't try. I did make an effort to give some idea of his motivations. Cops liked that sort of thing.

"I guess he thought killing Aunty Mommy would free me to be with him, which was true. I've never dated. The Wicked Bitch liked to persecute my friends. I couldn't imagine what she might do to a boyfriend. Anyhow, he decided he had to take my uncle out too and then hung around in the hopes that my parents would show up so he could kill them."

"What made him think they would?" Ballard asked.

"And why did he want to kill them?" Jeffers added.

"I guess Mason had told them about the Wicked Bitch and where to find me." I was totally making shit up now. I hoped Mason's story would fit well enough. "I have no idea why he wanted to kill them. Maybe he thought they wouldn't approve of his plan for me. Or maybe he's just fucking nuts."

Both detectives were writing notes. I told them how Damon and the girls arrived and that Garrett had seen me kissing Damon before he took me. I told them he flipped out and took a gun to kill them when they came in. The immobilizing drug had worn off enough for me to go after him. I'd struck him on the back of the head with a heavy vase, and then he'd slammed me to the floor and kicked me a couple of times. But by then, Damon had a hold of him, and that was pretty much the end of my tale.

I breathed a small sigh of relief when they seemed to buy my story.

"What did the doctor say?" Ballard asked, eyeing my face with sympathy.

"He said I should stop hurting myself. I broke my nose but not the rest of my face, and I may or may not have broken ribs."

"Ouch."

"Yeah, I could go with never running into a psychotic asshole again."

'Course, I'd been raised by one, and it was quite possible that the magical word bred them like mice.

"Sounds like you've had more than your share," Jeffers said.

I raised my brows. Or rather, I tried to, but with my face so swollen, they didn't move much. "Why, Detective, you almost sound like you don't think I killed anybody anymore."

He grinned. "Never did."

"Right," I scoffed. "You were ready to lock me up and throw away the key."

He shook his head. "Naw. But you weren't telling us everything. I had to take off the gloves." He winked. "Bad cop, you know."

"And here I thought you were just a giant prick."

His grin widened. "I may be that too."

"May?" Ballard asked. "I'd say she's got you pegged."

Somebody knocked on the door, and Damon, who'd been leaning against the kitchen counter through all this, went to answer. Two waiters rolled in three carts of food. Damon signed off on the ticket and they left.

"Guess we'd better get out of your way," Ballard said, rising.

"Stay," Damon said. "You've been up all night. I ordered plenty."

The detectives exchanged a look and then shrugged.

"Not protocol," Jeffers said. "But if I don't eat soon, I might pass out."

"No you won't. You've got enough gut to keep you going for years."

Ballard patted his stomach. I chuckled when he slapped at her hand.

"Mind your own business."

"You are my business, partner."

Damon uncovered the offerings, and we took plates from the stack the hotel had provided. There were eggs, bacon, sausage, pancakes, toast, biscuits and gravy, hash browns, fruit, and four different syrups. And two carafes of coffee with a tall pitcher of cream.

I piled my plate and filled my cup, settling in to stuff my face. Eating proved to be a lot more painful than I expected, so I ate slowly. Jeffers and Ballard continued to ask questions.

"That reminds me," I said. "Garrett said he was the one responsible for vandalizing my shop and loft. He'd come looking for me and when I wasn't there, he got pissed."

"Really," Jeffers said. "I'm going to have some questions for him. Like how he did such damage. Or did he say?"

Oops. Maybe I shouldn't have mentioned that.

"Afraid not, but if he tells you, I'd sure like to know," I lied.

"He lawyered up in the hospital," Ballard said. "Bastard's not answering any questions. Doesn't matter. We've got solid evidence on kidnapping, false imprisonment, assault, and attempted murder. With any luck, we'll find evidence he murdered your aunt. We'll have time to make the case, though. He'll be in jail awhile for all the rest."

I wondered how the magical legal beagles would take

possession of him. Inwardly I shrugged. Not my problem, so long as he was locked up far away from me.

Ballard and Jeffers stayed another half hour and then left after telling me that my phone and purse were in evidence but they'd probably be able to get them released to me by the afternoon. That left me and Damon alone. He'd hardly spoken two words since breakfast began. I was getting a little annoyed at the silent treatment, but I wasn't in the mood to force him to talk to me.

Instead I decided that I really wanted to go for a walk. Actually, I wanted to go shopping for shoes and go running, but my body wasn't up for that. Again. Plus, I didn't have any money or ID. I headed for the door, calling for Ajax.

Damon cut me off as I reached for the door. "Where are you going?"

"Out. You want to get out of my way?"

"I'll come with you."

"Thanks, but Ajax and I'd rather go alone."

That haunted look came back. He was strung tight as a banjo string. "The danger isn't over," he said roughly, looking away.

"Yes, it is. Garrett's all locked up."

Damon scraped his teeth over his lower lip and wiped his hand over his jaw. I'd never seen him nervous before.

"What's going on?" I asked, trying not to let worms of worry start crawling through my veins.

"You're still a target," he said finally, reluctance dragging out the words.

"What do you mean?"

"Anybody who wants to kill your mother and father need only come after you. Two birds with one stone, and you're the stone."

As soon as he started talking, a headache began throbbing behind my eyes. I'd already figured out this little revelation. Didn't mean I was going to go into hiding.

"I know."

He blinked at me. "Did you know that Garrett won't be the only one who wants to grab you?"

"Figured that one out too. My DNA is everybody's wet dream."

"You can't just go walking around like you're safe. You have to protect yourself."

"I know that too. But I've lived my whole life to suit somebody else's psychotic ideas about me, and I'm not doing that anymore. Somebody wants to come after me, they'll find out I won't go quietly. I'm not giving up my life."

"Beck," he started.

I held up my hand to cut him off. "Is that why you stayed up drinking instead of cuddling up with me?"

He flushed and swallowed jerkily. "You've been through hell. How was I supposed to tell you it's just beginning? And your families don't to want me around. They're going to do everything they can to pry me away so they can bring you into their folds."

"Yeah? Well, it is what it is. Haters are going to hate, and I'm going to have to deal with it. Presupposing you aren't giving up on me?" I had to admit the possibility had me worried.

"Not a chance."

He pulled me into a gentle embrace, his lips brushing butterfly soft against mine. It hurt but I didn't particularly care. I leaned into his heat, delighting in the hard strength of his chest and the way his arms held me as if I were the most precious thing on the planet. I opened my lips and our kiss was crazy hot. Delicate, tender caresses ignited a fire in my belly and made me want to throw myself into his arms. My fingers tightened on his shoulders where I'd grabbed him for balance. I lifted myself on tiptoe, but he still wouldn't give in to the harder kiss I craved.

By the time he pulled away, I was panting and all my girl parts were aching to be touched and fondled. The lack of a bra only increased the sensitivity of my breasts. He'd run his hands along my back and discovered my secret. I was pleased to see he was breathing just as hard as I was.

"A walk," he said and I couldn't tell if that was a reminder or a question.

"Or?" I asked, standing on tiptoe to run the tip of my tongue along the top of his collar. His pulse jumped and danced beneath the caress, and his arms tightened convulsively. It hurt but I wasn't about to let him in on that secret. He'd just push me away, and I really didn't feel like stopping this right now.

"Or I take you back into the bedroom, strip you naked, and make you feel really, really, really good."

He punctuated the *really*s of that statement with hot little kisses along the sensitive tendon of my neck. I shivered and gasped.

"If that's an argument against walking, it's a good one," I rasped as tremors started running down my legs.

He sighed and rested his forehead against mine, his hands sliding down to settle on my hips.

"As much as I want to have my wicked way with you, I'm pretty sure you'd regret it, and I don't think my heart could stand that," he said.

God, did he have to put it that way? I couldn't even get

mad, even if he was right. Well, maybe right. Just now, I wasn't certain about anything except I had aches that I knew he could make feel a lot better and I desperately wanted him to play doctor with me.

"You're probably right," I said but made no effort to push away. "But then again, you could be wrong."

"Don't tempt me, Beck. My control is very, *very* thin."

I decided that we both probably should step back from the precipice. When we went over—when *I* went over—I wanted to choose it and not let my hormones do it for me.

Sometimes I hated me.

We took Ajax over to the park where I'd met Ben. I wondered how he was doing. I was glad he had gone home before Garrett went Norman Bates. He'd certainly have killed Ben and chalked it up to collateral damage. I'd been shielding myself since I learned how and made a mental note to send a big thank-you to the young doctor-to-be for teaching me. I'd have to get Damon to teach me to anchor it to something so it would work 24/7.

We stopped at a coffee cart and then walked around the park.

"We missed our dinner date," I said.

"We'll make it up tonight." He glanced at me. "Or whenever you feel up to it."

"I'll feel up to it," I said, determined that I would. "How's Mason doing?"

"He's good. It took a little work to counter the mesmer dust, but no long-term effects as far as I can tell."

"That's good news." I was getting to like Mason. So far, anyhow. It's not like I knew him all that well.

We kept walking and I deliberately went for small talk. Just about every conversation we'd ever had focused on my family or magic or some other crisis. I barely knew anything about Damon. I asked where he'd gone to school, his favorite foods, hobbies, dream travel vacations, all the while veering away from any discussion of the contract-baby system or any other landmines.

Damon seemed just as happy to keep it low key, asking how I'd met Stacey, Lorraine, and Jen, and how I'd learned to cook and my favorite foods.

We strolled around the park twice, with Ajax sniffing and peeing and watching squirrels skipping across the ground and barking at him. On the way back, I noticed a new exhibit display for my favorite local museum. They tended to get eclectic and unusual exhibits that were always fascinating. This one was the history of oil drilling in California. The display board had photos and captions describing some of what could be seen in the exhibit.

"Wow. There are tons of working oil derricks in L.A. In people's backyards, even. Look, there's one in a shopping center."

I continued to examine the photos and read the captions. I'd just looked at several similar photos when a realization struck me.

"Oh my God! I know where they are! Come on!"

I whirled and started running back toward the hotel. Every jolting footstep sent a spasm of pain through my chest and head, but I didn't care. I wanted to hurry to see if I was right.

Damon overtook me in just a few strides. He didn't try

to stop me to question my sanity or anything else. He just kept up.

"What are you doing?"

I was out of breath. My ribs refused to let me breathe, so I could barely talk. "Aunty Mommy's house. I know where she hid them."

Damon didn't ask any more questions. When we got to the hotel, he asked the valet for his truck and then gently rubbed my back as I continued to wheeze.

In a few minutes, we were spinning down the road. But not headed toward the Wicked Bitch's house.

"Where are you taking me?" I decided not to be mad yet and to give him the benefit of the doubt. He'd proven himself more than once in the past few days alone.

"Going to make a stop at the sanctuary. I know," he said as I started to protest, "you don't want to go in. That's fine. I'll go grab some water and bring it back. You'll be glad I did, and it won't take more than twenty minutes."

It took twenty-five, but who was counting? By the time Damon returned to the truck with several sport-sized bottles of water, I was climbing the walls. Wordlessly he handed me one.

"You too," I said. "For your hand."

He took a breath as though about to argue then shrugged and started drinking. I followed suit. When I was done, he held something out.

"Here. The buddha sent this for you."

On his palm was an orange-red rock about the size of a runt walnut.

"What's that for?"

"I don't know. He just said to give it to you. He likes you. Wants to protect you."

I frowned at it and then took it. It was cool but almost

instantly warmed. It turned to liquid and then circled my middle finger and hardened into a ring. It continued to radiate warmth. I went to take it off, but Damon wrapped my hand with his.

"Leave it on. Maybe it will help you heal along with the water. The buddha has been very worried about you."

I remembered that night in the pool, listening to the buddha talk and decided Damon was right.

We headed in the direction of Aunty Mommy's. This time Damon wasn't content to be silent.

"Where do you think the gargoyle females are?"

Excitement sparkled inside me. "Hiding in plain sight. Did you see how they built towers and buildings around the pumpjacks in L.A. to hide them? That one by the high school was all covered with pretty flowers. That made me think about the Wall. It's big enough, and plenty close."

He nodded thoughtfully. "It's a possibility. Close but the magic it would take to keep the gargoyle males from sensing their mates would be astronomical."

"More than Aunty Mommy was capable of?"

He shrugged. "Hard to say. There's always the possibility that she had outside help to set a containment spell. Mason's sure she had help to create the dimension bubble for her secret office. I want to warn you we need to be very careful about getting inside the Wall. That kind of magic could do a lot of damage if improperly released."

"Bring it on. I'm done letting the Wicked Bitch do damage," I said. "She doesn't get to fuck with me or the people I care about anymore."

"Unfortunately, dead or not, she may not agree."

"Good thing I'm not asking her, then."

There were five cars parked out front of the massive house when we pulled in. I recognized the gray BMW Mason had been driving, but none of the other four. Damon parked behind a lemon-yellow Jaguar. We got out and Ajax went and peed on the Jag's rear tire.

"Who else is here besides good ol' mom and dad?"

"An attorney, a few others." Damon kept his gaze on the house.

"What's wrong?" He'd clamped his teeth so hard, he might break them. "Damon?"

"Everything's fine."

I rolled my eyes. "Yeah. I can tell." It irritated me that he didn't want to share, but I didn't push. He was entitled to a few secrets. I'd certainly kept plenty from him, and he had little reason to trust me. It still hurt, though.

"Let's get this over with," I muttered and stalked toward the grand entry.

Damon strode along beside me, and I could feel his tension rising. He'd squared his shoulders and thrust his chin out, the muscles in his arms and chest tightening. He had all the bearing of a man walking into the middle of a war zone. What was he expecting?

"Do my parents get along?"

"I don't think getting along applies," he said cryptically.

I stopped and turned to look at him, my hands on my hips. "What the hell does that mean? And this time, how about a straight answer?"

He considered his words, obviously trying to sort out an answer. "Their relationship came about because of a birthing contract. They conceived swiftly and lived together non-romantically or sexually until the birth. The participants in a birthing contract never think of each other as man and woman or friends or anything else. They are simply short-term business partners. I doubt they'd met each other more than a few times before the contract was signed, and after Osterraven's shenanigans, I doubt they've had any since then. Under ordinary circumstances, they would be neither friendly or unfriendly. However, given all that's happened with your birth and kidnapping, there is tension."

The way he said the last word was loaded with meaning that I couldn't understand. "I don't suppose you want to clarify? Because my head hurts and all this birthing contract crap is making it worse."

He pursed his lips. "The politics at play between the families means that their friendliness or lack thereof is not a matter of personal choice but politics. You're about to step into the world of the ruling families, Beck, and you're going to hate it."

"Tell me something I didn't already know." I folded my arms over my chest, wincing as pain spiraled down my rib cage. "Are you suggesting I can't handle this?"

For the first time since we'd left the sanctuary, he cracked a smile. He reached out and brushed a few loose strands of hair from my face.

"Oh, no. You will handle this. You're just going to come out feeling like you bathed in horse shit."

"Better than dog shit, any day of the week. Come on. Let's go get this over with."

This time I grabbed his hand, linking my fingers between his. I kind of felt he needed the support. He disentangled himself.

"You probably don't want them seeing us together like that. It could make things difficult."

I scowled. "Why is it any of their business?"

His lips curled. "Like I told you before. They don't want me with you. I'm not of the proper class for you to consider as a sexual partner. In case you should get pregnant."

"And chalk another one up under 'sentence I never imagined I'd hear said.' I take it that means that they don't like your mutt bloodlines and I shouldn't be slumming?"

"Something like that."

Anger swarmed through me. Who the hell were they to judge Damon? He was beautiful, brave, kind, generous, thoughtful and a whole lot of other things any child could hope for in a father. Not that my DNA donors cared about actually parenting. Well, they could go fuck themselves, and I was going to tell them so. That's when I got an idea. I chuckled wickedly and grabbed his hand, dragging him forward. "This is going to be so much fun."

I could have sworn I heard him mutter, "Oh, shit."

The staff was still off. I opened the door, and we went inside. Somebody had cleaned up Garrett's spell circle. The wall I'd smashed him against was still caved in. Other than that, there was no evidence a psycho had ever been planning a killing spree here.

I was more in a hurry to check the Wall than meet my DNA donors, but I didn't get a choice. They were in the garden room with Mason and four other people. Mason pounced on me before we'd taken two steps into the room.

"Beck," he said with a huge smile. He pulled me into a

hug. "I'm so glad to see you up and about." He stood back and looked me over, frowning. "That looks ugly."

"Hurts too," I said. "Worth it, though. I'm glad nothing happened to you."

He sobered. "I'm afraid you may be less glad when I tell you what I've done."

I reached for Damon's hand. "Oh?"

He pulled a thick envelope from the breast pocket of his blazer and held it out. "I've signed over everything that belonged to Adriane to you."

I stared at the envelope as if it were a cobra. I looked back up at him. Hurt and betrayal drilled through my heart. I don't know why I should have been surprised. Or why it bothered me so much. My eyes started to burn, and I blinked furiously. I absolutely wasn't going to cry.

Mason stepped toward me, his voice dropping. "I did this because it's the right thing. Give it all away if you like. There are many charities that would be grateful. I know you hate this house, but keep in mind that the gargoyles are bound to this place. I know you would want them to have a safe home. You could give that to other creatures as well. You could create a rescue haven here."

I hadn't thought of that. I could do a lot of good, and if I sold this place to someone, if they had any taste at all, they'd pull down the gargoyles and sell them or more likely, destroy them. I couldn't let that happen. Not until I figured out how to free them from their binding. I wasn't convinced it couldn't be done. Lots of impossible things happened all the time.

"Thank you," I said, taking the envelope, and then leaned in to kiss his cheek. "You are a gem," I murmured. He looked startled but pleased. I looked at Damon. "How do you feel about being my lawyer?"

"I already dumped all my clients. I'm all yours."

I frowned. "Seriously? All of them? Why?"

He shrugged. "Mason is—was—my primary client. He took most my time." His hand tightened on mine, and his blue eyes were deeply earnest. "I can't have any conflicts of interest. I need you to trust me."

"I do." I handed him my envelope. "I'll let you handle this, then."

"Yes, ma'am," he said with a wink and slid it into a pocket.

"Let me introduce you around," Mason said. "This is Ethan Osterraven, your father, and Elena Wyler Symms, your mother."

My mother looked a lot like Aunty Mommy, though softer and warmer. Definitely less militant. I tried not to hate her on sight, but it was hard to separate her from the woman who'd tortured me all my life. Elena dressed in flowing green designer clothing. She looked elegant, her eyes thoughtful in an oval face, her expression vaguely wistful. When I tried to meet her gaze, she averted her eyes.

My father was tall with light brown hair threaded with silver. He had a bold face, angular with a square jaw and was well preserved for his age. In fact, he was quite handsome. He eyed me with a certain amount of speculation, as though looking for flaws. He seemed to like what he saw well enough because he developed a pleased smile that was in no way fatherly. Then his gaze ran down to where Damon and I held hands. A furrow dug between his brows.

"Welcome to Hell," I said to them. "Did Mason show you the basement? You've got to check it out if not."

"My sister was not kind to you," Elena said.

"Now you're not giving her enough credit. Your sister was an evil bitch who got her rocks off torturing me," I said.

"But that's water under the bridge now that she's dead. I never did pick up her ashes from the crematorium. Was planning a grand funeral too. Something super tacky with a dash of trailer trash and a giant cherry of hillbilly on top. I was so hoping to make her spin in her grave. Well, if ashes could spin. You get the point. Anyhow, if you want what's left of her, you're welcome to it. Save me the trouble of flushing her down the toilet."

I was talking a mile a minute, obviously confusing both of the 'rents. I wasn't what they'd expected, though you'd think that my little e-mail to the Proclamation Server would have given them a hint. Maybe they'd thought this little reunion was going to be one of those Hallmark moments where the child runs into the loving arms of her long-lost parents. Not that there were any loving arms around here. Except maybe Damon's.

"I'd go to that funeral," Mason said with a conspiratorial smile. "I hate to say it, but it's no more than Adriane deserves." His usual reserve had vanished, and he seemed far less uptight than normal. I liked the new him. I hoped he stuck around and let the old him wander off into oblivion.

"Your treatment at the hands of your aunt was unforgivable," Ethan said, his voice deeper than I'd expected. "I've come to take you home—to your real home—where you can be properly cared for."

Wow. Condescending much? "No thanks," I said and then focused on Mason because that was sure to be annoying. "Who are the rest of my guests?"

"This is Hannah Wyler Symms, your cousin by way of—"

"Hi," I said, interrupting. I didn't care about her parents. I wouldn't know who they were. The woman had long brown hair that was pulled up behind her head. I figured she was probably in her thirties, with tanned skin and a mouth that was used to smiling.

"Hi," she replied and held out her hand. "Welcome back to the family."

I shook her hand and appreciated her firm grip.

"She does not belong to your family," Ethan declared arrogantly.

I turned to look at him. "And just who do you think I belong to?"

If he'd had any sense of self preservation, he would have realized that I wasn't going to put up with anybody claiming me. I belonged to myself and only myself.

"You were contracted to the Osterraven line. You are a member of *my* family."

Mason made a choking sound that might have been a laugh. I could feel Damon growing icy cold beside me, and if looks could kill, dear old dad would already be six feet under.

I tipped my head as I looked at Ethan. "No," I said and turned my back on him again. I swore I heard him gnash his teeth. Clearly people didn't ignore him.

"And you are?" I said to another man who looked a little bit like a cross between Clint Eastwood and Robert Redford. In other words, he was really pretty. In fact, they all were.

I glanced at Damon, who was still glaring at Ethan. "You people sure grow them pretty. Or is that a selection criteria for contracts too?"

"Pretty?" He glanced at me in surprise.

"Look around. Everybody in the room could be a model. Well, except for me, unless I'm modeling for *Horror Movie Today*."

"You're beautiful," Damon said, sounding offended that I would question that.

"Relax, Tarzan. I don't have self-esteem issues."

"Doesn't mean you get to insult yourself in front of me," he said, his indignation adorable.

"All right. I'll insult other people if that makes you happy."

He snorted as I turned back to Clint Redford.

"Sorry about that. You are very handsome, as are the two of you." I looked at the other two men. One of them was about my age, lanky, with long blond hair caught up in a ponytail and a foxy face. The other looked like him but older, with short hair.

"Thank you," the first man said solemnly.

I couldn't tell if he had a great poker face or a bad sense of humor.

"I'm Kenneth Silverthorn."

"What brings you here?"

"I accompanied Ethan."

"Let me guess—you're his contracts attorney."

Now he smiled. "I'm afraid so."

"It's too bad you came all this way for nothing."

"Oh, I wouldn't say it's for nothing. I'm rather enjoying myself. At the very least, I have the admiration of a pretty young woman."

"Yeah, I'm looking hot today," I said, rolling my eyes. "I can tell you're trouble."

I looked at the elder of the last two men. "And who would you be? Bodyguards? Personal fluffers?"

The younger one just about choked on the last. I grinned.

"I'm afraid we requested to join this expedition to get to

the bottom of my son's involvement in this situation." The elder one frowned with obvious worry.

"Son?"

"Benjamin. You used his account to send your e-mail to the PS. I'm Soren Sharpentier, and this is Marco, Benjamin's cousin."

I grinned and reached out to shake both their hands. "Oh! So very nice to meet you. Ben is a terrific kid, and we've become good friends. He's very sweet."

A look of relief ran over Soren's face, and his gaze darted past me to my parents. There was probably some sort of power thing going on here. I thought of Garrett's complaints about the drop in his family's status. It looked like his family wasn't the only one who feared my two families. Having known Ethan for all of a couple of minutes, I could understand why. The man was obviously arrogant and controlling.

"Well," I said, turning around. "It's nice to meet you all, but I'm afraid I've got some business to take care of right now. Mason? Will you come with us please?"

I headed out the glass doors onto the patio. I stopped a second to glance up at the gargoyles and took a deep breath. God, I hoped that their mates were inside the Wall. I hoped Mason and Damon would know how to free them if they were bound in magic.

"What's going on?" Mason asked quietly as we pattered down the steps to the lawn and headed toward the Wall. Behind us, I could hear the others following. I didn't particularly care, unless they tried to interfere in this rescue.

"We think the female gargoyles are hidden inside the climbing wall."

Mason considered that information then nodded. "It's definitely possible, though the magic containing them would have to be very strong to prevent the males from sensing them."

"Think she rocked that kind of power?"

He nodded. "It's quite possible. Or she had help."

I didn't know if that was a good thing or not. Good because that meant we would find the missing gargoyle females. Bad because freeing them might prove very difficult. But then, Mason had freed the males. With all three of us pooling our power, we should be able to manage this. I said so.

"I hope so," Mason said, but his voice carried a note of uncertainty.

"Do you think Marco is single?" I asked Damon as we walked around the Wall, looking for an access point.

"I have no intention of sharing you," was his hot response.

"Right back at you. Oh, and I'd get over any ideas of birthing contracts if you want to be with me. But I'm not sure the girls would forgive me if I didn't mention Marco to them. In fact...."

I pulled out my phone and texted Stacey, Jen, and Lorraine: Family reunion at the Wicked Bitch's house, plus some pretty male scenery. May have found the gargoyles' mates.

I hit send and pocketed my cell.

"What's going on?" Hannah asked as my visitors came inside the cage. She looked around at the water cannons and the cage. "What an odd place."

"You don't know the half of it," I said. "We're trying to

see if we can find a hidden entrance. Seems Aunty Mommy forced the gargoyles on the house to offer an eternal blood binding by threatening their mates. Then she hid the females, and the males can't sense them."

From the look on her face and everybody else's, this was a stunning and horrifying revelation.

"She also spelled the males so they couldn't transform unless the place was threatened and required defense," Mason added as he came around from the rear of the Wall. "Entirely despicable. We released them from the transformation-blocking spell, and Beck believes that the females might be hidden inside this monstrosity." He gestured toward the Wall.

"No sign of a door, though," Damon said as he returned.

"Let's knock a hole in it, then," I said.

"Too risky," Soren said, clearly understanding better than I did the nature of the magic Aunty Mommy had used.

Marco, Kenneth, and even Ethan nodded agreement. Daddy Dearest looked angry, the kind you get when someone gets bullied and you want to do something about it. Maybe he wasn't such a bad guy after all.

"So what do we do?"

"We work from the outside in and dismantle the spells," Elena said, speaking up for the first time. "I'm familiar with the way Adriane worked magic. I should be able to help tear apart this ... evil."

"You have no idea," I said under my breath. She couldn't tear down the memories of me on that wall.

Damon slid an arm around me and pulled me close. From the harsh set of his jaw, he was probably thinking the same thing. The trouble was, Aunty Mommy was already dead and there was no way to kill her any deader. A shame, really.

"You don't know how to raise the dead, do you?" I asked hopefully.

"She's cremated. There's nothing to raise, even if I could, which I can't, so don't get any crazy ideas," Damon said.

"A zombie cockroach army...." I said thoughtfully.

"You watch too many horror movies."

"I don't watch enough, actually."

"Focus."

Elena was formulating a plan with the others. It sounded like a bunch of nonsense, but then, they were all trained with magic and I was a total newbie.

"Are you going to be pissed when you can't help get inside?" Damon asked.

Duh. "Yes."

"You going to throw a tantrum over it?"

I whirled to face him. "Excuse me? Did you just say *tantrum*? Do you *want* me to kick you in the balls?"

He grinned and I realized he was pushing my buttons on purpose.

I crossed my arms over my chest. "You're suicidal, aren't you?"

"I just want you to remember that you've got plenty of help here for the magic. That's not going to be the problem. Female gargoyles are exponentially more dangerous than the males. They are the protectors of the young, the defenders of the home warren. The males go to war and offer services in the world. They serve in other people's wars. But the females fight personal battles, and this is going to be very, *very* personal. They've been separated from their mates and calves for years."

"Wait a minute. Where are the gargoyle children all this time if not here?" My stomach plummeted into my shoes.

"Oh my God. You don't think the Wicked Bitch destroyed them, do you?"

"Given all you've told me and what I've seen, I wouldn't put it past her. But I'm praying she didn't get the chance because if she did, then the females are going to attack mercilessly, and the males will be blood bound to defend us."

Oh, fuck. "Mason!" I sprinted over to him, pulling him aside. "Did you learn anything in the room? Anything about the gargoyles at all?"

He shook his head. "Nothing."

"So no mention of their children?"

"Their calves? No."

I plowed my fingers through my hair, yanking on it. "Shit."

"Do you want to wait? See if we can find out something about the calves?" Damon had followed me over.

I didn't even hesitate. "No. That would be cruel, and maybe their kids were never involved. Maybe they're safe somewhere."

"Then it's all going to come down to you."

I frowned at Damon. "Why do you say that?"

"The gargoyle males knew you. There's a chance the females do too. They have a stronger ability to sense beyond themselves and may recognize that your aunt was your enemy also. You can build on that. The rest of us have no chance to reach them. They'll see us as the ordinary rank and file—same as your aunt—and they won't trust us. The trouble is, you may not get a chance to talk before they try to kill you."

"I guess I'd better talk fast, then." I looked at Mason. "Will you need to do another spell like the one you used to free the males?"

"I don't know. It depends on how they're being held."

"We're ready," Elena said, coming up to stand beside me. "Rebecca, Mr. Matrovani, will you be taking part?"

"Call me Beck and no, I won't," I said.

"I will," Damon said.

"You should withdraw to outside the fence," Elena said to me. "It'll be safer there for the time being."

The woman who had given birth to me had a kind of faraway look to her eyes, like part of her was somewhere else. She turned to her brother.

"Mason, you're to maintain the anchor and be prepared to take point on a secondary spell. Mr. Matrovani, you'll do the same. The rest of us will join you and anchor in rotation in the case we can't detach once we've begun. Osterraven will take third point with Hannah, and then it will be my turn again."

She carried herself with a kind of quiet confidence that said she was sure of her own skills and had no fear. I wished I didn't have fear. I felt like I was swimming in it.

I gave Damon a quick kiss, well aware of my father's disapproval, and then did as told, retreating outside the fence with Ajax. He'd been watching everyone with a quiet predatory stare, assessing and measuring. I wondered what conclusions he'd come to.

He sat between me and the fence, staring intently as everyone else began their spells. Damon and Mason had gone to the other side of the wall where I couldn't see them. Osterraven was on the right side with Elena angled toward the left. Hannah, Marco, Kenneth, and Soren stood between them.

I didn't hear it begin. Elena held her hands out to the sides, her palms angled toward the wall. She chanted something. The words grew louder, and more voices joined hers.

Then she turned to the right and began a patterned walk, swaying as she went, her hands moving in graceful arcs and bends. The others followed her as she made the circuit, and though they chanted, they merely walked, their hands interlaced together and held to their chests as if they were all praying.

They made three circuits and then stopped. When they did, golden light flickered along the ground along their path. Elena continued to circle, weaving in and out of her companions, who now faced the Wall, their hands extending from their sides, palms pointed downward. Magic flowed from them down into the gold, and the circle grew brighter until I had to look away before my retinas burned.

I kept trying to sneak peeks through slit eyelids, but it was no good. Strangely, the light didn't bother Ajax. He'd risen to his feet, watching the proceedings without any difficulty at all.

Electricity filled the air. It felt as if a giant storm were about to hit, complete with crazy lightning and a dozen tornados.

It was hard to breathe, the air was so thick. I felt a spiraling from inside the circle, a drawing inward, winding tighter and tighter. It pulled on my heart and muscles, the marrow of my bones. I stepped forward before I could stop myself. Then I took another step and another, until my face was pressed against the chain links of the fence and I couldn't go any farther. I curled my fingers through the wire and tried to pull it apart. To my surprise, it tore like wet toilet paper.

I pushed through the opening and started walking again. Now I was staring at the glare of magic, and it no longer seemed so bright or painful. It called to me like sunlight on a warm ocean beach. Ajax pressed against my legs, keeping pace with me.

The closer I came to the Wall, the stronger the pull on me grew and the faster I needed to go. It wasn't a slow build. Need slammed into me, and I catapulted forward. The molecules of my body separated, and I became smoke. I streamed through the building magic of the spell and then through the Wall and inside.

I couldn't see. I wanted light and it came to me. Or rather the cloud of me began to glow. The gargoyle females had been stacked like cordwood on top of a thick rubber mat. Each was covered in a shell of plastic resin two inches thick. Layered inside the resin were patterns of wire, leaves, stones, and who knew what else.

The magic that drew me wound around the stacked females, continuing to tighten its pull. I flowed toward them. It didn't occur to me to resist. I probably should have. Self-preservation is clearly not my strongest suit. Though I had escaped Garrett's death curse and hiked miles for help, so it wasn't my weakest suit either.

Following the flow of spooling magic felt right. I snorted inwardly. Because danger always feels dangerous, right? Yeah. It was too late for logic, though, because I'd committed and couldn't pull free now.

I came to the spindle at the heart of the winding magic. It glowed with opal light. I wondered what this had to do with what the others were doing outside the Wall. I decided it didn't matter and slid inside the spindle core.

I formed back into my own shape and hardened, though I wasn't entirely solid. I was more like a ghost. I found myself in the center of a group of angry gargoyle females who weren't altogether there either.

"Hi," I said. "I've been looking for you."

"We recognize your being. Who are you?" demanded one of the gargoyles. She was slender and graceful, with a face that reminded me of an Egyptian cat. Her ears thrust tall and tufted, her muzzle elongated and pointed. She had wicked talons like an eagle, and the fur on her head melded into feathers on her body. Her feet were lion paws. She didn't look at all pleased to see me.

"You recognize me?"

"Your being," she corrected. "You have often been near. We have tasted your blood, sweat, and tears. They have strengthened our prison."

The news hit like a punch to the gut. I'd helped the Wicked Bitch keep them captive. The idea disgusted me beyond all reason. I didn't have time to think about it. I needed to focus on getting them free. Telling them I was related to Aunty Mommy and why I was scrambling up the wall outside seemed like a really bad idea at the moment.

"That's a long story," I said. "Right now, we need to get you out of here. There are magic practitioners outside trying to dismantle the containment spells. What can I do?"

The gargoyle speaker wrinkled her nose, showing a scary mouthful of needle-sharp crystal teeth. "You can do nothing."

"Fuck that. There has to be a way."

She gave a chuff of bitter humor. "She who bound us reinforced the prison spells for years. Now only she can remove them."

"She's dead," I said bluntly.

The gargoyles went still. I could feel the horror and resignation sweeping over them and settling like a heavy cloud. It filled the small space to suffocating.

"Then we are trapped forever."

"No. You're not," I argued. "If we can't figure it out, I'm

told that the elements will erode the spells. If nothing else, I'll go drop you in the river, and it will free you."

"It would take a thousand years. By then, our bodies would be worn away to nothing."

She was full of all kinds of happy news.

"Then we'll break the damned spells. I promised your mates I'd find you and bring you back."

They all jerked closer to me, their eagerness palpable.

"They live? They are free?"

"The Wicked Bitch wasn't particularly nice to them, but they are alive and mostly free."

Her lips peeled from her teeth in disgust. "The blood oath."

"Yep. I'm working on figuring a way around that one too."

She looked away and, though I got the impression she didn't like to show emotion, her hatred and loss were too much to hide.

"At least they're alive."

The look she turned on me was glacier ice. "But not free. Never to go home; we have no mates." Her eyes flamed.

"The hell you don't. All of you will get to go home together no matter what it takes. Now what can you tell me about the spells holding you?"

She hesitated, clearly trying to decide if it was worth it to bother with answering then decided to humor me.

"The spell draws magic to reinforce itself. From us, always, and from any who try to break it. Even now they will find they are caught in the trap and will be emptied of power."

My breath caught. "They won't die, will they?"

She shrugged. "Maybe. Maybe not."

Not reassuring. Suddenly my sense of urgency woke up and hit me with a baseball bat.

"Why are you here?" I looked around at the ghostly gargoyles. "I mean, why are your spirits separated from your bodies?"

"Dividing our flesh from our spirits made it possible for us to be bound so tightly. The enchantress forced us from our bodies and then contained them in shells implanted with magic to keep us from returning. If this magic nexus is destroyed, our spirits will disperse and our bodies will be nothing more than dead stone."

"So you're saying that I have to take the resin and spells off your bodies before I try to break the prison spells or your spirits will go flying off into the wild blue yonder?"

"Yes."

Well, fuck. I'd thought knowing what needed to be done would make it easier. I'd been stupidly hoping that I'd get some instant grand idea of how to save the day. Instead, I felt caught between a rock and a hard place with a clock ticking down to Armageddon.

Still, how hard could it be? Movie action heroes managed to save the day at the last minute all the time.

Clearly I watched too many movies.

"I'd better go see what I can do." I tried to sound confident and wished to hell I could get some advice from Damon. But all I had was me, myself, and I, and that would have to be enough.

Still in smoke form, I tried to exit the core of the winding magic but I couldn't. Every time I started to make headway against the incoming flow, I got dragged back. After a few attempts, I gave up. I didn't have time to fight a battle I couldn't win.

I examined the weird little space we were crammed

into. Opal light formed the walls. Below us, I could just make out the stack of bodies in their resin prisons. I looked up.

The light flared outward from beneath our feet, rising up in a balloon before closing high overhead. In the center of the closure hung a beaten gold disk inset with concentric bands of what looked like lapis lazuli and turquoise. There were six each of those and solid circle in the center. The middle stone was the size of dinner plate and glinted with streaks of gold, red, and tarnished silver, almost black.

The binding spells had to be tied into that. I flowed myself up closer. That's when I realized the disk wasn't inside the spell nexus at all. It was above it, hanging like a weird disco light from the indent in the top of the Wall where I used to huddle to hide. Where I'd bled and cried and sweated and apparently fueled Aunty Mommy's evil. Driving me up the climbing wall had been more than just torture; it had been a means to an end.

God, but that pissed me off.

I floated back down.

"You see?" The speaker for the gargoyle women glared at me. The others remained eerily quiet, watching with hopeless eyes. "You cannot escape the light unless you can break the spells. But the spells are outside where you cannot reach."

Couldn't I? Knowing that Aunty Mommy had been using me—using my pain, my blood, my sweat, my tears—all to torture innocent wives and mothers…. It ignited a rage in my belly. The kind that had driven me to climb the Wall no matter how often I fell, no matter how bad I hurt. The kind that drove me to run, to swim, to beat the Wicked Bitch by never surrendering. I'd never done it yet, and I wasn't starting today.

I asked my body to turn solid. The gargoyle females recoiled as I turned back to flesh.

"What are you?" the lead one asked again.

"If there's any justice, I'm your ticket out of here," I said and plunged into the wall of coruscating light.

Something clamped over and lit my body on fire. I stumbled out, falling down on top of the pile of gargoyle females. Blood trickled from hundreds and hundreds of little wounds, no bigger than the tip of a pencil. They covered every inch of me. Blood trickled into my eyes, a film of red coloring my vision. I'd lost the light and called it back. Once again, I became my own glow stick.

The framework of the Wall was steel. An easy enough climb. I scrambled up to the top in less than five minutes. The wounds on my hands and feet turned my grip slippery, but it was nothing compared to the water cannons.

Once I reached the top, I swung my way across the roof to the disk, catching the steel beams and throwing myself forward like a kid on the playground monkey bars. I dropped down on top of the metal plate, expecting it to swing or shake, but it remained solid as rock. Solid, but not indifferent. The moment I touched down and my blood hit it, the gold surface lit orange and heated up. It was like standing on the burner of a stove. If I didn't do something soon, I'd be French fried.

I didn't have time to think. I knew what I had to do— well, I knew what the results had to be. So I just did what I always did. Decided what I wanted and made it happen.

I took my magic and slammed it against the disk. My invisible club melted into the flow and turned against me. I hadn't really thought it would work. Had to try, though.

Now to do it the hard way.

Blood mattered. It held its own magic—of life, of

dreams, of passion. It also meant sacrifice and pain—a kind of giving that went far beyond money or canned goods on Thanksgiving. Blood was essential and the more you gave, the greater the sacrifice.

I got on my hands and knees, centering myself over the central stone. Blood dripped onto it like red rain, hissing and spattering. Magic flowed into the stone and radiated downward. I sucked in a breath and held it. Remembering what Ben had told me about focus and intent, I put all my strength of imagination into willing my magic to form a blade in my hand. The flow pulled on me, but I refused to let it win, to let *her* beat me. I felt my magical blade take shape and harden in my hand. Before it could dissolve, I slashed though the flow.

Strands of magic split and tangled into balls of power that popped and wriggled wildly through the air. I slashed again and then again.

More threads, more tangles.

Now the disk grew white hot, and the stones began to crack and flake loose from the gold. Freed magic turned into flailing whips that cut through my clothing and into my flesh. I didn't need to have experience to know the spell was done for. It was an eighteen-wheeler plunging down a mountain road with no brakes. I had maybe a minute or two before it gave way altogether. Not enough time to climb down and crack open the resin shells on the gargoyle bodies. Not that I could. My hands and lower legs were burned to a crisp.

Might as well make the damage count. If I died, I was going out a winner.

I took my magical blade and sheared through the four chains holding up the disk. It plunged sickeningly, crashing on top of the stack of gargoyle females. The impact sent me flying. I hit the rubber mat on the floor in a twisting belly flop and stuck the landing.

I couldn't breathe and I was in so much pain, I couldn't even think. Sheer stubbornness pushed me up to my feet. I staggered to the stacked gargoyles. My magical blade was gone, and I couldn't seem to call it back. I couldn't concentrate through the pain. But I didn't have to destroy the shells. I just had to make a hole. It didn't even have to be big. A hairline crack would be enough to give the gargoyle spirits access to their bodies. Traveling as smoke had taught me that much.

I put both hands against the clear resin then lost my strength and wilted against it. I pulled up all the magic I had, wishing I could somehow tap in to the storm whirling around me. Maybe I could have, but I wasn't sure I'd survive long enough to make a hole. I decided to go with better safe than sorry. Oh, who the hell was I kidding? I'd hit sorry a long time ago. Didn't make me even think about stopping.

I focused all my magic into my hands, ramming it down and through. For a few seconds, nothing happened. I dug deeper and thrust harder. All of a sudden, I felt the resin shell give. Cracks radiated out between my splayed fingers. I laughed.

"Take that, bitch," I said and thrust again. I imagined Aunty Mommy under my hands and unleashed everything I had. The resin exploded and shards went everywhere, spinning and cutting. At the same time, the rest of the binding spells finished unwinding. Fireworks burst. Sparks sprayed. I flew back and hit the iron framework of the Wall.

I woke on grass. Sunlight bathed me. A warm body snugged up against me, and a weight pressed on my chest. I blinked. My vision was hazy. I didn't feel any pain. That was unexpected. I thought dying would hurt more.

The weight lifted off my chest.

"Beck? Can you hear me? Talk to me, sweetheart. *Please wake up.*"

Damon. He sounded terrified, his voice hoarse with desperation and dread.

"Did it work?" I asked. Well, that's what I meant to ask. Mostly I croaked something that sounded like a sick cat in heat.

"Thank God," he rasped and his fingers brushed my cheek. "You scared the living shit out of me."

I licked my lips, though fat lot of good it did me. My tongue was sandpaper. "Did it work?" I asked again and this time he seemed to understand.

"The female gargoyles are free."

"Good."

Darkness pulled me back under, and I let it take me.

The next time I woke up, I could hear Jen, Stacey, and Lorraine. They were pissed.

"Haven't you fucking people hurt her enough? You have to try to kill her harder than her own fucking mother did?" Stacey.

"I don't give a fuck if that cunt *was* her aunt." Lorraine said in response to a rumbled voice. "You people won't rest until Beck's dead, will you?"

She used the c-word. Lorraine. She *never* did that. She had to be in a rage.

"Not on our watch," Jen declared and of the three, she was the only one who didn't sound pissed. Which meant she'd gone past rage into the kill zone, and you did *not* want to be in her crosshairs when she got that way. "You are all cordially invited to leave. If you choose not to, I will personally rip your hearts out and shove them down your throats before dousing you in gasoline and lighting you on fire. You. Are. Not. Welcome."

I tried to say something. I don't know if I wanted to explain to the girls this was all my fault or if I wanted to tell them not to kick Damon out. I ended up calling his name.

"Right here." His breath whispered across my face, and his hand wrapped mine. He didn't sound any better than before, as if his vocal cords had gone through a cheese grater.

I tilted my head toward his voice. "You okay?"

He made a choking laugh. "Fuck no, but I'm a hell of a lot better than you. The hospital is going to think you need to be locked up for your own safety. I'm pretty sure they'll be right."

I didn't have a good argument for that one.

"It's over now," I said, as though that made it all better.

I felt him bend over me, his shadow darkening my hazy vision. He brushed a kiss over my lips. It stung. I didn't care.

"Please, God, I hope that's true," he said in a heartfelt prayer. "I can't keep almost losing you."

"Okay." Though what I was agreeing to, I wasn't all that sure. I thought a second. "Ajax?"

"Right beside you."

Ah. The warmth against my side.

"Are you busy right now?" I asked.

Damon snorted. "Hell yes. I'm taking care of you, and don't get any stupid ideas about telling me to shove off. I'm not going anywhere."

I smiled. I think. "You should take me to Banana Buddha."

He didn't even answer. He just scooped me into his arms and levered up to his feet before marching away.

"How come I don't hurt?"

"Your mother spelled away the pain."

"That's nice."

He just snarled something extremely rude and kept walking. A chorus of voices shouted out to him. He didn't stop. He took me through the house and out the front door to his truck.

"Front or back?" he asked.

"Front."

He opened the door and laid me on the seat, shutting me in. The back door opened, and I heard Ajax leap up. There was a rustling sound and the door closed. Damon came around to the driver's side and yanked open his door.

"Where are you taking her? To the hospital?" Lorraine asked. "I can call and let them know you're on the way."

"She asked to go to the sanctuary," he said, sliding into his seat.

"Sanctuary?"

"It will help her," he promised. "I won't let anything else happen to her."

"You let this shit storm happen," she snapped. Then, "I'm sorry. I know it's not your fault. Just help her, okay?"

"I'll call you after," he said. "And you were right the first time. I shouldn't have let this happen."

Oh hell to the no! I managed to lift myself onto my elbow. "Nobody tells me what to do anymore," I rasped. "Had enough," I added and then collapsed back onto the seat.

"Like I said," Lorraine sighed. "Better get going. I'm going to go keep Jen from committing mass murder."

Who was going to stop Lorraine? I didn't have the energy to ask.

Damon started the engine and put the truck in gear. I wiggled myself so my head rested on his thigh. He stroked his fingers over my hair.

I didn't pass out again, though I was too wrung out to talk. Damon drove fast. Really fast, which probably said a lot about how bad I looked. Or maybe it was how bad I actually was. It seemed only a few minutes before we bumped off on the little side road and parked. Damon lifted me out and carried me past the mushroom circle and down to the pool, walking into its chill waters.

I felt the cold only a little bit. Maybe the effect of the anti-pain spell. I lay across Damon's strong arms, closing my eyes as the clear water washed over me.

"What's happened?"

I opened my eyes and blinked. I still couldn't really see. The Banana Buddha was nothing more than a gold blotch hanging above me.

"Hey," I said. "I hurt myself."

"So I see."

I could have sworn he sniffed disapprovingly. I started to laugh, but water filled my nose and mouth, and I sputtered and choked as Damon lifted me up into a sitting position.

"Thanks," I said when I'd gained control.

"Try not to breathe the water anymore," he said sardonically. "It seems to be bad for your health."

"Funny."

"I have missed seeing you," the buddha said.

"What? No other naked girls have come to hang out here?"

Another sniff. "I have no interest in whether you are naked or not."

"I do," Damon said in a growly voice that made my insides go all quivery. "Though I'm not liking the hamburger look. Plus, it's messy."

"Hush," I told him, attempting to look stern, but it was hard to say if I managed. My face was just as numb as the rest of me.

"How long before this starts to work?" I asked.

"Your exterior wounds are not severe," Banana Buddha said. "They will heal quickly. The carnelian ring I gave you began already. Your internal injuries will take more time."

Which in no way answered my question. He should have been a lawyer. "Care to give me a ballpark estimate?"

"No."

I groaned. "You must have been a cat in another life."

"My people do not believe in resurrection of souls."

"That's right. You're a buddha, not a Buddha."

"Exactly so."

"I'm getting a headache."

"I'm surprised that you didn't already have one with all your injuries."

"Damon, make him stop." I was whining. I hated whining.

"I'm finding this conversation entertaining," he said. "I see no reason to interfere."

"Aren't you freezing?" Maybe I could just get the subject changed.

"I'm keeping myself warm."

"What happened after I tore down the binding spells and opened up the resin coffins?"

Damon didn't answer right away. I blinked. He was still a blur. The haziness of my sight wasn't clearing up all that fast. I contemplated sticking my head under water.

"Earth to Damon, come in, please."

"The climbing wall cracked, and pieces sloughed off. Then the female gargoyles rammed through, flying to freedom. We found you collapsed against the bottom of what was left of the structure. You were covered in debris. I pulled you to safety."

He sounded very angry. Well, actually he sounded like he was reading from a newspaper account. No emotion at all, which translated into seriously pissed off in Damon-world. He and Jen had that much in common.

"Thanks," I said.

"I was in the neighborhood," he said dryly.

"The gargoyles said that the spells were pulling magic from all of you. That you could die." My voice cracked, despite my efforts to act as matter-of-fact as he was.

He didn't answer, which told me the gargoyles had been right. That I'd been right not to dawdle in destroying Aunty Mommy's spellwork. Emotion rose in me, and my throat tightened. To distract myself, I tipped my head back so my eyes went under the water. I blinked a couple of times before Damon pulled me up.

"What the hell are you doing?"

"I was getting water in my eyes. I can't see very well."

He started swearing again, a litany of imaginative curses centering on the Wicked Bitch and spreading out to my families, magic, gargoyles, himself, and me. Pretty much he covered all possible territories with marvelous creativity and zest.

Eventually he ran out and glared at me. I could feel it.

"Can you not just get well, stay out of trouble, and stop scaring me shitless?"

"Ducking my head halfway under the water was scary? I have to tell you, you set a ridiculously low bar on what constitutes the 'what terrifies Damon' category on this episode of *Beck Jeopardy*."

He muttered something and I thought I heard the word *spanking*, but my ears were half full of water and I couldn't be sure.

"I'm tired."

"Guess you should have stayed in bed today, shouldn't you?"

"Your lack of sympathy is noted."

"Good."

After that, I drifted off into a half sleep, unable to keep awake. I faded in and out, the murmur of Banana Buddha's and Damon's voices mixing with the lap and rush of water to lull me to sleep.

"Beck? Beck, come on now, time to wake up."

Damon shook me gently and tilted me up upright against him.

"I wasn't asleep," I lied groggily.

"It's time to go."

"I'm healed up?"

"Enough. I can do the rest."

I yawned and my stomach made a fierce growling sound. "And pass out so I can go gallivanting off where I want without you knowing?"

His teeth ground loudly together. I could see him clearly

now. The numbing spell had worn off, and I ached all over, but nothing like I should have. My ribs didn't hurt nearly as bad as I thought they should have, especially after I'd been tossed around like a rag doll. I bet my belly flop onto the floor or my flight into the side of the wall at the end had made sure all my ribs broke.

I didn't have the heart to look at my hands yet. They'd been cooked extra-crispy style, and I couldn't handle seeing the damage. I kept them in the water as Damon held me.

At some point, he'd stripped off his shirt and tossed it onto the shore. He radiated warmth, likely thanks to magic, but since I was starting to shiver, I melted against him, sliding my arms around his waist and snuggling against his satin skin. His heart beat strong beneath my cheek, and I couldn't resist the urge to lick him. His arms contracted sharply and then loosened.

"You won't go gallivanting. I'll set the girls to keep watch. I don't think you'll be getting past them," he said, totally ignoring the lick.

I made a face. "You don't have to sound so smug about it."

"I know, but why fight it?"

"Payback's a bitch," I threatened.

"And how are you enjoying it?" he taunted me. "Come on. Let's go before you start gnawing on my arm. The way your stomach's been growling the last hour, I wouldn't put it past you."

I glanced upward to the sky. It was still day, but sundown wasn't so far off. "How long have we been here?"

"Six hours, maybe seven."

That long and he'd been here in the water with me the entire time? "Thanks."

His brows rose. "I love the hell out of you. Where else would I go?"

I couldn't get any words out through the knot in my throat, so I pushed out of his arms and swam to the pool's little beach. Ajax leaped up, wagging fiercely. He barked and hopped up and down, bouncing his front feet in the water. I sat next to him and put my arms around his neck. He licked my face and then thrust his nose into my bare belly. I complied with the silent order and scratched his ruff. My fingers felt pretty good for being charcoal. I sucked up my fears and looked at them.

"That's not even possible," I said, turning my hands over and examining them. "Not even hours in the water could fix the damage I did to my hands." And yet they were perfect. Pale healthy skin covered webs of muscle. I looked at Damon. "How?"

"When you aren't under a death curse, I am quite able to help," Banana Buddha said, shimmering out of thin air.

He hung above the water just in front of me. His smiling face was shaded with irritation and something like ... hurt. Because I'd refused to come back? I mentally kicked myself. Why wouldn't he be hurt? He'd made this place for me. It was a gift I'd cherished my whole life and never even knew he existed. He was like my fairy godfather. He'd looked out for me the best way he could, and I'd run off and stuck my head in the sand so I wouldn't have to deal with my feelings. Stupid feelings, at that. I'd felt so betrayed—by Damon, by the sanctuary itself for letting him enter, and maybe even by the little buddha who'd been there spying all those years and never told me.

But was it spying if he honored my wish to be alone? And Damon—he'd blundered in where he had no business, but he'd apologized, and I knew he'd never meant me harm. As for the sanctuary, it had always been faithful to me; always here when I needed it. The betrayal I felt wasn't because of any of them. It was all on me because I'd somehow decided that the very place I'd always felt safe couldn't be that if anybody else came inside. I'd been so used to going it alone, to handling all the pain and the hate and the horror of my childhood all by myself, that I hadn't realized I didn't have to. I had the girls. I had Damon. I had Ajax. I had Banana Buddha and Kenny and Monica and Ben and maybe even Ballard and Jeffers. They might not have understood my pain, but they certainly understood and cared about me.

How about that? I had a weird and wacky family that wanted the best for me and were there to help me along the rough roads. I wasn't alone at all.

In short, I was an idiot. A really big one. Luckily, I wasn't so stupid I couldn't learn.

"I'm sorry. Will you talk to me when I come back? Tell me about yourself?" I kind of felt like I was asking him out on a date.

His smile was positively dazzling. He clapped his hands on his knees, and his yellow flesh jiggled. "I would like that very much."

One down, several to go.

I looked at Damon, who still stood in waist-deep water, just behind the buddha.

"What would you say to helping me throw a little party? Tonight."

It's amazing what can be accomplished in a matter of a couple hours when everybody wants to help. I started calling people the moment I got back in the truck. I decided to hold the party at Aunty Mommy's house for lack of a better location. Only it wasn't her house anymore. It was mine.

I called in the staff and told them what I was up to. A shocked Dierdre and Linus promised to come in and do what they could as far as decorations. I sent the girls, Kenny, and Monica for food after calling around to various restaurants to see what they could provide on short notice. Next I texted and called to issue invitations. I ordered Ben not to come if it would in any way screw up his homework or tomorrow's classes.

I had Damon phone Mason. When my uncle was on the line, Damon passed his cell to me.

"How are you?" Mason asked, sounding worried.

I smiled. "I'm actually pretty good. Listen, I'm throwing a party in just a few hours at the house. Do you think you could let Elena, Ethan, Marco, Soren, Hannah, and Kenneth know? And maybe you could make sure everybody stays away from the Wall. It's probably dangerous."

Damon had said it looked as though someone had set a bomb off inside, which was fairly close to the truth. Debris littered the ground inside the cage, and a residue of magic continued to swirl and pulse. We'd have to clean that up, Damon told me, or it could turn into something ugly. But that was a chore for tomorrow ... or maybe the next day.

I'd decided to stage the party in the garden room and back patio to take advantage of the warm evening. I wanted to head over there and start getting it ready, but Damon took me to the hotel instead.

"Go shower and get changed. I'll be back for you in a while."

"Where are you going?"

"You'll see. It's a surprise."

He pulled me into a long, slow kiss that made my bones melt and then pushed me out the door and left me on the sidewalk as he drove away with Ajax in the backseat.

He came back for me an hour and a half later. I'd fallen asleep on the bed and woke to his closing the door on the bathroom. I heard the shower start. I got up and found Ajax in the little kitchen having dinner. It looked like a hash of steak, rice, and yellow squash. He ate it all. I shook my head. The dog was not going to like the idea of kibble. Not that it would ever show up in his bowl. I could afford to feed him gourmet food, and I didn't have any problem doing it, especially given how tough his life had already been.

After he finished, I sat on the floor and petted him, scratching his stomach and chest. I couldn't feel his ribs so easily anymore. We were both healing, inside and out. Thanks to the sanctuary pool, the bruises and swelling from my fight with Garrett had all but disappeared, and those I'd gained in rescuing the female gargoyles were already turning green and yellow. All in all, I'd made it out of the week all right.

Damon came out ten minutes later. "Are you ready?"

"Yep."

I got to my feet. He grabbed my hand and pulled me out the door and downstairs before I could say anything else. The time in the pool had erased the bruises on his hand, and his bones showed whole beneath his skin.

We drove up to the house just after sunset. Pinks and

oranges still streaked the sky in a lovely watercolor, and the night twined thick with the scents of flowers and the lush green smells of nearby irrigated pastures.

The circular driveway was already filling with cars. Damon parked and we hopped out. I headed for the front door, but he grabbed my hand and guided me around back. We retraced our steps of that day when the cops had questioned me and I'd revealed what Aunty Mommy had done to me on the Wall. It seemed like a year ago.

The Wall was gone. Where it had stood was now a bower of trees and vines and cascading flowers.

"Illusion," Damon said as I gasped and stopped to marvel.

"It's lovely."

He smiled, clearly pleased at my reaction. "Come on."

He pulled me onward and around to the back of the house. I stopped dead, my mouth falling open. Glittering flowers of light in every color sparkled and shone on the house and overhead in a fairy canopy. Vines twisted and twirled over invisible supports. Glowing butterflies fluttered from flower to flower while puffs of gold sparks floated across and fell like stars.

"It's stunning," I whispered.

"I hoped you'd like it," Damon said in his deep, rich voice.

A thrill of pleasure and excitement ran through me. "You did this? For me?"

His hand tightened on mine. "I wanted to remind you that magic can be beautiful. It isn't always blood and agony."

I turned and put my arms around him, a knot growing in my throat, my heart swelling. "Thank you," I whispered against his neck. "Thank you so much. I love it."

He wrapped his arms around me, snugging me against his hard form. He kissed my forehead and cheek.

"I thought I lost you today," he said, his voice rough. "You looked so broken. I didn't think you were even breathing."

"I'm sorry." Not that I would have done it differently. He knew it too. "Did anyone talk to the gargoyle males?"

"Mason. They already knew their mates had escaped. They were grateful."

"They shouldn't be. They should be pissed as fuck that they were all turned into slaves and victims."

"Trust me, they are. But they also know that you risked your life to free the females."

"It doesn't feel like nearly enough."

"It's hope like they haven't had since your aunt captured them, and that's a lot. You told them you'd try to free them, and I think they believe you now."

"I hope so. I am going to find a way. Are the females coming back ever?" I hoped so.

Damon shrugged. "Likely, but hard to say when. Your aunt didn't harm their calves, so they will have gone to reunite with them. Anyway, come on. You're late to your own party."

It was a lovely evening. Just about everybody I'd invited came, including all my employees. Even Jeffers and Ballard put in an appearance, both startled at my swift healing. Since I couldn't rationally explain it, I didn't try. Instead I pointed them to the food and drink, then Lorraine, Jen, and Stacey descended on me and pulled me aside.

"You're okay?"

"On the road to recovery."

"You scared the life out of us," Stacey said and she started crying.

I hugged her. Her tears were catching, and my eyes burned. "I'm so sorry."

"We got here just as all hell broke loose," Jen said. "You should have seen Damon. He was a force of nature. He pulled you out of the wreckage, and if you could have seen his face…. He looked gutted."

"He wouldn't let anybody near you except us and Ajax. He was kissing your hands and begging you to wake up. It was a breath of relief when you came to and asked what happened, but then you passed out again," Lorraine said.

"We told him you had to go to the hospital," Stacey said. "He was about to, and then Elena—your mother, I guess—offered put a spell on you to numb out your pain."

"We kind of got in the faces of your so-called family," Jen said, not at all apologetic.

I grinned and pulled them into a group hug. "I heard. I was awake. You guys were spectacular. I was a little surprised you let Damon take me."

They all gave me one of those looks that totally questioned my mental capacity.

"He knew where this sanctuary place was. Plus, like I said, he was wrecked," Jen said. "The man was more than desperate. He was out of his gourd. He's got it bad for you, Beck. Really bad. You're going to have to seriously consider keeping him. Otherwise I might have to take him off your hands."

Stacey snorted. "As if. He can't even see another woman but Beck."

I'd started blushing and decided it was time to deflect. "Did you meet Marco?"

"You mean Sex-On-A-Stick-Man? Oh, hell yes. Don't tell me he's bad news. Or maybe do. I like 'em bad," Stacey said, sliding the tip of her tongue along her upper lip suggestively. "Bad is lovely when it's temporary."

"I don't know if you've got a chance, Stace. He was eyeing Lorraine like she was a lollypop he wanted to lick all over," Jen said.

"Oh, please," Lorraine said. "He's a tomcat. Every time you two turn your backs, he's checking you out."

"Maybe you should talk him into a foursome," I suggested.

Stacey shook her head. "Too many vaginas, not enough dick."

We all broke out laughing.

I made the rounds, talking to everyone, stuffing my face with as much food as would fit into my stomach, and generally enjoying the fact that I was still alive. Breathing is a wonderful thing.

At some point, I had to talk to my mother and father. They approached me separately, Elena first.

"Thank you for the numbing spell," I said.

"I'm glad it helped. You look much better."

"I am." She was clearly curious about how I'd been healed, but I wasn't going to enlighten her. I had no reason to trust her, nor any desire to.

"I would like to know you," she said. "I have no other children."

My brow furrowed. "I was one of triplets, or so I'm told."

She bit her lips and looked away. "I'm allowed no claim to the others."

"So? They're adults. Call them up and have lunch or coffee or something."

Her lips curved. "That is forbidden."

"That's stupid. Why would you sign a contract like that?"

"It was ... a good contract, and my family desired it."

"Did you?"

"It was a good contract," she said again.

"If you say so." I took a swallow of wine to clear the bad taste out of my mouth. "So what do you want from me?"

"To get acquainted with you."

"What exactly does that mean? Understand that there's no way in hell I'm moving anywhere. Not with you and not with dear old Dad."

Her smile held a hint of triumph. Maybe this counted as a win over Ethan. Or revenge. Maybe it was something else. Whatever it was, it repelled me.

"I can visit here. Perhaps take a house here."

Take a house? She wasn't talking anything short term. "I'm pretty busy, especially rebuilding my shop and pulling my business back together."

"I'll be pleased with whatever time you can offer."

She smiled again and I wondered if letting her into my life was a big mistake. Or maybe the better question was how big a mistake it would turn out to be.

"It looks like Ethan would like to speak with you. Excuse me."

She walked away, to be instantly replaced by my sperm donor.

"I'm glad to see you so much better," he said.

That was a general theme of the night. But when he and Elena said it, it felt more like they were glad their prize pig wasn't damaged beyond use.

"Thanks."

"How did you break the binding spells?" he asked. "And get inside the climbing wall? None of us saw you pass."

"Trade secret," I said without batting an eyelash.

He didn't like that even a little bit. "You must tell me," he sputtered, clearly affronted by my refusal.

"Why?"

"I am your father. By contract, you belong to me."

"Belong?" I looked up at the ceiling, trying to collect myself before I slapped him silly. I drew a couple of deep breaths and then looked him dead in the eye, speaking slowly so he'd understand. "Let me put this to you as clearly as I can. Fuck. Off. I don't belong to anybody but myself, and if you even try to push me around, I swear to all that's holy and unholy that I will put you in your grave."

He made a rude noise, gesturing dismissively. "Don't be ridiculous, Rebecca. You will come home with me, and this business with Matrovani is over as of now." He shot a disparaging look at Damon. "His family is not good enough to clean our toilets. Stay away from him."

I had to admit, I was so surprised that my mouth just dropped open and for a few seconds, words failed me. Then my brain caught up. I stepped into him, my voice dropping as I poked him in the chest.

"Leave my house. Right now. Don't come back. You are not now nor will you ever be welcome. *Daddy*," I added sarcastically as I stepped back. "Oh, and think about stopping at the hospital on the way to the airport and see if they can get your head out of your ass. It's pretty far up there, but it's worth a shot."

I didn't wait for an answer. I stomped away, but I'd started giggling before I'd gone three steps. He'd looked so *shocked*, as if he'd really expected me to fall in line with his demands.

"What's so funny?" Damon blocked my path, casting a dangerous look over my shoulder at Ethan.

"Seems I'm a rebellious and difficult daughter, and I am not good with authority whatsoever."

He smiled, settling his hands on my hips and pulling me closer. "That's one of your best qualities."

"I'm pretty sure you've told me otherwise. If you've changed your mind, we have to get you in to a shrink. You may have some mental issues."

"If so, then so do the girls and Ajax. And Ben. He seems to think quite a lot of you. I'm in good company."

His slow grin was sexy as hell, and my toes curled. He didn't bother to mask the desire in his eyes, and his hands slid around to the small of my back. My lady parts tingled and throbbed, and I had the sudden urge to drag him off to the closest bedroom and finally get some relief.

Focus, Beck. I tried to remember what we'd been talking about.

"Lunatics, all of you. Oh, and Mister Sperm Donor said he would very much like me to drop you like a bad habit."

His hands tightened on me, and his jaw turned to rock. The line of his jaw was so very kissable. "Did he?"

"Mm-hmm." I slid the tip of my tongue over my suddenly dry lips, and I shifted against him. It only made the ache between my legs worse. If Damon only knew what I was thinking. No way was I letting Ethan get between us. "If I ask the gargoyles to keep him away, do you think they would?"

A slow smile spread across Damon's lips. "Why don't we ask them right now?"

Arms around each other, we went outside. I didn't think Ethan would give up, any more than Elena would. But I knew I'd deal with whatever they threw at me. Aunty Mommy had taught me well. And this time, I wouldn't be going to war alone. I had the family of my heart, and with them at my back, I couldn't fail. I wouldn't.

THE END

**Keep reading for an exciting excerpt from Beck's next adventure, *Putting the Chic in Psychic*!**

# PUTTING THE CHIC IN PSYCHIC
## EXCERPT

I couldn't deny I was having a damned good start to the day. My fake mother—aka Aunty Mommy—remained dead and had thus far been unable to rise from the grave and haunt me; my savagely vandalized business was under reconstruction; nobody had tried to kill me recently; my dog, Ajax, loved me unconditionally, as did my three best friends; and I was enjoying the nectar of the gods—aka an extra-large 9-1-1 espresso—with a gorgeous man.

Yeah, maybe I had a few problems, but at the moment, I could ignore all of them and enjoy the lovely weather and the very fine specimen of masculinity sitting across from me.

I sipped my ultra-caffeinated brew, eyeing Damon over the rim of my cup. He was flat out hot. Like HAWT. I'd seen him mostly naked and could attest to six pack abs, broad shoulders, and thighs that could crack walnuts. And his ass. It could make a nun wet her panties. With that body, his dark blond hair, stormy blue eyes, and chiseled jaw, he could have been a model. The fact that he was eyeing me with the same orgasmic appreciation I'd just given the first sip of my coffee made me want to lick him like a lollipop.

Just at the moment, my life was closer to perfect than it had ever been, which of course meant that everything would shortly be going straight to hell. Murphy's Law and Mercury in Retrograde are the ruling forces of my life. Trouble was always lying in wait just around the corner. At least it meant life was exciting. Often hideously painful, but still exciting. It also meant I knew enough to enjoy the good while it lasted.

I am an almost twenty-eight-year-old business woman and witch. I run Effortless Estates, a high-end estate liquidation business. I hold wealthy estate sales and have a showroom of the more valuable pieces. Or I did, before a former colleague destroyed it out of frustration, all because I refused to die when he was trying to murder me. Luckily he did succeed in offing Aunty Mommy, which made me almost willing to forgive him for my attempted murder, except he'd also tried to kill my three BFFs—Stacey, Jen, and Lorraine—not to mention Damon and my recently discovered uncle.

Nobody fucks with the people I love and gets away with it. Nobody.

Anyhow, my business had really taken off in the last few years, growing like a weed on steroids. Damon's a lawyer. My lawyer, as of recently. I'm his only client. When Aunty Mommy kicked the bucket, all sorts of cockroaches crawled out of the woodwork, including my real parents and a bunch of other family, also all witches. I'd also learned I was the product of a birth contract, and that the entire witch world revolved around bloodlines and eugenics, and my eggs were in high demand. All of which was enough to make me throw up in my mouth.

But I also inherited a convoluted mess of money and property, and Damon had taken on untangling and managing it all, so I wouldn't have to. If I'd had my way, I'd have refused to take it. I considered it blood money—specifically *my* blood—but I had to be practical, one of my least favorite things to be when I was pissed off. It turned out I wasn't the only target of Aunty Mommy's, just her favorite. She'd been a category nine tornado and had left a whole lot of damage in her wake. Since nobody else would, I had to try to fix what I could, and that meant money and plenty of it.

Between the money, the fact that I'd never been trained in magic, and my current lack of a home (my ex-colleague had destroyed my apartment along with my showroom), Damon and I were practically glued together these days. He was super protective of me, and though he hadn't said much, I knew he was scared some witch family—or just as likely my own—would kidnap me and turn me into an Easy-bake Oven for magically powerful babies. He'd been giving me a crash course in witchcraft. Not that I didn't have good command of my power—I did. I just didn't know how to create spells or what ingredients to use for what, nor did I really know the dangers, or even what I could or should be doing to protect myself. Other than that, I was in good shape.

His concern and me being his only client made it hard for him to peel away from me, which was both flattering to my female sensibilities and annoying as fuck. I didn't need him under foot twenty-four/seven, no matter how pretty he was, or how much I enjoyed his company. The constant togetherness had started to feel claustrophobic, which could be totally normal, or could be me panicking over being in a relationship.

Just at the moment, however, everything gleamed shiny perfection.

"What are your plans for the day?" He asked, interrupting my rambling train of thought.

"I'm going to check on the construction progress, and I have a couple potential clients to meet with about sales this weekend. Later, I'm having dinner with the girls. What about you?"

"More of the same. Sorting out your aunt's financial estate. It's like picking apart a gordian knot."

"Sounds horrifying."

The corners of his mouth kicked up. "I enjoy puzzles. There's no satisfaction like solving a difficult one."

"I like puzzles just fine, but that mess is sheer torture."

"Which is why you have me to sort it out for you."

"Lighting it on fire would be more satisfying."

"But far less profitable. Anyway, you can bask in the knowledge that your aunt would have hated knowing that you are the sole beneficiary of her financial empire. Milking it for all it's worth is the best sort of revenge."

"I don't know. Peeing on her grave felt pretty good. The girls and I plan to make it a regular thing. Weekly maybe."

"I'll keep bail money on hand. Just in case you get caught."

He smirked, unfazed by the idea of me, Jen, Stacey, and Lorraine out in the cemetery and squatting on Aunty Mommy's grave. Chalk up another reason to keep him around.

"Have you thought any more about what you want to do with the estate?"

"Much as I'd like to burn it to the ground, my Uncle Mason is right. Until I can free the gargoyles, I have to keep it. I don't suppose there's any way to curse Aunty Mommy, is there?"

Damon shook his head. "There's no reaching across the veil, I'm afraid."

"Karma has seriously let me down. I hope there's a hell, and she's burning in it," I complained.

He lost his smile, his gaze turning dark. He still hadn't come to terms with the things my aunt had done to me. Not that we talked about it. As far as I was concerned, that part of my life lived behind a locked door, and I was never opening it again. Out of sight, out of mind. As a coping mechanism, it worked most of the time. Like when I was awake.

"Believe me, if there was a way to get at the bitch, I would already have done it," he said in a stone voice.

"I know. And I appreciate it." I stroked my fingers over the back of his hand. He grasped mine. "The idea of making the estate a sanctuary appeals a lot to me," I said, returning to the subject at hand. "Lorraine could potentially move her vet clinic there and focus more on rescues if she wants, and I could fund the whole shebang. I've got to talk to the gargoyles, though. The place is their home more than mine, and they deserve the deciding vote on what happens there."

He nodded. "They will appreciate your consideration."

I shrugged. "It's the right thing to do."

"For you. Many would disagree."

"Apparently, many are psychopaths, then."

"Agreed."

Just then, his phone bleeped with a text notification. He glanced at it and his expression darkened. His jaw knotted. "Excuse me a minute," he said. "This can't wait."

I watched him stalk away, lifting his phone to his ear.

Damon's entire body radiated tension. Foreboding stirred in my gut, an all too familiar feeling.

I drew a slow breath and let it go, trying to relax. No good. My rational brain had lost all control, and my primal self had taken over. A life of constant threat combined with endless torture had honed my survival instincts. It didn't matter how nebulous my uneasiness was, or that I had no good reason to think trouble was on its way. Primitive me had decided to circle the wagons, raise all the drawbridges, and load all the weapons. In the space of a few seconds, the new, defenselessly happy me vanished and the old me—scarred, jaded, and suspicious—returned.

In an effort to distract myself, I sent a couple of work texts while keeping a covert eye on Damon. He'd begun to pace, his free hand balled into a fist. Ajax, my giant wolf-dog, made a protesting sound, his ears pricked like little satellite dishes as he also watched Damon.

I stroked his head, infusing my voice with a calm I didn't feel. "Easy now. Everything's okay."

He visibly relaxed, and he looked up at me, his light brown eyes softening. He rolled onto his side so I could scratch his stomach. I obliged with a little chuckle. His eyes drifted shut.

Ever since I'd helped Lorraine rescue him, he and I had pretty much been inseparable. He'd become just as much family to me as Jen, Stacey, and Lorraine. Luckily Damon didn't mind sharing the bed with both of us, as Ajax tended to want to snuggle at night.

I smiled to myself. Even if Damon did mind, he'd have to get over it. Though how we were going to manage to have sex—if and when that time came—I didn't know. I didn't want an audience, furry or otherwise, and if we locked him in another room, I don't know if Ajax would rip down the wall, thinking I was under attack or something.

I planned to be a noisy lover.

"Something funny?" Damon returned to the table. He didn't sit down and his dark expression was the polar opposite of his lightly spoken question.

"What's going on? You look pissed, and I want to note for the record, this time it wasn't me."

He didn't even crack the slightest smile. I wasn't sure he even heard me. He was tapping out a text. "Problems at home. I've got to fly back, and I don't know how long I'll be gone."

I hadn't known Damon long. A few months is all, and he'd seen me through some near-death experiences, so we'd bonded pretty quickly. Enough that he'd told me he loved me a few weeks into our acquaintance, plus invited me to live with him while my loft was getting rebuilt.

I'd begun to think of him as a fixture in my life, as reliable as the ground or the air, so with that kind of news, I naturally expected to anticipate missing him. What I didn't anticipate was the shaft of hurt that stabbed through me, threatening to double me over. For a second I couldn't even move.

*Problems at home.* The phrase rattled around in my skull like a pinball in a clothes dryer. Because his home was not here. Damon actually lived across the country and had houses in Europe and South America. On top of that, he'd been looking for real estate around here. It hadn't occurred to me that he'd leave eventually and I wasn't prepared for the idea.

He just said he didn't know how long he'd be gone, I reminded myself. He's planning to come back. You've been whining about having some time to yourself. Now you get to have it, so quit being such a baby.

Oh, for fuck's sake. I was reading way too much into the situation. I was a walking soap opera, not to mention a complete nutcase.

I decided that silence was the best way not to make a total ass of myself. I got up and disposed of our garbage. Damon was still tapping away on his phone as we started back toward the hotel. He fell in beside me, barely looking up from his screen. Since he was in a hurry, I kept a brisk pace, Ajax trotting happily beside me.

I'd already decided I didn't want to figure out new doubts to torture myself with while Damon packed. As we approached the elegant boutique hotel where we'd been living, I slowed. "I'm just going to head out." I nudged my chin toward the entrance to the parking garage. "You don't need a ride to the airport, do you?"

He tore himself away from his phone long enough to glance at me. "No. I'll have the hotel shuttle take me."

Shuttle. As if. It was a limo.

"Well, have a good trip. Hope everything's okay." I winced. Lame. Could I have come up with anything more impersonal? Maybe if I'd said Dear Sir or Madam at the beginning. Or To Whom It May Concern.

His attention had returned to his phone and he didn't seem to notice my awkwardness.

"Everything will be fine," he said.

"I guess I'll see you when I see you then," I said, uncertain whether I should interrupt his focus for a kiss goodbye. I waited a few seconds for him to say or do something, but it appeared he'd forgotten me. I gave a little shrug and left, squelching my hurt and self pity. Damon wasn't given to hysterics, so whatever was going on had to be pretty bad.

The situation wasn't about me at all, so I just needed to get over myself.

I waved at Josef, who was currently alone at the valet stand and kept going, the cool, dark air of the garage closing around me. They'd long ago gotten used to me parking and unparking my own car, back when my car was a gorgeous classic Thunderbird in near mint condition. But then the attack on my business had happened, and the car had been a casualty. I hadn't decided yet if I wanted to use magic to fix it. Garrett Sandrini, a secret witch and my would-be murderer, had chopped it in half long ways. Fixing it using ordinary methods wouldn't be feasible.

Every time I thought of replacing it, I felt guilty, like I was betraying it. I'd been contemplating using magic to fix it, but change the paint and interior colors. Then I could claim it was a different car altogether.

I sighed. Stupid to get so upset about a car. I should just suck it up and find something else. Maybe a Ranchero or an El Camino. Or a Mustang fastback. Anything but the Toyota Highlander I'd been renting. Though to be fair, it was nice enough and had a lot of room for all the things I had to carry to and from sales. It just didn't have much by way of charm, not like a classic car.

I'd walked down the ramp to the second level when I heard rapid footsteps behind me.

"Beck, wait."

I stopped and waited for Damon to approach. His brow was furrowed and his jaw looked like it was sculpted from granite.

"What's up?"

He grimaced. "I'm sorry."

"For what?" I was acting a little too innocent, but I didn't want him to know I'd been hurt.

"For being a dick to you."

"You weren't a dick," I said. Okay, maybe a little bit, but I was frequently a bitch and a half, so I couldn't very well complain.

He raised his brows in clear disbelief. "I was, and I'm concerned that you aren't calling me on it."

I shrugged. "Whatever you have to deal with is clearly upsetting you. I don't need to make it any worse."

He tipped his head, his eyes narrowing. "That's very adult of you."

"Now you're being rude."

"I was rude outside, but that didn't seem to bother you."

"And what should I have said? Don't ignore me? Don't shut me out? Who am I to make those kinds of demands? Anyhow, it's clearly none of my business."

His mouth tightened and his eyes flashed with fury. "Is that what you really think?"

"I think if it were my business, you'd talk to me about it. You haven't, so...." I shrugged again. I knew I was pissing him off. I knew I sounded like a grade A super bitch. At least I was an elite bitch and not middle-of-the-road or mediocre. I probably shouldn't have taken pride in that, but gotta take credit where credit is due.

His jaw knotted and I could practically see steam rising from the top of his head. I tried to feel sorry about that, but I couldn't. Riling him up meant he wasn't ignoring me any more. So much for being an adult.

"It's family business," he said in a clipped voice.

"Okay."

"I have to go help sort it out."

"You said that."

"I don't *want* to go, but I don't have a choice."

Well, if that wasn't mysterious, I didn't know what was. "Okay," I said again. I wondered if he noticed he hadn't offered any details. Whether he meant to or not, he *was* shutting me out.

"Could you maybe say something more than just okay?" He growled.

"Like what?"

"Maybe that you'll miss me? You don't want me to go? Anything besides the cold fish act?"

"I *will* miss you," I said. "And I don't particularly want you to go."

"But?"

"But nothing."

He glared. "Talking to you is like trying to get gold out of Fort Knox. Sometimes I wonder if you're a robot."

My teeth clenched together. And here I thought we'd been getting along. I stepped back so that I wouldn't slug him. "You're going to miss your flight."

"That's it? That's all you have to say?"

I considered him as I tried to formulate what I wanted to say. I edited out the *fuck you, asshole* part. "I think," I said instead, "that this is probably a stupid argument that's quickly going way off the rails. Whatever is wrong, you clearly need to go handle it. I'll be here when you get back and we can fight about something stupid then, if you still want to. In the meantime...." I closed the space between us and put my arms around his waist. See? I can adult.

He snatched me close and nuzzled my hair as I pressed my face into his chest and drew a deep breath. He smelled of himself, fresh air, and the spicy soap he used. It made me want to rub all over him like a cat.

"Christ, but I don't want to leave you," he muttered in a gravelly voice.

"I'd go with you, but I have too much to do."

I felt him shake his head. "Last thing I want is to take you back there."

I pushed back, looking up at him. "My manners aren't *that* bad," I said. "I rarely ever pee on the furniture or chew shoes anymore. And I know how to use *all* the silverware."

# TO MY READERS

Thank you for taking the time to read *Putting the Fun in Funeral*. Without you I could not do this thing that I love and I am eternally grateful that you've chosen to take a chance on my book. I hope you loved it as much as I love writing it. I laughed the entire time. If you enjoyed it, please consider leaving a review on Amazon or Goodreads. It makes a huge difference in other readers finding my books.

If you'd like to keep in touch, I send out a semi-regular newsletter wherein I share news about releases, give you snippets and other free things, tell you all about my puppies and the silliness that they stir up, and whatever odd bits of information I collect and love to share with all of you in the privacy of your own mailbox. Sign up for it on my website: www.dianapfrancis.com

You can also email me using the contact form on my website. I love getting fan email!

# ACKNOWLEDGMENTS

I had a lot of help in the making of this book. I can't even begin to tell you how grateful I am for all they've done. If I forget anybody here, please know that I am eternally thankful for your help and I am sorry if I've left your name out. Thanks go to: R.J. Blain, Christy Keyes, Sherwood Smith, Andrea Howe, Jennifer Stevenson, the BVC community, Megan Thyagarajan, Heather Osborn, Lyn Forester, Devon Monk, Kristine Smith, Barbara Cass-Mills, Robin Owens, Julie Fine, The Word Warriors, SF Novelists, and most of all, my family. Without all of you, this book would not be possible.

# ABOUT THE AUTHOR

Diana Pharaoh Francis is the *USA Today* and Amazon Bestselling writer of fantastical, adventurous, and often romantic fiction. She holds a Ph.D. in Victorian literature and literary theory. She's owned by a corgi, a mini blue heeler, and a blue-eyed corgi mix. She spends much of her time gardening, airbrush painting, herding children, and avoiding housework. She likes rocks, geocaching, horses, knotting up yarn, and has a thing for 1800s England, especially the Victorians. For more about her books and to sign up for her newsletter, visit:

**www.dianapfrancis.com**

### You can also find her on:

**INSTAGRAM:**

www.instagram.com/di_pharaoh_francis/

**PATREON:**

www.patreon.com/dpfrancis

**TWITTER:**

twitter.com/dianapfrancis

**FACEBOOK:**

www.facebook.com/Diana.Pharaoh.Francis

# ABOUT BOOK VIEW CAFÉ

# BOOK VIEW CAFE

Book View Café is a professional authors' publishing cooperative offering DRM-free ebooks in multiple formats to readers around the world. With authors in a variety of genres including mystery, romance, fantasy, and science fiction, Book View Café has something for everyone.

Book View Café is good for readers because you can enjoy high-quality DRM-free ebooks from your favorite authors at a reasonable price.

Book View Café is good for writers because 90% of the proceeds goes directly to the book's author.

Our authors include New York Times and USA Today bestsellers, Nebula, Hugo, Lambda, Chanticleer, National Reader's Choice, and Philip K. Dick Award winners, World Fantasy, Kirkus, and Rita Award nominees, and winners and nominees of many other publishing awards.

Book View Café's Newsletter includes new releases, specials, author news, and event announcements. Go to our website to sign up.

www.bookviewcafe.com